GOYA. THE VINTAGE. (PRADO)

The Romance of
ALEXANDER
AND ROXANA

Being one of the

Alexandrian Romances

"Alexander the Prince",
❋ "Alexander the King" & ❋
"Alexander and Roxana"

by

Marshall Monroe Kirkman

Author of "The Romance of Gilbert Holmes"
"Primitive Carriers" and "The Science of
Railways" in sixteen volumes.

Illustrated by August Petrtyl

COPYRIGHT, 1909
BY
CROPLEY PHILLIPS COMPANY
———
Entered at Stationers'Hall, London, England

All Rights Reserved

The Lakeside Press
R. R. DONNELLEY & SONS COMPANY
CHICAGO

TABLE OF CONTENTS

ILLUSTRATIONS

INTRODUCTION

The romantic love of Alexander for Roxana has interested mankind for two thousand years, and will continue to interest it as long as the world lasts. Scarcely less interesting are the picturesque events connected with the tragic lives of Darius, the Persian King, and his beautiful Queen, Statira, of which this story has much to say. The romance deals with the lives of many exalted men and women, not because they are exalted or of historical interest, but that they form a part of the love story.

This story, like the others forming the ALEXANDRIAN ROMANCES, was suggested by studies of the times of Philip of Macedon and Alexander, and it was because of the interest they excited, and not the desire to write an historical romance, that they had their origin. The stories lie apart, and such interest as attaches to one, it is proper to say, is no way dependent upon the others. M. M. K.

CHAPTER I

THE DEPARTURE

MACEDONIA was in tears, and its war-like capital bowed in the dust, as if captive to some cruel and irresponsible monster. Throughout the city and beyond its walls, in the verdant plains and amid the secluded valleys and mountain solitudes, there were silence and mourning. For the invasion of Persia, so long foreshadowed, was at last a thing ordained, and because of it women wept for husbands and sweethearts, and fathers and mothers for their sons gone with the standards, their faces turned toward the east. Not lightly did they grieve, as in past years when some near-by conflict disturbed the nation, but as for something

1

unknown and terrible; the swallowing up of loved ones in a distant war, the length and vicissitudes of which no one could foretell.

Those who went considered it lightly, their minds filled with visions of new countries to be seen and strange adventures to be encountered; and of the glory to be acquired, who could tell! Thinking thus, they marched away with clanking armour to the sound of flute and fife, swallowed up in the smoky plain, while those left behind watched their departure from the battlements of Pella with beating hearts and streaming eyes. A hated country was to be overrun and conquered, all knew, but of its untold riches, and vast stores of gold that its parsimonious kings had hoarded for centuries, and that now in the desperate emergency of the imperilled state its sovereigns still foolishly withheld, they little dreamed. Nor could they foresee that the obscure and impoverished nobles of Macedonia would be honoured and enriched beyond all belief, and that the common soldiers would be accorded largesses by the conquering young King in excess of all preconceived dreams of the world's riches. Of those who went many were to meet a glorious death on the field of battle; all were to achieve riches and renown, and others the undying fame that attaches to kingly office. But of such things the sorrowing multitude gave no thought, overwhelmed by the mystery and remoteness of the undertaking, and the belief that few if any of those who marched away would ever return to comfort those who stayed.

Now only the King lingered, and on this soft April day when our story opens he, too, was to go forward to join the army ere it reached the Hellespont. Thus it was in the early morning when, amid the strident blasts of the trumpet, the drawbridge of the citadel beyond the Lydias was lowered, and Alexander came forth surrounded by the royal guard and his attendant pages and officers. Reaching the streets of the city, he found them crowded to their utmost limit by those who watched and waited his coming, eager to pay him honour. Not with joyful cries alas, as heretofore, but sadly and with the silence of death, as if conscious that they were bidding him farewell forever. Fearing this, all Macedonia was there to witness the melancholy spectacle and offer a prayer to the Gods for the safety and good fortune of their heroic young King. Halting with bared head on the edge of the picturesque river, he surveyed the vast multitude in silence, overcome by their sorrowing faces and tear-dimmed eyes; but the guard presently having cleared a path, he went forward with scarce room for his horse, so closely did the people press upon him. Some there were so fortunate as to lay hold of his hand as he slowly made his way, and this they remembered and told in after years, while others less forward were content to touch his horse or glistening armour.

Crowding the adjacent streets and from windows and house-tops, wherever a glimpse might be caught of the departing King, people waited in silence, intently watching, thinking themselves fortunate if they but caught a glimpse of the moving spectacle. And beyond from the summit of the walls, and far out on the extended plain, men and women stood with upturned faces watching the young King, as with bowed head and clouded eyes he at last emerged from the great gate of the city. When in this way he had reached the open country those who waited, remembering all too late, raised a mighty shout, conscious that their young King needed some voice of loving encouragement from out their hearts to cheer him on his uncertain and desperate venture. Hearing it and smiling, he turned and doffed his plumed hat in token of thankfulness for the gentle favour; and thus he passed from the sight of his countrymen, never again to hear their cheers and cries of joy as in the months and years that had passed.

It was the second year of Alexander's reign, filled to the full with unexpected happenings and glorious deeds. Coming to the throne on the assassination of Philip of Macedon, his father, he found his country beset by enemies on every side, openly defiant and aggressive, and in outspoken contempt of his youth and inexperience. All these he had overcome in open battle, and now, his power firmly established

and his country secure, he meditated the conquest
of Persia, a thing his father had dreamed about, but
dying untimely had happily left to him to carry out.
Persia! Synonym of oppression! The hated power
that once held Macedonia in thralldom and had
finally compelled her to take up arms against a kindred people! Now, at last, the day of reckoning had
come, and, unexampled was to be the punishment of
. the cruel foe!

When at last the warlike city and its sorrowing
multitude was hidden from view the King sighed
and spurred his horse to a gallop, the object of his
dreams and prayers at last attained. Not the conquest of Persia alone, but that and something more!
Something, indeed, of which mankind little thought,—
the regaining of his betrothed, the gentle Roxana,
from whom, as a Prince, he had been forced to fly
for his life, pursued by the soldiers of an angry King;
and afterward, when recalled from exile, it was to find
to his lasting sorrow that Philip, disapproving of the
union, had banished her from the country.

Thus discarded and humiliated, she had returned to
Bactria, her native land, on the further confines of
the Persian Empire. But of its remoteness the
King took no thought. What mattered it? Wherever she might be he would seek her, and finding her
claim her as his Queen as he had pledged himself;
for of her abiding love and trusting fidelity he had
no manner of doubt. Now at last his face was turned

toward her, and little he recked of the months and years that might intervene ere he should again clasp her in his arms as on that day when they had loved, and plighted their troth in the smiling Vale of Tempe, indifferent to Philip's will. Thus it was that, venturing all, he set out on that April morning to conquer the ancient world, and, conquering, make it all his own.

Of Asia Minor men knew much; of middle Persia, little; of what lay beyond only the fragmentary accounts of infrequent and hurried travellers. Of eastern Persia, of far-off Bactria, the home of Roxana, the King knew not a thing save her account of a country of fertile valleys, snow-clad mountains, and desert wastes. But what did its remoteness signify? Nothing. His invincible army would find a way, and the greater Persia's strength that intervened the greater would be the glory of its conquest. For love of glory vied strong in the heart of Alexander with remembrance of his betrothed, each passion flaming the higher because of the other. Animated by such thoughts, and crying aloud in exultation, he urged his horse to greater speed that he might the sooner overtake his beloved army of which he expected so much.

About the King rode his officers, and as they watched his face and eager manner they commented on what they saw and the strange situation in which they found themselves.

"There is something beyond our ken, something beside Persia's conquest that spurs the King on thus untimely in the face of an empty treasury," Philotas, Parmenio's son and the commander of the Companion Cavalry, exclaimed with impatient voice to Lyncestes, a Lyncestian Prince, and thought to have been implicated in the assassination of Philip, the late King.

"What is it!" Lyncestes asked, surprised at the other's words.

"What think you?" Philotas rejoined, evading the inquiry.

"I know not, unless it be his foolish vanity," the Lyncestian ventured, knowing Philotas to be insanely jealous of the young King.

"That were indeed enough and to spare," the commander of the Companion Cavalry sneered.

"And is that it, indeed!"

"No."

"What then!"

"A woman."

"That may well be, for Persia's women are the most comely in all the world 't is said," Lyncestes answered, with a smirk.

"I know, but there is only one of whom he thinks."

"Only one where there are so many to be admired?" the other laughed.

"Yes, and that one, the Princess Roxana."

"What, the Bactrian maid who visited Macedonia

with the Persian Embassy; she of the soft eyes and purring ways, to whom Alexander as a Prince gave himself up on his return from Cheronea!"

"Yes, and no other."

"Bah! He has never mentioned her since Philip sent her flying, bag and baggage, from the country."

"Flying! Rather with an honoured escort of twenty ships."

"That was like Philip," Lyncestes laughed.

"If he has been silent it was not without cause, for with whom could he speak of her unless it be Hephestion? Nor would it be like him to divulge the secret of his heart, only to be laughed at! Come, if you doubt I 'll lay a wager of a talent that it is as I say."

"I need the gold, but you would make a foolish bet, for Alexander remembers and treasures only the selfish ends he has in view," Lyncestes jeered.

"That is only partly true, for he does not forget his favourites any more than he forgets those he dislikes. He loves Hephestion and hated Attalus; the first lives and prospers, the other died untimely and is forgotten!"

"And by your hand?"

"It may be," Philotas assented, with a scowl.

"I have a disposition something like the King's myself, and would I had his power — if only for an hour," Lyncestes exclaimed, with surly discontent.

"What would you do? Nothing! When the hour struck and you might have accomplished much —

made yourself supreme, it may be — you shrank from your purpose, and, kneeling, saluted Alexander as King! His power! He starts out to conquer the most warlike country in the world with sixty talents — a day's supply — confident the enemy will afford his army all it needs. Was there ever so venturesome a fool?" Philotas particularized, scarce able to speak, so great was his jealousy and rage.

"Think you the Bactrian has remained true to him if it should chance that he still treasures her as you say?" Lyncestes asked, reverting to the former subject, not relishing the other's reference to his abandonment of his friends when Philip fell murdered by Pausanias.

"It may be, for the credulous say women are always true if their ideals be fulfilled, and I know not why it is but he seems strangely to meet their conceptions, although he will have nothing whatever to do with them," Philotas scoffed, for, being of a vain disposition, he was jealous of Alexander in this as in other things.

"It is said, though how truthfully I know not, that Roxana thrice refused Philip's offer to make her his Queen, promising her, if she would consent, to put aside all others."

"If she refused him, it was because she knew, the cunning wench, that he would quickly tire of her as he had of all others."

"Yes, and having failed to snare Alexander she has

long since married some Bactrian savage," Lyncestes prophesied.

"It may be, but I would I knew the upstart's thoughts and purposes," Philotas mused, eying the King, who rode in advance with upraised head and confident brow.

"They are an open book, my friend, as regards Roxana. He will have none of her. For seeking power and the kingship of Persia, what can help him so much as to make Darius' daughter his wife! 'T is there his thoughts dwell, Philotas, regarding marriage, as would yours and mine were we in his place."

"However that may be, he is a fool to venture abroad leaving his kingdom with no heir to succeed him should he die."

"There is plenty of time for a man of twenty-two to look about him."

"I know, but he is not the less likely to die because of his youth," Philotas insinuated.

"All men must die, and quickly if others be the gainers thereby," Lyncestes responded, meaningly.

"Yes, and he more likely than another."

"So I have thought, and so it will be if the Gods are not ungracious to obscure men like ourselves," Lyncestes scowlingly responded, touching his dagger.

To this Philotas made no answer, and so without more open speech they fully understood the desire of each — that the young King's venture should fail, and that he should die in the hazardous undertaking.

In this way, and at the very beginning of the conquest, a budding conspiracy was formed that was destined to run its course, and in its strivings cause the trusting King many anxieties and much grieving, and the doing of things abhorrent to him. Of all this, however, he was happily unconscious; the stars were out, the fragrance of the plain was as the perfume of flowers to his nostrils, and the flowing river and limpid lagoons that bordered its grassy edge were as if encrusted with a sheen of silver! For at last, the ambition of his life was to be attained, and so believing he gave no thought to the secret machinations of his enemies, his mind intent upon the vast undertaking that lay before him. Thus enlivened, and believing in the good faith of all about him, he overtook his marching troops, who hailed his coming with frantic cries as he drew rein beside their gleaming spears. Cheered by his presence and smiling countenance, the stride of the soldiers lengthened, and one more forward than his fellows, taking up the national anthem the whole army presently joined in the glad acclaim.

Such in part was the march to the Hellespont; one of continual rejoicing, for there were no sick or wounded to excite sympathy or regret, and at night camping by the sea the eager soldiers rested and gossiped contentedly of what was before them. And aboard the triremes of the King, anchored a little way off the shore, lights flashed, and above the murmur of the waves the soldiers could hear the laughter and songs of the sailors as they rested from their day's work.

Reaching the Hellespont, the King gave directions for the transfer of the army to Abydos on the Asiatic shore, after which he set sail for ancient Troy, sacrificing to Poseidon, the God of the Sea, as his vessel swung anchor-free midway of the noble stream. But as the ship spread its sails in the Grecian Sea a strange sadness came to mingle with his elation as he watched the tumbling waves from the vessel's prow. Was Roxana, his love, still alive? Of this he had not thought. And of the long years of silence— what did they foretell? Was she still a maid, or had some untoward event of the Persian King's planning forced her to wed another? He could not think it strange that no word had reached him, for Bactria was many months away, and between lay Persia and its hostile people. And if not one of his messengers had returned to bring back word or dispel the mystery of the passing years, that was nothing, for so dangerous a mission might fail, and fail again and again in its fulfillment. Her fidelity he did not doubt, and when this present pilgrimage was accomplished he cried aloud, looking forward to the plains of Troy, that there should be no further dallying, no turning aside, no hour's delay in penetrating the hated country that hid within its borders her he loved. Thus communing he approached the Trojan city with its sacred shrines and glorious memories, and reaching the shore

IN TOKEN OF POSSESSION

hurled his spear, burying it deep in the golden sand in token of the coming conquest and possession of the coveted country.

Hastening to the temple of Minerva, the Goddess of Wisdom, the King proffered sacrifices and libations at the sacred shrine, after which he sought the tomb of Achilles, his ancestor, where he offered up solemn libations in honour of the Grecian hero. These and attendant religious duties performed, he returned to the ship, and spreading sail set out on his return to the Hellespont.

Reaching the half-dismantled city of Arisbe, where he was to disembark, he was greatly surprised to find the quadrireme of his mother, Olympias, awaiting him in the roadstead. Of the Queen's coming he had no previous knowledge, having taken leave of her at Pella, seemingly content with the dignities conferred upon her and the hopes held out for the future. But unavailingly, it would appear, for she had followed on, and with some set purpose, it was apparent, other than to again bid him adieu ere he set out on his proposed conquest. Greatly disquieted, he entered his barge, and attended by Hephestion hastened to pay her a visit of respect and love. Mounting the side of the ship, the Queen received him in her arms, and after embracing him and making many loving inquiries led him to the seclusion of the middle-ship that their interview might be undisturbed. Taking instant advantage of his manifest delight on again beholding her, for his love for the imperious and cruel Queen was that of an affectionate son, she lost no time in making known the object of her visit.

"Do not tell me," she said, smiling upon him, "that you are surprised at my visit — that you expected that I, a Queen and the mother of Alexander, would submit calmly to Antipater's regency while you are abroad on this perilous mission."

"I thought everything arranged to your satisfaction; the honour and precedence of your exalted station having been accorded you," he smiled.

"What are such things my, son? Empty names! Shadows that make the absence of power the more galling," she protested.

"To possess power one must have the strength to exercise it," he answered, in excuse.

"Have I not strength? Has Antipater more? What do I lack; wherein am I weak?" she questioned with haughty mien.

"Yes, all the strength that ever fell to man or woman," the King acknowledged, admiring her resolute bearing. "But the enemies that beset the kingdom and the jealousies and unrest of our people make it necessary that a soldier with unsheathed sword should govern in my absence lest things go wrong and my present venture come to naught."

In this way did he evade expressing his real thoughts, for this great and terrible woman of whom, truth to tell, he like others stood somewhat in awe, had the strength and determination to govern the world; and except for her high and implacable temper would have made a safe ruler in the King's absence. But in all things, however trifling, where her will was opposed, or her passions excited, questions of policy were lost sight of in a passionate desire to punish. Nevertheless, could Alexander have forseen the crisis of the dynasty in the years to come it is possible he would have done as she desired, however cruel her punishment of those who transgressed her will. For as regent she would have had the courage and strength to crush those who afterward, in the dire emergency of the kingly house, traitorously abandoned its guardianship in the hope of benefit to themselves.

"You act wisely, my son, in giving Antipater command of the army, but doing so should put a bit in his mouth and this safeguard I, as regent, would supply," she persisted.

"No, it would weaken the government to deprive him of civil power, and end in both your and his destruction."

"Yet is it not better to risk something — though there is no risk — than that your interests and the perpetuity of the dynasty should be jeopardized by putting yourself or your successor in the hands of so crafty and ambitious a man!" she warned.

"What have I or those who follow me to fear from him, a creature of the hour?" he asked, frowning.

"This, my son; that should aught befall you in Asia, and you leave no one to represent the kingly interest having the strength to govern, Antipater will usurp all power, and so the structure no longer having your support will crumble and fall of its own weight," she pointed out, with growing vehemence.

"Empires like men must have an end," he retorted, conscious of the truth of what she said, but unable for reasons of state to change his present plans.

"Empires are born of men and exist for ages if wisely built, fostering the kingly house that reared them.   You, intent only on conquest, take no thought to transmit the kingdom you are building to your successor."

"Not so, for I shall live to perpetuate my power as others have before me," he excused, with some impatience.

" 'T is a brave thought, but having no heir should you die, which the Gods forbid, Antipater will grasp the crown or its substance, and so a new line of rulers will come, and with them what is entrusted to you as heir of the Dorian Kings will perish from the earth."

"Something must be risked, and I cannot now make other disposition.   Be content, exalted Queen," he smiled, striving to conciliate her, "for every honour shall be paid you, and by Antipater not less than others."

"The land of your birth will see you no more, my

son," she proclaimed, as if gifted with the spirit of prophecy, "and disregarding your duty as King, your neglect to provide for the succession, should you die untimely, will leave the kingdom a prey to military adventurers."

"Once Persia is conquered I will marry; let that content you," he answered decisively, hoping thus to quiet her.

"Why not now? 'T is a present duty, not a thing to put aside."

"Yet will I not respond to it. Why should it be different with me than with Cyrus, who founded Persia over which his dynasty has reigned undisturbed for two hundred years?"

"You, conquering in turn, have no son to succeed you as had he, and disregarding the danger leave the parent kingdom, in which all strength lies, in alien hands," she objected, striving to repress her rage.

"Am I so old that you should press me now to take a wife! When I have conquered Persia, and have a throne worthy of her I have chosen for my queen it will be time enough to marry," he cried, his vision filled with the image of the fair Princess who had so long engaged his thoughts.

"What! Have you then made a choice?" she questioned, surprised.

"Yes, oh Queen."

"And have not told me — your mother!" she chided, deeply aggrieved.

"My choice, oh Queen, has been known to you these four years," he smiled.

"What, Roxana, the Bactrian Princess?" she asked, after some pause, conjuring up the past.

"Yes, she whom you accepted and blessed as she knelt before you in tears, her hand in mine."

"I thought, as has every one, that you had ceased to remember her with your accession to the throne," she said, ill at ease.

"Why should that have changed me? Are the hearts of kings different from the hearts of other men?"

"She is but a recollection, my son, unsubstantial as a myth! A being who vanished into the unknown with her dismissal by Philip from the Macedonian court."

"Yet do I still treasure her, and searching the unknown and finding her, as I shall, will make her Queen of all the world," he cried, lifting his face to heaven.

"Tut, tut, how know you she is not already wed — perhaps a mother — for Princesses may not remain thus long unmarried in Persia."

"I care not how it is, and if her love be still unchanged I will make her Queen, though all the world oppose my choice," he declared, enraged at thought of losing her.

"Meanwhile you may die, for in every battle you risk your life, and in every cup there may be a poisoned draught."

CHAPTER II

Upon Alexander's return to his ship he gave orders to disembark, and this being quickly accomplished he set out with his retinue to rejoin the army, although it was near the hour of midnight. Beside the King rode Hephestion, the companion and friend of his youth, whom he loved above all others; and near at hand his secretary, Eumenes, who filled the office not from choice but by selection as he had in Philip's time. For this great souled man possessed military qualities of the highest order, but because of his modesty and the jealous crowding of those who made up the entourage of Alexander the fact was long in being recognized. Of all those trusted by the young monarch none, however, showed such unselfish devotion as this prince of men in the hour of peril, giving all he had and finally his life to the kingly house he served.

Directly behind the King rode the pages, the sons of princes and nobles, anxious to learn the art of war under the Monarch's immediate eye. Crowding close upon Alexander, and as if jealous of younger and more useful men, rode Lysimachus, the King's early tutor, now well along in years and not of robust health. But, notwithstanding this, and rather perhaps because

21

of it, Alexander would not deny him any wish, and so had responded to the old man's prayer to be permitted to accompany the expedition that he might behold ere he died the triumphs he had ever claimed were destined to mark the career of his beloved pupil. Behind those who surrounded Alexander followed a squadron of Companion Cavalry, clad in armour, as was the King and those about him; for they were now in the enemy's country, and feeling all the elation of the warlike venture committed themselves unreservedly to its hardships.

As the cavalcade mounted the hills behind the city, the lofty heights and wooded slopes of Mount Ida to the south were seen to be ablaze with the campfires of the Persian army; but whether they marked the present position of the enemy or were intended merely as a blind, the King could not tell. ' Stopping short, he fixed his gaze long and earnestly on the sacred mountain, but, unable to discern what lay behind the gleaming lights, he presently turned to the north, spurring his horse to a gallop. Seeing the direction the King took Lysimachus, greatly perplexed, exclaimed in piping tones:

"Why do you turn to the north, oh King, when the enemy awaits you in another direction?"

"What think you, unless it be to rejoin the army, good friend?" the King laughed.

"Have our troops not gone to the south, where the Persians rest?" the old man queried, surprised.

IN THE ENEMY'S COUNTRY

"No, they follow the Hellespont, and reaching its head will continue their march to the east," the King explained, making no effort to conceal the movement he contemplated.

Seeing no courageous purpose in this wide detour the old man cried out with manifest disappointment:

"Why this evasion, oh King, so much resembling flight when before you have always made straight for the enemy's lines?"

"The evasion is more seeming than real," the King answered amiably, for from habit and love he accorded the aged tutor the respect a son pays his father.

"How can that be," Lysimachus fretted, "when their army lies about Mount Ida of cherished memory, while our troops march in an opposite direction?"

"It may be the Persians still await us on Mount Ida, but to-morrow they will be in hot retreat when they learn the direction of our march."

"Why should we not seek them where they are; why put off the hour of conflict?" the old man, who knew little of the art of war, continued with garrulous persistency.

"Intrenched about Mount Ida, they have every advantage; by flanking them should they not retreat, we will attack them in the rear, and, overcoming them, may capture or destroy the whole force."

"I pray you have a care in the matter, for they number a hundred thousand men, commanded by the

Rhodian Memnon, while we have only a third that number," Lysimachus warned, a tremour in his voice, now that he saw a conflict was inevitable.

"It matters not who is in command, though were it Memnon his experience and cunning would entitle him to respect, but the jealousies of the Persian leaders will not permit him to have a voice in the conduct of the campaign, nor direction in the order of battle," Alexander explained.

While the King in high good humour, thus discoursed with amiable particularity as to his future plans, Perdiccas, an officer devoted to his royal master, and like Eumenes unhappy in his ending, hurriedly approached, and on being interrogated by Alexander explained that a spy who had just come in reported that the Persians had abandoned their position on Mount Ida and were in full retreat.

"In what direction?" the King questioned, not surprised.

"To the east, and in the direction of the River Granicus, behind which it is believed they intend to confront us."

"What particulars did he learn regarding the enemy's force?" the King asked.

"That there is no head, each satrap claiming precedence, while the grandees in their turn refuse all accommodation, every one protesting that his plan is the best."

"What about Memnon?"

"Nothing, for not being a Persian born he is discredited; nay, has but to propose a thing to have it scornfully rejected by the haughty nobles of the great King."

"Have they any definite knowledge concerning our force, think you?" the King asked.

"Yes, and such knowledge as could only come from some one within our ranks," Perdiccas cried, thinking of Lyncestes, whom he distrusted.

"Do they appear confident — or otherwise?" Alexander asked, disregarding the other's reference.

"They speak of you as the boy King, and hold your army thus commanded in slight respect," Perdiccas said, concealing nothing.

"Yet youth has something to commend it," the King smiled, amused.

"The spy making count of the enemy's leaders reports that Bessus and Mithrines are both with the Persian army and in command of considerable forces," Hephestion interposed aside, as if conveying information he thought of special interest to the King.

"The nobles who visited Pella four years ago in the train of Oxyartes, the Persian Ambassador?" the King commented, with constrained voice.

"Yes, and let us give thanks to the Gods that we are to meet them again — and on the field of battle," Hephestion added, recalling the unpleasant incidents of their sojourn in Macedonia.

"Bessus will not be found lacking in courage, but

Mithrines has no heart for fighting, and will fly ere a blow is struck," Perdiccas predicted.

"Yet I hope never to meet him except on the field of battle," the King rejoined, but not as if in reply to Perdiccas.

"Why not, if I may ask?" Lysimachus piped, remembering Mithrines' arrogance while in Macedonia and the tragic plot in which he involved Alexander.

"For the reason that should he yield I must treat him as a subject, with all outward courtesy, and that I by no means desire to do," the King sternly replied.

"Why in one case more than in another?" Lysimachus persisted with the freedom accorded him.

"That seeing my treatment of him others may be led to lay down their arms and serve our cause rather than that of Darius," the King explained, disclosing the policy that was to govern him throughout his conquests.

"I would run my sword through him, just the same," Perdiccas commented, under his breath.

"Know you whether Oxyartes is with the Persian force?" the King asked, turning to Hephestion, referring to the father of the Princess Roxana, who had visited Macedonia four years before in charge of the Persian Embassy.

"No, he is in disgrace with the great King."

"If that be true, it is as if the Gods had granted my prayer, that we may never meet except in amity," the King murmured, relapsing into silence.

Riding somewhat apart and in melancholy mood, there followed two young officers of the King, Demetrius and Medius, both favourites of Alexander, with whom they had served in all his campaigns. Looking back and scanning the lights that dotted the harbour, Medius exclaimed, with a sigh:

"When, comrade, shall we again look upon our beloved country?"

"When shall I again see my beloved Theba?" the other answered, with doleful voice.

"And I my sweet wife, Eurydice, whom I had scarce time to embrace ere responding to the King's call?"

"Think you the dear girls mourn our departure?" Demetrius questioned, solicitous of sympathy.

"Yes, with sighs and tears and prayers for our safety," Medius confidently responded.

"Shall we ever see them again," Demetrius sighed, looking away to the Persian camp-fires about Mount Ida.

"Yes — but I would our departure had not been so hurried."

"I can see no end to the war, the King's ambition runs so high; and because of it I look upon Theba as lost to me forever," Demetrius grieved.

"I know not how it may be, but for myself not many weeks shall pass ere I again clasp my love to my heart," Medius answered, believing it would be so.

"And is that why you sought a place in the King's train?"

"Yes — that I might be free, and he so understands it."

"You no longer care for glory, Medius?" Demetrius said, with lugubrious voice, as if it were indeed a thing to be ashamed of.

"Yes, but for my mistress more. It is enough for me to have won so dear a girl."

"And so you keep yourself free to go to her when you please?"

"Yes, whenever the mood seizes me, for her smile is more than all Persia."

"I envy you your freedom, Medius," Demetrius lamented. "Rich, you may go and come when you will, while I have nothing but my sword — and thee, Theba!" he mourned.

"Tut, tut, take it not so seriously, for the King has the heart of a lover, and you have but to ask leave to have it granted."

"Ask the King! Not I."

"Nor need you, for when there's a lull in the campaign he will send you home without the asking."

"Think you so — he who knows not the rapture of a lover?" Demetrius exclaimed, delighted.

"Yes, as certain as winter comes and fighting languishes."

"But if he should forget?"

"He will not forget, for there are many like ourselves, who have left their loves to follow his fortunes. Think you he did not see their tears and kisses at parting, and the anguish of it all?"

"I would he too had a sweetheart, Medius, 't is so sweet to love."

"Perhaps he has," Medius laughed, who knew the secrets of the King's heart as if they were his own.

"Yes — Persia."

"That, and another."

"Another?"

"Yes, but while you look back he looks forward — that is all the difference between you."

Much more they would have said of a tender nature, being but recently wed, had not other things claimed their attention as the scattered detachments of the army left to guard the road fell into line behind the King.

As the night waned and the cavalcade emerged from the cover of a small forest, the sky ahead was seen to be lighted up as from a conflagration. Thinking it arose from the unextinguished camp-fires of the army, the King and those about him gave it no thought, until, approaching nearer, the shrieks of women mingled with the execrations of men fell upon their startled ears. Spurring forward, they presently reached the scene of the conflagration, when the King was startled and enraged to discover a band of Macedonian soldiers gathered about a vat of wine, and near at hand the peasant proprietor lying murdered,

while his horror-stricken wife and daughters, their
garments half torn from their bodies, bent over his
form sobbing and moaning. Hearing the King approach the half-drunken soldiers, thinking it a body
of marauders, bent like themselves on plunder, cried
out with maudlin voices:

"Come hither, comrades, if your throats be dry,
for there's plenty and to spare!"

When, however, the King, coming on at a furious
pace, approached within the circle of light, they raised
a cry of fear and sought to fly, but Alexander calling
upon the Companion Cavalry to surround the marauders, the latter, unable to offer serious resistance, fell
on their knees and begged for mercy. Directing
Demetrius to make suitable provision for the stricken
women, the King bade his followers bind the offending
soldiers and conduct them to the camp, after which,
putting spurs to his horse, he continued his journey
at full speed.

As the sun arose on the succeeding morning, the
still angry King reached the edge of a wide plateau
that looked down on a spreading valley bordering
the inland lake, now known as the Sea of Marmora.
Beyond in the offing, and as if in contempt of the
invading force, a Persian ship with sails set was signal-
ling with columns of smoke to unknown watchers in
the interior far away. Looking down on the intervening valley, the King's face lighted as he beheld the
Macedonian camp, no measure of security necessary

to its safety in an enemy's country having been omitted in its placing or the attendant details.

Oval in form, it was surrounded by an embankment of earth four cubits in height, the outer side being protected by a wide ditch, an abattis of trees and pointed stakes adding to the security. At intervals near the camp, detachments of troops were stationed, and from these the picket-line was formed, extending in an unbroken circle about the vast enclosure. These armed guardians of the camp were stationed a few feet apart and curiously, as it would now seem, passed a bell from hand to hand to indicate to the officers in charge that constant watchfulness was being maintained; and not less curiously the patrol, whose duty it was to inspect the picket-line, carried similar bells. Farther away videttes guarded the camp from quick surprise, while beyond these alert bodies of light-armed horsemen patrolled the outlying district. At each end of the encampment and on either side a break was left in the earthen wall, and from these streets ran to the openings opposite. Near the centre of the camp where the roads crossed, the headquarters of the army were placed, the lofty tent of the King dominating all. Within the enclosure thus formed rested in their allotted places the five and thirty thousand troops forming the King's army, with their horses, baggage, pack-animals, and attendant slaves and followers.

Noting with satisfaction the orderly array, the King

went forward, his coming unobserved except by those who watched beyond the walls of the enclosure. Nearing the southern entrance to the camp he halted, and calling the officer in command, gave him directions in regard to the disposition to be made of the marauding soldiers of the previous night. Hearing him, the officer hurried away with downcast head to do as the King commanded, horrified, it was apparent, at the nature of the service required of him. Approaching the camp, the King stopped on reaching the sentinel, and laying his hand on the iron helmet of the soldier, exclaimed with high good humour:

"What, you will still march with your King, old friend, though your hair be white and threescore years mark your span of life!"

"Yes, my Prince, and with the hope of something to pay for services in the past, which brought me nothing but wounds," the veteran responded, delighted at the King's recognition and friendly words.

"Then you expect something from the present venture?" the King laughed.

"Yes, rich gains, and not as with the Illyrians or half-clad Thracians, who had nothing but their bodies to recompense the victor. No, no, my Prince," the old man went on with heightened voice, encouraged by the King's manner, "that 's not the reason I carry a spear, as you know, but that I have the habit of the camp, and could not sleep if I did not hear the sound of the trumpet when I close my eyes at night."

"No kings save ours have such followers," the Monarch cried, looking down on the old man and thinking of the great number of veterans of like age marching with the standards.

"No country save ours has such kings, my Prince," the old soldier answered, delighted.

Greatly pleased at the veteran's response, Alexander continued on his way, the troops being at the moment in the act of breaking camp. And this amid many discordant sounds, the crying of orders, the blare of trumpets, the neighing of horses, and the braying of asses, mingled with the oaths of the slaves as they fastened the baggage of the camp on the backs of the patient animals.

As the soldiers emerged from the abandoned camp, a strange and ghastly sight met their horrified gaze. For on each side of the road, high up and as if marking the way, rude gibbets had been erected, on which hung the still warm bodies of the plunderers of the previous night. Amazed at the horrid spectacle and ignorant of what had occurred, the soldiers halted, surprised and bewildered; but presently, knowledge reaching them of the reason for the King's action, they resumed their march, vouchsafing no word of approval or censure. It was plain, however, that they knew not what to think, for the condemnation of a soldier without trial was a thing that had rarely

happened before. Had not the young King acted
hastily? Would Philip have done such a thing? No,
that they knew. What, then, did it foretell? Thus
the comment ran, and Philotas, more outspoken than
the others, took no pains to conceal his disapproval
of the King's action. Marching at the head of the
Companion Cavalry, he halted to survey the grewsome spectacle, and calling Lyncestes to his side,
gave loud voice to his regret that brave men should
be thus punished for an act that the old King would
have regarded lightly. And his words, being quickly
conveyed from rank to rank, were received by many
with open expressions of approval, and by all with
contracted brows and sober eyes.

Thus the forenoon wore on, the uneasiness of the
soldiers growing with each passing hour; but of
their manifest discontent the King took no apparent
notice. Bringing up the rear of the marching column
with cheerful countenance, he commented with seeming unconcern on the beauty and fertility of the
strange country. But as the army resumed its march
after the midday meal, he took his station beside
the road, and as the different bodies approached, he
commanded them to halt, and dismounting, inspected
their arms and accoutrements, calling the old veterans
by name, and saying some pleasant word to each,
not forgetting to praise the soldierly bearing of all.
Then, ere bidding them resume their march, he addressed them, seemingly without intent, but in the

light of what had occurred the night before and the punishment that followed:

"Brothers in arms," he cried, "when we crossed into Asia we came to occupy the land, to make it our own, not to lay it waste. Only those who openly oppose us are our enemies. Those we will despoil, that men similarly inclined may be led to peacefully submit. All others we will treat with kindness. Thus conquering, prosperity will follow and the people everywhere hail our coming as friends. Comrades! Soldiers!" he went on, with strident voice, lifting his sword, "glory and riches await all who aid me in this!—dishonour and death those who are led to follow a contrary course! In the coming campaign," he continued, with more amiable speech, "I shall share with you the fortunes of war, asking nothing denied another, and in battle will not bid you go where I do not lead. Remember," he added, with exalted air, "that we wish not alone to conquer, but to make the world more sane; a world wherein men may live without fear, coming and going when and where their inclination leads," and smiling upon the now delighted soldiers, he waved them forward.

Hearing him, they struck their shields, crying with one accord:

"Long live the King!"

"Long live Alexander—the Great!" a veteran shouted, facing the King and lifting his spear.

"You may make me that—by your bravery,"

the King cried, in response to the cheers that followed.

Thus it fell out because of the King's determination, that wherever his troops went there was peace and safety for all who submitted, a thing before unknown of an invading army. And the words of the King being everywhere repeated, it followed that many cities and provinces yielded without a blow, and as it became apparent that his government was more kindly then that of Darius', and that his viceroys exacted less than had the satraps of the Persian King, the people became his friends, few indeed desiring a return to the old order of things.

Having reviewed the troops in the manner described, the King galloped to the front, where information was presently brought that the army of Darius had taken its stand beyond the river Granicus, some miles away; but it being now late in the afternoon, Alexander ordered the troops to camp, that they might be rested for battle on the morrow.

Thus the young King passed the first day with the army in Asia, a companionship that grew in love with the passing years and ended only with the lives of those concerned.

CHAPTER III

Discerning the trap Alexander was preparing to spring, the Persian forces hurriedly relinquished their position on Mount Ida, and took up their station on the eastern bank of the Granicus, at a place where the foothills merged in the plain below. Meanwhile it was arranged, after much dissension and jealous bickering, that Aristes, Satrap of Phrygia, the province in which the army lay, should command the Persian forces in the expected battle. This nobleman, brave to rashness, as were all true Persians, possessed the hot temper and arrogance that two hundred years of domination had bred in the grandees of his country, but in other respects deserved the confidence reposed in him by his royal master. Riding in advance of the army, he halted on reaching the fertile plain, and driving his lance deep in the ground, cried out with grandiloquent speech:

"Here, oh Persians, we will await the Macedonian, who in his youthful vanity has dared to throw down the gauntlet of war to the King of Kings."

About him and applauding his speech were gathered many of the princes and nobles of Persia, so great an assemblage of the exalted of the nation never

37

indeed having been known before when the King himself was not present. It was, moreover, as if they were come to a fête, so sumptuous were their accoutrements and so exuberant their speech and manner. Hearing Aristes' declaration, Mithridates, the son-in-law of Darius, cried out in derision:

"You will do well to look to your source of supplies, my friend, while we wait, for, take my word, it will be many a day ere the boy King appears to face our invincible army."

"Our coming will prove a fool's errand and rank waste of the King's gold," Rhiosakes, an exalted nobleman, added with a laugh.

"Yet Memnon, the renegade whom our master has been misled into honouring above all others, would have us fly without striking a blow, laying waste the cities and fertile plains of Phrygia that Alexander may not have wherewith to feed his army," Aristes responded, looking away to the smiling valley.

"An opinionated upstart, this Memnon, swollen to bursting with the respect paid him," some one called out.

"Yes, and now that we are determined to give battle, he advises that we place the Greek mercenaries in our front while we true Persians cravenly hide behind," Pharnakes, an illustrious prince. and kinsman of Darius, scoffed.

"Though our cavalry, the pick of the King's

forces, outnumbers Alexander's five to one," Mithridates added.

"By Mithras' might, I will break my sword as unworthy the King's service ere I hide behind the Greek hirelings," Mithrines, the master of Sardis, pompously proclaimed.

"Were I in command, I would draw our forces back from the river so that the barbarian should have no excuse for declining the encounter," Spithridates a grandee of the court, advised.

At this Bessus, a cousin of the King and destined to achieve an unenviable fame, unable to listen longer to their foolish boasting, cried out with angry speech:

"The Macedonian will not need invitation to attack you, Spithridates, once his spies carry him word that we await him here."

"Is he so brave, then?" the other asked, knowing Bessus had spent some time at the court of Pella and cherished, moreover, a deadly hatred against Alexander.

"Yes, he has the courage of the wild-boar, and believes himself set apart by the Gods to revenge the insults offered his country by the Persian kings in former days."

"And so rushes headlong to destruction, for, man for man, our cavalry is the equal of his in courage, while we have the advantage of numbers and position," Aristes commented, his gaze centred on the gallant array of horsemen resting at their ease on the sloping hills.

"Yet would I not neglect any needed precaution," Bessus urged, "and if it be Memnon's belief that the heavy armed Greeks should be put to the fore, do not lightly disregard his advice, for he has greater knowledge of the Macedonians than we; and besides," he added with a sardonic laugh, "you would be pitting savage against savage."

"Your present order of battle invites defeat, Aristes," Chærodemus, an Athenian general and exile, present at Darius' command, sternly criticised, "for wherever Alexander charges in person there your troops will give way, and, gaining entrance, he will split your forces, and destroying your order of battle gain the victory. Memnon is in the right. Oppose the Macedonian with the Greek mercenaries. These he cannot lightly break, and while he is thus engaged your twenty thousand cavalry charging his flanks may destroy his order of battle and so bring about his defeat."

"Bah! You overestimate the strength and adroitness of the young savage," Aristes hotly responded.

"Do not regard him lightly, friend," Chærodemus entreated, "for at Cheronea when but a youth he charged the Sacred Band which had before broken the power of Sparta, and when the conflict ended not one was left alive to tell of the encounter."

"Is he greater then than Parmenio and Calas,

Philip's veteran generals? Are his troops better than theirs, who scarce a month ago fled in terror before our invincible arms?" some one asked, with derisive voice.

"Disaster cannot attend Aristes' plans; yet should we suffer repulse, I will forever stop the Macedonians' progress before the walls of Sardis," Mithrines, the governour of the impregnable citadel boasted, looking about him.

Omares, who commanded the Greek mercenaries, encouraged by what Bessus and Chærodemus had said, now called out to Aristes, though with much hesitation of speech:

"It is apparent Alexander must attack from the river, and this being so I pray you place my heavy armed troops there to receive him. He will set on with cavalry, that being his way, and our infantry, thus placed, will be able to check his onslaught and disorganize his forces, after which you may destroy him at your leisure."

But to this there was such general and angry dissent that Memnon, who had joined the council, foregoing suggestion, exclaimed with deferential manner:

"In what I have hitherto proposed I had no thought save the King's good. Whatever you determine, I and my sons will second with our swords and such courage as we have," he concluded, shame-faced, glancing over the array of noblemen who scanned him from the corners of their eyes with ill-concealed jealousy and dislike.

"What think you?" Aristes asked, turning to Artabazus, a nobleman of lofty character, in whose judgment the King reposed great confidence, and who, moreover, knew Alexander and had been on terms of friendship with him.

"I have but this moment reached the field," he returned, "and so scarce know the disposition you have made, or the whereabouts of the Macedonian King. But of this be assured, that he is brave to rashness, and will offer battle without delay — and with such skill as Philip taught him," he added, unwilling to accord the young King any skill save that which he had acquired from his father's teaching.

"I have made such disposition of our forces as seemed best, the responsibility being mine, and if I have erred I will not live to be reproached for want of wisdom," Aristes now decided, and by his words forecasted his unhappy death by his own hand a few hours later.

Thus it was determined by these brave and ill-advised men whom centuries of domination had taught to believe that no one could withstand them in open conflict. But if such was their belief it was by no means shared by the brave Greeks, who had been led by the bounty of the Persian king to join his ranks in opposition to the forces of Macedonia. These sturdy soldiers clad in armour, with buckler, sword, and

spear, looked on impatient of what they saw, but
without voice in the disposition of their lives more
than Memnon and his two stalwart sons. Placed in
reserve some distance from the river, mere lookers-on,
they watched with anxious countenances the placing
of the troops and the spectacle of the battle that
followed. And as if in further contempt of their usefulness, they were placed in oblong masses according
to the custom of barbarians, without order or coherency, as it would be with men if their fingers grew
together and so could not be used apart as need required.

Such was the situation on that beautiful day in
May as the Persian army, divided in its councils,
confidently awaited the coming conflict. And presently, as if in confirmation of Bessus' words, couriers
were seen flying across the plain beyond the river,
and by their gestures and frantic cries indicating all
too plainly that the enemy was fast approaching.
But while Bessus and Artabazus loosed their weapons,
as if Alexander were already upon them, others
laughed, crying out that the scouts had mistaken
the herds of cattle that found pasturage on the plain
for the Macedonian army. Soon, however, in con-
tradiction, the spies, reaching those who waited, reported that Alexander was marching with all speed
straight for the Persian army, as if having exact
knowledge of its position. At this all wondered,
knowing how small was his force, but while they

doubted, scanning the distant plain, they discerned on its farther border a speck of white, not larger than a man's hand, rising like a mist from out the wide expanse. Watching, in doubt as to its purport, soon it took more definite shape, spreading and mounting like a cloud as it came on, and turning as it neared from gray to inky blackness. Seeing it, the veteran Memnon, who had watched the movements of armies on the deserts of the south, forgetting the disgrace in which he stood, cried out in fierce alarm:

"Comrades, the Macedonian army is upon us, and if you would save the King's honour let every one hasten to his post!" But to this appeal some one, still doubting, responded with a laugh:

"It is more likely a flock of sheep, Memnon, driven hither by the shepherd king to hide his quick retreat."

"I did not give him credit for so much sense," another commented.

Thus the foolish jeered, little regarding the significance of what they saw, or its purport to their royal master.

" 'T is as Memnon says," Aristes cried out at last, as a glimpse of the advancing army showed here and there amid the clouds of dust. "Hasten each to his place, nor loiter here like children watching a passing show!" he commanded, motioning them away.

At this all was hurry and confusion; those who scoffed, no longer doubting Alexander's purpose,

made ready their weapons, and soon amid the blare of
trumpets the Persian cavalry was marshalled beside
the river bank. And in its front the nobles and
grandees took their stand, that they might be the
first to meet the foe should Alexander have the temerity to cross in face of so formidable an array.
Thus they rested, eagerly watching the approach of
the Macedonian army, now in full view as its serried
ranks in glistening armour came on with swinging
stride, as if unconscious of the enemy in their front.

Nearing the river bank the oncoming mass in all
the glorious panoply of war opened like a fan, displaying in the movement the changing positions of
the various bodies of troops as dancers give place to
one another in a minuet. First the dimachias who
fought on foot or horseback as the fortunes of battle
decided fell back, and after them in picturesque display the slingers and darters were seen to melt away,
bringing into view the mounted bowmen, and following them the Phalanx with its upraised spears, fourteen cubits in length. These, receding in their turn,
revealed the hetairai or Companion Cavalry, that
incomparable body of horsemen, clad in complete
armour, with whom Alexander opened every battle.
As the Macedonian line advanced it was seen to separate in the centre, some portion of each arm of the
service being allotted to either wing. To the right
under Alexander's immediate command could be
seen four regiments of the Companions in glittering

array, and on their flank Peonian archers and Agrarian darters; and with them a body of Hypaspists, shield-bearing guards, the pick of the Macedonian infantry, to steady and sustain the advance in the coming onslaught.

With the left wing Parmenio, Alexander's general, rode, and as the various classes of troops moved with the precision of a machine to their allotted places the Macedonian King could be seen on horseback directing a change in the formation here or strengthening a position there. Acclaimed with ringing cheers wherever he went, he bade his soldiers be of good heart, crying out that the host before them was a bladder that they had only to prick with their spears to see it quickly collapse. While he was thus engaged marshalling his force for the coming struggle, Parmenio, cautious from growing years, approached him and saluting, exclaimed:

"It is now near night, oh King, and darkness will soon cover the plain; defer, then, I pray, the uncertain venture till the morrow."

"Not so, Parmenio," the King exclaimed, "lest meanwhile the enemy change the order of battle, for his present disposition could not be more to my liking if I had the planning of it myself," and waving him away the young King continued his review of the waiting troops.

At last every preparation for the attack being completed, Alexander rested for a moment, scanning

the enemy's lines with eager glance, deep silence pre-
vailing throughout the Macedonian ranks.   Thus
the two armies confronted each other.   One strongly
stationed on the high bank of the river, and the other
at a disadvantage, compelled to ford the uncertain
stream and reaching the opposite shore break through
the seemingly invincible array of cavalry that awaited
its coming.

Satisfied with what he saw, Alexander raised aloft
his sword, the signal to advance, upon which the
trumpets sounded and the eager soldiers, chanting
the pæan of their country, moved forward to the
attack.   Now indeed the Persians could doubt no
longer, yet so greatly did they outnumber Alexander's
force that they smiled grimly at his daring, thinking
that never again would they have so glorious an
opportunity to win the favour of their master, the
great King.   And so, smiling and commenting on
what they saw, they watched and waited the coming
onslaught.

Reaching the river bank the King plunged into
the turbulent stream, black and swollen by mountain
snows, his followers pushing and crowding, seeking
in vain to keep pace with his swift advance.   But
among the many who cheered and cursed, striving
to reach the farther shore, Demetrius and Medius
sat their horses, melancholy and abstracted, as if
having no part in the stirring scene.   And presently
with one accord they turned to each other as if

unable longer to remain silent, exclaiming as their gauntleted hands met in fervent friendship:

"If I should fall?"

Nor did they think their apprehensions strange though never before had such thoughts found a place in their minds when going into battle. But now, treasuring their wives, it was different, and Demetrius being first to voice his fears, exclaimed as he crowded close to his companion's side:

"It is the fate of battle, Medius — and one of us may die."

"And the other —"

"Shall carry the message of him who falls."

"Yes."

"And if I should die —"

"Or I?"

"See that Theba has my sword and war-horse — all I have save the ruby the King gave me at the taking of Thebes," Demetrius directed, with choked voice.

"Yes — if the Gods spare me."

"Tell her I die with her name on my lips, sorrowing that I should be denied the bliss of life now that she is mine," he mourned, with moist eyes.

"And should I fall, Demetrius — tell my sweetheart I loved her more than life."

"That she well knows."

"And as a love-token give her this chain that my father wore, and his fathers before him, when tribal kings."

"Yes, comrade."

"And one other thing," he continued brokenly, "when she caresses me it is her way to kiss my hair and praise its beauty."

"I will not forget to send her a loving remembrance."

"She will not think it vain," Medius excused, turning away.

Thus they discussed of their loves, thinking not at all of what was occurring about them until, nearing the centre of the river, they were recalled to the present by the missiles that darkened the sky and beat like hail on their upraised shields as their horses reared and plunged waist-deep in the uncertain current.

"God of War, this is something to remember," Demetrius cried, forgetting his sorrows as he plucked a javelin from his shield.

"'T is like the foaming Devol below the walls of Pelion!"

"Yes, but not like that either, for we were in flight with the wounded King bringing up the rear."

"As he now leads the advance, and with even greater haste," Medius cried, pointing with his spear to the waving plumes of the King, who neared the enemy's shore.

"Why does he hurry so? Why not let the fools waste their weapons on the empty air?" Demetrius fretted, as he watched the Persians hurl their javelins and lances in vain effort to stay the advancing column.

"See, the King has reached the shore and essays the slippery bank with upraised spear," Medius cried, spurring his horse.

"Yes — and alone! — God of Gods, why do the Companions lag behind?"

"Death of men, 't is not their fault, but his," Medius reproved, as the King's horse sank into the turbid stream, beaten back by the Persian nobles. "But see, he tries again — and with no better fortune," he groaned, as Alexander, overwhelmed by numbers, was a second time repulsed.

Watching with bated breath Demetrius presently cried out, exultingly:

"There! At last he gains the solid ground!"

"And holds it, every thrust unhorsing an enemy."

"But what will it avail?" Demetrius wept in despair, as the Persians swarmed about the King.

"Everything, for the Companions gain his side — and the landing 's won!" Medius screamed in a frenzy of delight.

"While we wallow here helpless and chattering, and impatient and breathless, looking forward to the struggling mass," Demetrius cried out in rage. "Make haste there, Comrades, or, God of Gods, give way to those who will," and, pushing and crowding, the two friends finally reached the bank, where they were instantly engaged in the deadly conflict.

Meanwhile, and ere the King reached the shore, Ptolemy, in command of the extreme right of the Macedonian army and because of his better position, first gained the opposite bank. But vainly, for here Memnon's force, wisely held in check, awaited his approach, and charging with sword and spear as the Macedonians reached the shore, drove them back in a disordered mass. Of this, however, no one thought, for the Persian nobles, noting Alexander's position by the splendour of his armour and waving plumes, hurried to the spot where he must land, that they might personally confront him. But the King, urging his horse with voice and spur, seemed oblivious of their presence as they crowded close upon the river bank, hurling first their javelins and then their lances in vain effort to stay his progress and those who followed.

Thus it was until at last reaching the shore the King essayed the steep ascent, the Persian grandees crowding forward emulous of each other, seeking to strike him down. Making use of his shield and thrusting-pike, the King, after being twice repulsed, at last beat back those in his front, and the more forward of the Companions reaching his side he was able to maintain a foothold on the yielding bank. Here, upon the brink of the river, strewn with the dead and wounded, the battle raged until those who followed the King coming up in numbers he was finally enabled to make some headway. Seeing the

Persians give way, Mithridates, furious with rage, rallying his followers, charged full upon the King; but Alexander, anticipating the encounter, met him midway, and slew the gallant leader in sight of all his followers.   Enraged at the sorrowful spectacle, Rhiosakes, the brother of the stricken noble, rushed upon Alexander from behind, and raising his cimeter half severed the King's helmet, wounding him with the stroke.   Whirling upon his foe Alexander beat down the other's lighter weapon, and poising his spear thrust the nobleman through the body.

At this, seeing a chance, Spithridates rushing in sought to strike the King ere the latter could recover his spear, but while his weapon was still uplifted, the veteran Clitus, who fought with the savage fury of former days, raised his sword, severing the Persian's arm with the stroke; and following the blow with insatiate rage thrust the fainting noble through the body, killing him on the spot.   Meanwhile, Bessus, freeing himself from the enemies who thronged about him, rushed forward to attack Alexander, but the King, meeting him midway, hurled him from his horse with a thrust of his spear.   Seeing this Artabazus, fighting singly and apart, conscious that the day was lost, now rushed in seeking to kill Alexander, indifferent to his own fate.   But the King recognizing him as he came on, warded his blow and unwilling to do him harm because of their previous friendship, turned to seek Mithrines, whose scared face appeared

some way back in the enemy's ranks. But that
wily noblemen, detecting the King's purpose, turned
his horse, and pushing this way and that forced a passage to the rear, and continuing his flight stopped not
till safe within the protecting walls of Sardis' lofty
citadel. Not so with Artabazus, who, pursuing his
headlong course, seeking death, was presently confronted by those who followed the King, and a spear
penetrating his thigh and another his horse, the
latter, maddened with pain, turned and in a frenzy
of fear carried the unfortunate prince from the field.

While the King was in the thick of the fight, and
beset on every hand, his spear being broken, a fresh
weapon was given him with which he continued the
attack, and with such energy that an opening was at
last made in the enemy's ranks. Closely followed by
the Companion Cavalry — as if all strength lay in
his presence and uplifted arm — the King charged
afresh full at the enemy's centre, and with such
furious savagery that the Persian nobles, losing heart,
abandoned the ill-fated field, recognizing that the
battle was lost. Seeing their leaders dead or in
flight, and Parmenio closing in from the north, the
Persian army waited not, but throwing down their
weapons fled in wild disorder.

Now there remained only the twenty thousand
Greek mercenaries, their weapons upraised, neither
advancing nor retiring, standing bravely, waiting,
knowing not what to do. Seeing them the King,

afire with the flame of battle, sounded the bugle afresh, and calling back those who were in pursuit of the fleeing Persians charged the desperate Greeks with such forces as he had in hand. His horse being slain, he mounted another, urging on the attack from every side, the Greeks continuing to fight with stubborn courage until barely two thousand remained alive. These in desperation threw themselves on their faces, letting the Phalanx pass over them, and in this attitude of supplication besought Alexander to spare their lives. This he did, afterwards sending them to Macedonia to till the soil as a punishment for taking up arms against their countrymen.

Of the gallant array of Persian nobles, scarce one escaped death or grievous hurts. Bessus, desperately wounded, lay long unnoticed among the dead, but taking advantage of the darkness crawled to the river side, and hiding beneath its sheltering bank finally effected his escape.

When at last the strife of battle had stilled, Alexander hastened to seek the wounded among his followers, cheering them by his presence, and personally looking to their wants, after which he sought his own tent where Jaron, his physician, bound up the many wounds he had received in the desperate conflict. In this way and as described the battle of the Granicus was fought and won by the heroic young King.

CHAPTER IV

A MESSAGE OF LOVE

Sardis, the hope of Persia, old in story and of legends innumerable, had fallen — a prey to the invading foe! The ancient capital of Crœsus, whose palaces still crowned the lofty cliff! The city of tragedies, of Solon's sojourn, within whose precincts gold was first coined and commerce made a robe to clothe the western world! Sardis, the metropolis of the West, the stronghold of Lydia, the seat of Government from remotest ages! The abode of Atys, wisest of kings, who in the long agony of his people putting grave things aside set himself to the planning of idle games that he might thus divert the thoughts of his famine-stricken subjects!

But such things the people no longer regarded, for, cowardly and all unnecessarily, Mithrines, the recreant Governour, had given up the city to the invading King. Not indeed since the Great Cyrus stormed

55

its walls and by strange chance discovered the weakness of its towering citadel had there been such bewilderment. Strange happening! Instead of stout defence, in the interval of which Persia might recover her strength, the city had surrendered, and with it the mighty fortress, a frowning rock buttressed about with triple walls that months and years would not suffice to undermine. All this without a blow, leaving the inhabitants panic-stricken, cowering in their houses or flying for their lives, fearing murder and sack.

When, following the battle of the Granicus, Alexander neared the famed stronghold, expecting to lay siege to the city, a deputation, met him beseeching him to halt his victorious army that Mithrines, the governour, might pay him a visit of respect and homage. Astonished to find submission where he had expected a hazardous and bloody siege, the King stayed his troops on the banks of the Hermus. And presently while he waited a squadron of Persian cavalry without arms or insignia of any kind approached at a furious gallop from the walled city. Halting some way off, they parted to the right and left, revealing a golden chariot containing the governour and his two daughters, maidens scarce grown to womanhood. Alighting, the sorrowful group made their way amid the breathless silence of the waiting army to the spot where the King stood, and reaching his presence threw themselves on their knees, the daughters in advance, as if in protection of their father. Raising his head Mithrines cried out with supplicating voice:

"I come, oh King, to make humble tender of these my daughters, and with them the keys to Sardis, and its protecting citadel."

Amazed and angered at the father's base offer, the King remained silent, frowning upon the traitorous governour. Terrified, the suppliants raised their hands, crying with one voice:

"Mercy, oh King! Mercy! Mercy!"

Taking pity on the affrighted maidens the King's brow relaxed, and advancing he lifted them to their feet, exclaiming:

"The gift of the city I accept, Mithrines, and in respect to your daughters the army welcomes their coming and extends to them its fatherhood and protecting care, exalted by their presence." Then, looking down on the recreant governour, he exclaimed with harsh voice and lowering brow: "Why have you brought these children here? Is it that you feared to come alone?"

"Yes, oh King, lest the offences of former years be remembered against me," he murmured, referring to his intrigues in Macedonia four years before.

"Nor have I forgotten, but the present leans not on the happenings of the past. Arise and go thy way, the gift of Sardis and its citadel I accept, but of these young and unoffending maidens they have no place within the camp," and backing away he seemed in the movement to spurn the offending nobleman.

"Do with them as you please, for they are in all things thy creatures, oh King of Kings!" Mithrines answered, with bowed head, giving to Alexander the sonorous title of the Persian monarch.

In thus offering his daughters, Mithrines yielded only what was the King's of right according to Oriental custom, but Alexander, vouchsafing no reply, looked about him, and espying Demetrius and Medius, who sat their horses scowling down on what they saw and heard, he motioned them to approach, and said:

"Attend these children to their home in the city, and that it may be notable and a token of the honour in which the army holds all women, Lyncestes, whom I have this day appointed commander of the Thessalian cavalry, will act as an escort with a detachment of his troops."

Afterward, when the blushing maidens would have knelt to take their leave, the King took the hand of each and led them to the waiting chariot, where he bade them adieu with expressions of good will and gracious wishes for their future happiness. Observing the kindly act, a deafening roar of approval went up from the staring troops, for the soldiers were very much in love with their chivalrous young King, and remembering the wives and sweethearts they had left behind, thought his act something to be applauded.

Turning again to Mithrines, Alexander directed him to return with the escort to the city and deliver up the keys to Asandros, a trusted officer, who was to be its future governour. Thus the surrender of Sardis was brought about, but of all that happened, including the giving up of the city, nothing so much astonished the army as the appointment of Lyncestes to command the Thessalian cavalry, a corps ranking next in honour to the Companions. For this scheming nobleman was everywhere distrusted and hated by the soldiers, who believed him to have been privy to Philip's murder, but because he was the husband of Antipater's daughter, and for reasons of public policy, Alexander had pardoned him, and having pardoned now trusted him.

Refraining from entering the stricken city, the King stayed with the army as it lay encamped in the plain beside the classic river. But, apprehensive that the surrender might be a trick to accomplish his destruction, and the treachery of Mithrines a trap to catch him off his guard, he set out at midnight with Hephestion to make the rounds of the sentinels lest some precaution necessary to the safety of the army should have been overlooked. Wrapped in a military cloak he left the camp, making a wide detour, stopping often to listen, as if expecting to hear the tramp of an advancing army from out the inky darkness of the surrounding plain. But of the presence of an enemy there was no sign, no sound dis-

turbing the stillness of the night save that of the
signals and answers of those who watched.   Going
forward within the pale of the glowing camp-fires,
a man suddenly emerged from out the darkness and
throwing himself at the King's feet exclaimed in
Greek, yet with some flavour of Persian speech, as if
he were accustomed to the use of both:

"If this be the King, I come, a friend, begging his
favour and protection."

"What would you have of me?" Alexander demanded, stepping back.

"I bear a message for thy ear alone, if such
favour be accorded me," the other craved, glancing
at Hephestion, who stood a few feet away with
weapon upraised.

"I have no secrets that he may not hear," the
King answered, curtly.

Hesitating a moment, the suppliant continued:

"My message is of such import, oh King, that I
may not divulge it save to thee, nor then if thy temper be not of like spirit.   Such are my commands,
admitting of no discretion whatsoever."

Thinking of Mithrines' base act and believing the
messenger conveyed an offer of like purport from some
exalted Persian, Alexander motioned Hephestion to
retire.   This he did, but only for a short distance,
standing alert with ready weapon should the intruder
offer the King harm.   Turning again to the stranger,
Alexander cried out in imperious tones, impatient at

the thought of further treachery, even though he profited by its exercise:

"Quick, slave, make known thy message!"

"It is of gentle import, oh King, and its bearer may not be received as if he were an enemy or bore a poisoned cup," the other protested, angered at Alexander's reply.

"Tell it, whatever its purport, and quickly, or go thy way," the King commanded, impatient at the delay when so many things claimed his attention elsewhere.

"It is a message of love, oh King, and devotion unchanged," the other hesitatingly explained, uncertain of speech.

"If its purport be of mercy, craved by one who has erred, speak, for I have no enemies save those in arms against me," the King responded, with gentler voice.

"It does not invite mercy, but return of like confidence and love. Naught but that, oh King; neither power, nor gift, nor favour of any kind besides," the other answered, ambiguously.

Surprised and at a loss whether to further interrogate the messenger or deliver him up to the guard, the King sought to make out the outlines of the stranger's face, but save a cloaked figure in the semi-darkness he could discern nothing.

"Mercy I may grant at will, but love and confidence are things that cannot be thus evoked. Tell me from whence you come, if indeed there is anything worthy of thought in what you say," the King demanded, mystified by the other's words.

"Know then, oh King, that I come from Bactria, though the delivery of my message has been delayed these many months."

"Bactria!" the King exclaimed, his voice losing its sternness, as his heart conjured up the image of Roxana, for to him that unknown and far-off country had no meaning save that it was her home.

"Yes, oh King."

"Bactria!" the King repeated, but checked himself lest the message be a snare devised by some one having knowledge of his passion for the gentle Princess. "Friends I had in Bactria," he went on coldly, "but of their present whereabouts or interest I have no knowledge. Is it from them you come!"

"Yes, oh King."

"From Oxyartes, it may be!" Alexander interrogated, after further pause, fearing to do that nobleman harm by remembrance of him now.

"No, oh King, but from one dearer to him than life itself," the other explained, with sober voice.

Hearing him, Alexander, overwrought, thinking of Roxana, cried out:

"Quick, tell me from whom you come and if your message be what you say all trust and honour awaits you as its bearer."

"I come, oh King, from the Princess Roxana.

Is it from her you would have word!" the other answered without further reservation. .

"Yes, though all the world claimed preference. And if it be be as thou sayest, then indeed art thou welcome, favoured in thy office beyond all mortal men," the King cried with impassioned voice, as if the messenger from out the night were sent by some favouring God in answer to his prayers.

"If that be so, oh King, then am I privileged to deliver the missive with which she entrusted me," the other said, reassured.

"Be quick, nor deny me longer," Alexander cried, forgetful of his kingly dignity.

"'T is here, concealed within this staff," the other said, as he knelt and presented the stick to the King.

Breaking the staff, there fluttered to the ground a letter, which the King seized and read by the flaming torch which Hephestion brought.

"Roxana to Alexander: Greeting. As I was, when we parted, in love, so am I now in love and trusting confidence all thine own, and so I will be as long as I have life to love thee."

Reading it, the King cast the torch from him, and Hephestion, suspecting the nature of the missive took the hand of the messenger and silently led him away. Thus they left the King, holding the letter in his hand, erect and motionless, his cloaked figure dimly outlined against the summer sky. No longer, however, was he King, but again the Prince Iskander — her love-name — holding her in his arms as on that night when they had pledged their love anew and so were parted; he fleeing for his life, an exile; she weeping and disconsolate. Pressing the missive to his lips he lived over again in the stillness of the night their days and hours of loving intercourse; the pledges they had interchanged; all they had promised themselves which promises now, the Gods favouring, he was at last to consummate. Thus hours passed, and when late in the night Alexander returned to his tent he hastened to question the messenger concerning Roxana and his journey.

"It is many months, oh King, since I left Bactria; a year — perhaps longer," the other replied to an inquiry of Alexander.

"What! Do you not know the time?"

"It was a three months' journey to Sardis, but after that I can only guess the time that has elapsed."

"What mean you by that!" the King questioned, surprised.

"I reached Sardis without interruption save by the outlaws of the country, who indeed did me no harm. Concealing myself in a cave, I hid my staff, after which I visited the city to seek for food and make inquiries concerning affairs in Macedonia. For ere I left Bactria, oh King, word had been signalled that Philip was dead, but of the succession nothing whatever was vouchsafed. My inquiries unhappily led to my arrest as a spy, but on being brought before

Mithrines and questioned, nothing was determined, and so he bade them detain me until he had opportunity to question me further. Upon this I was taken to a cell beneath the citadel, and whether I was forgotten by Mithrines or left there purposely I know not; but months, and it may be years, passed without my being able to obtain a hearing or satisfaction of any kind."

"Think you he suspected your errand?" the King asked, with lowering brow.

"Yes, oh King, and that he instantly recognized me on my being brought before him."

"How recognized you?"

"As one who accompanied the Princess Roxana on her return to her own country from Pella."

"And did you so accompany her?" the King asked, astonished.

"Yes; with Ossa, my Prince, to whom I owed allegiance."

"I knew not that another went with him."

"Yes, when you commanded him to attend upon her with his life, as he would upon yourself, and she afterward returned to Bactria while you were in exile, I begged permission to accompany him, and she, graciously assenting, I became from that hour one of her attendants, and so have remained to this day," the messenger answered, with simple speech.

"I knew not of this, as I say, nor do I now recall

your being with Ossa," the King said, perplexed, scrutinizing the other attentively.

"I am Orestes, who made your tutor Lysimachus a prisoner in the Vale of Tempe ere your encounter with Ossa, my chief," the other explained, smiling at the recollection. "Since then I have changed much, and purposely, as has Ossa, who is in appearance a true Persian."

"Why that?"

"That he may the better serve his mistress."

"The Gods favour him and you for the sacrifice!" the King cried, deeply moved, recalling his encounter with Ossa in the Vale of Tempe when a Prince, and Ossa's abandonment afterward of the life of outlawry he had previously led.

"Yes, immediately we left Macedonia," Orestes explained, with some show of pride, "we adopted the Persian language and dress, and so cannot now be distinguished from the natives of the country."

"You spoke a little while ago of your long imprisonment in the citadel?"

"Yes, oh King."

"How did you at last effect your escape?"

"This morning, at break of day, the guards, to our great astonishment, visited the cells of the citadel and released all the prisoners, and afterward drove them from the city through the southern gate that they might be dispersed ere you arrived, so it now seems, though their purpose did not then appear. Immediately upon being released," Orestes further explained, "I returned to my former hiding-place, and securing my staff hastened hither, hearing of your presence; but when I sought to pass the guard I was arrested as a spy and came near to being put to death on the spot. Making my escape in the confusion, I waited another chance, and remembering Philip's habit of making the rounds of his camp at night when in the enemy's country, and thinking you might do the same, I hid myself, and thus came upon you."

"Have you not known these two years gone that I was King?" Alexander asked.

"No, as I say."

"And the Princess?"

"She knew not whether you were King or still in exile, but immediately she heard Philip was dead wrote the message and bade me deliver it with all speed."

"The Gods bless her for the gracious act," the King murmured, under his breath.

"Though I set forth in some state, I lost all I had save my staff," Orestes continued, "and once came nigh to losing that, but waiting until night I killed the robber who stole it as he slept. Afterward disfiguring the stick so that it seemed hardly fit for a beggar to carry, I kept on my way, and save for Mithrines should have reached Pella ere you had been crowned half a year," he sighed.

"And I have been kept in ignorance all these

months because of Mithrines' act — and am now powerless to punish him," the King added, half aloud, regretting in his rage that he had pardoned the traitorous governour.

"Have you then heard nothing from the Princess!" Orestes asked, with anxious voice.

"No, and if other messages have been sent they have failed to reach me, as this came nigh to doing. And so it is, I fear," he went on, "with the many messages I have myself dispatched, but of which I have heard nothing."

"The Gods grant that they may have reached her ere this," Orestes cried, in deep distress, "for in sending me forth it was with much hesitation and as if she doubted the propriety of what she did."

Greatly agitated, the King embraced him, crying out with broken speech:

"Lest no word from me has reached her, you, more trustworthy than those I have dispatched, shall at once return to Bactria the bearer of such message as I will prepare.   And let not your going be delayed longer than necessary to rest and refresh yourself," the King added, giving no thought to Orestes, so great was his impatience to respond to Roxana's loving message.

"Let it be to-morrow, oh King, if that be not too soon, for I have been so long cramped within narrow walls that the adventure will warm my blood and build me up anew," Orestes begged, with cheerful voice.

"To-morrow then it shall be," the King said, and calling a page bade him prepare quarters for Orestes and attend upon him as upon himself. This office of love and hospitality performed, the King in devout thankfulness proceeded to the sacrificial altar and lighting the sacred fire offered up sacrifices and libations to the Gods for what they had so kindly vouchsafed him. Afterward seeking his tent, he gave himself up to thoughts of Roxana, and thus his attendants found him, and, doing so, could not but remark his great elation, for it was as if he were already conqueror of Persia, though assured, indeed, only of the undying love of her he treasured.

CHAPTER V

"Two years has Iskander, my love, been King and I have no word to cheer my heart or lighten the burden of my long waiting. And twice that time it is since holding me in his arms he bade me wait his coming, for no other, so he swore to the Gods of high Olympus, should be his Queen once he were King."

Such were the sorrowful words that escaped the lips of the Princess Roxana as she stood one autumn day looking forth from the Bactrian fortress of Arimazes, grieving over Alexander's unexplained silence.

"And I believed thee," she went on, disconsolate, "and still believe, yet somehow, sweet lord, thou shouldst have found a way to convey some token of thy love during all these waiting months. But I have not doubted, nor will I, though my father swears thy love is cold as the snow-clad mountains, and that thou dost look on me as one dead to thee. Yet it may well be, 't was so long ago, and thee beset on every hand by enemies, and Philip, thy father, foremost among them all. Thou didst stand in sore need of love, and I gave it thee without measure, and now, a King, thou art perhaps still more beset, yet I'll swear thou lovest me still though thou mayest have wed

70

another. Unhappy thy fate if that be so, yet in such things kings must oftentimes bow to the will of others, however their hearts may rebel at a thing so monstrous. Yet if it should be so I will still love thee, and always, knowing no change to the very end," she sighed, her gaze fixed on the half-hidden road that wound about the base of the mountain, and by which any message from her love must come.

While she thus watched and waited, as had been her daily custom for many months, her father, Oxyartes, approached unobserved, and gathering from her broken speech the purport of her thoughts, cried out with impatient voice:

"What, my child, will you forever sorrow for a love impossible of fulfillment; forever live apart, treasuring unrequited the memory of that inconstant Prince, to whom in mad haste and all forgetful of yourself and others you plighted your loving faith?"

"What would you, father? Can I be different from what I am, my heart being plighted to him then and now?" she answered, without removing her gaze from the mountain path.

"Yes, I would have you dismiss him from your thoughts, forever tear his image from your heart as a thing unworthy, and live again as before, happy in your life and the affection of those about you."

"I cannot if I would, for the heart knows no guidance in its selfish preference, and recks not of reason

In such a thing more than of the birds that circle above our heads."

"Your love is your shame, my child, for it is without avail; spent on the empty air. See, the very rocks on which you stand are worn with your watching and waiting for a message that will never come!" he sternly reproved.

"It may be so, but here will I abide, here maintain my vigil until the message comes, or failing, I die in my despair, there being naught else in life worth having save his love," she mourned.

"Is the love of your father, of your brother, of your mother nothing! Of the gallant men who would throw themselves from this dizzy height for a smile from your lips? Why delude yourself longer? A King, did he love, would have found a way to reach you with some word, some gentle token that he had not changed. But months and years have come and gone, winter has succeeded summer, and so again and again, and yet no word — nor will there be," he raged.

"Hush, father, you kill me with your cruel words," she sobbed, burying her face in her hands.

"And Orestes, whom you sent a too willing messenger to the forgetful King, inconstant, like the other, has made excuse of serving you only to find a way to return to his native land," Oxyartes scorned.

"Nay, father, I'll not believe it unless indeed my message of love to my dear lord, having proven fruitless, he has killed himself from very shame. For he could no more prove false to me, or my trust in him, than Ossa, whose patient service upon which his master sent him not even you can doubt," she answered, looking toward the sturdy chief who stood some steps away, attentive and alert, as if there ever rang in his ears the command of Alexander to guard and protect his mistress with his life. And so it had been in the years that had elapsed since leaving Pella with the Princess, each day adding to his devotion and his great desire for the approval of his master when he should at last call upon him for an account of his stewardship.

"Men stare and wonder," Oxyartes went on, less sternly, "that you find pleasure in no one, but live apart, melancholy of mood, as one deprived of reason, different from all others and from your former self."

"I cannot help their wondering, father, nor would I if I could, finding what comfort of life I have in thinking of the days spent with my sweet lord, in his own country, and of his great love and promised coming once he were free to exercise his will."

"'T is plain enough, my child, that Philip, enamoured of your beauty and thrice rejected by you, should afterward have thought to revenge himself by traducing you to his son, the Prince; and so, the latter misled and weaned of his passion, no longer treasures you," Oxyartes said, reflecting on what occurred at Pella at the time of their visit to that city four years before.

"I'll not believe Iskander could think me untrue to him, save from his own lips; nor could he be false to a vow more than the Gods we serve," Roxana protested, her eyes raised to heaven.

"Long you have waited and watched, and many have you rejected because of this vain passion, and I have remained silent," Oxyartes complained. "But now comes our sovereign lord, the King's viceroy, Bessus, admitting of no refusal, asking you to be his wife. Or, better still, his queen, for his power and estate in the east is little less than that of the King of Kings."

"I have listened to his prayer and thanked him, and so dismissed him and with that he must be content, for I have no love in my heart save for my lord, Iskander."

"You forget my debt to Bessus; that I owe him my very life and so cannot turn him away lightly, that you may continue to treasure your hopeless passion," Oxyartes reproached.

"I owe you all obedience, but life is not worth the having if with it I must wear a yoke so galling. No; sooner than wed Bessus I will cast myself from this wall, as I have been many times tempted to do in the past," she lamented, looking down from the lofty height.

"He cannot be dismissed thus, my child, for he is of no less royal blood than the King, being of the family of Darius, and so may not be refused what he demands."

"I care not for that, and were it Darius himself, governing all the world in undisturbed power, yet would I refuse him," she angrily retorted.

"Child, child, will you not listen to me, your father?" he supplicated.

"Yes, in all things save this, but if you would have me live speak not again of Bessus, or of any other who seeks me in marriage, lest, tormented beyond endurance and losing all desire to live, I throw myself from this rock and so end my unhappy life."

Hearing her Oxyartes drew back, long undecided whether to urge her further or await a more propitious hour, but as if at last convinced of her firm determination he turned away, leaving her to her sorrowful thoughts.

The fortress of Arimazes, of which he was the lord, raised its lofty front on the very confines of eastern Persia, and here on this impregnable rock, amid towering mountains and swift-flowing rivers, separated from the world by interminable wastes the Princess Roxana had her home. Here it was her father had found refuge from the deadly enmity of Darius, an enmity having its origin in his mission as ambassador to Pella. For the Persian monarch, misled by the distorted tales of Mithrines, his confidential agent, firmly believed Oxyartes had entered into a secret and traitorous understanding with the Macedonian King. And frightened by Alexander's threatened invasion, and fearing an uprising in the

far east, he determined to put the offending noble
to death.   But in this he was balked by Bessus, for
while that mighty and cruel prince respected no one,
not even the King, he loved Oxyartes with whom as
a youth he had been reared.   When, therefore, he
received Darius' order to put the nobleman to death
he made pretence of willingness, but secretly warned
his friend to fly.   Afterward, when the war broke out
and all was alarm and confusion, he gave Oxyartes
refuge in the fortress of Arimazes, reporting to the
King that the offending nobleman was free of offence
and active in his support — as was indeed true at that
time and during Darius' life.

No trace can now be found of the Sogdian rock of
Arimazes, but we know from the chroniclers of the
time every detail of the picturesque stronghold and
its rugged heights.   The face of the cliff whereon the
fortress stood was a mile in extent and two hundred
cubits in height, access being by a narrow path, cut
in the face of the solid rock and of such narrowness
and tortuous course that it could be effectively defended by a dozen men.   The castle, or citadel, wherein
Oxyartes lived, and where a last stand might be made
if necessary in defence of the fort, lifted its secure
front near the battlement of the great fortress, while
back of it, in picturesque confusion, were clustered
the wattled huts of the villagers and the more spacious
barracks of the garrison.   About the entrance to the
citadel, and giving it an air of comfort, a miniature

forest grew, interspersed with flowers and verdant shrubbery brought from the neighbouring mountains. Here in this sylvan retreat, undisturbed by the turmoil of the fortress, Roxana nursed her grief, and cried aloud to the empty air against the forlornness of her wretched life.

As Oxyartes ceased to urge Roxana and turned away, deeply disappointed, the sound of a horn, clear and sweet, arose from the valley below. Looking down, startled by the unwonted sound, Roxana beheld a company of Scythian nomads, armed with bows and arrows, according to the fashion of those primitive people.

"What means the presence of these savages, sister?" Itanes, the youthful brother of Roxana, asked, as he hurried to her side attracted by the bugle call.

"They form a part of Bessus' forces called to the war in the far west," she sighed, as the bugle sounded afresh and the hardy soldiers again took up their line of march.

"I had not heard of any war, — or is it merely the outbreak of some ambitious satrap!" the youth laughed, for he knew little of what was transpiring in the world at large, spending his time hunting and in idle dalliance about the fortress.

"They go to oppose the Macedonian King, who, to avenge some oppression suffered by his people, threatens the peace of Persia with a mighty army,"

Roxana explained, as if there could be no doubt about the cause of the war.

"Well, if that be all, our troops will make short work of the venturesome savages," he grinned.

"Savages! You know nothing of the Macedonians, brother, or you would not say that," she chided.

"That's true, sister, but what are they like?"

"Like no other soldiers in the world for skill in arms, and fierce bravery in battle," she said, conjuring up their conflict with the Theban band which she had witnessed in the plains of Thessaly.

"I doubt that, for I have always been told that the soldiers of Persia were the bravest in the world; or, what is more likely, those of Bactrian birth," he boasted, scanning the mountains as if men reared amid such rugged forces must be hardier than any others.

"The Macedonians are not brave merely, but are led by a young King who is great in war above all that ever lived," she praised, to the astonishment of Itanes, her intimacy with Alexander being unknown to him, or if some hint of it had reached him he had forgotten it, full of the importance of his own affairs.

"And has he invaded Persia to make war on the King of Kings?" Itanes questioned, incredulously.

"Yes."

"For the purpose of plunder?"

"No; that he may reign in Darius' place."

"Whew! I like that. Overthrow! Well, your

young King is n't burdened with modesty," Itanes laughed.

"He is both modest and brave, and has ambition to be something beside a huntsman," she scorned, in reproof of Itanes' idle life.

"There you go again; forever prating about my habits," he complained.

"This young King, you should know, won a great battle while still a youth, and now while scarce of age has crossed the Hellespont into Asia after conquering the enemies of his own kingdom, intent, as I say, upon becoming King of all Persia," she portrayed, with beaming face.

"Ye Gods, if Gods there be!" he jeered, as young men sometimes will, "I would I might meet him."

"Might meet him?"

"Yes, to see which is the better man," he bragged, tapping his sword.

"I would you could if I might be there to stay his hand," she smiled.

"Ho! Is he indeed so mighty?"

"Yes, for no man living can stand against him with sword or spear."

"Why have you not told me of him before, since you know so much?" he resented, as if she regarded him too lightly because of his youth and idle ways.

"I did not know you cared for wars or the exploits of brave men," she excused.

"You think I love this idle life, this pricking of

bears and wild hogs, when I would be like this young King, but have no chance," he complained.

"You have some ambition, then?" she questioned, with a smile.

"Is there any man who lacks it if he be not a coward — and is in love?" he ended, haltingly.

"Are you in love, then?" she sighed, as if it were a grievous burden.

"Can one know Ossillia, sister, and not be in love?" he asked, with crimsoned cheeks. "And if this young King has performed such brave deeds," he went on, "why may I not do something worthy?"

"I know not, but common men achieve so little," she answered, absently, her gaze fixed on the valley below.

"Come, sister, be reasonable. I'm not a child, and you know Darius flouts us. Shuts us out of the pale of royal favour; cuts us off from every chance of preferment, has condemned our father, and I, his son, to death — and so I owe him nothing."

"Well, what of that, for it has been as you say these many months?"

"Only this, that if you have favour with this young King, give me a letter or token by which he will receive me into his grace, and give me employment that I may use my sword and spear on something beside wild beasts."

"What! Would you join Iskander against Darius?" she cried, overjoyed, but in a voice so tremu-

lous that he stared, wondering, not knowing what
to make of it.

"Yes, if you approve, for only in the ranks of
Darius' enemies am I safe from his insane wrath,"
he cried.

"I would you might be with the brave King,
brother, and in his favour, but until we have some
further news of his progress you must dismiss the
thought. Or, if you treasure it, let it find no expression except in the practice of arms, so that if you
should finally go to him you may not disgrace our
people by your clumsiness," and lest she say too much
she dismissed him, turning again with a sigh to resume
her attitude of watchfulness.

Thus she remained until the music of the marching soldiers was lost in the windings of the mountains, and the stillness that heralds the night envel-
oped her. Yet still her gaze was fixed on the road as
it wound a thread of white beneath the cliffs, but as
she watched a trembling seized her, as had so often
happened before when some chance wayfarer approached the lonely fortress along the little-frequented highway. Now, thinking she espied a
traveller in the distance, she was yet in doubt, for
oftentimes she had conjured up such vision only to
find it the shadow of a tree or high-projecting crag.
All of a tremour, and uncertain of herself, she turned
to Ossa, crying out, discordantly:

"Come here, good friend, for my eyes are so wearied

with watching yonder path that I can no longer trust them to tell me if what I see be a man or only the shadow of a tree or shrub."

Approaching the wall, Ossa scanned the lonely road, and presently turned to her with stolid speech, in keeping with the character of a simple peasant he had assumed on accompanying her to Asia.

"Yes, mistress, it is a man or creature bearing the semblance of one."

"Then I was not deceived," she murmured, with heightened colour, fixing her eyes on the fast-darkening valley.

Thus they watched, saying nothing as the wayfarer dragged himself forward, seemingly overcome with age or fatigue. But presently, as he neared the lofty cliff, he raised his head, and espying Roxana outlined against the evening sky stopped and waved his hand as if in greeting or conveyance of some message.

"What means he by that?" she faltered, sinking down on her knees.

"Nothing, mistress; 't is the trick of a beggar or mountebank, that he may the more surely be received with favour," Ossa laughed, with seeming unconcern.

"No, Ossa, he has not the air of a beggar, though clothed in rags. 'T is a message he bears; a warning, it may be, to strengthen the guard against the onrush of some enemy," she said, seeking a reason for his coming different from what she hoped.

HEIGHTS OF ARIMAZES

"There is no enemy within a day's march, mistress, for had there been signals would have told us of their approach," he answered, with confident assurance.

"Then he bears a message. Look! Can you not discern his features? Stupid! . You who have the eyes of a wolf, say, is it not Orestes; he whom we have thought dead?" she screamed, knowing not what she said.

"Calm yourself, my mistress," he commanded, his stolid face giving place to one of lofty air; "and if it be he let not his coming be cause of any rash resolve," he added, drawing near her lest in her mad excitement she do some foolish thing.

To this she made no response, but tearing the veil from about her head leaned over the wall, waving it in welcome to the traveller, be he who he might.

"See, he looks up. Oh it is Orestes! He smiles — nay, is laughing, as if his coming would be welcome, and so it will be, Ossa; so it must be!" and losing the strength that had so long sustained her she fell forward in a faint. But as if the coming of her messenger lifted a burden from off her heart she quickly regained consciousness, her eyes opening as from a sweet sleep. Then, memory returning at sight of Ossa, her eyes sought the valley below and seeing no one, and believing what had occurred to be but a dream, she sprang to her feet and would have hurled herself from the precipice had he not forcibly restrained her.

"Release me, Ossa, for I can endure the agony of

life no longer," she moaned, struggling to free herself, her face flooded with tears.

"Would you thus requite Orestes for his long and perilous journey; thus rebuff our beloved King; cast a doubt, ere you know, upon his loving constancy!" Ossa reproved, with gentle voice.

Staring and bewildered, only half comprehending, she whispered:

"Is it true — has Orestes returned — was it he I saw?"

"Yes, mistress, and by yonder cries is hastening to your side," he smiled, looking toward the ascending path from which the shouts arose.

And hardly had he ceased speaking when Orestes, covered with dust and clothed in rags, ran forward, and throwing himself on his knees before Roxana gave into her trembling hands a jewelled casket, and such a one as Crœsus, in Sardis' glory, might have treasured.

"From him! The King! Alexander! Our beloved master!" he cried, and with the words sank fainting at her feet.

"Oh he is dead, Ossa!" Roxana cried, pressing the precious casket to her breast with one hand, while with the other she sought to nurse her faithful messenger back to life.

"No, sweet mistress, he has only fainted from exhaustion, as his sunken face and lank form too plainly show," Ossa explained, bending over the fainting man and bathing his face with the refreshing water that had been hastily brought. Recalled to life, Orestes quickly recovered his strength, and when he was quite himself she drew him down beside her, locking and unlocking the precious casket the while, longing yet fearing to look within.

"You are worn and tired with the long journey?" she absently questioned, not knowing she had spoken.

"No, I am refreshed by my coming as if rested by a night's sleep," he laughed, gazing contentedly about him.

"I fear you fared poorly on the way," she murmured, her eyes fixed on the casket.

"I lived on nuts and roots and every imaginable thing, sweet mistress, and thinking of it now, found them every way delicious," he smiled, as if his hardships were not things to complain of.

"You were so long absent that we have mourned you as dead," she went on, bending over and furtively pressing her lips to the precious treasure.

"It was not of my own will, mistress, but that of Mithrines, our old friend of years gone by, who, envying me my liberty, and perhaps guessing my errand, threw me into prison and kept me there."

"But you effected your escape, and so your journey was not in vain?" she questioned, eagerly scanning his face, as if fearing he had not, after all, seen the King.

"Yes; the approach of Alexander's forces frightened the craven, and I, with others, greater sufferers than myself, were at last set at liberty."

"Poor lad, how much you have endured in my cause," she whispered, half lifting the lid of the casket.

"No, if I have suffered it was only from the fear that I might never be able to deliver the message I carried."

"But when you were released by Mithrines?" she interrogated, with averted face.

"I at once sought the King, rested as if just setting out on a journey," he answered, draining a goblet of wine Ossa had brought him.

"And your return — in that you suffered no hindrance?" she murmured, striving to still the throbbings of her heart, her thoughts questioning the contents of the casket.

"That was little delayed, though I can scarce stand straight, I have so long played the part of a crippled beggar," he laughed, as he arose and limped away to show his skill.

"Did the casket give you no care?" she questioned, gazing on it with longing eyes, yet fearing it contained only some kindly remembrance, some token of kingly favour.

"Yes, more than my life, and many times I buried it while seeking food, or strangers approached, or I had lost my way.   'T was well, too, for I was often searched, the inhabitants being suspicious of strangers, thinking them spies of the King."

"Of our King?"

"Yes, Alexander."

"And this casket in truth comes from him?" she murmured.

"Yes, from him, the King, Alexander, sweet mistress," he answered, interrogating Ossa with anxious · look, astonished at her questioning. But the latter, his eyes filled with tears, made no response save to sigh and turn away.

"Did he himself give it you?" she whispered, her face ashy white.

"Yes, with his own hands."

"And it is surely for me, you think, and not Olympias, his mother, whom he so tenderly loves?"

"Yes, for you and no other."

"He said that — the dear lord?"

"Yes, and many things beside, but for your ear alone and at another time," he explained, gently.

" 'T is some toy, some piece of finery that he has sent me, for he always thought me vain?" she questioned, toying with the key of the casket.

"No, by the Gods, sweet mistress, I 'll swear he never had such thought of you."

" 'T is some bit of jewelry, some token of remembrance from Crœsus' treasures, perhaps. What think you, Ossa?" she asked, raising her eyes with trembling inquiry to the sturdy chief.

"I'll swear it's no such thing, sweet mistress," he answered, with choked voice.

"Is he quite well — the King?" she asked after a moment's pause, as if still fearing there might be no missive of love within the casket, and the sweet spell in consequence be forever broken.

"Yes, my mistress."

"Has he changed much — in looks, I mean?" she hurriedly added.

"No, or if it be he is fairer and of nobler form than then."

"Than then?"

"Yes, that night at Parcledes' hut when issuing from the river like a God, his armour glistening, following his flight from Pella."

"Why do you speak of that dreadful night when Philip's soldiers, seeking his life, drove him from my side?" she asked with anxious face, clasping his hand in hers.

"He bade me."

"Thinking I had forgotten?"

"No, but as a thing of which he always thought, about which he always mourned."

"Mourned?"

"Yes, the hurried parting with one he so greatly loved."

"Then he has not changed — in unimportant things?" she added.

"No, nor in anything great or trifling wherein you

are concerned, sweet mistress. But treasures forever in his heart every recollection of the hours spent
with you as if he found therein the sole happiness of
his life," he cried with beating heart, discerning at
last the secret of her hesitancy in opening the casket.

"My sweet lord!"

"Yes, and he would talk of nothing else, and with
such gentleness that I could have fallen down and
worshipped him."

"Was he in truth so kind?"

"Yes, and at mention of your name seemed no
longer to breathe, but stood as one enthralled by the
sweetness of the music that filled his heart."

"My true love," she whispered, her happiness complete.

"And when he mentioned your name it was as of
a being too exalted to be loved by mortal man."

"Then you think he has forgotten nothing, treasures every part of our former life?" she questioned,
with radiant eyes.

"Yes, and when coming upon him in the night I
told him from whom I came, he cried out as you have
done, 'then she has not forgotten,' and putting his
arms about me kissed me as if it were you instead."

"This casket, then, you think, contains some message from him in answer to my missive?" she whispered.

"Yes, and putting it in my hands he bade me give
it you unopened, protecting it with my life — nay,

treasuring my life that I might deliver it as if I carried his very heart," saying which Orestes sprang to his feet, his eyes overflowing with tears and turning to Ossa cried out, "Come, prince, to the kitchen, for I am starving," and putting his arm about the sturdy chief he hurried away.

Left to herself, Roxana, assured that she was quite alone, pressed the precious token to her bosom, and inserting the key lifted the lid, disclosing the letter it contained. Opening it she gave a cry of joy exclaiming:

"He calls himself Iskander — our love-name; surely he would not do that if he did not love me still," and striving to compose herself, she opened the letter and read, amid sighs and tears of joy.

"Iskander to Roxana: Happiness and greeting. I love thee, sweet, and the more that thou hast so long treasured me unquestioned in thy gentle heart. Though Persia's wide domain and bitter enmity lay between us, yet hast thou remained true; though Darius murdered my messengers of love and thou heardst naught from me, yet, waiting, thou didst not doubt, believing me still faithful to my vow. And, though months and years have passed, yet, trusting on, thy love lingered fresh and abiding in thy loyal heart. Could mortal man ask more of his beloved, or greater proof of her abiding constancy? Of myself, my cherished, though the silence has been that of death, and I was told that thinking lightly of the shepherd Prince of Pella, thou hadst sought greater station among Persia's royal sons, yet hearing, I still trusted and loved thee. And still I love thee, and will though empires crumble and the purposes of kings fail as do the hopes of other men. Thus it will be, beloved, till I die, but if the Gods spare me I will come to thee King of Kings, but more as thy true love, for 't is thee that makest the heavens radiant and the conquest of Asia a dream of love — FOR THOU, BELOVED, ART PERSIA — and 't is thee I seek, and, finding, will take to my heart as we pledged ourselves in the shadow of the sacred mountain. And this thou mayest never doubt, my love, my Queen, my very heart."

But as if this were not enough there was hidden away in the casket a diptych of panelled ivory, inlaid with gems, wherein the kingly lover expressed his passion in still more fervent words. Reading, she pressed the letters to her lips, only to read them again and again, and when at last darkness shut out all vision she held the loving tokens to her heart, all forgetful of the passing hours, until Ossa, returning to her side, lifted her up and conducted her to the castle.

CHAPTER VI

Our story takes us now to the famed city of Susa, beyond the Tigris, the winter residence of the Persian Kings. Of all the ancient and modern capitals of Persia, illustrating in their adornment the greatness of the empire and the might of former kingdoms, this was most loved by the great Kings; and here, accordingly, arose the most sumptuous of their many palaces. The stately edifice was surrounded by a spacious park bordered on the north and south by swift-flowing rivers having their source in the foot-hills and snow-capped mountains to the east. About the palace and as far as the eye could reach were pleasure grounds with spreading lawns in which lakes glimmered, bordered about and made picturesque by clustering groves of palms and every kind of tree native to the wide-spreading empire. At one side and apart were carefully cultivated gardens wherein orange and peach trees, indigenous to the Mesopotamian Valley, displayed their luscious fruit. Farther away and bordering the hills were verdant pastures in which troops of camels and herds of Indian-buffalo and highly-bred horses and cattle grazed in contented security, protected from intrusion by the great wall that encircled the private domain of the King.

From the great gate of the palace grounds there stretched away to the four points of the compass, like threads of silver, the King's highways leading to the thirty satrapies of the mighty kingdom. These roads were made secure throughout their length by garrisons located at frequent intervals where the King maintained relays of horses and fleet-footed dromedaries ever ready to answer the call of his hurrying couriers. In this way communications were kept open, and the wide-spreading kingdom with its varied nationalities, many sodden, ignorant, and half-savage, was held in check.

But for many years peace had reigned throughout the land, save some local disturbance, hardly worth the King's notice, and so the monarchs had dozed undisturbed in their palaces, waited upon by eunuchs and obsequious courtiers. At last, however, there had come a change—the invasion of Alexander in the far west—swift and terrible—and in consequence all was confusion and alarm in the regal palace. And because of it on an autumn morning following the fall of Sardis, the many roads leading to the palace gate were filled with hurrying men, the exalted of the land, called in haste to the King to take measures for the protection of the threatened empire. The hour of audience was fixed for twelve at noon, but from the first light of day the captain of the guard had stood at the great gate challenging the many that approached, and on satisfactory response being made

welcoming them in the King's name. Men there were
from every clime; princes and nobles from the satrapies and capitals of the empire in highly decorated
chariots drawn by richly caparisoned horses; blacks
with kinky hair and glistening faces (kings in their
own country) from the Upper Nile; swarthy Arabs
with protruding lances tipped with gold, mounted
on fleet-footed dromedaries; white turbaned Syrians
armed with spear and cimeter, glorying in the beauty
of their barbed steeds; black-browed princes sitting
upright and staring on silken canopied elephants
from the banks of the Indus; fierce-looking warriors
on Bactrian camels from the mountains of Sogdiana;
warlike Capadocians mounted on sleek, well-groomed
mules; cunning-eyed Armenians and Nomadic chiefs
from the deserts of the far east, supple and alert, in
rude chariots drawn by wild asses, harnessed now, it
may be, for the first time. These, with their retainers,
while seemingly countless in number, represented but
a part of the many tribes and nationalities of the vast
empire. As they passed the embattled gate one and
all cast glances of apprehension toward the distant
palace, for few there were, however high their station,
who felt assured of the King's good will or the real
purpose of their coming.

About the pillared entrance of the palace all was
confusion as the exalted guests dismounted and
patiently awaited their turn to be shown by the
servants of the King to the sumptuous apartments

DARIUS AND STATIRA

assigned them. Meanwhile the grooms of the stable, arrayed in the brilliant costume of their office, guided the retainers of those who had found entrance to the palace to the capacious tents provided amid the groves and slumbering lakes of the park. But not in too close proximity to each other lest strife arise, for many of the representatives of Persia's motley nations and tribes had no mind to keep peace with their neighbours, except as they were held in check by the power of the great King.

Such was the interesting situation without. But far from the confusion and noise, in a secluded part of the palace, Darius, the Persian King, reclined, meditating upon the invasion of his kingdom and in a mood so melancholy that Statira, his unhappy Queen, who strove to cheer him, found little to encourage her loving efforts. Gentle and unselfish, she knelt before him, holding his hand and ever and anon pressing it to her lips, vainly endeavouring to call forth a smile, or enliven by a spark his dull and lustreless eyes.

Of their surroundings they gave no thought, yet nowhere else in all the world was there such sumptuous splendour of life. For this, as the reader may already have surmised, was the stately palace of which Esther wrote in Sacred Writ.

Without, facing the approach, colossal winged bulls of bronze held high their heads in seeming guardianship, while about the emblazoned doors

glistening columns of marble, inlaid with lapis lazuli
adorned the wide-spreading porticoes and upheld the
fluted roof of peacock-blue.   Within and in adornment of the spacious hall were bas-reliefs of the royal
guards in their resplendent costumes, and appearing
by their alert attitude and upraised spears to keep
eternal watch over the sacred person of the King.
Beyond the far-reaching vistas of the extended hall
there lay an open court shaded by palms, in the midst
of which a fountain played, its marble basin supported
by tawny lions carved in stone.   About this secluded
enclosure, and as if guarding its quiet precincts, bas-
reliefs of Assyrian archers in their varied and attractive costumes completely encircled the spacious court.

Looking out on the sheltered spot were the private
apartments of the great King, their columned walls
adorned with marble panels inlaid with plates of
gold, half hidden by rare tapestries and purple cloths
of Tyrian pattern.   The floors of the lofty rooms were
of black marble, inlaid with panels of beaten gold, but
so deftly fitted that they seemed to form a part of
the glistening background.   Over these were spread
precious rugs of Indian and Accadian pattern, each
expressing in its geometrical form and mysterious
tracings some sacred symbol of the accepted belief
of the ancient and primitive people of the east.   Soft
perfumes diffused themselves throughout the rooms,
and in excess of luxury the couch whereon the King
reclined, half concealed by embroidered curtains of

Babylonian make, was of solid gold inlaid with precious stones. So, too, were the articles of daily use, the water-bottles, drinking-cups, vials, and ewers that rested on tables of ebony, each utensil in its formation and outline so softened and refined by the jewels that encrusted its surface that it seemed to be an object of art rather than an article of common use. About the apartments, and in further adornment, set in panelled recesses of gold, were jars of alabaster inlaid with obsidian, and intermingled with them vases of lapis lazuli and malachite of rare and graceful pattern.

It was amid such surroundings, telling of the wealth and power of the empire and in their every aspect inviting contentment of life, that the King rested. Not, however, as if secure in his exalted station, but with countenance embittered by a nameless fear, such as a hunted fugitive might have worn who had gained access to the sacred precincts of the palace, only to find himself still threatened by an implacable enemy. The Queen, whose resplendent beauty was the theme of courtier and poet, was as one bereft in her vain strivings to arouse the King and excite in him some cheerfulness of life. And, like her lord, the eyes of the unhappy woman, once so radiant and sparkling, had such haunted look of fear that the beholder involuntarily uttered a prayer in pity of her manifest distress. But of the reason of her settled melancholy none knew the cause, nor could they gain a clew, for she was known to be fortunate in the possession of a love such as no King had bestowed upon his Queen since the days of Artaxerxes of cherished memory. Nor was it till long afterward, when men had time to reflect on the sad happenings of Darius' reign, that they discovered the cause of the Queen's hidden sorrow, for she loved the King with a tenderness such as only women possess whose affections are not clogged by any rude or selfish motive. Hidden were her sorrows, for when abroad she simulated such air of gaiety and confident belief in the strength and majesty of the King that the wonder of her secret melancholy was the greater because of it. But in the seclusion of the King's room the veil was lifted, and the trusted attendants of the palace beheld Darius and his Queen as they were; he weak and unstable, and she brave and uncomplaining, striving in vain effort to support the broken and dispirited monarch.

Releasing the King's hand, which she held clasped in hers, the distressed woman put her arms about his neck and caressing his face and hair exclaimed with an air of seeming cheerfulness:

"Do not grieve, my lord, when the world is so fair and the exalted of the land hasten hither from every clime to offer you homage and hearken to your commands."

"It is because of their coming and the need of it that I grieve," he complained, with bitter speech.

"Why, possessing you," he went on, petulantly pressing her hand to his face, "am I burdened with a crown to rob me of the happiness that might otherwise be mine?"

"It is a gift of love and confidence, and nowhere in all the world is there one so fit as you to wear it; and if its present burdens be heavy they but forerun days and years to come when you will have naught to worry or oppress you," she answered, beaming upon him.

"No, there will be no such ending, for I am as one bound to a stake, helpless to save myself from the Macedonian savage who threatens me."

"What is there to fear, beloved," she pleaded, "when you have a million spears upheld by brave and loyal men to protect and guard your throne?"

"Yes, and going forth to battle, I must lead them."

"Why you, if you would choose another?"

"It will be so demanded! For 'tis said that at the Granicus the army had no heart in what it did, I not being there to reward its efforts," he answered, with fretful impatience.

"What does it matter? Your soldiers will be about you, and men seeing their King armed and in the field will count death a favour, he being there to smile upon the sacrifice. And 't will be but for a day — an hour, perhaps — to be followed by renown the greater because of it," she encouraged.

"I care not for the world or its approval, and hold you so dear a part of me that rather than risk my life upon the battle-field I would gladly relinquish the throne with all its foolish forms and garish pomp," he answered, pitifully.

"It is but to ride forth amid the clash of cymbals and the sound of fife and flute, surrounded by brave men, to return victorious and afterward pass the remainder of your days in peace, the happier for the brief hour of disquiet," she coaxed, striving with tear-dimmed eyes to infuse some courage into his timid heart.

To this he made no reply but started up, trembling and affrighted, and raising his hands to heaven cried out in anguish, as if beholding a vision:

"What all-revengeful fate, thou angered God, guided my steps to this accursed throne over the bodies of two murdered kings — I who, of all the world, am least fitted for so great a trust?"

"You shall not thus accuse yourself, my King; you so brave, so noble, so strong, so loving," she sobbed, her arms about his neck.

"Once I was as you say, fearing no man; but now the thought of danger sets my heart to quaking as if all the demons of the unknown were threatening me," he confessed, with sorrowing voice, constrained to openly disclose the cause of his distress.

"Your fear, beloved, is but a passing emotion born of the kingly office all new to you, and once you exercise your power afield, will pass like a distorted dream having no reality in fact," she pleaded.

"No, I am fated to be the last of the Akhæmenian kings, for so the stars decree and the magi have foretold," he exclaimed with a shudder.

"They lie; they lie, my lord, who seek to disturb you with such idle tales," she screamed in rage; "for no one can understand the import of the firmament, and the magi are but men and their prophecies the conjurings of half-crazed brains! You are unnerved, beloved, from lack of restful sleep and worn with the harassments of the crown, fearing lest men condemn you unjustly," she sobbed, stroking his face to hide her agony.

"I would it were so, and that I were the same in heart as when, of all Persia, I stood forth in the Cadusian war to fight the enemy's chosen champion, and killing him in single combat earned the title of the 'bravest of Persians,'" the King murmured, sorrowfully, thinking of the past.

"You are no way changed, my lord, unless it be that you are wiser and nobler now than then," she persisted.

"No, I am different, and because of the perversion of my nature brought about by the wretch Bagoas, who, ere he thought to kill me outright, made me the creature of his will by some subtle poison that destroyed the courage I before possessed," the King explained, with assured conviction, referring to a for-

mer eunuch of the palace, who, having murdered the
two preceding kings, sought afterward to poison
Darius, but being detected in the act was himself made
to drain the fatal cup.

"You have naught to fear from the invasion of the
Macedonian savages, my love, for others as brave as.
they have sought the overthrow of Persia and paid
for their temerity with their lives, as Alexander will."

"Their failure was due to Persian gold or some
lucky chance, but he, daring all, stands forth alone,
Greece and her conniving politicians having no power
to divert or stay his arm."

"What matters it? He is many months' march
away, and everywhere our forces intervene to stay
his progress. Meanwhile, and at your leisure, you
may collect the armed strength of the Empire and so
crush him ere he reaches the Mesopotamian plains,"
she smiled.

" 'Tis for such purpose that I have called the assemblage of princes and nobles, but it will avail naught,
for our forces are as men of straw when brought face
to face with the embattled ranks of Greece."

"'T was once thus, my lord, but now, taught
their mode of warfare, we may meet them on equal
terms."

"No, their armies fight as one man, together or
apart, each for himself, and foolishly for greater glory,
and to oppose them my soldiers have no common purpose, and hate each other hardly less than they hate

the Macedonian King," he explained, as if nothing more could be said.

"Yet with them Cyrus conquered and handed down his conquests even to our time," she encouraged.

"No, for of the Greeks he knew nothing, and when his successors foolishly went against them in lust of land our armies were destroyed as the tempest beats down the ripened harvest."

"Have we not Greeks within our ranks as brave as those of Alexander, and with these and our noble Persians, and you to give direction, we cannot fail to stay the march of the rash young King," she persisted.

"And would you, beloved, have me risk the stress of battle after what I have told you in the candour of my heart?" he asked, with half-hopeful face as if somehow her resolute courage made good his own weakness.

"Yes, dearest, for all the world does not hold one more brave than you, as was once heralded throughout the Empire."

"Pray to Persia's God, beloved, that I may be like that again, but my heart misgives me, for of the outcome I have no confidence whatever," he sorrowed.

"You shall not go forth alone, but I will go with you to the field, and though I may not take part in the strife I will be there to watch and guard you with my love."

"No, no, a thousand times, no!" he screamed, affrighted, clasping her in his arms.

"I will be in no danger, beloved, you being there supported by our invincible army. Terror of the Greeks," she hurried on, "has foolishly beset our people since the days of Xerxes, and needlessly, my love; for though the younger Cyrus, backed by Grecian hosts, reached unopposed the very heart of Persia, yet perished miserably once the King took the field against him; and so will Alexander perish opposed by you."

"God grant it may be as you say," he sighed.

"But such hour may never strike, for Alexander has enemies near his person who, encouraged by hope of preferment at your hands, must meanwhile contrive his death," she went on, with cruel voice, murder in her heart, so great was her love for her husband and so deadly her hatred of his enemy.

"Yes, I have had such assurance from trusted officers in his camp, but of which I had until now forgotten," he said, cheered by the reminder.

"And happy it is in this our dire emergency that he has such traitors in his confidence as you and every king must have."

"What mean you, Statira?" he questioned, paling at her reference to himself.

"Had we not Mithrines, trusted even before your own brother?" she explained, with reassuring voice.

"The accursed traitor — and that I should have been so deceived in him!" the King raged, springing to his feet.

"Yet he may still be of use to us — for once a traitor always a traitor!"

"Think you so?"

"Yes, and foregoing all thought of punishment promise him a throne, as you have Lyncestes, once the destruction of Alexander is compassed. And this he may easily bring about, for 't is said that the traitor's base act has so won upon the young King that he has made him one of his household, and so accessible to his person," she cried, exultingly, little understanding the politic object that governed Alexander in seeming to favour Mithrines.

"Though I am as I am, my Queen, and cannot be otherwise, yet am I so heartened by your words that I will abide the issue of battle, praying unceasingly that I may have courage when the hour of trial comes," the King exclaimed, with some show of firmness.

"In this resolve, my lord, you proclaim yourself the protecting King you are," she praised, clasping him in her arms.

"In that you much mistake me, for were Persia alone concerned I would cast the danger from me. No, 't is for you I fight — you who are more to me than all the world."

"And I will be there to cheer you when despondent and welcome you to my arms victorious from the battle-field," she whispered, striving to maintain her calm.

And thus it happened that she was afterward present at the battle of Issus, to the great surprise of all the world, and most of all to Alexander.

In this way, and as described, the weak King was led, little by little, by his brave Queen to such composure of heart that he was able to meet the assembled nobles of the realm with firmness and animation.

When the hour for the assemblage of princes and lords arrived the King set forth in regal state, accompanied by the Queen; the chief eunuch, strangely enough, in close attendance upon them. But not strangely, for these unhappy beings, the creatures of a melancholy fate, were ever the real directing force of the Persian Empire, save when the throne was filled by some mighty monarch — and oftentimes then — as in Ochus' case. Of all those in attendance upon the Persian Kings only the eunuchs had free access to every part of the palace, and so because of it became the purveyors of its gossip and the centre of every intrigue in which women bore a part. And the latter, as in every land, stoutly maintained their right to have a voice in everything that concerned their lords.

Cunning, hating the world, oftentimes unscrupulous and cruel, greedy of power, nothing was possible without the aid or connivance of the attendant eunuchs, and because of it and little by little they came to dominate those they were expected to honour and serve. Courted, feared and hated, the lives and fortunes of princes and nobles were oftentimes at their mercy, and it sometimes fell out that the King himself lay unprotected in their hands as in the case of Darius and his immediate predecessors.

Reaching the entrance to the throne-room, preceded and followed as the etiquette of the stately court prescribed, the Queen pressed the King's hand to her lips and whispering a word of love left him to seek the sheltered gallery from which, unobserved, she might still cheer the halting monarch with knowledge of her presence. When she had taken her departure the chamberlain of the palace threw back the purple embroidered portières of the throne-room, and the King, heralded by the shrill blast of the trumpet, stood revealed to the waiting assembly of princes and lords. Of commanding height and noble countenance, he looked every inch a king, and beholding him now, wearing the upright tiara, the assembly with one accord made deep obeisance, murmuring a fervent prayer for favour in his eyes.

The throne-room, or hall of audience where the assemblage occurred, was one every way worthy the exalted King and the purpose for which it was designed. Two hundred feet square, its gilded roof was upheld by massive beams of polished cedar, supported by marble columns, adorned throughout their length with delicate bas-reliefs, displaying in attractive colours the costumes of the various nations and tribes that made up the King's army. The walls of the great room were adorned with glistening plates of figured gold that covered their surface from floor to roof. Of seats or divans, however, there were none save that of the King, which was uplifted on a platform of gold supported by carved figures portraying the dependent nations conquered by Cyrus two hundred years before.

Casting a look of apprehension, almost of hate, at the canopied throne, the King descended to the lower step of the platform on which it rested, whereupon at a word from the chamberlain the waiting nobles, with bowed heads and according to their rank, approached the waiting King. Coming into his immediate presence they kissed the monarch's hand, and he, tall of stature and full of every kingly grace, smiled upon them as they made humble obeisance, saying to each some kindly word of recognition and welcome. But when Artabazus and Bessus drew near, still disfigured by wounds received in the battle of the Granicus, the King lifted them up and embraced them as if of equal rank with himself, making many inquiries regarding their hurts and the particulars of their escape and subsequent recovery.

Throughout the prolonged ceremony, according to the strict etiquette of the court, the Master of Ceremonies enjoining silence, kept his fingers outspread upon his lips, the assembled princes and nobles hiding their hands in the sleeves of their flowing gowns, in assurance that they meditated no covert act. When at last the humblest chief had done reverence to the King the latter mounted the lofty throne, about which there was formed a cordon of the royal guard in resplendent uniforms, wearing breast-plates of gold and having upon their heads plumed casques of like metal. When the monarch was seated the royal chamberlain advanced and in a loud voice disclosed the purpose of the gathering, for till then it was unknown save to a few, the King's summons having been signalled by columns of smoke and beacons of fire. When the chamberlain ceased the King arose, a thing unusual, and in a voice at once musical and commanding exclaimed:

"Again is the Empire threatened from the west, oh Persians, and as in the past aided from within by traitorous servants disregardful of their oaths or the King's welfare. Our forces defeated at the Granicus because of divided councils, Sardis which should have stood as a bulwark staying the enemy's progress was surrendered without a blow by Mithrines, our trusted governour. Afterward the invading King dispatched an army to overrun the Hellespontine district, compelling the surrender of the Æolic and Ionian cities, which, like Sardis, hastened to open wide their gates. Meanwhile the King himself took his course to Ephesus, and that city, which has ever enjoyed our royal favour, relinquishing all thought of opposition, cravenly submitted to his rule. So, too, Smyrna and all the fair cities on the Ægean Sea save Miletus and

Halicarnassus. The first, offering opposition, was quickly overcome and its people destroyed or sold to slavery in menace of any city that should thereafter remain loyal to the Persian King. Halicarnassus, stout of heart, closed its gates, and defending its walls with resolute courage long withstood the enemy. But finally, weakened by losses, was compelled to yield, save the outlying fortress, which point of vantage of all our fair possessions on the far west coast still remains in possession of the crown. Because of this the ships of Phoenicia, ever faithful to their trust, having no longer harbour or place of refuge must, perforce, seek anchorage to the east. In every city where unopposed success attends the enemy, and to tempt those still loyal to the crown, the Macedonian has remitted the duties heretofore gathered by the Persian treasury, substituting merely nominal offerings in their place. And this subserviency not being thought sufficient, he has given the governments over to liberal rule, the more effectually to wean men from the remembrance of their true King."

Hearing him the assembly stood spellbound, making no move, hardly comprehending the significance of his words, for he spoke rapidly and with heightening colour and voice, his heart filled with shame and rage at remembrance of the indignities offered the Empire and his sacred person.

"Such is the situation in the west, oh Persians," he went on, after a moment's pause. "Elsewhere the Empire is at peace, each province performing its allotted part, meditating no evil. And that those who remain loyal may not suffer harm, and that the kingdom may be maintained and its lost cities recovered, I, your King, command that after being rested and refreshed you hasten each to his own country and forthwith gather and arm the allotment apportioned to the various provinces. Having done this, marshal your forces and take your course without loss of time to join the combined armies of the Empire on the plains of Sochi, overlooking the Mediterranean, where we will await the coming of the enemy. And in this and in all you do, and in your every act of devotion to the throne, may Ahura-Mazda, the God of Persia, protect and guide you"; saying which, and without waiting for response or token of any kind, the King turned and abruptly left the hall.

Such was the gathering of the nation to oppose the Macedonian King, and such the splendour of Darius' surroundings. Yet, afterward, when Alexander came, clothed with the panoply of Persia's might, the dream of his life still unfulfilled, he lingered amid the splendours of Susa's royal abode scarce a day, but hastened on, the luxury of the great palace in no way appeasing the hunger of his heart.

CHAPTER VII

A settled gloom as of some certain and terrible calamity overhung the ancient city of Tarsus, that Tarsus from whence Saint Paul set out on his religious crusade three and a half centuries later. Few of the frightened inhabitants were to be seen abroad, and men scarce spoke to each other as they passed in the dark and tortuous streets. Houses were darkened as if abandoned, and the doors of shops barred, or if opened it was with reluctance and only to those known to be friendly. This fear, it appeared, had spread beyond the city walls, so that provisions were no longer brought in from the country, and because of it a famine threatened the terrified inhabitants. At every gate men and women, singly and in numbers, were leaving the stricken place, taking with them such goods as they could carry in their arms or on pack-animals, leaving the remainder unguarded in their homes and shops.

It was as if a plague prevailed or some terrible danger threatened, and truly enough in regard to the last; for Alexander, the conquering King, lay sick in the vice-regal palace, and his soldiers, disregarding all discipline, blocked the thoroughfares, sullen and

112

suspicious of all who came and went. The army halted in its triumphant progress, stayed as by the hand of an angry god. The disquieted soldiers asked themselves from whence came the mysterious sickness of the young King? The striking down of one who had never known ailment, whom no labour could fatigue, no hardship cause to murmur, no march so difficult or prolonged as to lessen his ardour. Most strange, the wise ones said. Poison, the common soldiers at first whispered, and then openly proclaimed in the camp and on the streets as the days wore on. Came this horror from an enemy within the royal household, or had the city, as many believed, poisoned the water wherein the King had bathed? The more superstitious believed it to be the work of sorcerers, for it was said there were dire rumblings of the earth and flames had been seen to issue from the river as the King emerged from his bath, shaking as with an ague. Woe to the wicked city if he should die, and the citizens, noting the temper of the troops, fled as from a pestilence, while those constrained to stay hid their treasures, and going to the temples offered oblations to the Gods, praying for the King's recovery and their own preservation from the danger that threatened them.

As the days progressed a new and frightful fear assailed the soldiers. What if the hosts of Darius should suddenly appear and overwhelm them! So long as the King was with them they thought not of their whereabouts, of where he led them, or of their remoteness from Macedonia, and the impossibility of succour should aught happen. But now they were as children, sheep without a shepherd, and in their fright told each other of the fate that had befallen the followers of Cyrus the Younger when deprived of their leader, as were they in the present instance. It was of no account that the generals sought to calm their abject fears; they listened in silence, and while no outbreak had as yet occurred, nothing, it was believed, could stay their mad rage if their beloved King's sickness should have a fatal termination.

It was amid such melancholy scenes in the afternoon of a summer day in the second year of the war that Jaron, the trusted physician of Alexander, arrived in Tarsus from Pella, whence he had been dispatched by the King, bearing presents and messages of love to his mother. Anxiously questioning the soldiers as he advanced concerning the King, he was unable to learn anything definite, but presently encountering Lysimachus he reined in his horse and accosted the aged tutor:

"What is this, Lysimachus, that I hear about the King's illness?"

" 'T was a sorry day, good leech, when we left our own Kingdom to invade this pestilential country accursed of the Gods and to the Greeks, a very graveyard," the old man censured, waving his hand aloft.

"Yes, yes, that is true, but what of the King's illness, good friend?"

"Speak no longer of him as living, Jaron, but as of an immortal; a being once known of men, but now enshrined and having the attributes of a god," the old man sighed.

"What! Is he dead?" Jaron gasped, his sunken features taking on an ashen hue.

"No, he still has some breath of life — but whence come you that you ask such foolish questions?" Lysimachus demanded, sharply, eying Jaron as if his inquiries had some sinister significance.

"From Macedonia on the King's business, as you well know."

"Yes, I now remember, a message to the Queen, about which there was much speculation at the time."

" 'T was not a matter of interest to any one save the Queen, who mourns unceasingly the absence of her beloved son," Jaron explained. "But tell me of the King's sickness, good friend; is there no hope of his recovery?"

"Ask it of the Gods if you would be sure, for I know not, there being so many contrary opinions."

"Have you not seen him?"

"Yes, within the hour."

"What think you, then?"

"I only know that he is bereft."

"Bereft?"

"Yes, mad."

"What mean you by that, Lysimachus?" the other exclaimed, surprised out of himself.

"That he knows not friend from enemy and so must be mad."

"A delirium, merely."

"So Philip the leech says, but I say he is crazy."

"His failure to recognize his friends means nothing, Lysimachus," Jaron commented, with less anxiety.

"That is not all, for he regards not the present or any material thing, but prattles like a child or raves like a madman of things having no pertinency, and so he must be bereft, stricken by the Gods for some misdemeanour or evasion of duty," Lysimachus asserted, doggedly.

"Nonsense, you know not what you say, for the Gods concern themselves not at all with the petty doings of men," the other rebuked. "Upon what does his mind dwell, of what does he speak in his delirium?" Jaron questioned, anxious to gain a clew to the King's malady.

"Yesterday it was of things done; of cities that had welcomed him, and of these he cried out that they were his children and should never suffer more from Persian oppression. Then his mood changing he would lift himself on his couch, and in a frenzy of passion call on his soldiers to follow as he led them through the breach of a crumbling wall or mountain-pass to attack the enemy that lay behind."

"Was that all?"

"No, presently starting up afresh he bemoaned with sorrowing voice the treason of Lyncestes, and so it went on without sense or coherency the whole day through."

"The treason of Lyncestes! What mean you by that?" Jaron demanded, awakened to fresh interest by Lysimachus' disclosure.

"What! Are you ignorant of that, too?" the old man piped, eying the other compassionately.

"Yes, I have been absent many months, as you are aware, and so know nothing of what has transpired," Jaron explained, with patient indulgence.

Chuckling to himself, greatly elated at the importance of what he was about to relate, the old man went on, but not too clearly, hoarding his news as a miser might a hidden coin:

"It seems, you must know, then, that Lyncestes, fattened by the King's bounty, has been all the while in correspondence with the great King."

"With Darius?"

"I know of no other."

"Yes, yes, to be sure; but go on, I beg, good friend," Jaron pleaded.

"Well it appears that Darius wrote to Lyncestes at Sardis in response to a traitorous letter the latter had sent him by the hand of Amyntas the Lesser, who fled from Macedonia at the time of Alexander's accession to the crown. In this letter Darius writes

Lyncestes that if he can contrive the death of Alexander he shall surely succeed him on the throne of Macedonia."

"That is being generous — with our goods."

"Moreover, the deed being done, Darius promised to sweeten the gift of the crown with a purse of one thousand talents of gold."

"How did all this become known?"

"Oh, 't was simple enough — Darius' letter fell into our hands."

"In what way?"

"How else think you than through the capture of the messenger who bore it."

"What did the King do when the plot was revealed to him?" Jaron went on, ignoring Lysimachus' irritable temper.

"Horror-stricken and incredulous, he set out immediately for Sardis in the guise of a common soldier," the old man laughed.

"Why should there have been any secrecy about it?"

"To avoid scandal, for the King hoped it might be untrue — a plot to ruin Lyncestes."

"What was the outcome?"

"It was as reported, and so Lyncestes was put to trial."

"Rightly enough."

"But when the soldiers condemned the traitor to death the King forbade it, and at most would only consent to his being placed under guard."

"That was like him," Jaron commented. "And he refers, you say, to Lyncestes' treason in his delirium?" the leech questioned, leading the old man on.

"Yes, as if the scamp were a brother."

"Poor King!"

"Well you may say that, but having worn himself out with sorrowing he lifted himself as if on horseback, intent upon fighting his battles afresh as if nothing had hitherto been accomplished."

"Exhausting the strength he so much needs to overcome the fever that consumes him," Jaron murmured.

"In his fury, surrounded by slingers and darters, he stormed the mountain fastness from whence the Pisidian robbers were wont to issue, and then seemingly quieted by the fierce battle that ensued told, as if reading from a book, how he traversed the pass where Mount Climax falls into the sea. But happily, and at a moment when the fierce north wind beat back the foaming flood, though the men waded in water up to their armpits, the tumbling waves threatening every moment to engulf them," the old man portrayed with garrulous speech, happy that the other would listen to him.

"Did the King thus endanger his army and himself?" Jaron absently questioned, reflecting on all he had heard.

"Yes, that he might surprise a fortified city beyond, which otherwise would have required a siege of many weeks."

"And did he succeed?"

"Yes, and obtained with it the key to the mountain passes to the north and west. With the fall of the embattled city the King cried out that now the coast of all Asia Minor was in his hands, and with that he ceased speaking and fell to picking his quilt as if searching the spot where some Companion had fallen in battle," Lysimachus related with sententious gravity.

"God of Gods, man, was naught done to allay this feverish distemper of the mind?" Jaron raged.

"Yes, but the narcotic seemed only to refresh his brain, and beginning anew, as if in a trance he recounted with laughter that made the blood freeze how with his bowmen and darters at midnight he surprised and captured the gap of Termessus, a path hewn in the perpendicular cliff that a hundred men could hold against all the world. Then hurrying on he told how they stormed the fortress beyond, and after a desperate battle put the barbarians to flight, giving over the robber stronghold to the flames."

"Did all the things occur that he relates?" Jaron asked, with patient indulgence, intent upon his mission of inquiry.

"Yes, and in the order described, for I rode by his side or near at hand," the old man added, cautiously, thinking of Alexander's many hand-to-hand encounters with the enemy.

"If all he says be true, then he is not mad. 'T is but a fever of the blood, and his mind being overwrought naturally recurs to things past that were of vital interest to him at the time."

"Call it what you will, I call it madness."

"You say he knows no one?" Jaron questioned, intent upon a new line of inquiry.

"No, or it is thought he sometimes recognizes Eumenes, who, sorely wounded, sits nearby with head bandaged, busily writing."

"Writing?"

"Yes, bringing up the correspondence, he says, but intent, I believe, on watching those about the King."

"Ever-faithful Eumenes!"

"Yes, he alone, save Hephestion, is unselfish; only these two would lay down their lives for the King, thinking it a favour."

"And Medius and Demetrius!"

"No, not now — their wives hold them."

"And properly, too."

"Yes, being still young and pretty. Oh, you need n't laugh, Jaron! I say young and pretty, but women might also be old and pretty — the fairies — if they would eat less or exercise more, and refresh their sweet faces now and then with a drop of oil. Why, bless the nymphs, they might be pretty at sixty if they had a mind," Lysimachus commented, petulantly, as if the carelessness of women in respect of such things were a personal offence.

"But —"

"And having foolishly wasted their beauty, the butterflies, they emphasize the fault afterward by wearing conspicuous raiment, that —"

"Yes, but—"

"Ending finally with —"

"What you say is all true, my friend, and sorry 't is so, but have you told me everything concerning the King?" Jaron interposed, impatiently, disregarding the old man's irrelevant speech.

"No, nor the half, for after an interval of silence and laughing as a boy might, the King told how on a dark and stormy night with the archers and spear-bearing guards he surprised and put to flight the Persian force that guarded the Gates of Cilicia, a narrow, rock-bound road three thousand feet above the sea. And afterward hurrying on brought his army to Tarsus, to save it from fire and sack that Arsames, the Persian commander, threatened," the old man chattered, seemingly refreshed by his long narrative.

Gathering up his reins Jaron turned away, vexed that in all he heard he could gain no clew to the King's sickness or how it was brought about.

"Why such haste, good leech? You have heard only the happenings of yesterday — to-day it is different," Lysimachus chuckled, staying Jaron's horse.

THE GATES (PASS) OF CILICIA

"Well, in what is it different?" Jaron asked, impatiently, laying down his reins.

"All is changed, for the King in his craze no longer leads his army, but implores the Gods unceasingly to give him life and strength to accomplish a purpose that lies near his heart."

"The overthrow of Persia's King!"

"No, and that 's the wonder of it, for he has never once referred to Darius in his sickness. No, clasping his hands in prayer to some unknown goddess, he continually cries aloud to the mysterious being not to doubt his love but to await his coming, though all men else prove false to their vows."

"That is strange."

"Yes, and oft-repeating himself, he will cry out with uplifted hands that though all the world intervene yet will he come at last to this divinity. Yes, I hold it most strange and a proof of his madness, for while goddesses are well in their way, I never prayed to one except she might be some dainty maiden of whom I was desperately enamoured," Lysimachus chuckled, stroking his chin.

"And Alexander?"

"Ere he became mad he prayed and sacrificed daily to the Gods, but no woman or goddess ever had place in his thoughts, or at least not since his callow youth, when he was enamoured of the Persian Princess Roxana," Lysimachus explained, thinking of Oxyartes and his daughter.

"Kings, like other men, are sometimes hopelessly enamoured of women," Jaron ventured.

"Yes, but he long ago ceased to think of the Bactrian sprite, and never since has so much as looked at a woman. But raving, as I say, in respect to this unknown divinity, he after a while fell into a troubled sleep, but only to awake presently to again pray and supplicate the unknown not to doubt his final coming."

To this the leech made no reply, but sat buried in thought while the old man prattled on, unconscious of the other's abstraction. At last, his face lighting up as if he had some clew to the King's strange prayer, Jaron asked:

"You say the King has never given a hint of this mysterious person or goddess when free from the delirium that possesses him?"

"No, and that's the proof of his madness, for of his battles and marches we know, but of this delusion which has possessed his mind at intervals since the distemper seized him, no one has the faintest knowledge."

"Not Hephestion nor Medius, his intimates?"

"If they have a clew they have said nothing. But there is no clew; he is mad, and his muddled brain conjures up things having no reality or meaning."

"That may be, but tell me without evasion, you whom he treasures as a man may the nurse who first guides his steps, have you no inkling of the King's true ailment or its cause?" Jaron demanded, facing Lysimachus with stern countenance.

"How should I when the doctors know nothing of his malady, or knowing, fear to act?"

"How fear to act?"

"Each leans upon the other, professing ignorance, loth to do anything lest if the King die the one blamed will be torn to pieces."

"Then all should be put to death — the cravens!"

"I know not the nature of his malady, as I say, but 't is claimed by many that he is dying of a poison," Lysimachus whispered, looking about him, distrustfully.

"Dying of a poison?"

"Yes, and in this dire extremity, Philip, the Acarnanian leech, only has courage to act; but when he would give the King some potent drug the other doctors in their insane fear or jealousy cry out that he is wrong and so nothing whatever is done," Lysimachus explained, dejectedly.

"Thus it is to be a King!"

"Yes, and save some harmless potion, having no strength or potency of life, the sickness runs its fatal course."

"The King to die at last like an abandoned dog!" Jaron cried, and gathering up his reins set off in a furious rage.

Traversing the narrow and winding streets of the city he found them everywhere deserted save by the soldiers, many of whom were gambling, but without speech and spiritless, as if it were a burdensome duty imposed upon them.

Reaching the palace where the monarch lay sick, he found it heavily guarded, as if an enemy threatened. Throwing the reins to an attendant slave he hurriedly entered, no one thinking to oppose or question him, for he had long been Philip's physician, and the latter dying, Alexander had taken him up and treasured him for his fidelity and skill. Thus he gained admission where another would have been denied, and passing the guard stationed in the vestibule of the vast structure entered the hall of assembly, where he found Philip, the King's physician, and others who had been called to his aid. And the latter much against their will, it appeared, for they stood apart in a body, silent and morose as if in deadly fear, as Lysimachus had intimated.

Grasping the extended hand of Philip who uttered a cry of joy at seeing him, Jaron hurried on, without speech, to the King's chamber. Surrounding the canopied bed on which the monarch lay he found Alexander's generals and close companions, and about the couch, alert and anxious-faced pages clothed in white tunics and noiseless of foot attending to the immediate wants of the stricken King. Stopping only long enough to survey the room, Jaron hurried to Alexander's side, and bending over scanned with long and earnest inquiry his worn and pallid face.

But of recognition the King gave no sign, his eyes, usually attentive and kindly, stared unmeaningly at the ceiling, aflame with the fever that consumed him. Testing his pulse and heart, Jaron found the first thin and high and the other fitful and uncertain, as if life, weary of the vain effort, no longer struggled against the inevitable. Satisfied, the leech arose and motioning Philip to follow him, returned to the physician's room, reaching which he asked, feigning ignorance of the situation:

"What are you and your associates doing, Philip, to cure the King's distemper?"

"Little, good friend, save to bathe him at frequent intervals, followed at stated periods by a gentle potion that my colleagues esteem sufficient."

"A gentle potion? God of Gods, man, can you not see that the King is dying of exhaustion; consumed by a fever that is eating him up?" Jaron cried, in seeming rage.

"Do you think it as bad as that?" one of the physicians in attendance exclaimed, crowding forward, followed by his companions.

"Much worse, for he will not live the night through unless some effective remedy be instantly administered," Jaron declared with meaning gesture.

"But consulting with these trusted physicians," Philip excused, surveying those about him, "we can agree upon nothing that is effective."

"Then dismiss them! Act! God of Gods, is the

King to die, that doctors may voice their foibles?" he stormed.

"I dare not, for they have been called to advise me and I have no power to dismiss them," Philip excused, startled by Jaron's words.

"Then the power be mine," Jaron cried, his eyes aflame, and turning abruptly to the physicians, who listened, astonished and angered at his words, he went on, purposely exaggerating the purport of what he had to say.

"The King is dying, exhausted; his life, trembling, hangs in the balance. Are you blind that you cannot see? Within the hour he may regain consciousness, the consciousness sometimes vouchsafed men ere death claims them. Fly, then, while you may if you would escape censure, perhaps death! Let the responsibility for the King's life rest on Philip and myself. If he survive you shall have the credit; if he die let the blame rest on us."

Hearing him, amazed, the faces of the physicians lightened, and after a moment's consultation they hastily gathered up their hats and cloaks and hurried from the room as if freed from impending death. Turning to Philip and embracing him, Jaron exclaimed:

"Now that we are freed from these parasites, prepare a potion for the King, and out of your own belief of what he needs, while I meanwhile refresh myself after the day's travel in yonder room."

"Will you not assist me — aid me with your advice?" the other pleaded.

"Yes, if need be, and share with you and with my life the responsibility of all you do. Call me," he went on, "when you have the draught prepared," saying which he idly took up one of the goblets that rested on the table, and smiling upon Philip sought the privacy of the room he had indicated. But not to sleep or refresh himself, as he had intimated, for no sooner had the curtain hid him from view than divesting himself of his cloak he drew therefrom a medicine chest, and selecting what he sought lost no time in mixing a draught, measuring and remeasuring each portion with infinite care and patience, as if his life depended upon the exactness of his labours. This completed, he turned to the door and cautiously parting the curtain fixed his gaze on Philip who was busy mixing a similar potion and seemingly with equal care and exactness. But of its contents Jaron could form no idea, and herein lay his fear, for there ever recurred to his harassed mind the startling inquiry, "Is Philip himself loyal? Does he stand apart from his fellows that he may the more effectively harm the King, assured of protection by some powerful faction in the army? Or is he honest in what he proposes?" Unable to decide, Jaron from the first determined to substitute the medicine he had now prepared for that which Philip was working over so labouriously, for upon the hour's action, it was plain, depended the King's life.

Philip, meanwhile; unconscious of Jaron's spying, went on with his work, and when the potion was at last ready for the King's lips he put down the goblet and buried his face in his hands as if offering a prayer to the gods for forgiveness or for their blessing upon what he was about to do. Thus he stood, when hearing some movement in the King's chamber he hastened thither to assure himself in advance that no delay need occur on Jaron's being called. The latter, overjoyed at this happy furtherance of his plans turned and grasped the potion he had prepared, but as he showed himself in the door of the half-darkened room a man heavily cloaked darted from an opposite chamber. And approaching the table whereon Philip had left the King's draught, he let fall into the liquid a transparent powder, and with the act turned and fled. But not before Jaron had detected beneath his hood the pallid face of Philotas, Parmenio's son and the trusted commander of the Companion Cavalry. Thunderstruck, Jaron stood still, amazed at what he had seen, but realizing that he had but a moment to act he hurriedly crossed the deserted room and grasping the goblet prepared by Philip substituted the one he himself carried. Scarcely had Jaron regained his hiding-place ere Philip called to him to hasten, to which he responded, trembling and deeply disturbed. Philip, surprised at his agitation and not understanding the cause, bade him calm himself lest it disturb the King, who was now conscious. For

Philip, who had before been timid, now strong in the integrity of his purpose and secure in what he was doing, no longer had any semblance of fear, and taking up the goblet entered the King's chamber. Recognizing him, Alexander received him with a smile of welcome and accepting the potion, handed Philip at the same time a letter bidding him open and read it. Doing as he was told, Philip found it to be from Parmenio to the King, warning him to beware of his physician, who had been bribed by Darius to poison him, the bribe being a thousand talents and the great King's daughter in marriage. Reading it through, Philip looked up to find the King had swallowed the draught, and when he would have protested his innocence Alexander, smiling upon him, exclaimed:

"Go seek the repose of which you stand in need, Philip. Jaron, who has so happily come, will attend me for the night," saying which, and already feeling the effect of the powerful drug, the King lay back on his couch, and after a little while fell into a deep and refreshing sleep.

All night Jaron watched with bated breath beside his bed, and in the gray of the morning, finding the King's temperature to be normal, he hastened to apprise Philip that no trace of the fever remained to retard the patient's quick recovery.

"It was like the King, chivalrous in all things, to trust his life to your hands, Philip, believing you to be his friend," Jaron exclaimed, referring to the incident of the previous evening. "Hasten now to his side and thank him, and in future guard him from another such attack, for 't is his youth and strength that have saved him, and lacking these he would have died."

"Think you so?" Philip questioned.

"Yes, he is not like common mortals, for as you may have noticed the hot and adust temperament of his body gives off the fragrance of a sweet perfume, unknown in other men. And if fever be added to this unnatural fire of the blood, and he have not youth and strength, he will be consumed as in a flame," Jaron concluded, and by his prescience anticipating by many years Alexander's last and fatal sickness.

In this way the King was cured, and for many days Jaron meditated on the course he should pursue in regard to Philotas, but being a prudent man he at last concluded to do nothing. And in this wisely, it would seem, for his word would not have stood against that of the King's trusted commander, whose family, through Alexander's indulgence and loving remembrance of Philip, filled all the more important places in the army. And so the matter rested, and Philotas went his way more vain and arrogant than before, making light of the King's sickness, and referring with much boasting to Parmenio's and his own services in having achieved all the things that Alexander claimed for himself. Afterward, however, on thinking the matter over and the danger the King ran, Jaron conveyed to his master a hint of what had occurred; so that thenceforth, without the knowledge of any one save the Sovereign and his trusted officers, some watch was put on the doings of Parmenio's vain and ambitious son.

CHAPTER VIII

High up on a projecting spur of the Amanic Mountains, where a summer palace of Xerxes had once stood, the lofty war-tent of Darius, the Persian King, now lifted its imposing front. About it were giant cypress trees, brought from the Lebanon Mountains centuries before, and from beneath whose spreading branches the placid waters of the Mediterranean were visible two miles away. Through the valley or plain of Issus that intervened between the mountain and the sea, the Pinarus wound its slow and tortuous way. To the north and south as far as the eye could reach a pastoral stillness reigned, in startling contrast to the crash of arms and the cries of armed men that were ere long to disturb the quiet of the tranquil valley.

Close about the tent of Darius a company of Median soldiers, clothed in scale armour and wearing burnished casques of steel inlaid with gold, guarded the royal family domiciled within. Beneath the trees, some little way off, a squadron of Persian cavalry rested, armed with cimeters and lances, and mounted on Nisæan horses of uniform colour and height. Brazen helmets, and breastplates ornamented with golden filigree formed their defensive armour, the waving

134

plumes of horsehair that surmounted their casques, adding to the picturesqueness of their attire. Further away and reclining at their ease there rested a band of Carduchian archers from the upper Tigris wearing leather helmets and tunics of quilted flax. These half-savage warriors were armed with bows six cubits in length, with arrows half that long and of such force that neither shield nor breastplate served to protect the wearer from their iron-tipped points.

Near at hand and in compliment to the bowmen a body of darters armed with javelins and carrying leather shields and short battle-axes stood at their ease, clad throughout in skins of panthers and having on their heads hats of similar description. That no element of the warlike age might be wanting, there was stationed near the foot of the mountain, as if designing an ambuscade, a band of slingers from the Taurus, carrying wicker shields and wearing hair tunics of gaudy colour beneath their goatskin mantles.

Such in part were the soldiers of the great King, whose duty it was to guard the Queen Statira, in her journeyings when away from the capital, as in the present instance. In explanation of her presence on the shores of the Mediterranean, it appeared that Darius had been wrongly informed as to the reason of Alexander's prolonged stay at Tarsus, and believing it was because the Macedonian King was afraid to meet him in battle, he had most unwisely abandoned the plains of Sochi, where he had collected his army, to seek the young King in the country bordering on the sea. Thus it was that with six hundred thousand men he had left the highlands and descended to the valley through the Armanic Gates, a mountain pass at the extreme northeastern corner of the Mediterranean.

But on reaching the hamlet of Issus great was his surprise to learn that Alexander's long delay at Tarsus had been occasioned by sickness and subsequent campaigns in Cilicia and Caria and not through fear. And having recovered his strength the young King had set out to find the Persian host, and believing it to be awaiting him on the plains of Sochi had passed through Issus, designing to reach the upper country by the Syrian Gates, a mountain defile to the south. In this way the two kings had missed each other; Darius coming down to the sea in Alexander's rear, while the latter was hurrying to the south to seek him in the highlands by another route.

All this was so contrary to what Darius had been led to expect that it threw him into the greatest alarm, though Charidemus, the Athenian general and exile from his country, had previously assured him that the Macedonian King would in his own time seek him wherever he might be found; and that only on an extended field such as the Sochian plain could the Persians hope to overcome Alexander in battle. Afterwards on the Athenian persisting in this, and being thought lacking in respect, the great King in a rage had grasped him by the girdle, the Persian act of condemnation and signal of execution. Accepting his fate without murmur, Charidemus turned back and he was led away to die, and mimicking Darius' manner, cried out:

"I fear not death, oh King, but would I might live to see thee and thy horde fly like sheep before the sword of the Macedonian."

These things Darius now remembered with regret, but of the miscarriage of his plans or Alexander's near proximity, the Queen and royal family, resting by the sea, were still in happy ignorance. For unfortunate in all he did, Darius in the victorious campaign, which the wise men of Babylon had foretold, planned that all his immediate family should be near at hand to share in the expected triumph over Alexander; and this, contrary to the advice of Statira, who had begged that only she should accompany him. Disregarding her wishes, when his army set out on the wide detour necessary to reach the sea he sent her forward with his mother, Sisygambis, and his children across the mountain to the valley of Issus by one of the little-frequented passes in the immediate neighbourhood. And it was in contemplation of this that he had caused the regal tent to be erected in the romantic spot already described, and here unconscious of danger the royal family rested.

Such was the situation on a November morning when the Queen, ever alive to the emergencies of her husband's troubled reign, was suddenly startled by the piercing blast of the King's horn as it echoed and re-echoed from the valley below. Looking forth, agitated and alarmed at his unexpected coming, she beheld the Persian monarch in his war-chariot approaching from the north at topmost speed. And hemming about as if danger threatened, there rode a regiment of the royal guard, kinsmen of the King, their glistening armour and upraised lances dazzling the eye with the reflected rays of the morning sun.

Nearing the royal tent, the imposing cavalcade turned abruptly to the left and without slackening speed ascended the intervening height. Drawing rein before the great pavilion, the King seemed not to see the attendant nobles grouped about the door in humble reverence as he hurried without speech to the apartment of the Queen. Striving to calm her fears, she hastened to meet him, but on seeing her he gave an agonizing cry and clasped her in his arms, as if fearing until then that he had lost her. But presently pushing her from him he sat down in utter abandonment, exhibiting none of the elation he had been wont to display when they had been long parted. Expressing no surprise at his strange manner, but soothing him with gentle speech and soft caresses, the distraught King presently relaxed, and little by little, encouraged by her words and calm demeanour was led to tell her of his apprehensions and the likelihood of an immediate and decisive battle.

"I feared from your hurried coming that you were ill or that some great danger threatened you," she smiled. But if she thought thus to quiet his fears her words were unavailing, for seeming not to hear he sat brooding, vouchsafing no reply. "Where, my sweet lord," she presently went on as if he had not heard, "is this barbarian Alexander if he be not in hiding, as we thought?"

"Where is he?" the King started, stirred to sudden life by the hated name.

"Yes, for I thought he meditated retreat, perhaps a return to his own country."

"May Ahura-Mazda, the God of our country, punish those who led me to such belief, as I have punished them for their treachery here on earth," he cried, his face distorted with passion.

"What does it matter, love, for you will be victorious wherever you may meet him, for so the Chaldean soothsayers foretell."

"Encouraged by a dream, I sought them out, and responding to my known desire and caring nothing for my safety or that of my empire, they prophesied as you say, and thus it happens that I am now entrapped."

"Why may they not have prophesied truly, for

all claim that the stars are as an open book to
them, and that they have the divine power to read
the future?" she protested, ready to accord them
every favour if thereby she might calm the King's
fears.

"Of Chaldean happenings it may be. but of
things foreign they are ignorant. What can they who
have no knowledge of men beyond the confines of
Babylon know of these Macedonian savages, who in
battle are without fear and regard not at all the
number opposed to them?"

"You have not told me the present whereabouts
of the Macedonian army, if the few men it numbers
may be called an army," the Queen answered, in
contemptuous scorn of Alexander's forces.

"Hearing of my presence here, Alexander is re-
tracing his steps in all haste from the south, intent
upon giving immediate battle," the King explained,
despondently.

"From the south! Impossible! From whence
have you such word?" she cried, affrighted, having
until then supposed Alexander was still in the neighbourhood of Tarsus.

"From my spies, who watch every movement of
the Macedonian army."

"And if by chance its coming should be as you
suppose?" she questioned, striving to regain her
composure.

"We cannot now draw off, but must accept battle

at a disadvantage, cramped within the confines of
this narrow valley."

"Why at a disadvantage? Here your very numbers must trample under foot Alexander's slender
force if you but set them in motion."

"No; thus clogged only a sixth of my army will
be available in battle, and so we are lost ere a spear
is raised."

"But our front, upon which the burden falls, will
still outnumber his three to one, and with soldiers
the equal in courage of any in the world," the Queen
reasoned, seeking to dissipate his fears. But in
vain, and discouraged and faint at heart she at last
bethought her to send for their infant son and
daughters, hoping thus to divert his mind and stim-
ulate his courage. And for a moment he seemed to
forget his fears in their soft caresses, but presently
relapsing into his former mood he waved them away,
and taking no note of their going sat with staring
eyes, unconscious of all about him. Greatly dispirited, and remembering the words of the King that
Alexander was coming from the south, the Queen,
in affright, hastened to the door of the tent, eagerly
scanning the valley in the direction from which the
enemy was expected. Seeing nothing, and reassured, she idly turned her gaze to the north, when to
her astonishment she beheld the Persian army in all
its array of gleaming spears and upraised standards
marching southward as if in haste to meet and over-

come the invading enemy. Assured that her senses did not betray her, she hurried to the side of the King, exclaiming: .

"Come quick, beloved, for our forces follow you and in all their mighty strength, hastening to meet and punish this presumptuous Prince who dares defy the power of your august majesty."

"Yes, it was so determined ere I left Issus," he answered, without animation or interest.

"Will you not go with them — spur them on to battle by your presence?" she questioned, seeing he made no move.

"Yes, but at present they go no farther than yonder rivulet," he answered, pointing to the Pinarus, that wound its way across the narrow valley.

"Is it there you will await Alexander; there offer him battle?" she inquired, scanning the level plain as a general might to judge its fitness.

"Yes, for retreat through the narrow mountain-pass with an enemy following is a thing impossible. And Bessus, whom I trust for his skill, has selected this spot to offer battle, in which decision Artabazus, whom I love for his fidelity, concurs. The river and its steep bank," he explained, with greater animation, "will retard the enemy's front attack, while our left will be protected by the mountain and our right by the open sea."

"Thus marshalled you will be victorious. Nay, it is as if the mighty God, offended at Alexander's presumption, here lures him on to his destruction," she cried, raising her hands to heaven, as if inspired.

"Think you so?" he questioned, grasping her hands and gazing upon her with staring eyes, as if indeed the Supreme God had made her his mouthpiece. For upon such childish conclusions oftentimes in that wildly superstitious age the fate of men and armies were made to depend.

"How can it be otherwise, sweet lord, for have you not always observed the God's command, and in your love erected altars to his glory throughout the land, upon which the priests ever keep alive the sacred fire of heaven?" she recounted, as if voicing the obligations of an attendant deity.

"It may be as you hope, but I like not the narrow confines of this sunken valley where the rays of the sun-god seem unable to penetrate," he objected gloomily, scanning the sky now overcast with clouds.

"He will favour you, oh King, will grant you victory," she encouraged, but with less animation, overcome by his gloomy forebodings.

"But lest it should turn out otherwise; lest our forces should be defeated despite his favour, I have commanded Arsames to arrange for your immediate departure for Damascus, where the court rests," he said, with choking voice as if the thought strangled him.

"What have I done amiss? How have I offended thee, beloved, that I should be sent away, leaving you to face the dangers of the campaign with no one near to comfort and support you?" she censured, clasping her arms about his neck and imploring him with her gentle eyes.

"Here there is danger.   There you will be safe — there the madman cannot penetrate," he cried, overcome.

"I do not wish to be safe, dearest, if you be in peril; and why such haste in the absence of all sign of Alexander's coming?"

"His present absence matters little, for the soothsayers who follow the fortunes of our Greek mercenaries, and claim to have knowledge of future events, all aver that the portents of their strange religion foretell dire disaster to our cause in the coming battle."

"What matter the portents of these savages? 'Tis but a cunning ruse to obtain some new favour at your hands, to force from you some new concession, some added darics to their monthly pay," she stormed, enraged and bewildered at this new peril she was called upon to meet. "However it may be, let me remain near you, my sweet lord, or if you will, make such provision as you think best for my departure should disaster overtake our arms.   This will not be difficult," she added lightly, "for the path by which I came may be reached in a moment's time, unobserved by the enemy."

"But should you by any chance fall into the hands

of this savage — better it were a thousand times that you were dead," he murmured, shuddering.

"The guard is ample for my protection, and commanded by the brave Arsames twenty Macedonian armies could not stay my flight," she urged, beaming upon him.

Thus it was determined, and presently the cries of men and the sound of bugle calls from the valley increasing to an uproar, the King and Queen turned their attention to the glorious panoply outspread before their eyes as the different classes of troops and the many varied nationalities that made up the Persian army took up their allotted places in the plain below. And in avoidance of the error of formation at the Granicus the Greek stipendiaries, thirty thousand strong, clad in scale armour with buckler, spear, and sword, held the front facing the river bank midway of the plain. On either side of these were thirty thousand Cardaces, men bred to war from their youth, shield-bearing guards armed with lances and Persian cimeters, their heads protected by helmets of steel. Clad in short cloaks of crimson cloth and holding aloft their glistening weapons, they presented so warlike an appearance that the King, forgetting his fears, clapped his hands in childish delight. Farther to the left and hugging the mountain-side, twenty thousand light-armed troops were stationed, ready as the battle progressed to descend and attack Alexander's flank and rear. On the other hand, far to the right, beside the sea, thirty-thousand iron-clad horsemen, the flower of the Persian nation, upheld their standards amid a forest of glistening lances.

Such was the warlike front that awaited Alexander's coming, and supplementary to it and directly behind the Greek mercenaries were stationed five and twenty thousand heavy-armed soldiers believed to be invincible, the Immortals and kinsmen of the King. In the midst of these and protected by them the great King, from immemorial custom, was to take his station and from his war-chariot observe and direct the course of the battle. Behind the forces described five hundred thousand soldiers of all arms were grouped in vast oblong bodies, according to their nationalities and the approved method of Oriental warfare. And herein lay the weakness of the Persian formation, as the units of service consisting of vast groups of men had no pliancy of movement save as a whole, while the Macedonian army, divided into innumerable bodies, each part was capable of separate and independent disposition, and so could be used when and where needed. Of inferiority in this respect, however, the Persians refused to believe, for so war had been conducted by their ancestors for hundreds of years. Or if they had some suspicion of inferiority, their pride and arrogant sense of superiority to all men prevented their profiting by the knowledge. Thus the day passed and night closed in as the King and Queen watched and commented on what was transpiring at their feet. But not wholly as spectators, for Darius, encouraged and cheered by Statira's brave demeanour, dispatched his aids from time to time to different parts of the field to command such changes in the order of battle as seemed to him proper.

As the chill night advanced, little by little the scene assumed a sinister aspect to the overwrought King, as the innumerable camp-fires of the army lighted up the vast plain. For, curiously enough, as viewed from the mountain-height, the soldiers, half disclosed by the flaming torches and blazing fires, took on a grewsome aspect, as if the plain were filled with gnomes and demons darting hither and thither without method or purpose. Shuddering, as if what appeared somehow foreboded evil, the King hastily entered the royal tent, murmuring as he looked back, trembling and affrighted:

"To-morrow at this hour I shall have recovered my kingdom — or lost it forever!"

Comforting him as best she could, the wearied King was at last led to seek repose, the Queen watching by his side in sorrowing silence. But of undisturbed rest the afflicted Monarch had none, for if lost for a moment in troubled sleep he would start up bathed in sweat, trembling and terrified, crying out that Alexander threatened him. Meanwhile the vast army, unconscious of the broken spirit of its King, wearied with the long march and expectant of the morrow, slowly sank to rest in the chill of the November night with only the sky for a covering and the bare earth for a bed.

CHAPTER IX

Little refreshed by the night's rest, Darius arose from his troubled couch with the first light of day, and soothed and cheered by Statira's encouraging presence donned his armour in preparation for the expected battle. When at last he was ready to mount and had taken leave of his mother and children, the Queen followed him to the waiting chariot, smiling encouragement and hope:

"Remember, dear lord," she whispered, "that the kings of Persia have never suffered defeat in battle when present to give confidence to their troops. Nor will it be different to-day, my love, if indeed Alexander's approach be not made in mere bravado of spirit."

"It was in such light that they viewed his coming at the Granicus — and to our utter undoing," the King responded, ungraciously.

"Had you, my lord, King of Kings, sovereign of all the world, been there to guide our forces on that fateful field, victory, not defeat, would have crowned our arms," the Queen protested.

"Not so, nor will my presence this day avail, for the army, disheartened by the unlooked-for battle, and I falling as I shall, will fly as one man."

148

"Dismiss your chariot then, my love, and fight on horseback, as does the Macedonian King. In that way your movements not being discernible from the field, no sudden fright will seize the soldiers, and so both you and your cause will prosper," the Queen advised, scanning the livid features of Darius, and fearful lest some sudden panic seizing him he should turn and fly, seeing which the army, losing confidence, would follow in his footsteps.

"That I would gladly do, but did I not show myself on my war-chariot, as is the custom of our kings, not one save the Greeks and my true Persians would lift an arm to defend the standards."

"Let them be scourged to battle then as in the olden time," Sisygambis, Darius' mother, who had followed, interposed with angry vehemence.

"As at Marathon, and with like fatal result, mother? No, I must take my station where all may see, and Alexander not less clearly than the others. For it is upon my person that he will direct his attack, and so has boasted, knowing that the army seeing the King fall will fight no longer."

"If he so directs his course then indeed your army will prove victor, my lord, surrounded as you will be by your invincible Persians, who will offer up their lives to a man rather than give ground before this boy-king," the Queen comforted, as if there could be no doubt of the battle's ending.

"Their courage will avail nothing, for Alexander's

army is not made up of men nurtured in the gentle usages of life, but savages, without fear, trained to fight and having no other occupation in life," the King resented, impatiently. Then, as if ashamed of his craven spirit and conscious of the unwearied efforts of the brave Queen to cheer and comfort him while her own heart was breaking, he suddenly caught her in his arms and lifting his pale face to heaven cried aloud in a voice of anguish and shame: "Oh, Ahura-Mazda, God of Persia, if indeed thou dost concern thyself with the affairs of men, watch over this, my beloved Queen, and give me heart to be worthy of her, bravest of all loving women!" and pressing his lips to hers, his eyes clouded with tears, he turned and mounting his chariot was gone.

Made inexpressibly happy by the King's words and tender parting, the Queen, followed by Sisygambis, took her station on the brow of the hill, from which place of vantage the valley in all its extent lay clearly revealed. And there with loving eyes she followed Darius' rapid course as he descended the mountain-side and made his way to the centre of the field amid the exultant cheers of the assembled army. Directing her attention to the south, the approach of Alexander's army was plainly heralded by the clarion notes of its trumpets, and this ere the marching troops came clearly into view. Not long, however, had the waiting Queen to watch ere discerning the enemy's blazing standards, as the different columns of the on-coming army fell into their alloted places as they neared the mountain stream behind which the Persian forces were stationed. Noting the smallness of Alexander's force, Statira's face lighted with something like an air of pity as she compared its meagre numbers with the innumerable host that surrounded the chariot of Darius.

"Surely the presumptuous King must be mad to think to overcome our army with so small a following," she cried, turning confidently to Sisygambis, who stood beside her with compressed lips and gloomy eyes.

"I know not, but 't is said that war in the west has become an art, and the knowing whisper among themselves that this young King surpasses all who have ever lived in knowledge of its secrets," the old woman growled, her eyes fixed with deadly hatred on Alexander, who with tossing plumes and clad in complete armour bestrode his war-horse Bucephalus, some yards in advance of his iron-clad followers. "And look, Statira, the presumptuous boy, scarce waiting to breathe his horse, turns his cavalry on those who guard the mountain-side — and foolishly, as he will presently see," the old woman chuckled, as the King leading the Companions suddenly charged in the direction indicated, amid the blare of trumpets and the fierce war-cry of his followers. But terrified and scarce making an effort to withstand the quick assault, the Persian left, surprised and panic-stricken by the unexpected attack, instantly gave way, retreating in mad haste to a less exposed position.

Astounded and furious at the cowardly act, Sisygambis cried out:

"See, accursed be Persia's God, our people fly before the savage horde like sheep pursued by hungry wolves! Oh, powers of evil," she screamed, as the troops of Darius threw away their arms in frantic efforts to escape, "give me duration of life that I may pursue the craven wretches to their homes till not one coward is left alive to taint the air of Persia!"

Greatly elated at his success, the Macedonian King, to the surprise of those who watched, made no effort to pursue his advantage, but wheeling about returned at a gallop to his waiting army. Giving his soldiers some minutes' needed rest, he made such changes as were necessary to meet Darius' order of battle, after which he raised his sword aloft as a signal to advance. Whereupon the Macedonian slingers and bowmen running forward let fly their missiles, and the darters, quickly seconding them, the sky in a moment was darkened by the multitudinous discharge. Retiring as suddenly as they came they were in a moment lost amid the advancing columns of cavalry and heavy-armed infantry that followed in order of battle, their exultant cries sounding high above the blare of trumpets and the resounding hoofs of the iron-clad horses. Confidently, and as if on parade, the Macedonian infantry entered the river and beating back after a prolonged encounter the Greek mercenaries who bravely opposed their progress, they gained at last a foothold on the opposite bank. Leaving the Phalangites to pursue the advantage thus gained, Alexander placed himself at the head of the guards and Companion Cavalry and turning again toward the mountain advanced at a trot, and presently circling to the left at topmost speed skirted the hill from which the affrighted women watched with bated breath.

"Accursed be the God of Persia who denies such courage to our troops," Sisygambis raged, as Alexander swept by with uplifted sword, cheering his followers to greater haste.

"Hush, mother, pray rather that strength be given us in this our hour of agony," the Queen reproached, falling on her knees as the young King and his Companions, continuing at headlong speed, broke like a tempest on the exposed flank of the Greek mercenaries. Bravely the latter met the onslaught, but as Darius had foretold nothing could withstand the fury of Alexander's charge. And of this his war-horse seemed to form a part, as with nostrils aflame, the noble animal beat down with mailed front all who withstood his progress. Impatiently casting aside his visor and helmet, and cheering his followers to victory with trumpet voice, Alexander spurred his horse into the seething mass, followed by the Companions, their gleaming swords cutting wide a path, until, with desperate rush and cry of fury, they faced at last the Persian guard surrounding the chariot of Darius.

Here the battle took on new access of fury and long and sanguinary was the struggle, the attacking force advancing, often beaten back, but ever gaining some slight advantage. In the desperate struggle many Companions fell, and many gallant noblemen who surrounded the chariot of Darius, but ever as they fell others equally brave crowded forward to take their places. In this way the conflict continued, uncertain of issue, Greek and Persian striving with equal valour and determination. In the savage encounter Alexander and Bessus twice faced each other in deadly hatred, and twice were parted by the fierce struggle of those about them. But of this no one took note, the Persians intent upon the defense of their King who fought irresolutely from the body of his chariot, while the Macedonians were equally intent upon reaching his august person with their long and bloody swords.

"See, child, the enemy weaken in their attack, hindered by the dead and the number of riderless horses," Sisygambis cried, as the Companions slowly gave way before the Persian forces. "Hold now, oh King — give blow for blow and victory is yours," the old woman crooned exultingly as the Macedonians

STATIRA WATCHING THE BATTLE OF ISSUS

fell into confusion, hindered by the ownerless horses that plunged hither and thither determined not to be parted from their companions.

"Pray God it may be as you say," the Queen exclaimed, rising to her feet, hope reviving in her tired heart.

But the Companion Cavalry, quickly rallying from the momentary confusion, cheered by the presence of the King who fought always in the van, now charged afresh, beating back with dreadful slaughter all who sought to stay their progress.

"Why does not the King abandon his chariot, toward which every sword is pointed?" the Queen chided, terrified at the danger that threatened Darius.

"'T is not the way of Persia's monarchs," the old woman reproached.

"Better it were," the other sighed.

"See, our guard waver and give way, leaving the King exposed. And look, Statira, for my eyes grow dim — what means the sudden movement of Darius?"

"'T is nothing, mother. He but retires a little from the centre of strife to bring up those who idly watch the battle from afar," the anguished Queen explained, her tear-dimmed eyes fastened on her beloved husband as his charioteer struggled to find an opening of escape from the desperate onslaught of Alexander's forces.

"If that be all, why do our troops rest — why does the battle slacken?"

"I know not unless the soldiers worn with strife can do no more," the Queen murmured.

"Tut, tut, they have received scarce a scratch," Sisygambis raged, shading her eyes in vain effort to discern what was occurring.

"Oh, God be praised! The King at last abandons his chariot," the Queen cried, with a sigh of relief, as Darius alighted and hastily mounted a waiting horse.

"Wherefore, child?"

"That he may the better guide the battle, free from the centre of Macedonian attack."

"And in good time, for scarce one in ten of our waiting troops has raised a spear," Sisygambis criticised.

"Hush, mother," the Queen excused, her eyes fastened on the King who, crazed with fear, sought, it was now apparent, only an avenue of escape from the ill-fated field.

"Hark, child! What is that swelling cry?" Sisygambis asked, after a moment's pause, holding up her withered hand in vain effort to distinguish the purport of the uproar. But to her questioning the fainting Queen made no response save with sighs and tears, and the aged crone, presently interpreting the ominous cry as it increased in volume, shrieked in a frenzy of hate and fear: "No, no, 't is false, 't is false, the King does not, will not, fly!"

But vain her rage and curses, for the fateful cry, "The King flies," presently increasing to a mighty roar, his followers quit their attitude of surprise, and, governed by a common impulse, threw down their arms and fled in the wake of the terror-stricken monarch. But still the sorrowing Queen would not believe, but waited with parted lips, dry and parched as from a fever, her bloodshot eyes fixed on her beloved husband as, spurring this way and that, with ever-increasing haste, he pushed aside or trampled under foot all who impeded his headlong flight.

Tardily indeed did the news of the King's flight reach the Persian Cavalry pursuing Parmenio's force to the south of the little river, but at last hearing it, and angered and disheartened, they turned like the others and fled, pursued by their exultant enemy.

Hushed now all the clamour of the field save the shouts of the victors or the smothered cries of hunted fugitives as they were cut down by the pursuing foe or trampled to death by Darius' guard as the latter sought to follow close upon their master's flight. Of such happenings, however, Alexander took no notice, but disregarding all else sought in frantic haste, furious with rage, to overtake the flying King, knowing that only through Darius' capture could the war be finally terminated. But vain his efforts, blocked as he was at every step by the mass of fugitives who crowded the plain in panic-stricken fear.

Thus the Persian army was put to rout, the victors

slackening not their pursuit until darkness put an end to the dreadful slaughter. But only with the approach of night would the loving Queen believe, and not till then did she give thought of her own peril. And all too late, for such part of her guard as she had not sent in haste to aid Darius, caught by the mad panic, had long since sought safety in the obscure recesses of the mountain. Thus it was that of all those whom the Great King had provided for her safety, only the nobles who commanded her guard remained faithful to their charge. These, on her turning about, hastened to her side, and prostrating themselves besought her to put them to death. And Sisygambis, releasing her dagger and scowling her rage, would gladly have done as they asked, but the gentle Queen, looking down upon them with streaming eyes, bade them arise and like the others save themselves by flight. But to the honour of men, be it said, not one obeyed, and forming a close guard about her person they conducted her to the royal pavilion where they kept jealous watch until Hephestion, coming up with a detachment of soldiers, took possession of the tent, assuring the waiting nobles that he would guard the safety and honour of the royal family with his life.

And thus it was when Alexander, wounded and worn in body, returned from the hot pursuit. Conducted to the royal abode, he was presently startled by the wailing of women in an adjoining room, and upon inquiring the cause was told that the Queen having learned that the King's chariot, shield, and robe had been brought to the tent now mourned her husband as dead. Hearing this Alexander, surprised and disconcerted (for until then he was ignorant of her presence near the battle-field), bade Leonnatus, one of his household, go to the sorrowing Queen and assure her of Darius' safety and escape. On the following morning, grieving over her unhappy state, he paid her a visit of ceremony and respect, accompanied by Hephestion, and in the interview that followed assured her that he did not make war on women, and that no meed of honour heretofore accorded her as Queen of Persia would be denied her now; and that in all things she and her children should be treated as if Darius and not he had been the victor. And thus it was to the end, but out of a chivalrous regard for the Queen's good name, and lest it cause her distress, he would never afterward, save on one memorable occasion, permit himself to see the unhappy woman.

CHAPTER X

"Itanes to Roxana; greeting and love:

"This in gentle remembrance to you, my sister, and my sweet Ossillia, in far-off Bactria while I abide with thy lord, the King, beside the bubbling sea.

"Thus I began, but wrote no more for a week, that I might have time to reflect; for while you have sought to teach me form, I know not what a letter is if, indeed, this is to be a letter. Rather I think, it will turn out what Orestes calls a chronicle; for you bade me omit nothing that Alexander the King said or did, and — so far as I could guess — what he thought. And besides, to see that he is not served as was his murdered father, Philip. Thus it is that I, a stripling, find myself letter-writing and a self-imposed guardian of the King, and such a King as the world never saw before and never will see again.

"It will cheer your heart to know that he welcomed my coming as if I brought him the crown of Persia, and, not to be outdone in kindness by her who sent me, ever seeks occasion to question me concerning you and your sayings and doings, nay your very heart-beats. Until now I had thought the gentle art of loving was a foolish passion, a thing set apart

160

for women and youths like myself, having no great
strength or purpose in life, but Lysimachus, a garrulous old man about the camp, says that the braver
and stronger men are the greater their passion when
caught by woman's wiles. This you would readily
believe of our King if I could recount the ways in
which he shows his passion. But of that anon; be
satisfied that it is real, and that my throat is parched
answering the questions of this mighty man, whose
sword hangs over the world, but who in love is a mere
willow. For in that he is not kingly at all, but just
a lover, asking the same things over and over, and
this, I'll swear, that he may but hear your name.
For a king in love, sister, is exactly like another
man, only more commanding and insistent; but
what he says in respect of his passion will no more
bear repeating than the sayings of a swine-herd. And
so it is with him whom men crane their necks to see,
and seeing will babble of till they die. But not many
are like him, so mighty that they may choose their
Queen because of their liking, holding the opinion of
men of no account whatever.

"Having got so far I laid this aside and went down
to the sea and watched it tumble and gurgle among
the rocks, for of its bigness and ways one never tires.
On our way here from Bactria, when we came to the
Tigris we thought it held all the water in the world,
but when we reached the open sea we stopped, thinking it a mist overspreading the land, and finding it

water — were speechless. And now before I take up
the serious things about which I came, and I can see
they will be serious, and maybe tiresome for a lad
fond of the air, I will tell about myself. Not for
you only, but for the home-folk, and more especially
that dimple-cheeked girl who lives in the thatched
hut by the fortress gate; and if you have any affection for your brother — an exile on your account —
you will watch over the little goddess with your life.

"Our journey hither, to recount some of the things
that occurred, took four months and was full of happenings, but nothing serious save the loss of two
javelin men; one killed by nomads in the big desert
while hunting a water-pool, and the other by robbers
in the Zagrus Mountains. The last, poor lad, met
death while defending me as I lay on the ground with
an arrow in my leg, and save for the chance passing
of a vagrant fly I would have got my quietus then
and there. But as the robber raised his spear to
slay me the insect chanced to light on the villain's
nose, and, it tickling him immensely, he stopped to
brush it aside, whereupon I thrust him through the
body with my javelin. My wound was grievous and
detained me a month, but while I rested, nursing
it, my companions passed the time hunting, and so
agreeably that they were loth at last to believe me
fit to continue the journey. Altogether our adventures were great and fit for talk about a camp-fire
at night in the mountains, for sometimes we trav-

elled as recruits going to join the Persian army, at
other times as traders, then again as hunters, but
more often as robbers. This last not from choice —
though the life isn't so bad — but from necessity when
game was scarce and the people unfriendly.

"After crossing the Euphrates a new danger beset
us, and one wholly undreamed of before. For soon,
to our surprise, we began to encounter the half-starved
and maddened soldiers of Darius in flight from the
battle-field of Issus. Before this, however, and to
our great astonishment, Darius himself passed us at
full gallop, sunken of face and shrivelled in body, surrounded by his retinue and followed by Bessus with a
body of cavalry, as if fearing pursuit. This was the
first we knew of what had happened, but learned
nothing definite, for they passed like phantoms in the
night, saying not a word; and oh the deadly pallor
and unspeakable agony of the King's face — It was
as one in Hades damned for all eternity. Afterward,
sorrowing at the distressful plight of the soldiers that
followed the King in wild disorder — for they were
pitiable objects to look upon — we gladly shared with
them our stock of food; but when we had no more to
give they would have taken our animals, and these
too we killed and divided with them, save one lean
ass. To gain possession of this they would have
murdered us, but fortunately they had thrown away
their arms, and so forming a guard about the brute
we pushed ahead, until the multitude having passed,

we killed the half-starved beast, and building a fire feasted on the savoury dish till we were full.

"Descending the mountain-pass Darius had traversed, we came all of a sudden on the battle-field of Issus, and may I be preserved from ever again beholding anything so horrible. The Macedonians had burned their dead, but of Alexander's permission given the Persians to bury their slain they seem to have taken no notice, save in the case of the great nobles. The others to the number of a hundred thousand or more strewed the plain as far as the eye could reach, and nothing so grewsome was ever before beheld by mortal man. Mostly the faces and limbs of the dead were horribly distorted; some, though, sat half upright, seemingly resting; others were prostrate on their knees as if in obeisance before the flying King. One stood half-uplifted, with arms outstretched, as if beckoning to me, so that I ran to him in all haste only to find him dead; but many of the slain lay at ease as if they had sunk down in peaceful repose, and so fallen asleep. About the place where the chariot of Darius had stood men and horses lay in windrows, countless in number, half consumed by wolves and jackals from the neighbouring mountains. At one spot where the pursuing troops crossed a deep ravine to intercept the fleeing Persians, they made a bridge of the dead, and passing with their cavalry at a gallop had trampled the bodies into an undistinguishable mass. About the dead, and hovering low in the fetid

air there were such multitudes of vultures and eagles
and smaller birds-of-prey as the tongue cannot tell of.
Not as we see them in the mountains of Bactria, sister,
hovering uncertain and hungry above some crippled
animal, but gorged to the full so that the loathsome
things made no effort to escape. Enraged, we killed
many with our spears as they watched us furtively
with fiendish cunning out of their half-closed eyes;
but tiring at last we sought the sea and skirting the
shore, suffocated by the odour, hurried forward till
we gained the country beyond. Such, my sister,
were some of our adventures, but of Issus and its
horrors not a word to her of the melting eyes,—my
love, my sweet Ossillia.

"Dejected, hungry and in rags, we finally overtook
the Macedonian army late one afternoon, and coming
up I sought Hephestion, he whom you so extolled
for his mild ways and unselfish love for his master.
I was able to gain his presence only after I had told
the guard that I was fleeing from Darius and had
some vastly important news to communicate regarding the Persian forces. Succeeding at last, I found
him clad in armour, for it was his day on duty, and
speaking apart I told him who I was and from whom
I came. Hearing me through, he embraced me as if
I were his brother, and straightway calling a slave
told him to prepare a bath and when I had bathed
he provided garments with which to clothe myself.
Then, greatly refreshed and thinking better of my

mission, I sat down to a sumptuous repast, and while
I ate he talked of you, and among other things how
you had once nursed him back to life in the plains
of Thessaly after an encounter with a band of out-
lawed Thebans, who it seems had attacked father's
embassy then on the way to Pella. I suspect if
another and one greater than Hephestion had not
straightway pressed his suit with the Bactrian maid,
and with the concurrence of the maid herself, that
Hephestion would not have been backward in making
known his own passion! However that may be, he
was most kind, so that I was at once at my ease and
greatly pleased to be thus favoured by so lovable a
man. When at last I could eat no more and had
drunk a goblet of their strong wine I accompanied
him to the King's tent, and bidding me wait without
he went in alone, but emerging almost immediately
told me to enter, which I did unannounced.

"The King's tent was lined with silk and had many
rooms, and this of necessity, for since Issus he has
become the heart of all the western world. When I
looked about expecting to find him crowned with the
upright tiara such as the great King wears, I beheld
instead a young man pale of face from recent wounds,
wearing a simple tunic of white linen, girt about by a
jewelled belt. His head had no covering save his
yellow hair, which is of such length and tumbling
luxury that it more becomes him than a crown.
Withal, too, he had attractive and lofty features,

and such mild, responsive eyes that it seemed impossible they should ever be animated save by the most amiable passions; and if it be otherwise — and truly it is — such outbursts are no more to be denied a King than common men. The simple-minded natives everywhere hail him as a god, and there is reason in it, for his comeliness and grace of body and limb can only be likened to a God — and the gods, I suspect, sister, were in the first place nothing more than perfect men.

"Reclining at his ease, intent upon a book, I knew him at once, for he had the air of one who will take no denial; a descendant of the Kings who preyed upon each other and their neighbours in the mountain fastnesses, knowing no safety in their homes or abroad, and, withal, so inured to danger that, like Philip, it no longer had a place in their thoughts. When I would have prostrated myself he put out his arm and drew me to him, for he was desperately wounded, and kissed me on the mouth. Thus he held me as if it were another, she indeed who sent me, and this for a long time saying nothing and I all abashed and trembling at being thus received by one whom, as I say, the simple-minded liken to a God. And holding me he choked and caught his breath, from the pain of his wound it may be, but it was as I have done an hundred times when coming unexpectedly upon Ossillia, my love; or when indeed she has granted me some favour I greatly craved. But after a while releasing

me he took hold of my hand and encircled me with
his arm:

"'And are you Itanes, Roxana's brother, come
hither to follow my fortunes?' he exclaimed, and upon
my assenting, glad that the silence which was smoth-
ering me was at last broken, he went on, gazing
intently into my face. 'By heavens, child, it is as
if I saw in thee Roxana's self, for thou hast in thy
features the very breath of her body.' And upon
my first coming into his presence, sister, I believe
he thought he clasped you in his arms, not knowing nor caring how you came, if indeed it might
be you.

"'And you come from her?' he presently went on.

"'Yes, oh King.'

"'And is she well — and happy?'

"'She is well, oh King.'

"'Why do you evade my question?' he asked,
starting up.

"'She is content, oh King — since the return of
Orestes,' I answered and at this he smiled.

"'I have greatly feared for Orestes' safety, no
courier of mine having been able to evade the watchfulness of Darius,' he responded, meditatively, as if
counting their number.

"'Many times Orestes was stopped, many times
threatened, oh King, but evading every snare, at last
reached his destination,' I answered, with more freedom, encouraged by his amiable manner.

"'She was pleased at his coming — and what he brought?'

"'Yes, overjoyed.'

"'But before that — for he was long delayed?'

"'Until then she scarce lived, shut up within herself, doing naught the day through but watch the mountain-path by which he must return,' I answered, concealing nothing.

"'And I not less expectant waited the years through for some sign, some token from her, some assurance of her love,' he murmured, half aloud, communing with his own thoughts.

"''Twas as if the fates conspired to prevent all intercourse,' I answered, remembering your complainings, 'but in the end,' I added (determined that no part of your heart's affliction should remain unknown to him), 'all the seemingly vain prayers were happily answered.'

"'The Gods be praised that it was so — and that she still regards me as on that night when we were parted on the river bank,' he went on, forgetful of my presence.

"'Yes, oh King, and she has life only in the thought of your coming,' I answered, pretending his words were addressed to me.

"'May the Gods protect her and give her patience,' he sighed, as if contemplating the period that must elapse ere he can reach you. For meanwhile, sister, all the intervening country must be conquered, no enemy being left behind, and above all, Egypt and the warlike cities of Phœnicia with their countless ships forever threatening. Thus the King went on, sometimes questioning me but more often communing with his own thoughts; but of Darius or news that I might have of Persia after traversing its wide extent, not a word. This indifference to his enemy's doings with no thought of any advantage he might derive from what I had seen or heard, I thought King-like; but in truth he thought only of you, sister, and your happiness.

"In the way I have described he questioned and I answered till the night was far spent, and when he could think of nothing more to ask concerning you he questioned me about my journey and its perils. At last, seeming to notice my weariness he made as if he would dismiss me, but with reluctance, it appeared, as if some thought oppressed him of which he was loth to give expression. At which I, fool that I am, all at once bethought me of the leaden casket you gave me, and which I now in haste and with burning face snatched from my bosom and kneeling, gave into his hands, crying out:

"'She bade me give you this, oh King, but until now I had forgotten, so little do I regard the purpose of my coming.'

"Striving to open it he found it sealed, at which putting his arm about me he kissed me and calling a page bade him provide me with quarters for the night. Thus I left him, ashamed of myself and red of face, but this he seemed not to notice nor any other thing save the casket which he held in his hand.

"And now, sister, a part of my business having been accomplished and having told you of the kindness of the King, I lay this letter aside, hoping to find a way to send it to you, but not knowing how nor when."

CHAPTER XI

"Itanes to Roxana; greeting and love:

"Most surprisingly an itch to write, to portray, comes over me. Lysimachus says such a thing is a distemper and needs little encouragement to blossom into a flower — or more likely a weed. The King, sitting by at the time and eying one of the scribes out of the corner of his eye — a lean, sallow-faced Greek, who follows the army to recount its doings — said, aside, that 'writing is an eczema, the humouring of which increases the flame like a fire nourished by the wind.' Watching the Greek, I had thought to filch the marrow of his work and so save myself some labour, but on reading his manuscript I found it had little pith and so dull that the ink dried ere I could transcribe the words. And if it be that men hereafter will know our King as this Greek describes him, then indeed will he appear to them as sapless and void of human interest and sympathy as an Egyptian mummy. More like a phantom than a man! Yet so it will be, I fear, for the scribes lack human weaknesses and, what is worse, by no means admire or love the King; and this because of things that happened away back in their own country.

172

"But it was not of such matters that I set out to write, but how I have become one of the King's pages, with a crimson cloak surmounted by a plumed hat, with a sword and scabbard of such surprising richness that I would Ossillia might see me wear them. And of her, the dear thing, keep me ever in her gentle thoughts, sister, for there are many comely youths about Arimazes who will seek her to my detriment if she but forgets me for an hour. The King said he made me a page that I might always be near him, for these lads are his couriers and aids and accompany him wherever he goes. But who I am or from whence I come no one, save Hephestion and the King, knows, for thanks to Orestes' teaching, so good is my Greek that men think I am a native of Athens, or maybe of Corinth, both famous towns in Greece.

"The King looks upon, his pages as his children, and does not hold himself in such reserve in their presence as with older men; and so I am able to be always near him and in some intimacy, but withal have little idle time on my hands, for he is never idle himself. When there is no business, though, to engage his attention he will humour himself by sitting at the table till far into the night, and at such times he likes to talk of wars and battles and sip his wine, but the last lightly and more in compliment to those about him than from any great love of it. The wounds he got at Issus have healed, but for days after the battle he was carried forward in a litter; but whether in that way or on horseback he is not like any one about him, but seemingly set apart by the Gods of his country from all other men.

"As we marched south beside the sea, the petty kings who rule over the different cities and islands sent embassies or came themselves, offering submission and bringing golden crowns and presents innumerable. This was thought remarkable, for some of these ancient strongholds never yielded themselves unreservedly to either the Assyrian or Persian monarchs. Now, as if recognizing a power greater than any known before, they gave up their cities and with them tendered the King expressions of confidence and friendship. In some cases minor princes represented their rulers in these overtures, their masters, who possess great numbers of ships-of-war, being at sea under mandate from Darius. But it made no difference, for the people, fearing Alexander's wrath and hearing of his generous treatment of those who yield, one and all compelled their princes to make peace with him. In this way the great island strongholds of Rhodes and Cyprus yielded, and so the cities of Aradus and Byblus and Sidon, she of the rich cloths and purple dyes, famed for the cunning of her people and their deftness in bartering — and on occasion when trade is threatened, for courage in open battle. Thus the King advanced, and it was like the progress of a Persian monarch, for the people knew no difference and prostrated themselves beside the road, and this to the amazement of the Macedonians who are not accustomed to see their ruler received with such homage. Some of our leaders laughed, but with others it excited anger and jealousy; and this in particular of one Philotas, who makes much of being the son of Parmenio, and carries himself with the air of a monarch, striving in all ways to excel the King in the splendour of his raiment and the luxury of his equipages — at which display the King indeed only smiles.

"Progressing in the way I have described, we at last came to Tyre, the queen city of Phœnicia, and, indeed, of the seas; and here they met us as before, with a golden crown and offers of submission. But when the King, because of some oracle or sooth-sayer's communings, expressed a desire to sacrifice to Herakles, his ancestor, at the ancient temple of that hero within the city, they would by no means sanction it, thinking, apparently, that it was easier to keep him without the walls than to exclude him once he had gained entrance. From this it was evident they did not contemplate complete submission like the others, but designed to retain their freedom so that they might be in a position to take advantage of any accident that might befall the King; or, indeed, might make barter of their offices as between him and Darius. Listening to all they had to say, the King persisted, and so the Tyrians retired, having, it seems, moved all their people and belongings within the walls of the city. This last lies on an island separated from the mainland by an arm of the sea half a mile in width and of considerable depth. And not without reason did the haughty traders defy the conquering King, for they possess two hundred war-ships and an army of thirty thousand fighting men within the mighty wall that encompasses their island city. The height of this wall is an hundred and fifty feet, and at the top fifty feet across, built throughout of cut stone; and so strong that both Assyrian and Babylonian monarchs were unable to effect an entrance after sieges of many years' duration. The King, no wise discouraged at the action of the Tyrians, called a council of his generals and pointing out how foolish it would be to leave the city with its army and vast number of ships in the rear, it was finally determined to lay siege to the place.

"The Tyrians — huckstering wasps, men call them — settled here so many ages ago that there is no account of their coming, nor from whence they came. But during all the passing years they have sailed the wide waters in their ships, bartering their wares and accepting in exchange such things as those who border on the seas have had to offer. Thus venturing and unmindful of their great gains, it has been their way when they had disposed of a cargo to fill the holds of their ships, when opportunity offered, with hapless

natives whom they afterward sold into slavery! Yet
these hucksters do not lack courage, nor ever have
when their trade or savings were threatened; and so
the prospect of a siege somewhat discouraged our
people, remembering how others had attempted it and
failed. But the King, undismayed, fixed his tent on
the shore, and losing no time gathered the able-bodied
men from all the country round about and set them
to work to construct a mighty mole two hundred feet
in width from the shore to the walls of the city. But
regarding this undertaking and other things concerning it, I am now too weary to write, and so put it off
until another time. '

"If you, sister, and my sweet Ossillia, still have
Itanes in the flesh you must know it is because the
Gods are mindful of him and disregardful of his
great vanity, which last came nigh to costing him his
life. For the King, wearied with the slow progress
of the siege of Tyre, and angered at the robbers who
infest the adjacent mountains, murdering his soldiers
and stealing his supplies, determined at last to make
war on them. Thinking to gain some extra credit,
I and some of the pages, with Medius and Demetrius,
two of the King's officers and great favourites with
everybody, set out in advance of the troops to do a
little fighting on our own account. But when we
reached the forest that covers the mountain like a
cloak there was all of a sudden a whir in the air and a

spear penetrating my shield bore me to the ground. Remarking the direction from which the missile came, my comrades, all unmindful of me, charged up the mountain, scattering as they ran, and being fleet of foot, quickly overtook and captured my assailants, three in number, all Cretans born, it appeared, and strangers to the country. Wondering at their presence here, Medius interrogated them, whereupon they explained that they had been engaged to do as they had by Bessus, the Persian viceroy —he who sought you in marriage! According to the agreement with him they had followed our army, hoping to come upon the King unawares, and so put him to death, and thinking from the waving plumes in my casque that I was the King, they sought to kill me as I have described. While we were deliberating whether we should hang or impale the rascals, the King came up, and listening to their story and pitiful pleadings he finally asked them if they served Bessus from choice or necessity. Then it came out that Bessus, being about to put them to death for deserting Darius' army, had offered to pardon them if they would make oath to the Gods to follow our troops, and, when chance offered, assassinate the King. When the King heard this he turned to Demetrius and bade him give to each of the Cretans a piece of money, and without further words dismissed them. But while all this was occurring, your brother, having found that he was unharmed, plucked the towering feathers from his helmet, cured of his vanity and no longer desirous of aping his master, the King.

"Continuing our march, we came at last on real enemies who met us in the open and from ambush, and we, pursuing and attacking wherever we found them, presently penetrated far into the mountains, where progress was slow and difficult. Thus it fell out late one afternoon, when a heavy snow had fallen, that Lysimachus, unable to keep up with the column, fell far behind; and the King waiting on his steps and aiding him, darkness found us (for I was with them) alone and lost in the mountains without fire or food. This did not seem important, but as the night advanced it turned bitter cold, and the King, seeing that Lysimachus suffered from it, presently took off his cloak and wrapped it about the old man, afterward making use of mine in the same way. But without much good so that he was greatly alarmed lest Lysimachus should die ere the night passed. While the King bent over the old man, striving to comfort and encourage him, I ran back and forth to keep life in my body, and doing so espied a camp-fire high up on the mountain, half a parsang from where we lay. Fearing it to be that of the robbers we were pursuing, I called it to the attention of the King, thinking there might be some danger. Hearing me he arose, and after eying the light for some time as if to fix its location, took up his spear and bidding me watch beside Lysimachus disappeared in the dark-

ness. But disobeying him in this, thinking it no
great harm, I grasped my spear and followed, keeping
out of sight. The fire turned out as I had thought, to
be the night camp of a band of the murderers and
robbers we were hunting. And the King, discovering
this to be so, continued on and reconnoitering as he
approached suddenly rushed the camp and taking the
robbers unawares killed two and put the others to
flight. Afterward gathering up the live coals in his
helmet he made his way back, I running on ahead,
so that when he reached Lysimachus I was seemingly
resting. But springing up in all haste, I kindled a
fire with dry twigs, and in a minute the old man was
warming himself by its side, believing the Gods had
in some miraculous manner intervened in his behalf.

"You have never said aught to me of Lysimachus,
the early tutor of the King, and strangely, I think, if
you met him while at Pella. He sometimes calls
himself Phoenix and the King Achilles, and without
much reverence or reason. For this Achilles, who
took part in a small war at Troy on the Asiatic coast
many hundreds of years ago, seems to have been a
very eccentric person, possessed of some courage but
with morals far from heroic and the very reverse of
our King's. His doings and those of his companions and the part the Gods took in the strife are
described in a book they called the 'Iliad,' by a man
named Homer, one of the greatest liars that ever lived.
The King thinks the book great and keeps it in a gold

casket and sleeps with it under his pillow at night, but as for me I can make neither head nor tail of the stuff. But Homer wrote another book called the 'Odyssey,' describing the adventures of a man named Ulysses, the King of a small island, and this, sister, I think immense.

"Lysimachus is much given to boasting and foolish talk, and is laughed at because of it, but notwithstanding the old man's weakness the King treats him with more respect than any one else, and will by no means sit down until he has been seated; and this, it is apparent, in remembrance of Lysimachus' kindness to him when a youth. But it is like the King in so far as the weak and helpless are concerned; for in respect to them it is as if he thought the Gods had made him their protector and guardian. But in respect to those who stand out against him — he is as a flame of fire."

CHAPTER XII

"Itanes to Roxana; greeting and love:

"Last night as I lay sheltered from the storm beneath a foraging cart I dreamed that Ossillia visited me. She seemed to have wings, and this not strangely, I thought, but as I advanced she receded, beckoning me to follow, which I did, until at last I awoke to find myself in a field drenched with rain — and the vision gone.

"We returned from the campaign against the mountain robbers, greatly refreshed by the adventure, to find the mole had been built far into the sea and equipped throughout with towers and mantlets and engines for throwing missiles. But day and night we were harassed by the enemy's ships and firepots and the flaming arrows they shot from the walls of the city. All this until one stormy night they contrived to anchor a ship filled with pitch and other combustibles beside the mole, and setting it on fire the flames caught and destroyed the towers and machines; and taking advantage of our helplessness they assailed the mole throughout, breaking down its supports and weakening it in every way. Then the same night as if the Gods frowned upon us a great storm arose,

182

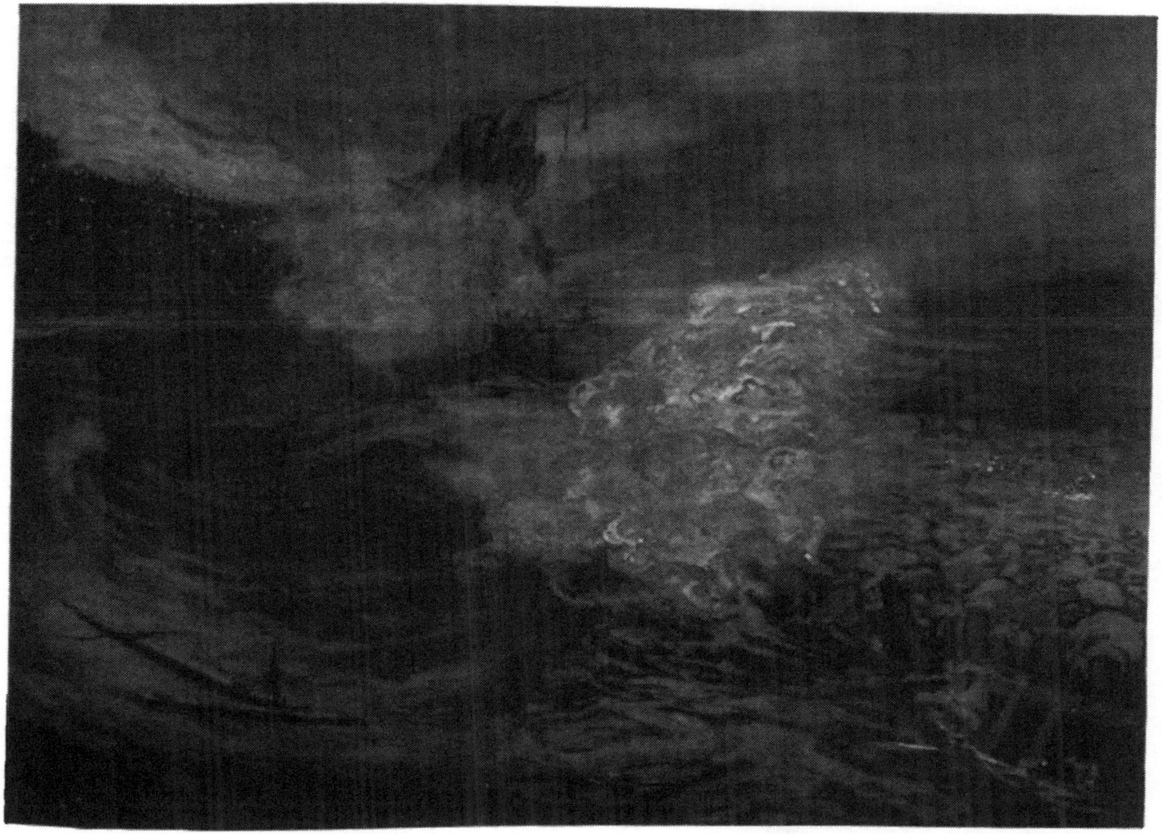

DESTRUCTION OF THE MOLE

the sea running mountains high, so that in the morning there was scarce a vestige left of the great undertaking.

"Had we possessed ships we could have beat the enemy off, and this the King saw, and after giving directions to commence a new and greater mole he betook himself to Sidon, and meeting the petty kings who rule over the island and coast cities, finally prevailed upon them to aid him with their ships. In this way he collected three hundred vessels, some of them having five banks of oars, and with these he set sail for Tyre. When the surprised inhabitants of the beleaguered fortress beheld him approach with the vast array — for they had not before believed that their sister cities would come to his aid in this manner — they straightway hid their ships in the harbour of the city, blocking the entrances with , sunken triremes. Now having command of the sea the King assailed the fortress incessantly from every side, but so mighty were the walls and so resolute its defenders, that for a long time nothing was accomplished. At last the Tyrians, thinking to weaken or destroy our fleet, suddenly emerged from the harbour and fell upon our ships, which lay some way off and unmanned, the sailors having gone ashore for their midday meal. But as it happened the King was with the remainder of the fleet to the south of the city, and the enemy's attack being signalled to him, he instantly set sail with all the ships at hand, and

skirting the walls suddenly fell on the enemy's flank
and rear.   And they not expecting anything of the
King, nor being able to get their ships in position to
repel the attack, he sunk or captured the greater
number of their vessels, putting the others to flight.
The enemy's fleet being now weakened by this disaster and no longer to be feared, the King assailed
the city with increased fury; and presently a weak
spot in the wall being discovered, our machines and
rams assailed it night and day.   This until a breach
was effected, and the King coming up, bridges were
lifted to the wall and the final assault commenced.
But not with any immediate success, for the Tyrians,
crowding the battlements, cruelly harassed our
soldiers with red-hot sand and boiling water.   Others
farther off hurled javelins or shot their arrows, while
those defending the breach assailed us with sword
and spear.   Three times we were repulsed — for I
was with the attacking party — but at last the King
leading and cheering his followers, beat back the
opposing force and gained a foothold on the wall.
Here we stopped to take breath, and being unable
to descend into the city because of the great height
of the wall we went forward along the battlements
until we reached the citadel, where we were at last
able to descend to the streets below.   Here the
enemy showed no less courage than before, and our
troops, enraged at the Tyrians for having put the
King's heralds to death and mutilated our soldiers,

would neither give nor ask quarter. In this way eight thousand Tyrians were slain and two thousand hanged on the great wall, the remainder of the inhabitants being sold into slavery. In respect to the last, however, a King is but a looker-on. Such spoil belongs of right to the soldiers, and he has no great voice, unless it be to rescue some gentle captive, as in the case of Timoclea, now the wife of Seleucus, the commander of the pages.

"Of all the helpless beings who have been enslaved since time began the Tyrians are the least deserving of pity, for they have always trafficked in the lives of men and women and children, as others do in cattle, and if they now feel the shackles on their own limbs they cannot complain. Of the great spoil there fell to me a brother and sister, but not of my own choosing; for while I stood looking on the hapless throng that filled the market-place, these two all of a sudden threw themselves on the ground and hugging my knees besought me to buy them. Why they did this I know not unless it was that some twitching of my lips might have showed my compassion. I smiled upon them as if pleased (for a man should look unconcerned, however much annoyed he may be, the King says) and did as they asked, giving five golden darics for the two. Afterward I did not much regret the purchase, though they were a great bother, when I found they could play on the harp and cithara and the soft-sounding guitar. However,

I do not look to bringing them to Bactria, for I expect I may not have the heart to keep them once we reach Egypt, their own country, for there they have relatives and friends. And, well sister, what would you do in such a case were you in my place? Of the part I took in the battle, though always near the King, I have no wounds to show save the scratch of a spear head. But being worn and sore I bid you adieu for the present, and in cure of my hurt beg a kiss and a word of endearment from my love Ossillia.

———

"Of the doings of Darius we know nothing, or if the King has any knowledge he does not make it known. But if the Persian monarch be not brave he is a facile scribe, for the King has received two letters from him, not altogether lacking in dignity yet having somewhat the air of a trader or patron. In the first he craves the return of his family, proffering money, and in the second offers his daughter in marriage and the sovereignty of all Asia west of the Euphrates, and with it ten thousand talents if the King will consent to make peace. Replying, the King wrote, 'I am now lord of Asia; come to me and I will give thee all thou canst ask, but if thou dost still deny my sovereignty then stand and fight for thy kingdom, for I shall seek thee wherever thou mayst be found.' The meaning of which is that he will deliver the Queen and her children into the hands of Darius and otherwise make abundant provision for the unfortunate monarch if he will submit himself to his grace, but of trading or compromising — no. When this offer of Darius was made known to Parmenio, he cried out that if he were Alexander he would accept, and the King laughed and said that if he were Parmenio he would do the same thing, but being Alexander, would not.

"Thus the letter-writing has ended but while the King will not listen to Darius' pleadings nor for good reasons allow correspondence between him and Statira, yet under cover of Leonnatus, one of his officers, he contrived a plan to further the Queen's great anxiety to communicate with her husband. An anxiety very natural, you will think, when you remember the fate usually accorded queens who fall into the hands of a conqueror. The plan was this, and so simple that those concerned will never know of the King's agency in the matter. For her wishes having come to his knowledge he bade Leonnatus contrive a way by which Bazares, a eunuch beloved and trusted by both the Queen and her husband, should effect his escape from the camp, and going to Darius carry any message the Queen might desire to send. And the plot falling out as the King intended, the bereaved Queen's heart was in some part lightened of its great burden (for she mourns her husband unceasingly) and Darius assured of the honour and security of his beloved wife. And it falls out daily in things like this, sister, that while some openly, and others covertly, accuse the King of cruelty or lacking in generosity, he only of them all has any real regard for the weak and afflicted. In regard to the Queen, it is apparent that he detains her and her children as hostages for reasons that. affect the safety of all those friendly to the Macedonian cause throughout the Empire. For otherwise the Persians would torture and mutilate all our people so unfortunate as to come into their hands, as at Issus, where Alexander had left his sick and wounded when he passed through the village on his way south.

"And speaking of the King, a funny thing happened that I had like to have forgotten and for which you would never have forgiven me. In our battles, you must know, we do not take many prisoners, but among those who secured this immunity at Tyre was a Persian nobleman whom the King determined for some reason to hold as a hostage. One day this nobleman speaking within hearing of the King, mourned in tears over the sorrow his captivity would cause his young wife — Roxana! At the name the King started up and straightway became interested in the man and a little while afterward called Hephestion to him and bade him supply the Persian with every needed thing and set him free. And this was done to everybody's great astonishment and the nobleman's most of all!

"After the siege of Tyre the King said that another such battle would make a man of me, and such

a one we have had, sister, yet my heart still inclines
to the peaceful vales of Bactria; and above all to
that sweet maid whom I see so often in my dreams,
and for a sight of whom I would give all I have in the
world. But of this great longing I say nothing to the
King lest he send me home and I thereby incur your
lasting displeasure.

"The battle about which I set out to tell was at
Gaza, a city of spices and frankincense and myrrh,
lying on the very edge of the world, and commanding
the desert and all that lies beyond. It was built on
a hill some distance from the sea, and above this they
had erected a mound sixty feet in height from which
the walls were lifted. Within the city was defended
by ten thousand Persian soldiers, and when we approached, Batis, the governour, a eunuch, mindful
of his master's interest, shut the gate in our faces.
But it being a great fortress and commanding the
road to Egypt, the King would by no means pass it
by lest it become a rallying point for his enemies.
Fixing his camp, therefore, he collected all the people
round about the country as at Tyre, and set them to
build a mound that should overtop the walls of
the city. This when completed was two hundred
and fifty feet in height, and in its building there were
many desperate battles in which we mostly got the
worst of it. When at last the mound was completed
and the machines placed thereon, the fighting became
incessant, but often the enemy making an unexpected

and furious sortie our works would be injured or our batteries destroyed. In one of these, toward the last, the King was wounded by an arrow shot from a catapult which, penetrating his shield and corselet, entered his breast. Enraged at this and the long resistance, for the siege had lasted two months, a general assault was ordered in which we were thrice repulsed, but still persisting the walls were finally scaled and the city taken. But the followers of Batis foolishly refusing quarter every one fell, sword in hand; and among the dead we found Batis, whom no danger weakened nor temptation caused to waver in his allegiance. Alexander, impatient and angry, watched the day's struggle from his couch, and at last directed his litter to be carried to the summit of the mound, and from there ordered the final assault. Of those who remained alive all were sold to slavery — save a girl stolen from a near-by city, who somehow had a look of my dear Ossillia, and she I bought and freed in remembrance of my love. And I expect it is because of Ossillia and much thinking of her and her soft eyes that I cannot look except with clouded face upon the killing and despoiling of those who have no part in the shaping of these wars. For the soldiers who fall I do not care: They die the death of brave men, and 't is a part of their life, they having mostly chosen it in preference to that of shepherds or other honest calling, and so their fate is not a matter to grieve over.

"Leaving a garrison in Gaza, the King, cured of his wound, set out on a hurried march to the heavily fortified city of Jerusalem, which had refused him submission. The people who inhabit that city and the neighbouring mountains and valleys are inclined to prophesy, and altogether different from others in this, that they claim there is but one God and that they are his Chosen People! Certainly they are remarkable, being much given to prayer, and in the intervals to a most surprising thrift. In the past they have been famed for warlike adventure in which they often suffered grievously, but more often it was their enemies who were worsted, for they are a wily and courageous race. While they have a king their real ruler is a high priest named Jaddeus, whose place of power is a great temple in the heart of the city. Advised of the King's rapid approach, and remembering the city's past misfortunes and above all the melancholy fate of Tyre and Gaza, Jaddeus knew not what to do. After a while, bethinking him and being both a wise and politic ruler, he prayed to his God and retired to rest. And while he slept he dreamed — and in this most wisely — that his God came to him and told him to decorate the city and go forth unarmed with all the priests and people and offer submission to the King's will. This Jaddeus accordingly did, to the great annoyance of our soldiers, who had anticipated much spoil from the sacking of the ancient and wealthy city. Seeing the multitude approaching, and advised of their errand, the King, highly elated (for he had expected to have to storm the city), went forward alone, and coming to the high priest who was clad in resplendent vestments with the cidaris on his head, prostrated himself in homage to the strange God that Jaddeus worshipped. Afterward with the high priest he entered the city, and going to the temple of Solomon offered sacrifices, according to the custom of the place, the people following and shouting hosannas to their God. Thus did our King, according to his politic way, pay respect and homage to the religion of these strange people, and this without any great knowledge of its merits.

"With the submission of Jerusalem the last of the great strongholds near the sea fell into the King's hands, and returning to Gaza he directed his course across the desert — a waste much dreaded by armies in the past — to Pelusium, an Egyptian city built at one of the mouths of the Nile. Here after a weary march of seven days we met Hephestion with the fleet, for the King, uncertain of the temper of the people, kept all his forces with him. But needlessly it appeared, for news of the downfall of Tyre and Gaza having preceded him, the country submitted without the flight of an arrow. Apprised of their peaceful intention, the King continued his march beside the river bank to Heliopolis, and thus to Memphis, the capital of the country. Here he sacrificed to Apis, the sacred bull, the object of Egyptian worship — following it with Greek games and musical entertainments conducted on a scale magnificent beyond words to describe.

"Presently leaving Memphis with a part of the army, he visited Canopus by the sea, and here laid out a city and called it Alexandria, designing when finished that it shall become the capital of the country. From there we marched two hundred miles to the west beside the sea, and from thence a like distance to the temple of Jupiter Ammon, in the heart of the Lybian desert. Of the purpose of this surprising and hazardous journey there is much speculation throughout the army, but of a truth it was to offer sacrifices at the shrine of the Supreme God, and receive in return, perchance, some insight into the future. This not at all strangely, for the King strives incessantly to learn the will of the Gods, and so sacrifices to them daily; nor will he do anything that the oracles forbid or the soothsayers declare to be unpropitious. His enemies, however, aver that his going was the outgrowth of a vanity that he might afterward claim that the oracle had proclaimed him to be not the son of Philip but of Jupiter himself. And this story being noised about and the ignorant thinking the oracle had so proclaimed, the King laughed but would say nothing, knowing the belief would be of great advantage to him among the superstitious people of the East.

"But of a truth, sister, I am much disturbed by the

ill-natured things said of the King by a little group
of leaders in the army, and of one Clitus in particular
— a remarkable man and long a favourite because
of his warlike valour. But now he gives himself up
wholly to wine and irritating thoughts, and while slipping back in the esteem of men thinks only he is wise,
and that the achievements of the King are hardly
worth regarding. His childlike reverence for Philip's memory has also bred a bitter jealousy that the
son, still scarcely more than a youth, should have so
greatly exceeded all the acts of his warlike father.
The truculence of Clitus and what it may lead to is
one of the real sorrows of the King. The enmity of
Philotas and his family is caused by jealousy, and
because of it they cannot understand his greatness
of mind and soul. This spirit of unrest I fear will
grow, and in the end culminate in the destruction of
the King — or his detractors! I write this not to disquiet you, my sister, but rather that you may be advised of affairs in the years to come when you shall
have become Queen! Of the common soldiers, however, you need have no fear, for their love knows no
bounds and grows with each passing day. Young
enough to be the grandson of most of them, they
nevertheless gravely salute him as Father, and indeed
he looks upon them all as his children. But many
of the petty officers who live on terms of familiarity
with the King are like a colony of field-mice, who
have their homes in the lair of a lion, and living thus

in such close proximity come to look upon the king
of beasts as one of themselves, sniffling disdainfully
when he roars or his might is spoken of as something
extraordinary! It is because of such small envyings
that the Persian kings always keep themselves apart
and in dignified seclusion — and wisely, too.

"From the temple of Jupiter Ammon the King
directed his course straight across the Lybian desert
to Memphis; though Cambyses, the son of Cyrus,
in attempting to do the like, lost his entire army of
sixty thousand men, not one returning to explain the
disaster by which so many brave men had perished.
Arriving at Memphis without mishap, the King has
set himself to organize a government for Egypt, after
which we will set out in search of Darius, who is said
to be organizing a vast army beyond the Tigris. And
here, my dear sister, and you Ossillia, my love, I
close my third letter, hoping to find a way to send it
forward with the others as we pursue our journey
eastward.

"I add this from on board the quinquereme Apollo,
a great ship with five banks of oars, and fleet of foot as
the winds of Bactria. For at the last moment before
marching, and to my great surprise, the King made
known his intention to send me to Pella with messages of love and respect to the Queen Olympias, his
mother; and also having in care presents for her and
many sacks of gold for Antipater, his governour in

Macedonia. And for myself, he presented me with such great riches that it took two asses to carry the burden to the ship's side!

"And now, my sister, and you, Ossillia, whom I so tenderly love, I must say good-bye, not knowing how long I will stay at Pella, or what the King intends for me when my errand is accomplished. The ship takes me to Byzantium, after which it will continue on to the Euxine, from whence the King's courier, bearing remembrances and messages of love to you, will go forward through the peaceable countries of the far north, and so at last reach Arimazes and those I so much love and long to see."

CHAPTER XIII

THE CAPTIVE QUEEN

It was now the fourth year of the war and Alexander, intent upon a final trial of strength with the Persian King, had sought the latter on the Upper Tigris, twelve hundred miles from Memphis, where we left him at the close of the last chapter. Here he forded the great river (then known as the Arrow because of its swift and treacherous current) some miles north of the ancient city of Nineveh. Above the ford Alexander formed a moving dyke of cavalry to break the current, placing mounted men below to catch any foot soldiers so unfortunate as to be swept off their feet. With these precautions he plunged his army into the swirling stream, he leading the way, the water reaching to his armpits. Immediately after the hazardous exploit an eclipse of the moon occurred, a startling thing in that rude age, and looked upon by every one with fear and trembling. In this instance, however, the soothsayers, wiser than their fellows, cunningly construed it as being favourable to the Macedonians, for the reason that Astarte — the moon — was an object of worship by the barbarians, and its eclipse therefore foreboded harm to the Persian cause. In this way the alarm in the Macedonian army was quieted.

197

Directing his course to the south, Alexander's spies soon brought him word that the Persian army, numbering a million men, awaited him on the plains, four days' march away. Thus at last a decisive conflict was at hand, and fraught with supreme peril, it was apparent to the Macedonians, far removed as they were from their base on the Mediterranean, with the Euphrates and Tigris in their rear, defeat meaning annihilation. And Persia, responding anew to the call of her King, had come to his aid with all her forces, confident that had they been at Issus that disastrous battle would have resulted in a glorious victory. Of boasting, however, there was none, or only among the younger and more sanguine, for Macedonia's young King was no longer an object of derision, every wind that swept the plains of Mesopotamia from the west seeming to whisper his name or tell some wondrous story of his might. Nor could Darius find fault as at Issus with the field of battle, nor complain if defeat overtook him, for it was on an extended plain, levelled by his engineers till it was like a beaten floor.

Approaching within a short distance of the Persian forces, Alexander halted to rest his army, consisting of seven thousand cavalry and forty thousand infantry, and here occurred events so surprising that this story of love and war would be incomplete were they omitted.

Agonizing indeed had been the intervening months

to Statira since she watched her husband, with breaking heart, as he fled from the battle-field of Issus. Now fearing the result of the pending battle, and no longer able to bear the agony of life, she lay sick unto death in her tent, and this despite the skill of her physicians, aided by Jaron and Philip, the King's doctors. Reclining upon her couch, she called in her delirium for Darius to come to her if he still loved her as before, but tiring, her mood would change, and sometimes with anger, but more often with tender pleading, she besought Alexander to bring him to her. And when he did not answer she fell to upbraiding him for his cruelty in permitting her to die without again seeing her beloved husband, whom he had so cruelly persecuted. Thus she raved until exhausted, when she would fall into a troubled sleep to awaken in her right mind, in which state she said nothing nor made complaint of any kind. And so it had been for many days, her anxiety and grief throwing her into a delirium, during which time all that filled her sorrowing heart found utterance in prayers and reproaches. But on this day there had been a change for the worse in her sickness, so that Jaron, listening to her pleadings and seeing that her death was near, could restrain himself no longer, and slipping away unnoticed, hastened to Alexander's tent to acquaint him with her short lease of life.

Reaching the King's pavilion he found the antechamber crowded with officers and couriers going

and coming, for the two armies lay so near each
other that accident or design might bring on an engagement at any moment. Continuing on his way,
he presently encountered Eumenes, and inquiring the
whereabouts of the King, the secretary nodded his
head toward an inner room, which Jaron entered
without waiting to be announced. Here he found
Alexander studying a rude map of the country, but
looking up and observing Jaron, whose usually cold
and impassive features were now pale and agitated,
he pushed the map from him and awaited in silence
the other's speech. Approaching near to the King,
that his words might not be overheard, Jaron exclaimed without in any way softening the dread
news he brought:

"I come, oh King, to acquaint you that Statira, Persia's unhappy Queen, lies in her tent dying, and this
without comfort or redress of any kind for her many
grievous afflictions," saying which he fell back a step
and waited as if to observe the demeanour of his master.

Surprised and dazed at the abrupt and startling
announcement, for her sickness was unknown to the
King, Alexander seemed not to comprehend, but
when Jaron had repeated his words he cried out,
protesting to the Gods that such ending of her life
were impossible.

"Not impossible, my master, but of immediate
accomplishment and justly favoured by the Gods,"
the leech asserted.

"Why favoured by the Gods?" the King asked, as if in a trance.

"That her sorrows may have an end, for until now the Gods have granted her continued lease of life, as if something in her behalf were yet to be accomplished. Dying, she supplicates Darius to come to her, but wearied with the unavailing cry, she couples your name with his and with equal gentleness, beseeching you to come to her, as if she had some favour to ask, which, hearing, you would by no means deny."

"Surely, Jaron, her illness cannot be so serious?" the King exclaimed, awed and unwilling to believe the Queen's sickness to be fatal.

"Yes, she is dying, a thing I have long looked forward to, yet hoped to defer to a more convenient season."

Comprehending at last, the King started up, crying out with staring eyes as if the Gods summoned him:

"Am I responsible, Jaron? Am I the cause?"

"No, oh King," the leech hastened to say, no longer intent upon questioning the King's heart, "she ceased to live when Darius fled at Issus and looked not back to see that she was safe. Nor was that the beginning of her ailment, for long before she had somehow discovered his weakness, and ever fearing what at last occurred, her strength wasted and all desire of life save for her husband's good died out of her heart. Thus it was, but had he redeemed himself at Issus, she would have been strong within the hour and welcomed captivity had it come to her, nay slavery and degradation, he being free and respected of men."

"I knew not nor dreamed that she so mourned her husband or thought him, ere Issus, other than a man of courage," the King murmured, with bowed head.

"He, himself, I think, must have acquainted her with the secret of his life, but this I know not surely, yet it made no difference save to add pity to her love. But since the day when first she knew, waking or sleeping, she has had him always in her mind, and thus sorrowing is at last wasted and about to die."

"I should have known of this ere now, Jaron; of her sorrowing, of her failing strength," the King reprimanded, overcome.

"It would have availed nothing, for the sorrowings of woman over the shortcomings of him she loves admit of no alleviation from without."

"Jaron, Jaron, may the Gods be merciful to me if in my treatment of her I have acted amiss," the King cried, lifting his face to heaven.

"Of such thing you cannot accuse yourself, for your gentle care of her, your denying her no prerogative of her exalted state, and nourishing and honouring her children as if they were your own, ever keeping them and her apart from the turmoil of the army, have preserved her feeble hold on life till now," Jaron answered, decisively.

"But now, you say?"

"She has but a day, perhaps not so long a time, to live."

"And I can do nothing?"

"Yes, you may contrive a way by which she will die in peace, more than that only the Gods can accomplish."

"You mock me, Jaron, by such speech," the King exclaimed, with impatient voice.

"I but speak the truth and what is in my mind."

"Quick, then, tell me the way if you speak not in idle vanity!" the King commanded, laying hold of Jaron.

"Bring Darius to her side — only in that way can you favour her," the leech answered, shortly.

"Bring Darius to her!" the King repeated, staring as if the other were mad.

"Yes, for 't is a thing easy of accomplishment."

"Yes — to-morrow it may be — as a prisoner," the King absently assented.

"No, not as a prisoner nor under restraint of any kind, for her heart will stand no further burden and the knowledge that he was a captive would kill her ere he could reach her side."

"She need not know, for I will keep her far from the camp so that no knowledge of what occurs will reach her."

"She would divine it, though no word be spoken, for she so loves him that the very currents of the air would convey the mishap to her. Then, losing all desire to live, she would die, for her present hold on life is only kept alive in the hope of seeing him and in all honour."

"Well go on — why do you stop — what is your plan, for I can gain no clew to it whatever?" the King, overwrought, cried in a passion.

"I have no plan save to bring Darius to her free and untrammelled," Jaron answered, vouchsafing no explanation.

"Are you bereft that you dare speak to me thus?" the King cried, enraged.

"No, and in this am more regardful of your honour than in anything I have ever said or done."

"Go on — say what you have to say — for I will no longer bandy words with you," the King answered, exasperated, wrought up to the highest pitch.

"What I say is easy of accomplishment, for Darius is scarce half an hour's ride away. Acquaint him with the Queen's fatal illness, and that she cannot die in peace without once more clasping him in her arms, once again listening to his words of love — and having done this bid him come to her," Jaron explained, as if it were a thing apparent.

"Go on, you do not propose this without having contrived a way," the King said, dully.

"I myself will be the messenger, will go to him, and if he but love her as 't is said, he will be with her ere the night ends," Jaron confidently affirmed.

"No, timid of heart, he will never trust himself openly in my power."

"He will if you pledge his safety — if you but order that he may come and go without question or hindrance."

"No, he so hates and fears me that he could not trust me if he would."

"He cannot doubt your good faith in this or any other thing, remembering the proofs he has of your chivalrous honour."

"And you will go to him," the King questioned, pleased at Jaron's speech, "knowing he is more likely to put you to death than listen to your story?"

"Yes, ere the ink is dry, oh King."

Smiling his gratitude, Alexander called to Eumenes, and bidding him write, he thus commanded:

"From Alexander the King. Greeting to all into whose hands this may come. And know that it is my will that Jaron the leech and whomsoever may accompany him shall pass the lines without word or hindrance; and to this I have pledged myself," and signing his name the King gave the order to Jaron, exclaiming as he bade him adieu, "May the Gods of Persia and Greece aid you in your mission!"

Emerging from the tent Jaron encountered Medius, the officer of the watch, and showing him the order, exclaimed:

"Quick, friend, a horse — on the King's business!"

"I will myself go with you lest some mishap occur," Medius responded, surprised at the nature of the order, and picking horses from the many that stood tethered near at hand Jaron led the way to the Queen's tent. Relinquishing his reins to a slave the leech lost no time in seeking Statira's couch, and happily finding her awake and of right mind he made believe he had no purpose in coming save to administer to her ails; but presently and as if giving expression to a purpose carefully considered he said:

"As thou dost know, exalted Queen, our wanderings for many months have been apart and in the wilderness so that we have had no opportunity to replenish our store of medicines; and now being wholly bereft we have no other way than to appeal to thy friends, for they have abundance. In particular there is in the Persian camp a leech who can supply that which I need, the procuring of which will instantly allay the strain upon thy heart and the fever of thy blood. Give me then some treasured token, a gift it may be from the great King, seeing which he will know that I come from thee and have thy confidence, knowing which he will instantly further my wishes in the undertaking I have in hand."

To this the Queen for a long time made no response but lay like one enthralled, looking Jaron steadfastly in the face as if to read his very soul and there determine whether he wished this favour that he might take advantage of her husband, or whether it was as he had said. At last, seemingly satisfied of his good intention, she removed the ring from her finger, the only jewel she had been known to wear during her captivity, and giving it to him, said:

"Thou hast been kind to me always, good leech, as has thy master, and I can think no wrong of either of thee. Go thou to the great King and give him this, which he gave me on our bridal day when we were happy and dreamed not of the crown and its burdens. Tell him," she went on, striving to stay her tears, "that I have but one wish in life and that is to know that he is well and happy," saying which she pressed the precious ring to her lips, and, sobbing, turned her face to the wall as if now indeed all desire to live had left her.

Scarcely less affected than the sorrowing Queen, Jaron assured her that he would do as she commanded, and placing the ring in his bosom returned to Medius, and mounting his horse hastened with all speed to the outer lines of the army. Here, when Medius would have questioned him at parting, he said:

"Await my return, I know not how long, for I cannot tell the hour. It may be," he went on, slowly, "that I shall never return, but coming, you and no other must be here that I may not be stayed nor questioned." Saying which he directed his course to the Persian camp, the presence of which was clearly discernible by the myriad fires which lighted up the heavens so that the whole firmament seemed ablaze.

Reaching the advanced lines of the Persian army he was halted and searched by the guard, but to all their questions he would make no other answer than that he came from the Queen with an urgent message to the great King.   After a while, wearied with their fruitless efforts, they admitted him within the lines, and as good fortune would have it, Darius, who was making the rounds of his sentinels, presently came unexpectedly upon them.   Thereupon the officer of the watch, prostrating himself, made Jaron's presence known and the object of his coming.   Bidding them bring the messenger to him, Jaron on reaching the King's side threw himself on his knees and holding aloft the ring besought the monarch to receive that which the Queen had sent him.   Recognizing the love-token, the great King for some moments remained silent, unable to speak, but presently recovering himself, waved back those who crowded about him.   When he was quite alone and had seemingly forgotten the presence of Jaron, he lifted the ring to his lips, his face wet with tears, and kissed it as if he were in truth thus reunited to her who sent it.   At last conscious of Jaron's presence, he turned to him, saying:

"Who art thou and how is it that thou bringest this to me?".

"I am Jaron the leech, sent hither by the King, that thou mayest grant the Queen her prayer."

"And did she give thee this and of her own accord to bring to me?"

"Yes, oh King."

"And for what purpose?" he asked, with trembling voice, as if Jaron's errand foretold some new sorrow.

"That she may behold thy face, may press thee to her heart, may again hear that thou lovest her," Jaron answered simply.

"Why now; why at this impossible hour?" the King asked, abruptly, all his suspicions aroused.

"That the things I have recounted, oh King, may be accomplished ere she dies."

"Ere she dies!" Darius cried, with choking voice. "Yes, oh King."

"What dost thou mean, man, by speech so abrupt and foolish?" the King gasped, bending over, scarce able to sit his horse.

"It is as I say, oh King. She has scarce strength to last the night through, and so I come without her knowing the purpose of my visit that thou mayest not be left in ignorance of her condition, and so may do as she begs of thee."

"That I come to her?" the King murmured, as if in a dream.

"Yes, and within the hour if thou wouldst see her alive."

"Within the hour! To-morrow it may be, if meanwhile I overcome my enemy," he said, starting up.

"No, now, for of the result of the battle we cannot tell; nor will life wait on our purposes, for the Gods take no account of the affairs of men, however exalted they may be," Jaron responded, not yet ready to divulge his plan.

"Why dost thou come to me, then, knowing I cannot answer her prayer?" Darius exclaimed, impatiently.

"But thou mayest, and now, oh King, if it be thy wish."

To this Darius made no reply, staring unmeaningly at the other; whereupon Jaron continued, presenting the King's order:

"Yes, and to that end Alexander sends thee safe conduct; his plighted word that thou mayest pass his lines without question or hindrance."

"Fool! Think thee I will do this thing; will trust myself in his power?" Darius asked, irritably, after reading the order.

"Yes, without further waiting or questioning, knowing that Alexander will keep his word though the heavens fall," Jaron retorted, sharply, angered that Darius should question his master's honour.

"What assurance have I of that?" the other asked, yet seemingly ashamed of the question.

"What assurance needst thou? Hast thou not seen in the months and years that have passed such evidence of his exalted honour that no man can question it?" But the King making no response, Jaron, irritated beyond measure, cried out: "If he permitted thee to visit thy Queen months since, disguised

as an attendant, think thee he would break his word
now when he gives thee permission to visit her openly?" Jaron concluded, referring to a visit, contrived
by Bazares, the eunuch, that Darius had made Statira
some months before, of which Alexander had knowledge, but out of pity and unwilling to take his
enemy in a trap would not take advantage of, and
so let the sorrowing King take his departure without hindrance.

Amazed at Jaron's words and Alexander's forbearance, Darius no longer hesitated, but interrogating
the leech, said:

"And if I should conclude to go with thee?"

"Bid the escort await thy return here, for of preparation thou needst none, the distance being scarce
half an hour's ride, so that thou mayest go and return
ere the dawn."

Sitting his horse in the stillness of the night the
King long deliberated, but at last making up his mind
he called to the officer and bidding him await his coming, turned to Jaron, exclaiming:

"Go on, good friend, I will accompay thee," and
without further words turned his horse's head toward
the Macedonian outposts. Reaching Alexander's
camp; they found Medius awaiting them, but without
drawing rein Jaron and his mysterious companion—
for the King's features were hidden by his military
cloak — proceeded on their way at headlong speed.
Reaching the Queen's tent Jaron took the King's

bridle, and pointing to the door of Statira's tent, exclaimed with broken voice:

"There, oh King, thy Queen awaits thee."

Making no response and seemingly bereft of his senses Darius threw himself from his horse, and bidding Jaron await his return hurriedly entered the tent.

CHAPTER XIV

Long Jaron waited, and not until the gray of morning did Darius come forth from Statira's tent, but of what had passed between him and the dying Queen, of their unavailing tears and tender caresses, of vows renewed, of prayers uttered no one ever knew. Holding up his hand to restrain the other's speech, the Persian King, his face wet with tears, mounted his horse, and like one in a sleep set out at a gallop for the Persian encampment. As they neared its outposts he stopped and facing the east, now aglow with the coming day, the sorrowing King lifted his arms to heaven, exclaiming in a voice broken by sobs:

"If it be, oh thou God of my people, that I am not worthy to wear the crown of Cyrus, grant that Alexander, my greatest enemy and my greatest benefactor, may succeed me on the Persian throne!"

With this prayer, as if in relinquishment of the crown, the King turned to Jaron, and taking a chain of gold from about his neck gave it to him, exclaiming:

"Thank thy King in my behalf for the gracious kindness he has accorded me. For thyself, accept this in token of my favour, and that thou mayest be remembered because of it I make thee a prince of the

213

realm," and putting his arms about Jaron's neck kissed him on the cheek. Then gathering up his reins he spurred his horse into a gallop, and without stopping or looking back regained the outpost of his army.

Sorrowing, Jaron returned to the Macedonian lines, and bidding Medius acquaint the King of his safe return and the successful accomplishment of his mission, he rode on to the Queen's tent, where he found her impatiently awaiting his coming. Acquainting her with Darius' safe return to his army, she thanked him, and bidding him seat himself beside her questioned him long and earnestly regarding her husband's strength and ability to endure what lay before him. When at last she could think of no further question to ask she laid her hand on his, and looking into his face with pleading eyes exclaimed:

"Much thou hast done for me, good friend, for thy medicine has indeed lightened my heart and reconciled me to death, but ere I die I have another favour to ask of thee — and say that it will be granted ere I ask it," she added, as if afraid if she did not thus pledge him he might refuse her request.

"Fear not, oh Queen, to ask, for I swear to thee by the Gods of Thessaly, my native country, that anything thou askest, whatsoever it may be, that will I do," Jaron answered, falling on his knees beside her couch, grieved that one so exalted should thus plead with him.

"It is not much, and such a thing as becomes the prerogative of a Queen, and yet I greatly fear it may not be granted me."

"Naught that thou mayest ask if in the power of mortal to grant will be refused thee," Jaron protested, moved to tears.

"And canst thou speak thus confidently for thy King?"

"Yes, though thou didst claim thy freedom."

"Freedom to me would mean nothing, for I am already in the keeping of the mighty God," she whispered. "No, it is not of that I would speak.".

"Whatever it may be, oh Queen, ask that I may the sooner fulfill thy commands," Jaron urged, lest she die ere preferring her request.

"Thou art kindness itself — and yet I fear," she said, still hesitating.

"In the name of my master, the King, I swear that whatsoever thou askest shall be accorded thee," he affirmed, lifting his hands aloft.

"It is to him I would speak — it is to him I would prefer my request — for only he can grant my prayer. And if it be that thou canst prevail upon him to come to me, then indeed will I have had all I could ask," she hurried on, scanning his face with anxious glance.

"If that be all, then I pledge thee that thy prayer shall be granted so soon as I can reach his side."

"Will he be long in coming, think thee?" she asked, as if indeed her span of life were short.

"He will come to thee instantly; this I know as I know his heart, which to those who grieve is as thy own."

"Haste, then, I beg, lest I die ere he comes," she pleaded.

To this the Prince (for Alexander confirmed Darius' act when Jaron made it known to him) made no response save to hurriedly take his departure, and happily finding the King in his tent he at once made known to him all that had occurred.

"Did not the King's visit revive her strength and quiet her sorrowing heart?" Alexander asked, when the other had done.

"It brought her joy unutterable, and, happily, release of the misery of life. Now having seen him she no longer struggles against the weakness that overpowers her, and so looks forward to the end once she has preferred her request of you."

"Then you still think she has but short lease of life?"

"So short, indeed, oh King, that unless you hasten you shall not find her alive to greet you."

"Why then have you detained me with this idle talk?" the King cried in a rage, knowing not what he said; and quitting his tent mounted a horse and followed by Jaron set out as if life and death were indeed dependent upon his haste.

Reaching the Queen's tent, her attendants, apprised of his visit, received him with every show of honour and respect, and admitted to her presence he found her eagerly watching the door by which he would enter.

"At last, oh King, it is fit that thou shouldst come to me," she exclaimed as the King threw himself on his knees, and taking her hand reverently raised it to his lips; "thou to whom I owe so many kindnesses of which, indeed, I cannot now speak, but which, dying, I still remember with fervent gratitude," she whispered, in a voice so weak as to be scarcely audible.

"I come to thee, gentle Queen, in sorrow at thy plight, and as I would to my mother or sister, to do thy bidding, asking not in advance what it is thou wouldst have of me," the King exclaimed, his heart stirred to its utmost depths at sight of the dying Queen once so exalted, now so forlorn.

"Then I may ask of thee freely?" she queried, as if still in doubt.

"Yes, as if I were thy brother; as if indeed I were Darius, thy loved and honoured husband," and in this the King spoke truly, and as to one exalted above men.

"It is of him indeed that I would speak," she sighed.

"Speak then, for whatsoever thou askest I swear to thee I will grant," Alexander cried, neither knowing nor caring what request she might prefer if it but quieted her.

"What I have to ask, oh King, seemeth not much to me, for he is in all things a most gentle and lovable man and every way worthy thy friendship and regard," she mourned.

"That I know, oh Queen, for so all men speak of him. What is it, then, that thou wouldst have of me?" the King urged, in all gentleness.

"It is this, oh King, that if by chance the God of Persia relinquishes him into thy hands, I pray that thou wouldst treat him as thy brother and no longer as thy enemy," she pleaded, half raising herself and grasping his hand.

"What thou askest I swear before the Gods I will do, granting thy husband not only life, but respect and honour and such independence of living as becomes one so exalted of birth," the King promised, rising to his feet and lifting his arms to heaven, appealing to the Gods to hear and record his vow.

"That is more than I dared ask of thee," she wept, voicing her gratitude. "It may be," she went on, sobs choking her utterance, "that in the coming battle my husband may regain his own, yet will he none the less honour and love thee all his life in this that thou hast treasured that which to him is greater than power or kingly favour."

"The Gods alone know the future — alone determine the fortunes of men, oh Queen, but if by chance my cause be favoured it shall be with thy husband as

I have pledged myself," the King answered, stirred by her deep love.

"I know not how it will be, nor may I await the outcome, but much I fear, for except in his great love for me he is not as in his youth. But is so worked upon by some dire distemper foreign to his blood, and for which he is in no way accountable that he hath no longer complete power over himself when deeply stirred. Because of this he is not as other men who may command their will, and of this thou knowest something, though not the cause thereof. And so I would have thee, to whom I owe so much, treat him, if he fall into thy hands, as one afflicted for some divine purpose, but which we mortals may neither fathom nor question," the Queen went on with desperate energy, as if she could not die nor have the King depart without thus justifying her husband's honour in his sight.

"Thou hast had cause to rejoice in his love for thee, exalted Queen, and however grievously stricken in other ways, yet in that thou hast been blessed above all women in the world," the King exclaimed with clouded eyes, amazed at a love which held back death that it might find excuse for the one it treasured. For now the Queen was surely dying, but beating back the fatal weakness with a last effort of her will, she grasped his hand and drawing him down to her kissed him tenderly on the mouth. Then, as if in this last gentle act of trust she had forever sealed the compact between them, her hand relaxed and breathing a gentle sigh she died.

Sorrowing, and in fervent prayer to the Gods, the King long knelt beside the body of the unhappy Queen. Then, reverently covering her with his mantle, he gave directions that every respect due to the exalted in life should be paid her, and that her body should be embalmed and taken to Persepolis, the burial place of Persia's kings, there to be interred in all honour.

Grieving over her troubled life he took his departure, and approaching the camp, his mind occupied with what had occurred, he was startled into being by a great commotion observable throughout its wide extent. Coming nearer, he was astonished to discover Bessus, the Persian Viceroy, haranguing the soldiers and extolling Darius for his generosity in proffering half his kingdom and thirty thousand talents to be divided among Alexander's followers if the Macedonian King would but give up the contest. Perceiving that Bessus availed himself of his mission, whatever it might be, to create discord in the army by proffer of so great a gift of money, Alexander pushed his way to where the Persian stood, and confronting him cried out with stern displeasure:

"From whom comest thou with this unmanly offer, already twice refused by me?"

"From my master, the King of Kings!" Bessus answered, abashed, perceiving Alexander for the first time.

"When was this mission to my camp determined?" the King asked, anxious to know if it had been conceived by Darius after his return to the Persian lines.

"Yesterday evening, oh King," Bessus answered, wondering.

"Was it of his own will or at thy instigation?" the King questioned, restraining his anger.

"I do admit that desiring to secure some remnant of his empire to the unfortunate King, and assure the security of my own provinces in the far East I and my colleagues urged him to act thus," Bessus proclaimed, as if believing the offer might be accepted.

"I thought it might be so, but know," the King cried in a voice of thunder, "that I, Alexander, rightful King of Persia, will accept naught from Darius, for the Empire and all its treasures belong to me by right of conquest. Take this my answer and depart, for I swear if thou art within my lines a half-hour hence I will hang thee for thy impudence."

Entering his tent, angered at the attempt to create dissension in the Macedonian ranks under cover of a peaceful envoy, the King bade Parmenio order the immediate advance of the army, designing to force a battle in the early morning. And thus it would have been, but delays occuring the attack was deferred, the intervening time being given up to a survey of the field and the establishment of a camp in which to safeguard the baggage and prisoners during the coming battle. However, when darkness had fallen and the two armies confronted each other, Parmenio, who was to command the left wing as in the previous battles, came to Alexander's tent and advised him not to await the morrow, but to take advantage of the enemy by a night attack. But to this Alexander would not listen, answering laconically:

"No, I will steal no victory," knowing moreover that it was only by defeating Darius in the open day and on ground of his own choosing that the Persians could be deprived of all excuse if they should again suffer defeat.

Thus it was determined, and Alexander retiring to rest did not awake till some hours after dawn, and then only upon Parmenio's arousing him and telling him the army awaited his coming, marshalled for battle. Awakened to life, the King arrayed himself in a tunic of Sicilian pattern and over this a cuirass of quilted cloth. In protection of his throat he wore a gorget of steel set with precious stones, and about his waist, to which was attached his sword, was clasped a broad belt of exquisite workmanship, heavily embossed. Light greaves protected his limbs, and on his head he wore a helmet of polished steel, adorned with ostrich feathers. Thus accoutred and with shield and spear he reviewed his soldiers, encouraging them with confident speech, assuring them of victory and empire if they but fought as became the followers of Philip and Alexander. Having reviewed the army, he placed himself at the head of the Com-

panion Cavalry on the extreme right, and all being
in readiness he signalled with uplifted spear the order
to advance.

The Persian army, which meanwhile had made
no move, numbered a million men, and confronted
Alexander drawn up on a plain thirty miles in extent,
the array being marshalled in three lines of battle
extending to the north and south far beyond the wings
of the Macedonian force. Each line was formed of
oblong masses or squares, the different classes of
troops and nationalities forming the several chains,
presenting in the brilliancy of their warlike fittings
and picturesque costumes a scene of unexampled
splendour.

In the centre of the Persian force the chariot and
person of Darius were visible to both armies, surrounded as at Issus by the Immortals and kinsmen of
the King, fifteen thousand in number. As Alexander
advanced and was observed to turn to the right —
which he did in avoidance of the spiked balls with
which the Persian engineers had strewn the intervening plain — Darius, fearful the combat might be
transferred to ground unfavourable for manoeuvering
his vast force, ordered his centre to charge, preceded
by one hundred scythed chariots designed to confuse
and break Alexander's line. Interspersed with them
and in stately array (and to the great wonder of the
opposing force) were fifteen war-elephants, from the
backs of which Indian soldiers clad in crimson armour

showered arrows and javelins on the Macedonian front. Not, however, with the resulting panic Darius had been led to expect, for the Macedonians, evading the onslaught of the elephants, put the huge animals to flight with showers of missiles. Opening wide their ranks (as Clearchus had done at Cunaxa seventy years before) the Macedonians allowed the chariots to pass through their lines when they were unable to intercept and turn them back in flight on the Persian front. Thus nothing was accomplished by Darius' ingenious devices.

Alarmed at Alexander's continued oblique movement to the right, he ordered Bessus, who commanded the Persian left, to move forward his first line of troops to intercept and stay the Macedonian King. Doing as commanded, he beat back a column of cavalry Alexander caused to threaten Darius' extreme left, but in the movement Bessus' second line for some reason failed to move forward to take the place of the one he had advanced to stay Alexander's progress. Thus there intervened a weak spot in the Persian left center, which Alexander perceiving instantly charged, forming for the purpose a wedge of the Companion Cavalry supported by a body of Phalangites.

For a time the Persian troops bravely held their ground, animated by Darius' encouraging presence, but the armour-clad Companions, charging again and again with thrusting-pike and sword, supported by

THE BATTLE OF ARBELA

the long, protruding spears of the Phalanx, at last broke through the weakened line. This accomplished, Alexander turned abruptly to the left and charged the serried ranks formed in a mass about the chariot of Darius, and beating down those in front directed his course straight for the person of the great King. At this moment, when the battle hung in the balance, Alexander, having approached near the Persian King, hurled his spear full at Darius' body, but missing the mark the weapon transfixed the charioteer of the great King instead. Whereupon Darius' followers thinking it was he who was stricken, raised a cry that the King had fallen, and the alarm spreading the timid instantly took to flight; and this disorganizing the array of those more courageously inclined, they in turn gave way, leaving the unhappy King alone and unprotected. The Persian centre and left wing being now broken, and those about Darius in panic-stricken fright, no recourse was left him save submission or flight. Choosing the latter he wheeled about and reluctantly abandoned the field, seeing which Bessus, angered beyond all measure, sought no longer to stay the failing battle, but turned and followed with all speed upon the heels of his master.

At the opening of the battle, Mazæus, in command of Darius' right wing, observing the gap in the Macedonian centre caused by Alexander's wide divergence to the right, ordered his cavalry to charge the weakened line. Beating down all opposition, the Persian troops passed through the Macedonian ranks, reaching at last the camp beyond. Here they found the members of Darius' family, and would have carried them off, but frightened at the wild turmoil of the field and fearful of the result of the battle the royal children would by no means accept the friendly offer.

Gratified at the success of his manoeuvre and the desperate plight of Parmenio, Mazæus collected his remaining cavalry and ordered it to charge the Macedonian front, and this it did with such headlong fury that Parmenio, fearful of the result, dispatched courier after courier to Alexander to come to his rescue lest his forces be destroyed and the day lost. This summons reaching Alexander while in hot pursuit of the flying King, he reluctantly turned about and presently encountering those who had penetrated his centre, a fierce struggle ensued, ending in the extermination of the Persian force. Taking fresh heart, Parmenio massed his cavalry and charged with hot anger upon the hitherto victorious Mazæus, which assault the latter, weakened by the defection of the main army, found it impossible to withstand, and so evading the conflict drew off his forces in the direction of Babylon, of which city he was the governour.

Immediately upon Mazæus' abandonment of the field, Alexander, angered at the delay and Parmenio's lack of skill, set out afresh in pursuit of

Darius, whose capture meant the close of the disastrous war. But on arriving at Arbela, seventy miles distant, the following morning, he found the unfortunate King had passed through the village several hours before, having abandoned his chariot for a horse, the better to expedite his flight.

Thus the fateful battle of Arbela, on which the Empire of the east depended, was fought and won.

CHAPTER XV

"Itanes to Roxana; love and greeting:

"Of my visit to Macedonia, about which I wrote you from Memphis, and of my stay there I have no time now to tell, only that I rejoined the army as it neared Babylon, it having marched thither from Arbela, where there has been a great battle. The King received me with kindness, and when I had delivered the messages with which I had been entrusted at Pella he bade me don my uniform and join him without delay. This I did, and as it happened that the other pages were away upon some business of the King, I took my place by his side. Thus we approached the mighty city which, in circumference, you must know, is four hundred and eighty stadis, so great a distance indeed that one may hardly compass it in a day, though riding at a trot. The King led the advance, clad in armour, with buckler and spear, as were the Companions and guards, thinking we might have a battle or need to lay siege to the place as at Tyre and Gaza. For Babylon is like no other city for strength, being surrounded by a wall two hundred cubits in height and fifty in width at the top, and about it, and in further protection, a deep moat filled with water,

228

and beside the outer wall there is an inner one, but not so high or strong as the other.

"As we neared the city in battle array, and were looking eagerly forward expecting to see the walls crowded with soldiers, the brazen gates were suddenly thrown open and from one of them Mazæus, the royal governour, emerged, attended by his suite. Immediately behind marched the soldiers of the garrison to the sound of trumpet and cymbal, their silver-tipped spears garlanded with flowers. Following them in stately array came Chaldean priests in the gorgeous robes of their office, and after them the people of the city, clothed in white. Seeing this peaceful array the King's face lighted, and drawing rein he awaited in silence those who came to welcome him. When, however, the soldiers saw the multitude and knew that the place was to be yielded without a struggle there was such a shout as can only come from the throats of these bronzed and war-worn veterans.

"When Mazæus and those about him had come to where we stood, they all, with one accord, prostrated themselves before the King, making submission and offering presents, according to the custom in such cases. Smiling, the King bade them arise, whereupon the governour came forward, and doffing his plumed hat presented the keys of the city on a plate of gold. These the King accepted, after which the satrap gave place to the waiting priests, who, lifting up their altars, proceeded to sacrifice to Belus, the Babylonian God.

While this was occurring, the people parting to the right and left formed a wide avenue through which the King was to approach the city, and over this they scattered flowers.

"While these bewildering things were taking place a group of beautiful maidens came forward with garlands to decorate the King's horse. And as I sat beside him looking on, amused and unconcerned, all of a sudden I espied a face I knew or thought I knew, yet doubting I stared blankly, wondering, all in a tremour of hope and fear. But, as I first thought, it was she, my love, Ossillia, and like the others about her intent upon strewing the path before the King with flowers. When I could no longer doubt I was as one dumb, but quickly regaining my senses slipped from my horse and running to the dear girl clasped. her in my arms and kissed her mouth and then her eyes, the lashes of which were longer and more be- witching than ever. Then I kissed her again and hugged her the harder, asking the while innumerable questions, not one of which I waited for her to answer. Thus it was, and the King presently espying me — for I was conspicuous among the white-robed multitude because of my crimson cloak — he stared in amaze- ment, seeing which the multitude also looked, and beholding Ossillia clasped in my arms they gave a great shout, thinking her one of their own number. At last the King took up his reins, and bidding Mazæus mount and ride by his side he went forward,

but as he passed he plucked a rose from the garland
about his horse's neck and leaning over stuck it in
Ossillia's hair, laughing, but saying nothing at all.
And indeed what could he say, not understanding
what it all meant more than those about him.

"Crowded to one side by the marching column, we
waited, and the officers and soldiers as the army
passed presently espying my uniform and plumed
hat, and remarking Ossillia and her beauty and that I
had my arm about her, they cried out with laughter
and cheers, 'Itanes, oh Itanes.' And one snatching
a flower from the road threw it at my love, and the
others seeing him do this did the same, so that we were
presently buried in the fragrant blossoms. At this
I was filled with gladness that Ossillia should see that
I was known in the army, and that it regarded me
with some consideration notwithstanding my youth —
about which some people in Arimazes are so much
concerned! It was plain that she was pleased and
immensely proud of me, for she clung the closer to my
side, which you could hardly have thought possible if
you had seen how I pressed her to me. But you must
remember that it was two years and more since I
had seen my love, and she was now somewhat grown
and more beautiful than ever, if that were possible.
And to find her in this strange place, as if awaiting my
coming and with no particle of her love for me gone
out of her dear heart — for so she whispered over and
over in my ear — how could I do otherwise than

hold her tight lest somehow I should lose her amid the vast multitude?

"When the cavalry and guards, followed by the Phalanx, had passed, I espied the bronzed chariot of Darius drawn by four milk-white horses. But not caring whose it might be, I bade the charioteer halt — for a page may do anything he pleases and be favoured in it by the common soldiers — and running forward lifted up my love and quickly following her I took the lines in my own hands. Thus we went forward, the horses tilting and prancing under the whip, and she clinging to me with both her arms about my body as if in fear of her life. The people observing this and thinking I must be a great prince laughed and shouted themselves hoarse, and I pleased that my love should receive so great an ovation — for they cried out continually at her beauty — doffed my plumed hat as the King is wont to do when they cheer him. This they thought very polite on my part, and so they shouted the harder, and thus it came about that our progress was something to be proud of as well as immensely funny.

"Nearing the wall there was a great jam, and here we were detained a long time, and so I had opportunity to look about me. Directly above the bronze gate before which we waited there was a ragged place where the wall had been torn away, and this my love, seeing that I observed it, took occasion to explain while we waited. It seems, so she said, and there was music in her voice, that many years ago a Babylonian queen named Nitocris had caused her body to be laid in a tomb above this particular gate. And that her sepulcher might not be disturbed, she fixed a plate of brass on which she implored the kings who should succeed her not to disturb her body nor the treasure resting there, unless they were indeed in sorry plight. In this way her body reposed for many generations until there came the King Darius, son of Hystaspes, and he being avaricious of money, though having wealth beyond all needs, opened her tomb to despoil it. But doing so found nothing whatever except her bones and these written words: 'Hadst thou not been insatiably covetous and greedy of the most sordid gain, thou wouldst not have opened the chamber of the dead.' Thus the laugh was on Darius, at which he was exceedingly wroth. Because of this act and others like it the people called him 'The Trader,' and this title seems to have been a good one for most of his successors, for the Akhæmenian kings have never been great, save Cyrus, the others being mere idlers and misers, more lovers of gold than kingly exploits.

"At last the road being cleared, we passed through the gate into the eastern part of the city, for Babylon is divided in the middle by the river Euphrates. Reaching a great temple with eight towers, one superimposed upon the other, we came suddenly upon the King, who was sacrificing to the Babylonian God

Belus, to the great surprise and delight of the people. When the sacrifice was completed he mounted his horse and proceeded on his way across the river into that part of the city where the King's palace is, and where the more prosperous live, some of their houses being embellished beyond belief. The royal abode is of vast extent and surrounded by a high wall with towers and brazen gates, within which there is a park with a shimmering lake and attractive lawn, dotted with waving palms. The palace stands high up like a white cloud floating in the summer sky, the sides of the terraces upon which it is uplifted being clothed with verdure and trailing vines brilliant with blossoms. From the level ground broad steps of pure marble ascend to the palace entrance, so wide, indeed, that an ile of cavalry might ride the height without breaking ranks or drawing rein.

"When we reached the park about the King's palace I let go my chariot, and taking Ossillia's hand we sought a shady spot far away from the noisy throng, and there, after I had again embraced and kissed her to make sure that it was certainly she and not a shadow, I asked her how it happened that she was in Babylon when I thought her in attendance upon you at Arimazes. Then as I reclined on the yielding turf, my face resting on her soft hand, she told me how her father, who loves war better than watching his flocks, being seduced by Bessus' offer of a troop of Parthian Horse, marched away to join the

great King at Arbela, she accompanying him. In
the battle he fought, so good fortune would have
it, under Mazæus, and when that gallant man gave
up the struggle and fled to Babylon he followed.
But before the battle he had sent Ossillia here to
await his coming, and on our approach, not knowing what the future had in store, she went out with
the others to propitiate the King as I have described,
her father riding with Mazæus, uncertain of what
would follow.

"It was in this way that she happened to be in
Babylon, and I, by the favour of the Gods, having
avoided the blandishments of Pella, was here to meet
and protect her if need be. But the last was not
necessary, for the King, pleased at Mazæus yielding,
and knowing with what gallantry he had fought under
Darius at Arbela, not only forgave him and all his
followers, but made him governour of the city! Thus
I was to my great happiness reunited to my sweet
Ossillia. But of the coming hither of my love it
seems you thought to make a use, for when I asked
about you she shyly drew from her bosom a silken
bag, and when I inquired if it were for me she shook
her head and laughed. No, for your faithful messenger who had risked his life you sent nothing, but for
the King this dainty thing wrapped about in a crimson
cloth of silk. Nevertheless, harbouring no anger, I
begged it of her, and taking it, warm with the
perfume of her sweet body, I pressed it to my lips

in remembrance of you, but more, ungrateful sister,
in love of the dear thing who bore it.

"Having much to say to each other, we lingered
beneath the palms until night came and the moon
arose, when the noise of the city and the murmurings
of the camp recalled us at last to our senses. Getting
to out feet in some alarm we hurried, hand in hand, to
seek Zapetes, her father, whom we found at last in
the governour's palace. He was much surprised at
seeing me with Ossillia, but when we told him how it
came about he received me, but with no great spirit,
I thought. It being now late, we all hastened to the
King's palace to see what was doing there, and upon
our approaching the entrance, my uniform — the
dear thing — gave us instant admission. Following
the throng of nobles and princes, clad in gorgeous
robes, we presently reached the presence chamber, and
here, as if he were indeed Monarch of all Persia, we
found the King standing before the throne with the
upright tiara on his head, and wearing the royal
robe of white and purple stripes fastened across his
breast with ropes of rubies. Nor was the sumptuous
raiment of the Persian monarchs in any way slighted
by our King, for his dress was in all things like theirs,
and like them his wrists and ankles were encased
with bands of gold inlaid with jewels, and from his
neck and arms there hung massive chains adorned
with precious stones. This not in vain display, I
thought, but that the people might know that he

was King and that thenceforth there could be no
divided loyalty. But Lysimachus, who stood near
us and who thinks the King should never doff his
armour, cried out pompously to Medius, so that
many heard him:

" ' 'T is a shame to be thus attired, he who rides the
battle with flaming sword and directs its course as
the Gods hold the sweeping winds and all-devouring
hurricane.' At which speech some laughed and
others stared, but of a truth the King looked like a
God as he stood at his ease beneath the purple canopy
raised above the jewelled throne.

"Coming near the King we bent to the floor in
obeisance, as we would have done, forsooth, before
a Persian monarch. Recognizing me, I thought he
showed pleasure that I, your brother, should honour
him as I would have done Darius in his place, but
thus all Persians approach Alexander, thinking such
ceremony belongs to him of right, as indeed it does,
as Persia's King. The Macedonians, however, will
by no means countenance it, and look askance with
angry scowlings at those who thus render obeisance,
as if somehow it separated them from their King,
or weaned him from the rude custom of his own country, where men scarce bend their heads when they
approach the throne. All this most unhappily I
think, for if he is to rule in peace and with loyal
men about him, he must conform to what the Persians
think a king should be, and exact from all what the

people believe is due to him; for they will by no means render him obedience if he permits men, whatever their rank, to approach him as an equal.

"Immediately the King saw us he bade the royal chamberlain bring us forward, and on our approach he put his arms about Ossillia and kissed her before the whole assembly; and this to her and my great astonishment. But it appears it had already come to his knowledge, though I know not how, that the dear girl was my betrothed; which by the way she is, and already I call her father Papa Zapetes — not before his face, you will understand, but only when Ossillia and I talk of the future and what we will do.

"When the King would have dismissed us, all of a sudden my love bethought her of your letter, and so searched for it in her bosom, her face all the while aflame with blushes. At last getting hold of it she drew it forth and gave it to him with so much modesty and grace that I wanted to embrace her then and there, so captivating was the act. The King received it smiling, wondering somewhat, I thought, and straightway broke the seal as if it were some grave matter of state. But when he saw what it was the colour flooded his face, which recent happenings have rendered somewhat pale. At first he made as if he would put it aside, but thinking better of it tore the missive open and proceeded to read it, while every one stared in silence, thinking it was a petition or some-

thing of that sort. Presently becoming unconscious
of where he was, the King stood like a statue, smiling,
going from one page to another and then back, as if
for reference, and then on again, all forgetful of the
great assemblage that stood waiting and watching
still as death.

"At last when he had finished he bent over and
kissed Ossillia on the mouth, and this disregardfully;
for a Persian King may not favour any one in that
manner, nor may one Persian thus kiss another not
their equal in rank. But in all such trifling things
I think your King, sister, will establish rules of his
own, as in Ossillia's case. Saying some word of
thanks to her he dismissed us, but doing so bade us
await him in the King's room, where he presently
joined us. There, being free and unobserved, he
talked and laughed like a boy, and well he might.
For while he seems very old to me, yet five and twenty
is not so awfully old for a man who has fought to
establish himself on his throne, and afterward conquered the greatest country in the world. However,
he seemed to have forgotten all that, and turning to
the chamberlain of the palace bade him spread the
table where we were so that we might sup alone. Not,
my sister, as in poor Bactria, but reclining at our ease
upon gorgeous divans inlaid with lapis lazuli, and attended by obsequious slaves who served the food and
drink on dishes of gold, for the kings of Persia, you
must know, will have no other. The floors and walls

of the palace were also laid with plates of gold, and of like metal were the curiously-wrought candelabras, the fragrant oil with which they were fed filling the room as with the perfume of a garden.

"Looking about him when we were seated, the King remarked some curious article that seemed to be neither ornamental nor useful, at which we laughed, and this somehow put us at our ease, and Ossillia presently regaining her accustomed manner the dinner passed off with such gaiety and abandon that we altogether forgot with whom we dined. The King asked her many things about Bactria, but more about you, and she being now at her ease answered back with such aptness and wit that he, who so seldom laughs, was often convulsed at what she said. When we had supped, he sent for Papa Zapetes, who came in greatly embarrassed, but the King at once put him at his ease, and soon set him to talking about the battle of Arbela and the part the Parthians had taken in the fight. All of which greatly pleased the King, for there is nothing he loves so much to talk about as battles and the part he or another has taken therein. Certainly Papa Zapetes must be a very gallant man, for the King commended all he said, and ended by telling him that he would give him command of the Parthian Horse near his person, if those terrible warriors of the desert cared to serve under his standard.

"In this way the evening passed, and as they talked and sipped their wine Ossillia and I wandered through

the spacious rooms that make up the King's suite.
And often when we were examining the precious
objects in some unobserved nook or corner our lips
would meet and we would fall to talking of the future,
as if our marriage were a thing agreed upon. Thus
it is, for in this I will have my way, and if you object,
the King, I warn you, will side with us, and justly, too.
Though for that matter I am little worth so precious a
treasure as Ossillia, but in respect to this, bless her
heart, the dear girl is all unconscious.

"When long past midnight the King dismissed us,
he called the chamberlain and bade him assign us
quarters within the palace, with waiting women to
attend upon Ossillia. And as good fortune would
have it, her apartments fell near those of Demetrius
and Medius, who were domiciled in the palace with
their young wives, Theba and the Princess Eurydice.
These great ladies were left behind in Macedonia
when their husbands marched away, but when they
heard that I was about to leave Pella to join the army,
nothing would do but that they must come along,
although Queen Olympias sought in every way to
dissuade them. When at last they joined the army
as it neared Babylon, there came near to being a riot,
so great was the surprise and joy of their husbands,
and so wild the cheering of the soldiers, who had not
seen a woman from their own country for months.
The sweet creatures have taken a great fancy to Ossillia, and she to them, and indeed no one can help admir-

ing and loving them. The King, too, holds them in particular affection because of happenings in Macedonia, and so has given them charge of the inner palace life, and it has become their duty to receive and entertain the great ladies of the city and pay visits of ceremony. But the honour seems to be a burden to them, taking up time which it is apparent they would much rather spend with their husbands, for indeed the four are like people just wed.

"When the King ordered me to lodge in the palace he graciously relieved me from all duties about his person while we were in Babylon, saying there were many things that would interest me, and besides that I would need to look somewhat after Ossillia. This was great in him, for the army has tarried in the city a month, and they have been days of bliss to every one, undisturbed by war or thought of it, except on the part of the King, and filled to the full with wonderful things and doings.

"For Babylon is not like any other place in the world, but so old and worn and tired that it has forgotten to be good or to have any desire to be better than it is. And that is poor indeed, for mankind comes here from every part of the earth as to a hiding-place, enlivening and colouring its life with their varied costumes and quaint and wicked ways. For days after our coming all business was given up, the people flocking to the streets, gaping and talking, rejoicing that the city was spared, and giving the soldiers of all they had, even the ornaments from off their bodies, so great was their delight.

"My sweet Ossillia and I never tire of the wonderful city; of watching the caravans of lumbering camels bearing perfumes and spices and frankincense from the west, or returning loaded with costly rugs and precious jewels, the white-robed drivers sitting high on the backs of the patient animals, drowsily guiding their course. The city is a very babel of noise and confusion, loose-robed Chaldean priests parading back and forth chanting their prayers undisturbed by the cries of the jugglers, sorcerers, fortune-tellers, and fanatics. In the market-places men and women forever cry their wares, and on the streets there is the ceaseless clatter of mules and asses bringing food to the city that we may not starve, or carrying away bales of cloth that the people in the country may not go naked. And who shall say what there is behind the garden-walls! For if you but stop to wonder and guess you are overcome by the perfume of flowers as you listen to the splashing of hidden fountains and the soft sound of the lute or guitar from the latticed balcony of some hidden beauty.

"At night the streets are ablaze with torches, men standing about curious and bold of speech, while women with faces made tantalizing by draperies that conceal only that which they do not wish revealed, urge on the modest among those who gaze to more open demonstrations of approval. Many there are who never seem to sleep but stand about throughout the night, or wander hither and thither aimlessly until the dawn, to be lost as before in the crowds that surge back and forth in pure joy that they are alive. Or if there be some space beside the street you will find a crowd of scented dandies in silken garments watching and commenting on the half-clad women who whirl and pirouette through wild fantastic dances to the clang of cymbals or the barbaric music of some far-off country. And about one of these groups I came near to losing my life as Ossillia and I one day stood idly watching. For thinking no harm, of a sudden a scented, silk-clad coxcomb with pallid face and drooping eyes, espying Ossillia and being enamoured of her beauty (for she will by no means wear a mask), stole up unobserved and clasped his arm about her with intent to give her a kiss; but being quicker than he she jerked herself free, and whirling slapped the scurvy knave in the face. At that I whipped out my sword, and he doing the same we were at it in a moment with a frenzy that made the sparks fly. But after a little his friends, thinking I was getting the better of him, drew their swords and rushing in joined the fight. While thus beset, and much concerned for Ossillia's safety, I was suddenly aware that a friend fought beside me, and with such fury and skill of arm and quickness of eye that his sword whipping the air shot back and forth like flashes of light, disarming a man here, or deftly

puncturing the skin of another there. In this way
he quickly cleared the space before him, but I, not
having the same deftness, made no headway whatever.
While I was thus hacking away my companion cried
out as if giving a lesson in fencing: 'Your defense is
too close, Itanes, and your thrust too high and not
given with enough force'; and as he spoke his sword
flashed past me like a stream of light, piercing the
breast of a brawny rascal I had been till then unable
to touch. And well it was, for hearing his voice I
was paralyzed, my sword falling limp by my side.
For he who had come to my aid was the King! Yes,
sister, the King! And Ossillia, recognizing him, let
out on the instant a fearful scream from where she
lay huddled at my feet to avoid the sword thrusts;
and the sound of her voice seeming to give her courage,
she screamed the louder until her shrill cries could
be heard half across the city. This in itself, being
unusual, attracted attention and a troop of our soldiers who were passing, turning about, recognized
the King, upon which they charged headlong into
the fray, calling out, 'The King! The King!' Upon
which our assailants, surprised and frightened, turned
and fled in every direction, dragging off their wounded
companions with them. Thus the affair ended without harm, and when the King was assured that neither
I nor Ossillia were hurt he put up his sword and
mounting a horse rode away. But ere he had gone
far he stopped and calling back told me to seek in-

struction of Demetrius, one of the best swordsmen in the army, and with that he laughed and rode off at a gallop.

"There, my sister, you have a glimpse of Babylon; but when we tire of its noise and confusion my love and I go out into the suburbs, where we ride back and forth on the sleepy canals. For the country is full of them, you must know. Or we wander hand in hand beside the river, and when tired beckon one of the many boats that float down from Armenia with wine, and for a small piece of silver are taken back to the babbling city. These boats are not like any you ever saw, but round as saucers and covered outside with leather and tar and have neither prow nor rudder. Sometimes in play we make excursions on rafts made of hides inflated like bladders, for there are many such conveyances on the river, manned by hucksters in quest of trade.

"The King is much abroad, and the people never tire of watching for the young God with the crimson cloak and feathered hat. But the wars and the jealousies of the officers and the intrigues of the court have hardened him, I can see, and his eyes have lost something of their softness in repose. But he still clings to his ideals, and so, though his ministers urge him to wed Darius' daughter the better to cement his power, he will by no means listen, but says his Queen shall be chosen because of his love for her, as in the case of other men. And this, Ossillia says, is as it should be, the dear girl.

"Sometimes the King appears in the street on a Median horse, dressed in a long close-fitting coat, with baggy trousers and upright hat — the Persian symbol of kingship — and when he does this then there is something worth while, for the multitude simply go wild that he should thus honour his new subjects by appearing abroad in the costume that has been worn from time immemorial by their rulers. This adoration of the King by the Babylonians tickles the soldiers beyond measure, and no two of them ever engage in any kind of confab but you will hear them chuckling over 'Their Prince'! He who has become master of the world! Their King who loves war and leads them to victory! He whom they knew as a youth in Philip's day, riding the wild horses no one else dared mount, and so fitting himself for the kingship and the coming wars! But Philotas and Clitus, and he of the short cloak and long beard — the scribe Callisthenes — scowl and flout the prostrations of the people, as if the King being thus adored somehow lessened their own height, and presaged troublous times, as indeed it does, for them. For the anger of a Persian King is something for men to fear, and our King's temper will some day lose the edge of indulgence with those who flout him, and by their acts threaten the stability of his conquests. And Mithrines, who betrayed Persia's trust at Sardis and has lived without honour these many months! He, too, scowls, but is now happily banished to the petty government of Armenia, though the King would have much preferred to hang him.   But good riddance to the traitor, every one says!

"The scoffers grow not in number, however, for men are really pygmies beside the King.   And because of his forbearance to the weak, and his grand ways and the great things he does, he has won the hearts of all, so that whenever he goes abroad the soldiers cheer him till their throats are sore.   Thus the days of our stay have passed, and the King, having distributed among the officers and soldiers great largesses of gold, there has been no limit to what they have done.   Some indeed hoarded their treasure, but the more spent it in days and nights of indulgence, and this oftentimes with little show of reserve, for as I said the city has lived long and is old in sin and wantonness.   And because of the shameful goings-on, I have often been led to take Ossillia to the suburbs or hide her in the King's garden, where indeed we passed much of our time; for the doings in the streets and temples are oftentimes such as to grieve a gentle maid from the hills and vales of Bactria.   But with the passing days one can see that the King tires of it all, for bred amid the mountains, he longs for the open country, the winds and drowning rains, the birds and rivers, and the vales and wooded heights.   And the soldiers, ever attentive to his bearing, are burnishing their armour and sharpening their weapons, expectant of the coming order to march.   But no part of the great city has the King left unvisited nor the country round about it; and this as if he had a mind some day to make this the capital of his Empire. In these excursions he often takes Ossillia, and at such times speaks much of Bactria, saying it must be like his own country. And then he will fall to talking of you and your journey through Thessaly and what you did, and how you looked, for in that brief hour and what followed seems to rest all the real happiness of his life.

"Thus in the way I have described we have occupied ourselves during the stay in Babylon, but there are enemies beyond the Tigris, and it is rumoured that Darius is gathering another army about Ecbatana, the northern captial, and so the King is anxious to be away. But while we have tarried word has come that Susa, the favourite capital of the Persian Kings, only awaits our coming to surrender its citadel, and with it fifty thousand talents! And so the army being rested and having tasted of the things that the King promised it ere leaving Macedonia, the command has come to march. Because of this, my sister, we bid you adieu, for Ossillia has had much to do with this letter, I being always more inclined to listen to her voice than to obey your command to write."

CHAPTER XVI

THE CARRYING OFF OF OSSILLIA

When it became known that the King was about to leave Babylon, the sodden, worn-out heart of the great city gave a distinct throb of regret, for while the people feared and hated him on his coming, they heard of his going with a sigh. In truth, the pleasure-loving inhabitants liked the fair-haired Prince, for here at last, they recounted, was a real King, a man of blood and iron, but assuredly no trader nor mere effigy or saver of money. His kingly air, his mastery of men, they said to one another, evinced his divine origin; and his appointments and the splendour of his court, did they not already exceed those of the greatest of Persian monarchs? Never before, they gossiped, was there anything like the sumptuousness of his table, the magnificence of his belongings, the number of his chariots, or the jewel-encrusted trappings of his horses.

Thus the woof-worn city, where kings had come and gone for thousands of years unnoticed, felt for Alexander a distinct interest; something it had not known since the great Cyrus diverted the water of the Euphrates, and gained unexpected entrance to the sleeping capital through its mighty sewer!

When, therefore, the sun arose on the day appointed for the King's departure the people assembled in a mass to bid him farewell, strewing his path with flowers, and paying a like compliment to his soldiers as they marched in solid ranks to the wild clangour of cymbals and the shrill music of the pipes. Thus amid cheers and sighs the army took its way to the east, across the plains of Chaldea, then a fertile garden with fruitful orchards and spreading forests of palm-trees, now a desert waste given up to wandering nomads and half-savage herdsmen. Here wheat was indigenous, and watered by abundant canals each golden kernel reproduced itself three hundred-fold, and here the peach, lemon, and orange were native to the soil, while figs, grapes, and dates, nourished by the canals, grew everywhere in luxuriant abundance.

Through this blossoming plain the Macedonian army marched, its presence half hidden by the waving fields of wheat and barley that clothed the level country as far as the eye could reach. Midway of the plain the progress of the army was halted by the coming of a stately train of vehicles, guarded by Persian troops and drawn by mules with brazen harness and nodding plumes. These, it appeared, were purveyors of drinking water and provisions for the King's table, dispatched by the palace chamberlain at Susa, according to immemorial custom. The forward vehicle of this curious procession, as if in preference, bore water from the Choaspes, sealed in silver casks; another contained delicacies from the Susan palace and gardens, while confined in wagons in padded cells were delicately nourished animals and fowls fattened for the royal table. When told what the vehicles contained Alexander laughed and said:

"Thus it is to be a real king," but presently, turning to Eumenes who rode beside him, he directed that the water and food be set aside for the sick and wounded; for in the field the Macedonian King lived with his soldiers, sharing everything with them in common.

Several days' march from Babylon, Itanes, who had been missing from the King's suite, rejoined the army bringing with him Ossillia; and this, it appeared, after an adventure of the liveliest interest to every one, and the greatest possible excitement to the lovers themselves. Then it came to light, for few had known of it before, that on the eve of the departure of the army from Babylon, Zapetes, Ossillia's father, had come to Alexander and reported that his Parthian followers, having received private word from their King, were no longer of a mind to join the Macedonian forces. This news greatly annoyed Alexander, for aside from their being fine soldiers he had hoped their joining him might influence other warlike peoples to follow their example. However, appearing to treat the matter lightly, he ordered the Parthians to be disarmed and sent to their homes under guidance of Zapetes, their commander. This being agreed upon and their immediate departure provided for, Itanes and Ossillia, surprised at the unexpected order, hurried to the eastern gate of the city to bid Zapetes good-bye. Whereupon, much to their surprise and horror, he insisted upon his daughter accompanying him, intending after the completion of his present errand, as he explained, to return with her to Arimazes.

"But we are now husband and wife and do not care to be parted," Itanes remonstrated, quite overcome.

"Yes, papa, we are husband and wife," Ossillia affirmed, with quavering voice, pale of face.

"Husband and wife!" Zapetes exclaimed, astonished.

"Yes."

"Since when, babies?"

"An hour ago."

"And why such haste?" he raged.

"That people might not talk if I stayed after your going," Ossillia explained, sweetly.

"Nonsense! Nor will I sanction a thing so ill-timed and absurd," Zapetes cried, red of face.

"But the King will not think it absurd," Itanes said, hoping the name would quiet the enraged man.

"Does he not know of it?"

"He knows we are in love and are to wed, and thinks well of it."

"Yes, for he always laughs as if pleased when we speak about it to him," Ossillia explained, blushing.

"I care not whether he be pleased or no, and will have none of it, though he were a hundred times a king," Zapetes roared, no way appeased.

"But you have known all along that it was our determination to wed," Itanes persisted.

"At some future day, perhaps, but not until our return to Bactria," the other said, scowling.

"Why should we wait till we reach Bactria, when we love each other and were determined to wed?" Itanes questioned.

"Haste in such things is not seemly; besides, you are too young — mere children, in truth," Zapetes scoffed.

"What does that matter? We love each other, and those who love are surely of an age to marry," Itanes proclaimed, as if there were nothing more to be said.

"What do you know about love — you, a boy!" the other sneered.

"I am a man, and so the King proclaimed at the siege of Gaza, where I was among the first to mount the wall," Itanes cried with heat, lifting himself up.

"I care not for that — nor will you lose by waiting."

"I will lose my wife, and that I will by no means put up with," Itanes responded, resolutely.

"However that may be, you shall abide my will, even though you be wed," Zapetes thundered, and with the words grasped Ossillia in his arms and lifted her into a chariot near at hand, paying no attention to her cries and frantic efforts to free herself. And this action, it appeared, he had contemplated all along, for the Parthians on the instant surrounded the vehicle and at a signal from Zapetes set off at a furious rate.

Dumbfounded, Itanes stood for some moments, irresolute, overcome by what had occurred and the suddenness of it all. Then bewildered, he set out at a run, madly thinking to follow and reclaim his love, but being quickly left behind, threw himself on the ground, disconsolate, consumed by rage and grief. Thus he lay for a long time overcome by the unexpected misfortune that had befallen him, but at last, in his distress, thinking of the King, he sprang to his feet with a joyful cry and hurriedly made his way to the royal palace, where he threw himself on his knees before Alexander and recounted all that had occurred. Hearing him through, the King laughed, so youthful did the bridegroom appear, and so exceedingly droll the whole proceeding; but presently, restraining his merriment, he inquired when the marriage had occurred.

"This morning, oh King, Demetrius and Medius being present, with Theba and the Princess Eurydice as witnesses," Itanes related, turning to Medius, who happened to be with the King, to confirm his statement.

"According to what ceremony?" the King questioned, maintaining his calm.

"According to the Persian rite and in proper form."

"The Perisan rite?" the King interrogated, as if ignorant of its nature.

"Yes, and it is very short and simple, for you have but to kiss the bride with intent of marriage and she to return it in like spirit and you are wed," Itanes confided, as if nothing could be more conclusive.

"A device of lovers," the King smiled.

"Yes, and most fit," Itanes reflected.

"But looking on I thought such form of marriage inadequate and barbarous, oh King, and so had them wed according to the Macedonian rites, as well," Lysimachus, who was present, interposed, pushing himself forward.

"Observing every form?" the King queried, greatly entertained.

"Yes, oh King," Itanes exclaimed with great earnestness; "we knelt before the altar of Aristander, and pouring wine on a loaf of bread as a libation, afterward divided it, each partaking of a part; and thus we were wedded, the soothsayer being present to lend solemnity to the occasion."

"Does Zapetes know of all this?" the King asked, with serious face, for he was very fond of the youth.

"Yes, and he has known of our determination to

wed at some future day, but this morning, thinking the ceremony should be ere his departure, I had it performed on the spot, as I have told you."

"Why was he not present?"

"He was away collecting his Parthians, and I dared not wait, fearing we might not see him ere his departure," Itanes explained.

"And now that he has carried off your wife what do you propose to do?" the King smiled.

"It is about that I came; to beg you to give me an ile of cavalry that I may follow and bring her back. Or if you will not do that I will set out alone," Itanes sorrowed.

"A foolish adventure, Itanes, for he will never consent to give her up," the King said, to try him.

"He shall, and in the taking of her there will be little ceremony, for it was a scurvy trick to entrap me as he did and decamp ere I could draw my sword or call a soldier to my aid," Itanes cried out, enraged at the remembrance.

Angered at the insolence of Zapetes in not coming to him, and pleased at the youth's spirit, the King turned to Medius and bade him order a company of the Companion Cavalry to be placed at Itanes' disposal, as the latter asked. And Medius doing this, and every one being in hearty sympathy with the distress of the young lover, little delay occurred in making the necessary preparations. So that ere the day closed the troop set out in pursuit of the flying

Parthians, and their horses being superior to those they followed, they were so fortunate as to overtake the latter on the afternoon of the second day.

As they came up at a gallop with shields raised and spears in hand, the Parthians, being unarmed and unable to offer opposition of any kind, turned about and came to a halt. Sounding the trumpet, Itanes called aloud for Zapetes, whereupon the latter, much downcast, emerged from a covered wagon where he had concealed himself. As he approached, Itanes cried out impatiently:

"Make haste, old man — you did not lack in sprightliness yesterday!"

"Why this interruption to our march and contrary to the King's explicit order to me to convey the troop to Parthia with all dispatch?" Zapetes demanded, as if surprised at the other's action.

"I have no temper to bandy words, nor do I come to make excuses, but to claim Ossillia — my wife," Itanes explained, his voice breaking at thought of his love and her near proximity.

"Then you may return the way you came, for I will by no means give her up," Zapetes curtly refused, remarking the other's halting speech and mistaking it for fear.

"If that be your answer, then stand aside, for I'm not here to ask your leave," Itanes screamed in a rage, gathering up his reins.

"This is unseemly to me, an old man, in you — a

mere youth!" Zapetes chided, holding up his hand to stay the other.

"What! Is it unseemly for a man to claim his wife?"

"But the manner of it — and I her father!" the other rebuked.

"You stole her from me by a trick, and I am left no other course than to reclaim her by force, so stand aside and let me pass."

"How could I know she was your wife, it being all unexpected and I not present to witness the ceremony?" Zapetes expostulated.

"Well, if you doubted then you can doubt no longer." Itanes reasoned, anxious to come to terms with his father-in-law.

"But I know no more now than before."

"You know we are married, and with the King's consent; but if you doubt we will wed anew, here and now," Itanes argued, impatiently.

"No, that is impossible!"

"Why impossible?"

"Having had time to think it over she will by no means abide the foolish act and is now of a mind to have nothing more to do with you. Go your way, then, and disturb her no more with your childish importunities," Zapetes cried, waving the other off.

To this Itanes for some time could make no answer, so great was his fear that in some way Zapetes had prevailed upon her to deny her love. But reflecting that this could not be possible he presently cried out in a passion:

"Quick, old man, bring me to her before I ride you down, for by the Gods I will listen to no more idle talk."

"No, having deceived and entrapped her into a foolish marriage you shall never again come near her," Zapetes protested, backing away.

To this Itanes made no response but calling to the Companions to follow spurred his horse to the side of the chariot in which Ossillia had been placed by Zapetes at the gate of the city. Leaping to the ground he unloosed and opened wide the door, frantically calling her name, and she responding on the instant threw herself into his arms, sobbing:

"Oh Itanes — my boy — my sweet love, I knew you would come, though they told me you no longer cared!"

Holding her trembling form he quieted her with gentle words and soft caresses, and when at last she was reassured, called out to Zapetes in boyish triumph:

"Come, old man, and see us wed according to the Persian fashion, that you may go your way in peace," and clasping Ossillia's face in both his hands they pressed their lips together with such unmistakable love and abandon that a great shout went up from the waiting soldiers at the earnestness and drollery of it all. But Ossillia, looking with pleading eyes to her father, cried out:

"Be good to me, papa, and forgive Itanes, for you know I love him with all my heart!"

To this appeal, however, Zapetes, scowling, returned no answer, and Itanes, angered and defiant, lifted his bride to the croup of his horse and mounting rode away, her arms about his waist. And it was in this fashion that they rejoined the army, the bride's face aflame with blushes at the awkwardness of her position. At first the soldiers laughed, but presently taking notice of her beauty and modesty, they filled the air with their cheers and cries. And thus Itanes and his young wife approached the King, who in the spirit of the adventure sprang from his horse and lifted the bride to the ground, saying as he kissed her blushing face:

"Thus I welcome you and make you the ward of the army, that you may have no further cause to fear."

Hearing him and delighted the soldiers raised a mighty shout of approval, which they presently redoubled when Itanes threw himself from his horse and knelt with his young bride before the smiling King.

Afterward, as the army lay encamped for the night in a forest of palm-trees, the King gave a great banquet in Itanes' and Ossillia's honour, in which the common soldiers took part, every man being given a present of gold and double portion of wine, that he might remember and treasure the festive occasion. Thus the day ended amid general rejoicing, and the following morning the King, recalling the event, sent for Itanes and Ossillia and graciously set aside a chariot for the latter, with attendants and slaves to wait upon her. And this presently coming to the knowledge of the soldiers they showed their delight by the wild-flowers with which they showered her equipage as it made its way within the lines of the army.

Thus ended Itanes' remarkable campaign against the Parthians, as the adventure was afterward laughingly spoken of throughout the army.

CHAPTER XVII

Continuing his march, the King on nearing Susa was met by Abulites, the Persian satrap of Darius, with the keys of the citadel, which latter held the Susan treasury. Accepting the nobleman's good offices and bidding him ride by his side, the King directed his steps to the royal palace, where he installed Sisygambis and the children of Darius with every honour that could be bestowed; and this especially in remembrance of Statira, over whose unhappy death the King still mourned. Here he held court for several days, reviving the splendour of the Persian throne, that all the world might know that he came both to conquer and to reign.

While thus occupied, and busied with the affairs of the empire, fifty youths of Macedonia joined him as pages, hoping to win favour and learn through him the art of war. But the duties of these delicately nurtured youths were destined to be far more exacting than they had thought, and already there were murmurings of the severe discipline and exacting duties imposed upon them. Nor were these complaints destined to cease with the passing months, but to become more and more pronounced as the hardships of the war increased, and, in the end, encouraged by the King's enemies, to terminate in one of the most sorrowful of the many tragedies of the great conquest.

While Susa and Babylon had yielded without a struggle, acknowledging Alexander as King, Persepolis, the southern capital and the home of the Persian race, stood out, necessitating an immediate and arduous campaign in that direction. Accordingly, the King, after a brief stay at Susa, directed the course of his army toward Persepolis, he himself with a body of picked troops entering upon an active campaign against the Uxii, a tribe of savage robbers who commanded a lofty mountain pass through which the army had to make its way. And in this connection it appeared that from time immemorial these hardy mountain warriors had preyed upon the country round about, going so far as to exact in their arrogance tribute from the Persian kings whenever the latter had occasion to pass between Susa and Persepolis. Knowing no difference now, they dispatched a messenger to Alexander demanding the usual gratuity under threat of their displeasure. Patiently listening to their demand, the King told them in ambiguous phrase to come to the pass and receive their just dues. It was then that he determined to make war upon the outlaws, and although the mountains were deep with snow, yet undeterred he forced his way through the narrow and little frequented defiles of the rugged coun-

try and encountering the murderers in their native
stronghold, defeated them in the conflict that ensued.
Continuing his swift march through the highlands, he
came at last upon the armed body set to guard the
mountain pass; and here after a desperate battle, in
which victory long hung in the balance, he finally over-
threw and put the robbers to flight. Enraged at
their murderous nature and long-continued and cruel
oppression of the plains people, the King determined
to exterminate the savage tribe, but Sisygambis, now
grown old and somewhat tender-hearted, intervening, he was finally led to spare the remnant of the
band.

In this way a grave obstacle to his march was overcome, but further on it appeared a still more impregnable pass, heavily guarded, barred the way. This
defile, the entrance to Persis and known as the Persian
Gate, reared its towering walls fourteen thousand feet
above the plain. Four men only were able to march
abreast within its narrow confines, while from the
precipitous cliffs above an alert enemy was free to
assail the attacking force unhindered. In defence
of the gate, Ariobarzanes, a brave Persian noble, had
collected forty thousand men, all that remained to
Darius in the south after the disastrous field of Arbela.
Boldly entering the narrow defile, Alexander sought
to force a passage, but assailed in front and from above
with missiles of every description, he was at last compelled to withdraw with the loss of many men. En-

camping in the plain some distance away he learned from a half-savage mountain shepherd that the summit might be reached by a narrow and rugged path twelve miles distant. Leaving Craterus, a trusted general, to guard the camp, the King marched away when darkness concealed his movements, and preceded by his guide finally reached the summit of the mountain on the second day. Remaining quiet until darkness hid his movements, he took his course along the summit of the snow-clad mountain, capturing the various outposts of the enemy without his presence becoming known. On the following morning at break of day, he surprised the fortified camp of Ariobarzanes, and sounding the trumpet (the signal agreed upon with Craterus to renew the assault at the foot of the pass) the King charged the outposts of the astonished enemy with savage fury. Thus in a moment, and all unprepared, the Persians found themselves assailed from above and below. In this way, hemmed in between the two advancing forces, they were unable to offer effective opposition to either, and so were overcome, seven thousand only, with Ariobarzanes at their head, being so fortunate as to effect their escape in the direction of Persepolis.

Defeated and his army destroyed, the brave Persian, with the remnant of his force, hastened to the ancient capital, hoping to hold the citadel that guarded the palaces of Darius, or failing in that to effect his escape with the vast treasures of the Persian King.

But as it happened Tiridates, in immediate command of the stronghold, anxious to conciliate Alexander and fearful of his vengeance, sent word to him to hasten ere Ariobarzanes had time to rob the citadel of its treasures and effect his escape. Hurriedly collecting a body of cavalry, Alexander set out as night closed in, reaching the Araxes, forty miles distant, at break of day. Resting his exhausted force for an hour, he pushed on with renewed vigour, reaching Persepolis in time to defeat Ariobarzanes' purpose, the brave Persian losing his life in the encounter that followed. Thus Persis, the birthplace of the nation, fell into Alexander's hands, and with it the palaces and vast treasures of the Persian King, including among the latter one hundred and fifty millions of dollars in coined money and ingots.

The campaign having been one of extreme hardship, Alexander determined to rest his army for the winter months, but impatient of the delay, the King collected a body of light troops, and penetrating the mountain regions to the south and west carried on a hardy campaign against the Mardians, a savage tribe of robbers and murderers who had for centuries terrorized the fertile plains of Persia. And to add a new and terrible aspect to the war, the women were found fighting side by side with the men, and with the ferocity of savage beasts. However, pursuing the outlaws with relentless energy, they were driven farther and farther into the mountains, now covered deep with snow, where the King finally reached and overcame their last remaining stronghold.

"It is in these obscure and terrible campaigns against the savage enemies of mankind," wrote Itanes to Roxana, "that the King evinces his heroic character, his contempt of danger, and indifference to toil. For it is never his practice to direct his men, but to lead them, and in these wars, amid the cañons and mountain heights he fights on foot as a common soldier, bearing the worry of command with the fatigue and danger of an archer and slinger. Sharing in this way the hardships and dangers of his soldiers, it is no wonder he has become to them a very God. But of a truth he knows not what fear or fatigue is, and sleeps as soundly in the open air wrapped in his cloak as in a palace."

But of the particulars of these toilsome and dangerous mountain campaigns, many in number, the scribes who accompanied the army said little; for of a truth they knew little, being satisfied to remain in their tents, recounting merely the names of the campaigns and the savage peoples subdued.

Of the sumptuous accommodations of the King's court when in the field in the intervals of the war, as at Persepolis, the luxury of Darius was thought to have been mean and parsimonious compared with Alexander's lavish expenditure and the splendour of his Oriental appointments. Beneath his crimson tent adorned with priceless rugs and resplendent tapestries, a thousand guests supped each night, attended by as many slaves, the food being served on plates of gold. But in this, as in all other things, he exceeded everything before known of men. And properly enough, it was thought by his friends, for he loved the ornate luxuries of life, and the magnificence of the court surroundings diverted and refreshed his mind and body in the few hours of rest he allowed himself from the harassing cares of his vast empire and the immediate command of his victorious and every-growing army.

Such was Alexander's life at Persepolis, and now peace and good government having been established in Western and Central Persia, he mustered his army afresh and set out to complete his conquest, news having reached him that Darius had collected a fresh force and awaited his coming at Ecbatana, the northern capital. The great nobles of the further provinces, so it appeared, had rallied anew, and having been joined by the Scythian nomads of the north, the Persian King was reported to have mustered a great army which confidently awaited Alexander's coming in the plains of Media. Midway of the march to Ecbatana, however, Alexander, mindful of the opportunity, halted his army to conduct in person a campaign against the Parætacæ, a savage tribe of mountain outlaws, hitherto allied with the murderous Uxians he had subdued the previous autumn.

"For the King in his progress," Itanes gossips in a

letter to Roxana, "mindful of the future peace of the country, will nowhere leave an organized enemy of mankind in his rear. For he says the helpless denizens of the villages and plains are entitled to the same protection that those enjoy who inhabit the fortified cities — something never accorded them under the Persian kings."

Resuming his rapid march to the north after the subjection of the Paraetacæ, all was excitement and exultation, for the army, confident of victory, looked forward with eager expectation to the end of the war in the capture of Ecbatana, the summer home of the Persian monarchs, and the last of the great strongholds and treasure-houses of the Empire. In this belief the King, riding amidst his soldiers, happily shared, and looking away to the east, across the great desert beside which the army marched, he beheld in imagination the woods and mountain-slopes of Bactria, and so near did they appear that he had but to stretch out his arms to clasp the adorable woman who there impatiently awaited his coming. But from this dream of love's quick fulfillment, alas, the overwrought King was destined to an immediate and cruel awakening.

CHAPTER XVIII

THE BETRAYAL OF ROXANA

When Alexander was yet several days' march from
Ecbatana, unexpected word was brought him that
Darius had fled to the east, the armed forces he expected having failed him at the last moment, leaving
him no other alternative than flight or capture. Hastening his march, Alexander reached Ecbatana to find
the great capital in a turmoil of excitement and fear,
and the report of Darius' flight confirmed. Determined on pursuit of his enemy, Alexander was nevertheless compelled to give his troops needed rest after
the long march from Persepolis in the heat of summer,
and for much of the way in battle-array. Moreover,
the internal affairs of the Empire and the necessity of
establishing a stable government in Media compelled
him to delay his departure; and in this emergency
many were the men he thought of for governour of
Ecbatana ere he came to a decision. For the ancient
capital, with its protecting walls and impregnable
citadel, was the key to all northern Persia, and a weak
or traitorous governour might cause the state in-
calculable harm. Here, moreover, the vast treasures
of the Persian Empire were to be collected and safe-
guarded.

In this emergency most strongly did the King turn
to Parmenio, but while he meditated he remembered
Philotas' many treasonable utterances now long borne
by him with indulgent patience. Did Parmenio, the
father, sympathize with his son in his treason, treason
that a Persian king would long since have punished
with torture and death? Was Parmenio himself
loyal? And reflecting on the past the King remembered with a bitter heart that at Arbela he would
have effected Darius' capture and so ended the
struggle had not Parmenio recalled him from pursuit
of the flying monarch. And at the Granicus had not
Parmenio counselled delay, thus jeopardizing success
at the very moment of victory? And strangely, too,
had he not sought to ruin the leech Philip while the
King lay sick unto death at Tarsus? Angered over
the present flight of Darius, Alexander was inclined
to attribute his present embarrassment and the pro-
longation of the war to Parmenio's acts. Could he
then trust him as governour of Ecbatana and the
rich provinces of Media, while he, the King, was in
the far east, or perhaps in still more remote India?
But while thus holding the general in distrust, the
generous young king remembering Philip's love for
Parmenio and the latter's long service, could not find
it in his heart to humiliate him by appointing another
in his place.

Thus it was one evening that Alexander, worn with
the harassments of the day, rested within the lofty

palace of the first Median king, when an event oc-
cured that so excited his rage and grief that disregarding all else, he determined on the immediate
pursuit of the flying King. Strangely that which
stirred him and most unlooked for and startling was
a letter from Roxana, and not written from a place
of security or in any form, but disjointed and pitiful,
as if in secret and as opportunity offered. This was
so apparent that upon recognizing her writing he
became on the instant white as death, trembling and
disconcerted, stricken with a mortal fear. When,
however, presently mindful of the situation, he looked
up and remarked the bewilderment and wonder on
the faces of the officers and courtiers in attendance, he
motioned them to retire, which they did reluctantly
and with many anxious glances. Then slowly and
laboriously perusing the almost illegible sentences of
Roxana's letter, sighs filled his throat and tears clouded his eyes, or his mood changing, he would fall into
such fury of rage and half-articulate threats of vengeance that thought was for the moment denied him.
And this was Roxana's message, so unexpected and
fearful of import:

"Come to me, Iskander, my sweet lord, if thou
dost still love me as on that summer day when in all
truth we plighted our faith in the slumbering vale.
For thou, beloved, monarch of all the world, can alone
save me. * * * Yet why were we not born of
simple people, tending our flocks in the valleys, that

I might have claimed thee long ago for my own, and so been spared my present peril and the years of unavailing sorrow? * * * But now I call to thee in direful fear and in all thy strength of heart and arm, for, thou must know, I am held a captive in cruel bondage, broken in spirit and knowing not what the morrow may have in store * * * And only thou canst save me and from a fate the Gods can alone foretell. Hasten, then, if it be thou lovest me and would save me from thine enemies and mine. For thou must know, beloved, that I am a prisoner of Darius, a thing he planned ere the battle of Arbela, thinking if he but had me in his power he might force thee, because of thy love, to release Statira, his beloved Queen * * * And thus it would have been, I know, had events turned out as he expected, but ere he could accomplish his purpose Statira was dead and Arbela lost! And so when I was ushered into his presence he received me in tears, sorrowing over what he had done, and the futility of it all. And this truly, Iskander, for he is not bad, only weak — and to be pitied. * * * And so I forgave him and said as much, his provocation being what it was. But I was still held a prisoner, for when he would have released me, Bessus objected, saying they could not forego the advantage over you to be gained by my captivity. To this the poor King assented, and of necessity, I am sure, for he treats me as if I were a child and at Ecbatana assigned me a sumptuous pal-

ace and attendants with every honour that could
have been accorded a princess of the blood. This,
I think, Iskander in emulation of your gentle treatment of Statira. * * * While thus a captive, I
sought in every way to convey some word to you, but
being closely guarded no chance offered. And so I
awaited your coming, thinking that after the expected
battle I should be free, for I knew of a surety that
you would be the victor. But the battle, like everything Darius has planned, miscarried, and now he is
in flight and I a prisoner in his train, a hindrance,
yet watched and guarded as if the very Empire were
at stake. * * * But, unhappily the poor King is
held in slight regard by Bessus and his followers, and
this feeling grows with the passing days. And in that
is the peril, for I forsee that a conspiracy of the camp
will ere long deprive the King of all authority, and
this occurring, Bessus will become supreme. * * *
If this should come about, beloved, I am lost, for
Bessus has long sought me in marriage, and having
me in his power will enforce his wishes nor hazard
the chances of delay. * * * Ride, then, and with
thy guards, beloved, nor let Empire, nor heat, nor
desert waste, nor mountain wilds stay thy progress —
for I love thee. Do this if I still hold thy heart in
mine and thou wouldst make me thy wife as we did
plan, but oh, so long ago that I often start affrighted
fearing it is but a dream. And so it may be, but if,
perchance, thy love is real as thou didst once swear,

pressing thy lips to mine, come in all haste lest thou
come too late.   But come not without strong following, my sweet, that thou mayest not meet death at
Bessus' hands, for he is among men the most cunning
and cruel, and sleeps not for sinister plannings.
* * * Much more I would write thee, dear lord, but
dare not wait and so give this all hurriedly into the
hands of Zapetes, long a trusted follower of my father.
* * * Be kind to him, Iskander, for he has ventured much to aid me, and now risks his life in bearing
this, it may be, my last word to thee.   For as thou
mayest believe without the telling, I will by no means
survive the direful calamity that threatens me.   Farewell, I love thee dearest — and come, and in all haste,
if thou dost still hold me in thy heart, *Roxana*."

Overwhelmed, dumb with apprehension, the King
was for a long time as one crazed over Roxana's
unhappy plight, protesting over and over again with
sighs and imprecations his undying constancy.

"Yes, beloved, I treasure thee as on that day we
plighted our troth.   Nor canst thou doubt it, for
thou dost now know as well as I, that there is naught
that is real in life save trusting love, all else being as
a mirage having no substance save in foolish imagin-
ings.   And now indeed, my sweet, *I know that thou
art Persia*, for what comfort will there be in conquering if I do not at last find rest and happiness in
thy presence?"

Thus he mourned, pressing her letter to his lips

in bitter anguish, but more often with furious rage
that having conquered the world he should now be
denied the happiness he had thought was finally
to be his. In this way, overcome, he mourned with
bowed head, when suddenly from out the silence
of the night Roxana's sorrowing voice seemed to
call:

"Why dost thou wait, oh King, while the hours
pass, and tarrying it be all too late!"

Startled into life as if indeed it were her voice,
he lifted himself and calling an attendant cried
out:

"Quick, bring me the bearer of this message if
indeed he be not already gone?" holding up the letter
as if it were a talisman.

"He is still within the citadel, oh King," the other
answered, frightened at the King's distraught manner and savage voice.

"Then bring him to me on the instant!" Alexander
commanded, waving the other away.

Hastening to do as he was bid, the affrighted page
presently returned with Zapetes, attended by a guard
with drawn swords. Dismissing the soldiers, the
King turned to the prisoner and holding up Roxana's
letter cried out, little regarding what he said:

"Tell me how it happened that you became the
bearer of this distressful message."

"By the urgency of the Princess' need, oh King."

"Why should she have chosen you in preference

to another for so great a trust?" the King demanded, distrustfully, remembering Zapetes' ungracious behavior at Babylon.

"Because I alone, of her friends, was free to come and go, or knew of her relation to — you."

"How did you have knowledge of this relation if indeed there be any truth therein?" the King asked, perplexed.

"I learned it at Babylon."

"In what way?"

"From the idle chattering of Itanes and Ossillia."

"And was it this knowledge that led you to concern yourself with the affairs of the Princess?" the King asked.

"No, but out of friendship for her and from seeing her in the King's train and under restraint when I thought her at Arimazes. Disturbed, I sought the first opportunity to question her, but this I found most difficult, for she was closely guarded, though outwardly having seeming freedom."

"Poor child!" the King sorrowed, turning away.

"She welcomed me with sobs and throwing her arms about my neck begged me to befriend her."

"Go on, go on," the King urged, as the other hesitated.

"Inquiring the cause of her distress she told me her story, but this only at intervals, so watchful was her guard."

INTERROGATING ZAPETES

"Her story?"

"Yes, the manner of her abduction and the cause of her present anxiety."

"Her abduction?" the King interrogated, as if surprised, determined to probe Zapetes and his motives to the bottom.

"Yes, oh King."

"Tell me how it happened and the purpose of it," the King went on more gently, motioning the other to a seat.

"It appeared that Darius being anxious to gain possession of her person sent Boartes, a Bactrian noble, to Arimazes to effect his purpose, knowing him to be a man of resolution and highly esteemed by Oxyartes. Reaching his destination, Boartes was welcomed as one direct from the seat of war, and when at last he had ingratiated himself in the confidence of every one, he joined Oxyartes in a lion-hunt the latter planned. Thus they set forth amid rejoicing, but on the third day Boartes returned to the fortress in all haste, reporting that Oxyartes had been seriously wounded and fearing death from his injuries had besought him to bring Roxana to his side. She, overwhelmed with grief and suspecting nothing, set out immediately with her attendants, but when they were some distance from the fortress she was suddenly surrounded by a body of armed men, whereupon Boartes came forward and boldly disclosed the deception he had practiced, saying truly enough that it was by command of the great King. Afterward, refusing to listen to her prayers or grant her any redress whatever, he set out with all speed for Ecbatana."

"Was no effort made to rescue her?" the King asked, benumbed.

"Of that she does not know, but it is improbable, as her abduction could not have been known at the rock for several days."

"And how did she bear the fatigue?" the King questioned, conjuring up the long and tiresome journey.

"It seems that every care was taken by her captors to relieve the distress of the journey. For Darius, it appears, warned Boartes that if the Princess was so much as frightened or suffered in any way, he would flay him alive, being desirous, so he himself said, of treating her no less kindly than you had treated Statira."

"Oh, ye avenging Gods, why did I not put aside all thoughts of advantage to my people, all thoughts of policy and give back the unhappy Queen to her husband while it was in my power?" the King moaned in anguish, thinking of Statira's sad death and the captivity of Roxana that had grown out of her detention.

"To make more sure of the Princess' comfort and peace of mind," Zapetes went on, pretending not to hear the King's words, "Boartes cunningly contrived that she should be accompanied by all her attendants when she set out ostensibly to go to her father."

"All, say you?"

"Yes, both men and women."

"And who were there among the former?" the King asked, thinking of Ossa and Orestes.

"Those whose office it was to attend upon her."

"Surely you can name them, having seen the Princess meanwhile," the King said, with some impatience.

"I know only those who attended her ere I left Arimazes."

"It is of these that I would learn."

"Well, there was Ossa for one, a gentle, simple-minded giant," Zapetes reflected.

"Simple-minded, say you?" the King queried, astonished.

"Yes, or so he appears."

"Who were the others?" the King smiled, amused at the deception Ossa had practiced.

"Orestes, a player on the flute, and knowing naught else."

"He too, then, is simple?"

"Yes, as a child."

"They certainly accompany her?" the King asked, his anxiety somewhat lessened to know that these brave men were near his beloved.

"Yes, for I myself saw and spoke to them."

"And do they attend immediately upon her person?"

"Yes, but only as slaves, without arms and as carefully watched as the Princess herself."

"In what state does she travel?" the King questioned, comforted in what he heard.

"In a sumptuous chariot with her women in attendance, the others following on horseback."

"She is treated with all honour then?"

"Yes, and as a part of Darius' immediate household."

"What, then, is the cause of her fright?" the King asked, to try Zapetes further.

"That Bessus, whose power grows each day, may overthrow the King and so become supreme."

"Is there danger of that?"

"Yes, most pressing, oh King."

"To what country is it thought Darius will fly if nothing intervenes?"

"The Upper Provinces; Bactria and Sogdiana, the satrapies of Bessus."

"There to renew the struggle?"

"Yes."

"But if the King fall meanwhile?"

"Then Bessus, if alive, will surely continue the struggle in his place."

"Where did you leave Darius?" Alexander asked, referring to the subject uppermost in his mind.

"Eight days' easy march from Ecbatana, oh King."

"Is he hastening his flight?"

"No, seeming to have no fear of immediate pursuit."

"Which of the great roads does he follow?" the King asked, bending over a map of the country that lay outspread on the table before him.

"That, by the north."

"Think you if we march by the southern and shorter-road we may intercept him ere he passes the Caspian Gates?" the King asked, pointing out the mountain defile and anticipating the delays that would very likely attend the passage of this difficult and robber-infested pass.

"Yes, with well mounted troops, if Darius does not meanwhile hasten his flight."

"What strength has he?" the King asked.

"Nine thousand of all arms, many having deserted."

"Are those that remain loyal to him?"

"Only the followers of Artabazus are true; those under Bessus will do whatever their lord commands."

"If that be so, the Princess has indeed cause to fear," the King said, deeply moved. "What disposition did you make of the Parthians I commanded you to lead to their homes?" the King continued, thinking to make use of these incomparable horsemen in the present emergency.

"I did in all things as you directed, oh King, though they were at first inclined to rejoin Darius when we neared Ecbatana."

"After their oath to the Gods to take no further part in the war?"

"An oath is little regarded by a Parthian, oh King," Zapetes replied, shrugging his shoulders.

"What caused them to continue on to their homes at the last moment?"

"The news that Antipater, your general in Macedonia had met and defeated the Grecian army, and killed the Spartan King in a great battle fought at Megalopolis. From that my Parthians reasoned that there could be no further opposition to you in Greece, and so you would have a free hand to prosecute the war against Darius," Zapetes related.

"They thought it wise under the circumstances to return to their homes ?" the King smiled.

"Yes, as did the Caduchians and Scythians, and many others."

"And that was the cause of Darius' failure to remain and give battle at Ecbatana?"

"Yes."

"Why couldst thou not have anticipated all this, Antipater, and so have stayed thy hand until I could have again faced Darius in the open field?" the King murmured, half aloud, conjuring up the battle. "But why," he went on, curious as to Zapetes' motives and desirous of informing himself as to his present honesty, "did you go to Darius after dismissing the Parthians?"

"For lack of a better place, oh King, fearing you

would not receive me after my intemperate act in abducting Ossillia while under your protection."

"Thinking thus, what then induced you to undertake your present errand?" the King demanded.

"The desire to aid the Princess, my former mistress, in her great distress, and my longing to be again with Ossillia, my beloved child, believing you would forgive my former foolishness, knowing it grew out of my great love for her," Zapetes explained, much affected.

"And in that you thought truly," the King smiled, stirred by the other's distress.

"And moreover I hoped my desire to serve the Princess would be a thing in my favour," Zapetes continued humbly.

"Yes, as it is — everything," the King answered quickly.

"Then you forgive me?" the other asked, looking up.

"Yes, and if all you tell me prove true I will treasure you in my heart and enrich you beyond the wildest expectation of mortal man," the King cried. Hearing him, Zapetes threw himself on his knees, tears streaming from his eyes, but lifting him up, the King embraced him and taking a chain from off his neck placed it about that of the other, saying:

"Go seek thy daughter, good friend, but let no word of what thou hast told me escape thy lips."

CHAPTER XIX

Immediately upon the withdrawal of Zapetes, the King called an assembly of his officers, determined to set out in pursuit of Darius at dawn of the following day.

"Let your preparation be conducted with secrecy both as to the time and direction of the march," he commanded, when he had made his determination known. "In organizing your force take only men of courage and heart, for the pursuit will be without rest day or night, wherever the flight of Darius may lead. Cull the horses as you do the men, and see to it that the armour of man and beast is both light and serviceable. Having conquered Persia," he went on, "we must now gain possession of the person of Darius to insure peace in the far east, for only his voice will quell the hot blood of his half-savage subjects in that remote region," he concluded, dismissing the astonished officers, for until then they had thought a considerable interval would occur before setting out in pursuit of the flying King.

Afterward, calling for his secretaries, the King completed such business as required his immediate attention, appointing Parmenio governour, and Harpalus,

286

who had shared his exile while a Prince, custodian of the vast treasures of the Persian King. The appointment of Harpalus was most unfortunate as it afterward turned out, but in all respects like Alexander, who in every emergency of his life remembered and favoured those who had in any way befriended him. When the business before him was completed he bade his chamberlain admit all who sought audience, and to these he patiently listened, nor did one of those present suspect the anxiety that oppressed his heart or that he contemplated a campaign on the morrow, the hardship and strangeness of which has no parallel in the annals of kings.

After dismissing his attendants he gave himself up anew to thoughts of Roxana and her distressful plight, and thus the attendants found him when they gained admission to his presence in the early morning. Wondering, they helped him to don his armour, after which, emerging from the palace, he mounted his horse and set out while it was yet dark to join the waiting troops in the plain below. As he approached in the gray of the morning, the soldiers hailed his coming with cheers, but without waiting or speech of any kind he gave the signal to march, and in a moment the column was off at a gallop that full advantage might be taken of the cool of the summer day. Far in advance the King rode, and about his upraised spear there was entwined a silken veil, its embroidered ends fluttering in the morning breeze.

Seeing it the soldiers stared, for to no one save Hephestion was its significance known; only he knew it to
be the love token Roxana had given Alexander in the
plains of Thessaly while he was yet a Prince. Now
in honour it became his guidon, under which he
sought as on that day long past to rescue the Princess
from the perils that threatened her.

To the brave men who followed Alexander, the
capture of Darius was the sole object of the hurried
expedition, but to the anxious Monarch the fate of
the panic-stricken King was only a part. And as
days and nights followed, unrelieved by anything
to lessen the anxieties and hardships of the forced
march, the vision of Roxana that always urged him
on to greater effort. Spurred by the two-fold object
of the pursuit, he gave his troops no rest save at long
intervals when the torrid heat rendered further endurance impossible. Then a respite was taken, but to
the King this boon was denied, or if he slept it was to
arise unrefreshed to busy himself anew with the affairs of his overwrought soldiers. Seeing this not
one made complaint, and when men sank down
exhausted beside the road they still cheered as others
hardly less worn leaped from their horses to leave
food and water, and mounting in all haste sped on
lest they, too, should be left behind. Thus the pursuit continued amid mountains and deserts until the
eleventh day, when the King reached Rhagæ, the
deserted capital of ancient Media, with such part of

his following as had been able to withstand the hardships of the terrible march. Here, amid limpid pools and in the shadow of crumbling walls and tumbling columns, he halted to refresh his soldiers, but to the King himself, occupied with the welfare of his troops and the rescuing of those who had fallen by the way, there was no rest whatever.

While thus busied news reached him through native scouts that the Persian Monarch, making straight for Bactria, had reached and passed the Caspian Gates. This was a grievous disappointment to Alexander, who had hoped to overtake or head off his enemy ere the latter could enter the narrow and dangerous defile. However, assured of the direction of the King's flight and his followers being somewhat rested, he immediately set out with such force as he could muster and in a hurried march of fifty miles reached the entrance to the coveted pass. Entering the defile, disregardful of any trap the Persian King might have laid for him, three hours' hard riding brought him to the open desert beyond. Encouraged by his good fortune he continued on with unabated speed until the succeeding day, when he was met by two Persian noblemen, from whom he learned that through a conspiracy of the camp the fugitive King had been dethroned by Bessus and was now in imminent danger of his life.

From their account it appeared that Bessus had corrupted the guard of Darius and seized the person of the King and bound him, in mockery of his rank, with the golden chains that adorned his person. Afterward they hid him in a cart which they covered with the raw skins of animals, the more completely to conceal what they had done from the officers and soldiers who were not in sympathy with the conspiracy. Thus what Roxana had feared had come to pass, but of her fate neither of the noblemen could give any account, having fled from the camp as soon as knowledge of what was transpiring reached their ears.

Invoking the wrath of the Gods on the heads of Bessus and his fellow-conspirators, Alexander hurriedly selected a body of picked men from his remaining troops and at once set out in pursuit. Thus for two days and nights the chase kept up, and when the King's horse could no longer respond to whip or spur the impatient monarch, leaping to the ground, ran beside him; and the others following his example the weary beasts were rested and so able to continue without stopping. In this way the flying column reached Thara, where the Perisan King had been deposed, and here Alexander found Darius' interpreter sick and abandoned, who confirmed all that had been told. But of particulars the secretary knew nothing, being ill at the time, and so had been left behind without excuse or aid of any kind. Nor could the unfortunate man give any particulars concerning Roxana, save that she had been shown every honour by Darius during his hurried and prolonged flight; but of her disposition after the arrest of the unfortunate monarch he knew absolutely nothing. To further heighten Alexander's fears, information was brought him by deserters that Bessus and his confederates, having learned of the King's tireless pursuit and being in deadly fear, were now hastening their flight by night as well as day marches.

Apprehensive of Bessus' escape, Alexander inquired of the frightened peasants if there was not some shorter road, however difficult, by which he might hope to overtake the recreant nobleman. In reply they told of a little-used path across a waterless plain, much shorter than that followed by Bessus, but because of the roughness of the country and the depth of the shifting sand no one save the nomads of the desert ever attempted the difficult passage. Undeterred, the King procured a guide, and late in the afternoon set out with five hundred men, all that remained of the gallant array with which he had marched from Ecbatana. Striking across the desert, black with the shadows of the night, the King led the advance as he had throughout the long pursuit, and there being no abatement of the mad speed, many of those who followed were lost in the interminable waste or sank exhausted in their tracks.

With the coming of day the King, eagerly scanning the desert before him, discovered Bessus' retreating army, a speck on the horizon, making its way along the foothills that skirted the desolate plain. Slowing his horse Alexander looked back to see what number of his troops followed, observing which Itanes, who rode close behind, white with the impalpable dust of the desert, cried with cheerful voice:

"There are sixty, oh King, if none have fallen since the dawn."

To this Alexander made no response either of elation or despondency, and bringing his horse to a halt awaited the faithful few whose courage and strength had withstood the fearful ordeal. As these came up one by one cheering as they drew rein, the King loosed his sword and pointing to the enemy exclaimed:

"There, friends, are our foes flying in a disordered mass like drunken men in fear of the night-watch. In your still enduring strength and courage rest the life of Darius and the peace of the Empire his capture will insure! As we advance, extend wide your line so that your number may be magnified, for the dust of the plain will hide all behind you. When you reach the enemy's line," he went on with grim determination, "charge at topmost speed, neither giving nor asking quarter of those who stand to oppose you."

As the brave men gathered about the King and observed his drawn and pallid face, one more provident than the others slipped from his horse and carrying in his helmet the little water he had hoarded, raised it aloft and offered it to the Monarch. Thanking him, Alexander refused the proffered cup, and resting his hand on the soldier's head exclaimed:

"Why should I drink, comrade, when you are dying of fatigue and thirst?"

Seeing him refuse the cup, Medius, looking to those about him for approval, cried out with choked voice:

"Command of us what thou wilt, oh King, for we are no longer mortal when thou dost lead!"

Smiling his gratification Alexander waved his hand to the brave band to extend its line, and the order being instantly obeyed, he raised his sword and in a moment the slumbering plain resounded with the thunder of the charge that was to end in victory or annihilation.

CHAPTER XX

Bessus, who was not lacking in courage or alertness as a soldier, on being informed of Alexander's approach caused the trumpet to sound, and hastily dispatched aids to marshal his widely scattered and disorganized troops. But in this he met with little encouragement, many of the soldiers in their weariness having thrown away their arms, while others in fear of Alexander refused outright to further endanger their lives by attempting to beat back the onslaught of the seemingly invincible King. Seeing that resistance was not likely to prove effective, Bessus hastened to the cart in which Darius was confined and throwing back the filthy covering discovered the unfortunate King asleep on the floor of the rude vehicle. Surveying him for a moment with a scowl of deadly hatred, Bessus cried out, striving to infuse into his voice some show of deference:

"Awake, oh King, for the enemy is upon us!"

Lifting himself up, bewildered, Darius made no response save to stare unmeaningly at the impatient nobleman.

"Arouse thyself, oh King, for the barbarian approaches intent upon thy capture," Bessus continued, taking hold of the Monarch.

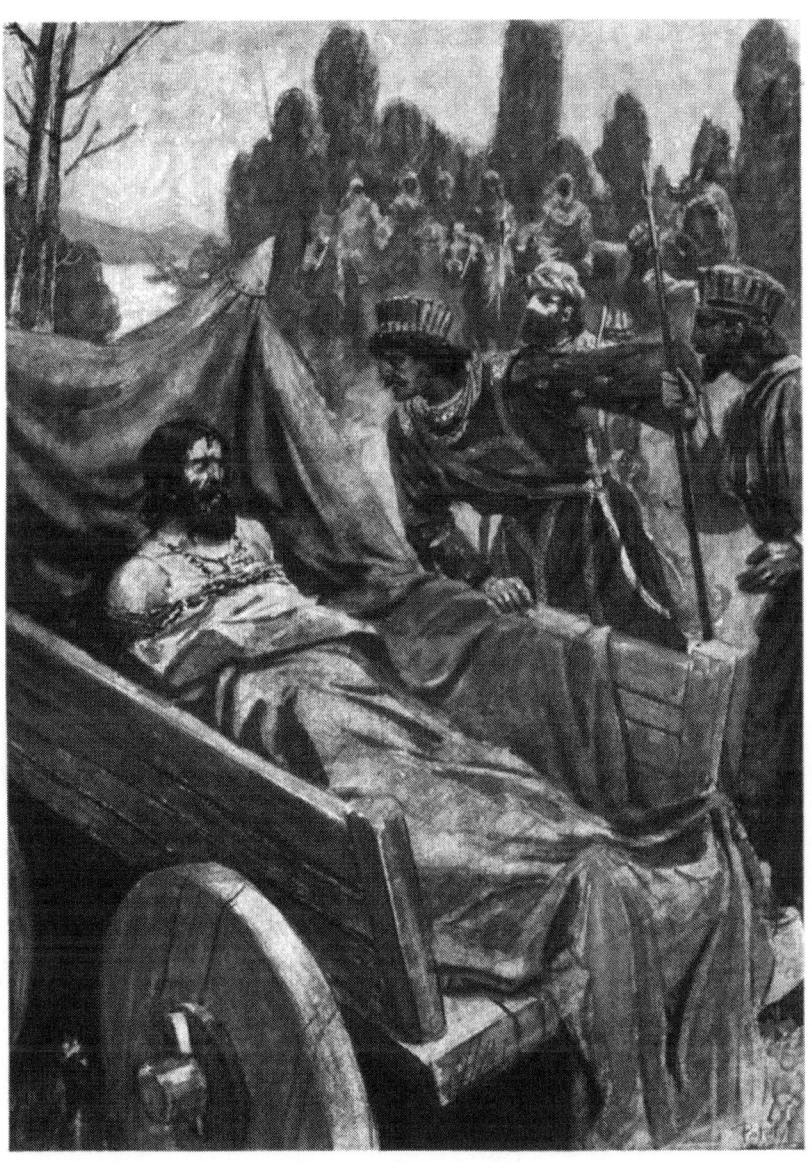

DARIUS AND BESSUS

"Alexander!" the other murmured, his face lighting as if in welcome of a friend.

"Yes, but happily you have time in which to mount and effect your escape," Bessus explained, bending low in obeisance.

Regarding him for a moment with ill-concealed, disfavour, the King said:

"No, Bessus, this is the end, for I will make no further effort to escape!"

"But your freedom — the crown — nay, the very Empire is at stake!" Bessus expostulated.

"Escape will avail nothing, for I cannot avoid my fate more than another man — as witness these chains and the degradation I suffer," he sighed, holding up his hands and scanning the sordid quarters in which he was confined.

"In that I have grievously sinned, oh King, and in reparation will reinstate you on the throne and cause you to be honoured and obeyed by all men," Bessus entreated with truculent voice, frightened lest Darius should fall into the hands of Alexander, foreseeing the leniency with which the Persian King would be treated, and the peaceable use that would be made of his person.

"No, Bessus, dethroned and a fugitive, I will make no further effort to regain what I have lost."

"What! You no longer wish to reign?" the noble scowled, disconcerted.

"Thou hast said it, Bessus. Having lost the substance I will no longer struggle for the shadow. All that I most prized I have lost in vain effort to avoid a fate ordained of the Gods from the first, and so I will continue the struggle no longer," the King said, decisively.

"Your fate is still in your keeping, oh King, and in the rugged mountains and impenetrable deserts of the far East, with hardier and braver men you may accomplish what has been denied you in the West," Bessus soothed.

"Urge me not — The God of Persia no less than those of his own country favour the fortunes of Alexander, and nothing mortal can withstand his arms."

"The Gods but try your constancy and courage, oh King, and under a more favourable sky will smile upon you as they have for centuries on all who have filled the Persian throne."

"No, 't is their will that he should rule, and I lacking in strength should play a lesser part. I should have yielded at Issus, and while losing my kingdom have saved my beloved Queen," he sorrowed, with bowed head. "Lacking wisdom there and again at Arbela I should have given myself up at Ecbatana, nor waited to see my followers fall like autumn leaves in a mad effort to escape a fate unalterable."

"The lives of men lie in the hazards of war, and for those who have fallen you are no way censurable nor are they to be lamented," the haughty Prince answered, contemptuously.

" 'T was a cruel waste, Bessus, and now when Statira is dead and my kingdom lost and all too late I have wisdom given me. No, foregoing further strife, let us await the coming of the master, for so all Gods declare him. Go, then, Bessus, and bid the soldiers lay down their arms and acclaim him King ere there is further slaughter!" the Monarch commanded, motioning the other away.

"I cannot, oh King, nor would the soldiers obey, for you only may bear the sacred title," Bessus objected.

"Titles mean nothing except to the strong, and Persia's strength is as a reed beaten by a torrent. Let us yield while we may, that men may again live in peace and the sun once more cast its rays on our distracted country."

"No, neither I nor my followers will yield, though in the end not a Persian be left alive to mourn his country's fate," Bessus threatened.

"Hush, cousin, such boasting ill becomes a fugitive flying for his life. Yield now that a worse fate may not befall thee and those who look to thee in confidence for guidance and protection," the King reproved, as if foreseeing Bessus' fate.

"No, far from here I will continue the struggle alone, if need be, though Alexander's strength were multiplied a thousand-fold," Bessus cried with savage fury.

"Not if I, thy King, command thee to yield," Darius exclaimed, with something of the dignity of former days.

"Yes, a thousand times, yes, thou craven!" Bessus raged, losing all control over himself. "What care I for thee or thy commands? A trader and saver of money, it is because of thy parsimony and cowardice that the princes and nobles of Persia are to-day scattered to the four quarters of the earth with no one so poor as to do them honour!" he screamed, unable to longer hide his rage and contempt.

"Yet have I never knowingly harmed any man, cousin, nor failed of duty where the God of my country did not deny me strength," the King murmured, overcome.

"Ignoble descendant of an illustrious race, yield then in thy weakness to me, that through my strength our country may yet be saved. For thou knowest that the blood in my veins is not less kingly than thine, and thy following being mine I will drive this Macedonian back to the wilds from whence he came!"

"What wouldst thou have?" the King whispered, stilled by the other's vehemence.

"I would have thee mount and fly, that together we may seek the fastnesses of the far East where, surrounded by sturdier men, we may once more renew the hitherto unequal struggle."

To this the King for some time made no response, but at last seemingly having weighed what the other said, exclaimed:

"It would avail nothing and to continue the struggle elsewhere will be to further harm our hapless friends without betterment to ourselves. Let us rather yield now, that by so doing we may be of service to those who have so long followed our failing fortunes."

"No, I'll not yield, nor shalt thou, though all Persia were here to crave it as a boon," Bessus sullenly asserted.

"Dare thou defy me thus, thy rightful King?" Darius demanded, in a rage, forgetting his unhappy plight.

"As my King I followed thee in all obedience as long as thou faced the enemies of my country with upraised standard; but yielding and timid of heart, I cast thee off."

"Yet am I still thy King, and thou but a subject and so bound to obey, however bitter the draught," Darius reprimanded, with lofty air. "Let us relinquish the unavailing struggle while we may, and doing so lay down a burden Persia is too weak to bear," he went on, his sorrowing eyes fixed on the fast approaching column of the Macedonian King.

" 'T is not for thee, Darius, to decide a thing so great, and again I ask thee to mount and fly, that thou mayest still preserve thy honour and the integrity of thy kingdom," Bessus urged, with meaning glance toward his confederates, who had been impatient listeners to all that passed.

"Go thy way, if that be thy determination, but I,

thy King, will do as I have said," Darius persisted, without anger.

"And I, thy subject, again beseech thee to join us in our flight," Bessus demanded, laying hold of his weapon, with menacing gesture.

"And I, thy King, again refuse," Darius answered, impatiently, turning away.

"Then die, thou craven, that Persia, through the efforts of braver men, may yet be saved!" Bessus screamed in a frenzy, burying his javelin in the body of the helpless Monarch. Seeing this his companions, applauding the deed, rushed in with cries of rage and contempt, hurling their spears in like manner at the unresisting Monarch.

Thus perished the last of the Akhæmenian kings, and his murderers, spurning his body with no vestige of pity in their hearts, mounted their horses and fled as Alexander's advancing column in a whirlwind of dust showed itself scarce an arrow's flight away.

CHAPTER XXI

THE ESCAPE

Abandoned by their leaders, the followers of Bessus stood irresolute and trembling as the column of Alexander burst like a thunderbolt on their disorganized ranks. Some among the more resolute sought to withstand the onrush, but when many had fallen, the remainder turned and fled, or throwing down their weapons craved forgiveness of the conqueror. But far the greater number, worn and disheartened, offered no opposition whatever, but threw themselves on the ground and with sobs and tears besought the King's mercy.

When all opposition had ceased, Alexander, thinking of Roxana and Darius, commanded his followers to bring before him all who were imprisoned or held against their will. In this search the King took part, spurring his horse amid the disorganized and terror-stricken mass, seeking in every direction for some trace of those he had ridden so long and hard to rescue. At last when hope had given place to dejection, Polystratus, a Macedonian soldier and favourite of the King, came running up, exclaiming that he had found Darius.

"Quick, lead me to him!" the King called out.

"It is some way apart and as if his custodians in their flight had sought to drag him with them," the soldier explained.

His anxiety allayed, Alexander made no response, save to urge the other forward, believing the whereabouts of Roxana would by equally good fortune be presently discovered.

"I found him reeking with filth and half concealed by raw skins," the soldier went on, with garrulous freedom, as they made their way through the frightened throng.

"Did you leave him thus unguarded?" Alexander questioned, fearing the fugitive might after all effect his escape.

Looking up surprised, the soldier answered shortly:

"He needs neither guard nor attendant, oh King, for he is dead."

"Dead!" Alexander cried out, horror-stricken, stopping short.

"Yes — dead."

"Murdered?" the King interrogated, overcome, comprehending Bessus' extremity.

"Yes, in cold blood, bound and unable to defend himself!" Polystratus answered, stirred by the recollection of the tragic scene.

"Did he utter no word, give no sign, ere he died?" the King questioned, spurring his horse to a gallop.

"Yes, lifting himself and looking about in fright, as if fearing the return of his assassins, he begged me

not to leave him. Telling him he had nothing further
to fear I gave him water and sought to revive his
failing strength, but all in vain. After a while, feeling
that he was dying, he clasped my hand and besought
me to thank you for your treatment of his beloved
Queen, adding, but not as if speaking to me, that he
was grateful the throne lost to him was to pass to so
generous a man. Then begging me to lift him up, he
turned his face to the rising sun and thus died, murmuring a prayer to Ahura-Mazda for mercy for himself
and happiness for his afflicted country."

"Did he divulge the name of his murderer?" Alexander asked, his eyes clouded with tears at the melancholy ending of the great King.

"Communing with himself in his delirium as he lay
dying he reproached Bessus, his kinsman, with the
foul crime."

"Peace to thy manes, thou King of many sorrows,"
Alexander prayed, his mind busy with what had
occurred and Darius' unhappy ending.

Coming at last to where Darius lay, Alexander,
overwhelmed at the grewsome spectacle, threw himself from his horse and knelt in tears beside the prostrate body, striving to revive the stricken King.
But when at last assured that his efforts were vain, he
raised himself and taking off his cloak reverently
covered the body of the fallen Monarch. Then in
rage and pity he raised his sword aloft and calling
the Gods to witness, swore eternal enmity to Bessus,

the King's murderer. And in this oath which he was in due time to execute with terrifying violence, there was much of personal concern, for the capture of Darius alive had meant the yielding of Persia to its utmost boundaries, and with it the saving of unnumbered lives and the avoidance of years of devastating warfare.

Directing that every honour accorded a Persian King in death should be paid the body of Darius, Alexander mounted his horse and set out anew in search of Roxana. And this with greater confidence than before, being assured by those who witnessed Bessus' flight, that no one had accompanied him save his immediate followers. But further than that he could learn nothing from the frightened men who grovelled in the dirt or stood sullenly awaiting whatever fate he might have in store for them. Thus he traversed the disorganized line, until nearing the end of his search there was brought before him a Median in chains, who upon being questioned as to his offence, answered after some hesitation:

" 'T was for permitting a captive of Darius to escape, oh King."

"If through any act of yours a follower of mine has regained his freedom reward not punishment awaits you," Alexander said, thinking the Median referred to the escape of a Macedonian prisoner.

"I would it had been a friend of yours, as you say, oh King," the other lamented.

Disappointed in the prisoner's reply, Alexander gathered up his reins to depart, whereupon Itanes, who rode by his side, thinking it might have been some Bactrian noble unfriendly to Bessus' cause, cried out:

"Who was this prisoner, then, for whose escape you were put in chains?"

"I know no more than you save that it was a woman attended by a retinue of slaves — if slaves they were," the Median vouchsafed.

"A woman!" the King cried, awakened to life, reining in his horse.

"What! Will you, too, put me to the torture?" the frightened wretch moaned, shrinking back in terror.

"Of that have no fear if you tell me truly who this woman was," the King promised.

"I know no more than you save that Darius held her in respect, though keeping her apart and under guard."

"What manner of woman was she — her name — her country, her history?" the King cried aflame, flinging himself from his horse.

"She was fair of face with eyes of purple-blue, but of her name or country I had no hint. I believed her to be a princess in disfavour, but my comrades thought her a Bactrian, the daughter of some refractory noble," the other described, frightened at the King's manner.

"Go on, go on, tell me all you know — all you thought," the King demanded, impatiently, as the other ceased speaking.

"I have nothing more to tell, oh King, save that not one of us had ever before seen woman of such beauty or gentle ways."

"And you say she escaped?" the King murmured, with a sigh of relief, no longer doubting that it was Roxana.

"Yes, and most surprisingly," the other vouch-safed with more freedom, seeing the King's face relax.

"In what respect?"

"Its manner — and those who aided in it."

"Go on, tell me how it was," the King urged, thinking of Ossa and Orestes.

"'T was her slaves who planned it — the half-witted Greeks who attended upon her person."

"Did they also escape?"

"Yes, and for that I should be accorded favour, oh King, they being your countrymen," the other pleaded.

"And such favour you shall have if you conceal nothing from me," the King promised, motioning the soldiers to remove the chains from the Median's limbs.

"What more would you have me tell?" the other asked, with cheerful voice, released from his bonds.

"Tell me about the slaves of whom you speak."

"I know not whether their names were real, but one

called himself Ossa, a simple peasant, and the other Orestes, fair and slight of form, who knew nothing save to play the flute."

"These men aided her?" the King interrogated.

"Yes, and except for them she would still be a prisoner in yonder chariot," the other explained, pointing to a sumptuous vehicle some way off.

"Tell me, good friend, how they brought it about — these simple Greeks?" the King asked, in rapture.

"The princess — for so we called her — somehow found that Bessus had dethroned and imprisoned the King. I think Darius himself called out to her; anyway it was in the night and the sky overcast and all about dire confusion because of what was occurring. But in a flash the two Greeks, who had somehow possessed themselves of weapons, fell like fiends upon the Princess' guard, and sooner than I can tell it, put them all to the sword."

"And you?" the King asked, gazing upon the other, pleased at the exploit.

"I, as it chanced, happened to be some distance away, but coming up on the instant the Princess commanded them to spare me because of a kindness I had shown her while in captivity."

"And because of it I, too, will spare you and reward you as well," the King interrupted with unsteady voice. "But tell me," he went on, "how did they finally effect their escape?"

"They worked with such quickness and skill that

ere the commotion about the King had subsided, the Princess and the Greeks had mounted and were off like fireflies in the darkness."

"And you?"

"Ere going they locked me in the abandoned vehicle," the Median answered, laughing, as if it were a pleasantry.

"What direction did they take in their flight?" the King inquired, hoping to gain a clew to the Princess' present whereabouts.

"To the north — the direction Artabazus had taken."

"Did he, too, abandon Darius in the extremity of his life?" Alexander asked, with flaming eyes.

"Yes, having only a small force, but not till after he had warned the King of Bessus' designs and offered him the protection of his arms."

"Did the Princess design seeking him, think you?" the King went on, delighted at everything he heard.

"I know not, only that she went that way."

"What did Bessus do when he discovered the Princess' escape?" the King inquired, deeply interested.

"Stormed and raved like a madman, sending out bodies of mounted men in pursuit. But they accomplished nothing, and he, apparently fearing to delay his flight, ordered that the retreat should thereafter continue day and night."

Believing Roxana safe, and overjoyed at what he

had heard, the King ordered the Median to be released and every favour accorded him. After this
and insensible to fatigue, he headed an expedition in
person in search of the missing Princess, and thus
many days were passed. But fruitlessly, for he could
gain no trace of her or Artabazus, save that the latter
had sought a hiding-place in the forests bordering the
Caspian Sea. Much cast down, the King returned
to his camp, where he busied himself day and night
in preparation for the war he meditated against
Bessus, who had proclaimed himself King of Persia
under the title of Artaxerxes, a name held in high
honour throughout the Empire.

While Alexander was thus occupied, Artabazus and
his three sons unexpectedly rode into camp, and
throwing themselves on their knees besought the
King's protection and favour. Greatly delighted, he
accorded all they asked, and the more willingly as he
had formed lasting ties of friendship with Artabazus
when that nobleman visited Macedonia with Oxyartes
and Roxana during Philip's reign; a friendship now
renewed and destined to continue throughout both
their lives. Moreover, Artabazus' loyalty to Darius
when others had betrayed him or sought safety in the
Macedonian camp greatly heightened the esteem in
which Alexander held the exalted Prince. Welcoming and embracing the nobleman, the King lost no
time in questioning him concerning Roxana and her
present whereabouts. Whereupon it appeared that

she had joined Artabazus the morning after her flight from Darius' camp, and doing so had besought his friendship and protection, both of which he gladly accorded her. It further appeared, however, to the King's great disappointment, that after remaining with him a short time and hearing nothing of Alexander, she departed with her attendants, Ossa and Orestes, lest somehow she again come into the power of Bessus. But whether she intended returning to Ecbatana or would attempt to reach Arimazes, Artabazus could not tell, as she gave no hint as to the direction of her flight lest it should reach Bessus' ears.

Thus the long chase had ended, not as the King hoped, but in the murder of Darius and the failure to rescue Roxana and afford her the protection of his arms. And as many days had now passed since Roxana left Artabazus' camp, it seemed futile to send out further scouting parties with the hope of coming upon some trace of her movements. This the King, however, did, selecting for the purpose the most adventurous of those about him, and mounting them on Nisæan horses, famous for their speed and endurance. But with no better result than in the case of the previous expeditions, no clew being obtained as to her safety or the direction of her flight.

Somewhat comforted because of the presence and guardianship of Ossa and Orestes, the King, hiding his grief, set about to build up his army anew, preparatory to the coming campaign in the little known region to which the combat was now to be transferred.

Much he was with Artabazus during this period, and questioning him concerning the conspiracy in Darius' camp, the nobleman explained that the Persian King had it in mind after passing the Caspian Gates to turn about and give battle to Alexander, thinking he was the stronger and so might regain all he had previously lost.

"It was a kingly thought," Alexander assented, pleased that Darius had conceived so resolute a purpose.

"However," Artabazus went on, "he determined in the event he was again defeated that he would strive no more, but forthwith submit himself to your will."

"What prevented his giving me battle?" Alexander asked, greatly concerned.

"The refusal of Bessus, his evil genius, to acquiesce in his purpose."

"Surely Bessus did not lack in courage!"

"No, it was his fear lest the King should succeed in the undertaking."

"Might defeat me?" the King exclaimed, mystified.

"Yes."

. "That, it would seem, should have led him to concur in the design."

"No, for had Darius proven victor it would have

frustrated Bessus' plan to gain possession of the East for himself."

"Then he already contemplated the treason that followed later?"

"Yes."

"For yourself, did you encourage the King to give me battle or did you seek to dissuade him?" Alexander laughed.

"I encouraged him with all my heart, believing that the weaklings having been weeded from our army we had a chance of defeating you; and Bessus, thinking the same, held back, knowing that if Darius were victor the latter would be again all-powerful. Much incensed," Artabazus continued, "the King threatened him with death, but Bessus, making humble submission, the thing was smoothed over and Darius' forgiveness accorded. However, surmising the traitor's purpose, I advised the King to entrust his safety to my command; which was loyal to him. And of this he thought well, but put it off, and Bessus, presently hearing of it or suspecting some such purpose, caused him to be suddenly arrested and hid away, as you know."

"What did you contemplate doing had the King put himself under your protection?" Alexander asked, highly entertained.

"I would have separated my command from that of Bessus, and in the wilds of the North have awaited a favourable opportunity to renew the war."

"A brave thought, Artabazus, but did the Princess explain to you the manner of her escape?" the King inquired, returning again to the subject of his beloved, seeming never to tire of asking questions concerning her.

"Yes, her conveyance was near that of the King and he, mindful of her safety, called out that he was under restraint and could no longer afford her protection."

"That was a kindly act and worthy of him," the King murmured, deeply affected.

"And her servants hearing the cry did not wait to ask her permission, but fell upon those who guarded her person, putting them to the sword, while Bessus, all oblivious, was looking to the imprisonment of the King," Artabazus explained, confirming the story of the Median prisoner.

"Brave men! Well have you redeemed my trust in you!" Alexander exclaimed, half aloud, his heart stirred at the recital.

With the gathering of the army about the King, there came to the camp one day, to the great delight of every one and all unexpected, Ossillia, whom Itanes had mourned as one dead to him. For he had refused to be comforted throughout the long and forced march from Ecbatana, his heart filled with distrust of Zapetes, and this notwithstanding the King's forgiveness of that unfortunate nobleman. Afterward, when the pursuit was over, he moped about the camp,

a shadow of his former self, meditating a return to
Ecbatana, contrary to the King's will, hoping thus
to rescue his beloved, as he had done in the plains of
Babylon. It was while he thus mourned, that a
detachment of Hypaspists arrived from Ecbatana,
making a great display of their bright armour and
glistening spears as they marched into camp amid the
cheers of the soldiers and the welcoming smiles of the
King.   And in their midst, as if in sacred guardianship, there towered a mighty dromedary topped with
a canopy of silk and nodding plumes, to the wonder
of all beholders, for these animals had not up to that
time been much used by the Macedonian soldiery.
Little interested in what was occurring, Itanes stood
idly watching the marching column, when a hand
suddenly parted the silken curtains of the howdah
and there appeared the eager face of Ossillia.   Seeing
her he drew back with a cry, thinking it an apparition,
so great was his bewilderment.   But she looking
this way and that, with anxious eyes and presently
espying him, pushed the curtain aside, and disregarding all ceremony or formal method of alighting, thrust
her body through the opening, and so shot to the
ground.   And this with such display of dainty lingerie
and Babylonian hose that the soldiers turned away
their heads as they laughed and cheered the coming
of their favourite.   Thinking not at all of the indeli-
cacy of her hurried descent, or the merriment it
caused, she ran with all speed to where her lover

RETURN OF OSSILLIA

stood, and throwing herself into his arms, cried out
with a sob:

"Oh, Itanes, tell me it's you and that you still
love me!"

Thus the youthful lovers were once more reunited,
and this amid the acclaim of the army, every man of
which looked upon the trusting love of the two children as a part of his own heritage. Clasping her in his
arms Itanes kissed her, too choked for words of welcome or affection, but presently taking account of
where they were he put his arm about her and led her
away to the quiet of his tent.

CHAPTER XXII

With the tragic death of Darius, the Persian King, we approach the close of our story of love and adventure, and with it that part of Alexander's warlike career which has appealed to the imagination of mankind for twenty centuries and more — the conquest of the World at an age when other men have been content to study the art of war, or at most, put forth their efforts in the attainment of unimportant things. For while he was afterward to carry his wars into India, the conquest of that country loses much compared with the splendour of his former achievements, and so does not excite the picturesque interest of his earlier deeds. In his own estimation, the glory of his conquests lost its glamour with the melancholy death of Darius, the great King. And while he was thereafter ready to hold out the olive branch to his enemies, he grew impatient that men should longer sacrifice their hapless followers in vain effort to withstand the irresistible course of events that his will foreshadowed.

Because of this he was angered by the warlike preparations of Bessus, but confident of victory, collected his forces anew, and traversing the lonely shores

316

and wooded slopes of the Caspian Sea, took his way to the east, which for a thousand miles bristled with the hostile arms of open or covert enemies.

But now at twenty-six, it was clear to those about him that the weight of the world and his private griefs had greatly aged the young Monarch. The establishment of governments among a strange and hostile people, the long and exhausting marches, the battles in which everything was hazarded, and finally the fatiguing campaigns attending the subjugation of innumerable predatory tribes, had told on his strength and temper. For it was noticed by his soldiers, and much commented upon by them, that the buoyant spirit that characterized him in other days was gone, and his eyes, once mild and companionable, were now cold and expressionless.

Melancholy and abstracted when not concerned with the affairs of the army or the interest of the State, he was no longer elated, it was apparent, by what he achieved or the hope of what he might accomplish in the future. Something was lacking, and this, as Hephestion knew, was the non-fulfillment of his dream, the imagery of his life, to which it was plain he no longer looked forward with his former confidence. With the conquest of Persia, bloody strife should have given place to peace, to gentle companionship, but instead a new and sordid war, cruel and void of glory and without advantage to mankind, lay before him. For from the barren steppes of the far north to the

Indus in the still more remote south, amid mountain fastnesses and desert borders, bloody battles and still more cruel marches plainly awaited him. Nothing then had really been accomplished, nothing had turned out as he had pictured, save the pomp and glory of war, and that at best had offered only momentary satisfaction.

Emperor of the World he was one apart, denied the solace of common men, the loving companionship of woman — the forgetfulness of self in the soft content of her gentle presence. That had been the secret part of his life, the better part that was to follow war and conquest. And was the vision after all to elude him? Was this expectation never to be realized, leaving only the storm and stress of conquest, the uplifting of the sword and spear?

As if in sympathy with the King's melancholy, something akin to disheartenment filled the minds of his followers, for looking forth on the wastes of Parthia they murmured and hung back, asking where it was all to end. But they only wanted to be urged by their glorious King, who always led and who bore so much more than his share of the burden. And so they again went forward when he asked it, but the disloyal saw in these mutterings of the soldiers an awakening of discontent with the King, such as they themselves had long felt. And mistaking the mood of the army, the enmity of the disaffected at last flamed forth in open treason to be extinguished in blood and dire reprisals by the angered King.

For it was amid the hardships and dangers of the far East that treason first openly flaunted itself, and strangely and unaccountably it found a place among the King's pages — fostered by the caviling Greek, Callisthenes. A conspiracy of youths to assassinate the King as he lay asleep, secure in the guardianship of their presence. This in forgetfulness of the treason of Philotas that had preceded it; Philotas the pampered one, who after years of half-concealed disloyalty had openly sought to bring about the assassination of the King. But detected in the crime had been put to death, his sympathizing father and the Prince Lyncestes sharing his fate.

But most grievous to the King's heart was the drunken truculence and open treason of Clitus, the friend and courageous soldier of Philip's time. Disloyalty of such menace that only punishment swift and terrible could still the poisonous distemper that threatened to spread throughout the army. But in the exercise of the kingly office that followed, for Clitus was put to death by the King's own hand, there was in truth much of primitive savagery — the rude awakening of the primeval instinct in man to save himself. And with it all the flaming rage that possesses the most tolerant men when they are at last convinced that their hard-earned renown excites only deadly hatred among those once their friends but less

fortunate in their lives — a jealous hatred that grows
with each day's passing and that nothing can ap-
pease. And so the sword fell with the swiftness and
terror of the lightning stroke, and this that trusting
loyalty might not be estopped or led astray in the
remote and unfriendly land in which the army found
itself.

Thus Clitus died, but punishment having been in-
flicted the King's heart melted and the slanderer
and seditious brawler was forgotten in remembrance
of the once loyal soldier. For the pathos of Clitus'
death appealed to the King more strongly than any
one else, and retiring to the seclusion of his tent the
unhappy Monarch, denying himself to all, mourned
for days in bitter anguish the loss of the friend of other
and happier years. But when the soldiers in their
rage would have cast the traitor's body to the dogs,
denying it sepulchre, the King, intervening in his
sorrow, gave the dead such honourable burial as
he would have received in the days of his greatest
strength and glory.

In the surprise and horror of these unexpected and
tragic happenings, however, the King's belief that the
loyalty of those about him was as the truth of the
Gods was forever swept away. And coming, as they
did, amid the new war and the solitude of the far-off
country, they disheartened Hephestion — the other
and gentler soul of Alexander — so that when news
was brought that the provinces bordering upon

India had been stirred into unexpected revolt by Bessus' far-reaching intrigues, he sought the King, exclaiming:

"What is to be the end, Alexander? Have the Deities condemned you to eternal strife? That being in truth the God of War you shall forever feed its gaping jaws, denied the solace of that love which we dreamed the ending of all ruder ambitions? Can it be," he went on with melancholy frankness, for they were as brothers in all things, "that the Gods, having given you so much, will forever deny you this greater favour?"

"The Gods concern themselves not at all with the loves of men, Hephestion," the King censured, half angrily; "or if they deny me the solace of other men, I will pursue the favour with such undying energy that they must at last smile approval."

"Is this vision of your life something real, or is it but a phantasy of the mind, forever to delude you, having no reality in fact?" Hephestion questioned.

"If a dream it is none the less real, not the less true, that the future must treasure the being of whom I have dreamed," the King confidently affirmed.

"And what if after all the expectation fail you?"

"Then life will have been robbed of its solace, for the ambition born in me to conquer the world was but a part, and long ere Cheronea, as you know, I nourished that other and gentler hope, to be loved at last by her whom my ardent fancy portrayed."

"And the hope still holds you as in your youth?"

"Yes, and with greater longing than before, Hephestion, as the barrenness of all other things is made apparent."

"And will this being abide in truth the passing years, the tempest of war that seems to have no end?"

"I know not, but if it prove otherwise then will the hidden desire of my life be denied me."

"To me this vision of entrancing love has lost all semblance of reality; this belief in an ideal being having her home upon the farther confines of Persia, whose possession would follow conquest and give solace to a heart which glory had tarnished by a too great fulfillment! And the end being reached, what if this vision that has always evaded us, and now evades us, proves to be only an illusion of our youth?" Hephestion asked, with a look of sympathetic interest.

"Then the glory which I craved and have found as a man is a valueless thing," the King sighed.

"But this idealized woman you believe will surely await you?"

"Yes — if she still lives," he answered, conjuring up a vision of Roxana, a fugitive and wanderer on the face of the earth. "Yes, this love which you question has shown such resource of life that I am only concerned as to the interval that must elapse ere its final fulfillment if, happily, she survives the perils that surround her," the King concluded, but without animation.

"And these years of waiting, of endless strife, have no way abated the romantic desires of your youth?"

"No, the unavailing years, void of all save glory, have clothed the dreams of youth with a more eager desire, born of the knowledge that in their fulfillment all real happiness in life is centred."

"With its consummation, this dream of love so long concealed and so little suspected, men must at last believe in."

"Why should they have doubted its existence, I being a man, like themselves?"

"Because thy love, so often tempted to assert itself, has been as if it did not exist," Hephestion answered simply.

"Tempted?"

"Yes, has not the witchery of woman in every alluring form and in every land sought to ensnare you, while you, most tempted of us all, have alone escaped untouched?" the other confessed.

"You always had a light opinion of woman, Hephestion, distrusting alike her acts of grace and gentle inclination, but of a truth I have not been tempted, for to be tempted one must first desire," Alexander said.

"What I say is not in disparagement of women, for my estimate of them has ever been heightened by their great desire to enlist your favour."

"And that they have always had."

"But not one your love."

"Not one, say you?"

"Well not one save her, the idealized being of your life."

"What could I wish beside? Only idlers and debauchees have time to treasure more than one, Hephestion."

Remembering the questionable morals of the Macedonian officers and the scandals of their lives, Hephestion did not pursue the subject further, but reverting to the strife in the far East, said:

"What will be the outcome should you lose in this new and remote war?"

"I will not lose," the King cried, "but, pursuing these new enemies will overcome them as I have the armies of Darius. And first, and of greatest urgency, I will put down the uprising in the south, and that accomplished, will turn to the north, subduing as I go all who are disregardful of their loyalty to Persia's rightful King."

And so it was determined, and as a fitting prelude to the coming campaign, the King caused all his personal belongings to be taken from his tent into the open square of the camp where, amid the sound of flute and fife, and as if in celebration of a festival, he himself applied the torch to the piled up mass. Watching the spectacle, astonished, the soldiers after a while appreciating the suggestion and the urgency that called it forth, followed the example of the King amid cheers and laughter, as if it were a holiday. In this way the army was again placed on a war-footing and fitted for the campaign before it, in which vast distances were to be traversed and desperate marches encountered wherein men would sink down in despair, and only the strong survive.

When everything had been arranged and the army reorganized, it continued its way across the Parthian desert, overcoming the rebellious chiefs in its rapid progress. Afterward turning to the south it continued its triumphant march for a thousand miles, until not an enemy that Bessus had conjured into life in that remote region remained to dispute the King's will. Then turning to the north in search of the arch rebel, winter found the army encamped in a sheltered valley protected by the southern slopes of the Paropamisadæ — the mighty range we know as the Caucasus. Here for the moment, the centre of the political world, Alexander established his court. And here it was with the approach of spring, while the King was preparing for his campaign in the north, that there came one night to his tent — and to his great surprise and alarm — Ossa in rags, disguised as a shepherd of the plains. Welcoming him, Alexander exclaimed, as he viewed the other's sordid garments:

"What sufferings and humiliations, oh Prince, hast thou been called upon to endure in my behalf!"

"Not one, oh King, but if I had 't is only fit, for thou didst make life a happiness to me by thy kindness and generosity," Ossa answered, referring to his former life in Macedonia.

Thus they met, and the King, recognizing no distinction of rank, put his arm about the other and led him into his tent, where he listened to the startling news concerning happenings at Arimazes. For it appeared that Roxana, with her attendants, Ossa and Orestes, after many months' wandering and many wonderful adventures had at last reached the great fortress in safety! Questioning Ossa further as to events at Arimazes, it appeared that Bessus had caused it to be proclaimed that Alexander, tiring of the war in the northeast, had given up the conquest of the hardy provinces to find a more fruitful field of action in far-off India. Because of this, and the belief that it was true, the King's friends were in deep distress, and among them Oxyartes who could no longer trust the loyalty of his followers as in former days. Already an uprising had been attempted within the fortress, which he had suppressed with difficulty. And now as a further incentive to the garrison to abandon its lord, Bessus had established a close investment of the great rock, hoping for a favourable opportunity to gain possession of the height. It was amid these perils that Roxana had secretly dispatched Ossa to Alexander to acquaint him with the situation and to crave his immediate aid.

What further passed in the King's tent no one knew, but ere the dawn Ossa departed as silently and

SURMOUNTING THE CAUCASUS

mysteriously as he had come. With the rising of the sun, however, and in quick response to Roxana's summons, the shrill call of a bugle sounded from the portico of the King's tent, giving notice to the camp that orders to march would immediately follow. And thus it was, for on the succeeding morning the army set out on its way to the north, the crossing of the lofty mountain seemingly easy of attainment because of the genial warmth of the early spring. But midway of the height and without warning the rugged mountain was swept by a furious hurricane which lasted many days, clogging the rude paths and filling the passes with snow and ice. Harassed and delayed, the army made little progress, so that ere the summit of the great range was reached the provisons were exhausted and the wearied soldiers compelled to subsist on the flesh of their half starved animals and the roots of the stunted shrubs they found amid the rocks. In consequence of this and the bitter cold, great numbers became crazed, or in despair of life, hurled themselves from the dizzy cliffs; others blinded by the snow wandered away and were lost in the cañons and crevasses of the mountain, while still greater numbers perished from weakness and hunger or were frozen where they lay asleep, wood with which to build fires being unobtainable.

It was amid such hardships, the horror of which was added to by frequent and destructive avalanches of snow and ice, that the soldiers slowly surmounted the storm-swept height.   And to add to their dejection, on reaching the plain beyond they found it devastated by Bessus' troops and so devoid of shelter or food.   Encouraging the drooping spirits of his followers, the King, who marched among his men, sharing the hardships of a common soldier, led them at last to a more hospitable land, where they were rested and refreshed.

Fretting at the delay, so destructive to his plans, the King waited until the army had regained its strength, when he again set out in pursuit of the regicide Bessus. But that wily Prince, apprehensive of the result, did not wait his approach, but fled northward to a more secure region beyond the Oxus.   In the pursuit that followed, and as if the very presence of the traitorous Persian brought disaster to Alexander, many soldiers lost their lives in crossing the waterless desert that lay to the south of the great river beyond which Bessus had sought safety.

For in the march across this desolate waste, into which the King had been entrapped by treacherous guides, great numbers of his followers perished from thirst and the intolerable heat.   And if any survived the terrible ordeal it was due to the action of the heroic King and the courage of the seemingly helpless Ossillia. ᐧ For this favourite of the soldiers had continued with the army that she might be near Itanes, and in the present peril, fearing for his life, she collected the women of the camp, who were mounted on dromedaries, and arming them with javelins after the manner of the Amazons of the North, led them, with all speed to the edge of the desert. There they found the King intent upon the rescue of his soldiers, and aided and encouraged by him they filled the water-skins they had brought, and mounting their dromedaries returned in all haste to the perishing army. In remembrance of this the soldiers presented their rescuers with girdles of golden darics, adding a crown of beaten gold to that of Ossillia. And this not being thought sufficient, it was decreed that her howdah should thereafter bear the device of an eagle in place of the dove that had previously decorated it!

Terrified at the relentless pursuit of the King in crossing the apparently impassable mountain and the wastes that followed, the confederates of Bessus, deeming it impossible to escape Alexander's vengeance, threw down their arms and yielded up their leader to the pursuing King. And now in punishment of his crimes it fell to Bessus' unhappy lot to reap in his own person, and as a warning to all Persians, the barbarous cruelties that so many Greeks had suffered at the hands of his countrymen for two hundred years. For so it was decreed, after which the cruel Prince was sent in chains to Ecbatana, where he was put to death before all the world as a punishment for the murder of his sovereign.

Peace being at last seemingly attained, Alexander

set out for Arimazes, word having reached him that
the investing army still threatened the lofty fortress.
But the conspiring nobles of the disaffected provinces,
no way intimidated by the fall of Bessus, and relying
upon the Scythian hordes of the North to aid them,
made haste to dispatch messages of insult and open
defiance to the conquering King. As it was impossible
to leave these formidable enemies in his rear, Alexander,
foregoing his present purpose, turned his arms against
the new array, attacking and dispersing one by one
the armies organized to oppose him. Thus he at
last reached the extreme northern border of Persia,
and not waiting the movements of his enemies crossed
the Jaxartes upon floats and rafts and, having effected
a landing attacked with savage fury the Scythian
army beyond, driving it broken and disheartened into
the wastes of Tartary, from whence it came. Aflame
with battle, the King recrossed the great river and
hastened to invade the country of the Massagetæ,
(the inhospitable and barbarous land where Cyrus the
Great had met his death) and attacking the hordes of
the desert, who meditated the invasion of Persia, put
them to flight as he had their savage neighbours to
the East.

Now at last there was an end to the long conflict
and the wearied King sought permanent peace by
inviting the princes and nobles of the conquered
provinces to meet and form a government that would
be acceptable to them. But the disaffected leaders,

no way appeased, caused it to be proclaimed throughout the country that the King's only purpose in calling the meeting was to gain possession of their persons that he might put them to death! And this being credited by the half-barbarous inhabitants, rebellion instantly sprang to life afresh in every part of the territory, rendering ineffective all that Alexander had hitherto accomplished. Furious with rage, and despairing of all gentle measures, the King marched into the rebellious country, and traversing its broad extent swept it from end to end with fire and sword, no one being spared who in any way opposed his will. Thus at last amid flaming cities and sanguinary battles the turbulent and half-savage provinces of the far East were stilled and Persia was once more a peaceful and united country.

CHAPTER XXIII

THE ROCK OF ARIMAZES

It was amid the distressing scenes related in the last chapter that the fierce struggle in the eastern provinces came to an end. With it, however, word reached the King, as if peace were to be forever denied him, that the disloyal among the garrison at Arimazes, taking advantage of the recent outbreak, had risen in revolt and made themselves masters of the great fortress. But of the fate of Roxana and Oxyartes not a word was vouchsafed. Deeply stirred and enraged that any one in this hour of victory should invite his displeasure by so untoward an act, the King waited not for the warmth of spring, but set out at once on the long and difficult march. And it was as if the Gods smiled upon him, for the day was one of resplendent beauty, but soon, as in the Caucasus, fierce storms arose in the mountain-topped country, filling the valleys and passes with rushing torrents, and afterward with avalanches of snow and ice. In this emergency he abandoned his horses and equipages to the crippled and frostbitten soldiers and went forward on foot, forcing the advance with such of his troops as were able to withstand the hardships of the terrible march.

On the twentieth day, after incredible hardships, the great fortress came into view, but the King, ignorant of the approach, marched with the more backward of his soldiers, the better to hasten their progress. And it was not until word was brought him that the advance had reached the rock, and on its coming had been assailed with savage cries and the flight of arrows, that he knew that the end was reached. Mounting a horse he hastened to the front, and reaching the fortress sounded a parley. But when he demanded that the rock be given up, offering pardon and free exit to all who desired it, the herald responded that the fortress was assailable only by winged soldiers and to no others would it yield. And when the King sought to prolong the conference in order to come to a peaceable accommodation, his words were drowned in the cries and imprecations that assailed him from the towering fortress.

While he waited, angry and irresolute, the Princess Roxana, apprised of his presence, and evading the revolting soldiers in the confusion that existed, suddenly appeared on the walls waving him welcome from the lofty height. Looking up, entranced by the presence of her he had so long sought, the King cried out in rapture, as one enthralled:

"Is it a vision vouchsafed by the Gods, Hephestion, a voiceless spirit of the air, or she whom I have so long sought?"

" 'T is Roxana, my sister, oh King!" Itanes cried

with boyish excitement, attracted by Alexander's fixed gaze, but even as he spoke, the figure vanished as suddenly as it came, giving place to a body of armed men.

"The Gods be thanked that no harm befell her in the garrison's revolt," Alexander murmured, his face uplifted, expectant of her return.

"No, nor need such thing be feared," Hephestion mildly affirmed.

"Why do you say that, as if you knew?" Itanes cried in heat, his fears for his sister's safety excited by the manifest danger that surrounded her.

"She is the spirit of the place, and well the rebels know that should harm befall her, not one would be spared once the fortress is re-taken," Hephestion confidently responded.

"I know nothing about spirits, only that she is surrounded by murderers and traitors," Itanes fretted, no way appeased.

The King, hearing and not hearing, sat his horse, scanning with angry glance the lofty promontory from which the rebellious garrison so openly defied him.

This mighty rock, with which history has made us familiar, was ages ago shattered by mountain rains and winter frosts, all trace of its presence being lost in the wilds of Turkestan. Three hundred feet in height, it was approachable only by a narrow path hewn in the solid rock that wound about its rugged side. Looming behind the fortress a sheer precipice arose to a still loftier mountain that looked down upon it like a watchful sentinel. To this overlooking height the King presently directed his gaze, and after long and careful scrutiny set out at a gallop to make a circuit of the double-capped mountain, hoping to find a weak spot by which the rock might be successfully assailed. On his way he encountered the disconsolate soldiers of Oxyartes, who had been expelled from the fortress by the revolting troops, and now lay encamped at the foot of the guarded path that led to the summit above. These he interrogated, but one and all declared that the rock was unassailable, and that it could only be taken by winged soldiers, as the rebels had proclaimed. Satisfied that the fortress could not be assailed in front, the King determined to force an ascent of the less precipitous mountain in the rear, hoping to gain an advantage, notwithstanding the perpendicular cliff that intervened between the greater and lesser height. Accordingly on his return to the army, he caused proclamation to be made inviting all who had knowledge of mountain climbing to come forward and attempt the difficult ascent. In reward of their efforts he offered twelve talents to him who should first reach the summit of the overlooking mountain, and to others who followed lesser sums in proportion. Immediately upon this becoming known, there was great commotion throughout the army — for each prize was a fortune in itself — and ere the day closed three hundred men came forward, eager to make the attempt. When they had assembled, the King addressed them, saying:

"Comrades, those who have disloyally possessed themselves of the mighty fortress will yield only to winged soldiers! 'T is a barbarous conceit but fits well with the fortress' unassailable walls. But if we may not storm the height with winged soldiers, you may show them the front of brave men from yonder overlooking mountain, and that with the rising of to-morrow's sun. But that their surprise may be complete, let the ascent of the mountain be delayed till darkness intervenes. Meanwhile," he went on, turning to Hephestion, "the better to allay the suspicions of the garrison, let the army withdraw from before the fortress and fix its camp in yonder valley," indicating a spot some distance away. Then thanking those who were to make the dangerous ascent, and bidding them be of courageous heart, he dismissed them that they might rest and refresh themselves until the hour for making the attempt.

Thus it was arranged, and at the appointed time, amidst a violent storm of wind and rain, the three hundred men supplied with tent-pegs and ropes, set out on their dangerous mission. And being skilled in such adventure, and taking advantage of the crevices and inequalities of the surface, or where there was no such advantage driving their iron pegs deep into the frozen ground or solid ice, the summit was

at last reached. But in the attempt many becoming
confused or benumbed with cold, or meeting impassable barriers and unable to retrace their steps,
lost their foothold and were precipitated to the
depths below. Thus many perished, but those who
survived, reaching the summit as the sun arose,
ranged themselves on the edge of the frowning precipice that looked down on the fortress below, and
here, in derision, raised and lowered the sleeves of
their tunics as if they were indeed winged men.

Meanwhile, and unknown to the waiting army,
most surprising things had happened in the great
fortress, the possession of which the King sought by
such hazardous means. For it appeared that while
the soldiers loyal to Oxyartes had been previously
overcome and expelled from the fortress by those
unfriendly to him, other residents of the rock were not
disturbed; and among these were Ossa and Orestes, the
supposed half-witted attendants of Roxana. These
courageous adherents, when darkness set in, Roxana
summoned to her presence in the thatched hut of
Zapetes, where she had sought refuge after the be-
trayal of the rock, bidding them come clad in iron as
if intent upon some desperate enterprise. When
they had responded to her call she addressed them,
and this sometimes with elation, but more often with
sighs and tears, so that those who listened were wound
up to the greatest possible pitch of excitement when
she had finished.

"The army of our lord, the King," she sorrowed, "refused admission to the rock, rests upon its arms before the fortress after expending its strength in traversing the mountain passes filled with snow and ice. Where he should have found welcome, the conquering King, lord of all Persia, finds the gates of the fortress closed, while we, his friends, look on in helpless bewilderment. And all this vain display of the rebellious soldiery in foolish bravado, for what the exalted King wills no one can deny, for so it has been and so it always will be. But I would not see these misguided creatures who have denied my father and taken possession of the rock slaughtered like cattle or dealt with harshly though they be arrant rebels. For they are not so because of any malice, but from being misled and the desire born in every hill-man to be free, as in the days of the tribal kings. Nor would I have the King come to woo me in armour amid the note of war with blood upon his sword and an army embittered by denial! But weaponless, with a wreath about his brow and clad in shimmering silk as befits a lover intent upon gaining the favour of his mistress. Thus it should be, and so I have dreamed and planned, until this foolish revolt springing up I am denied the happiness of welcoming him as I had thought. But somehow, gentle friends, the petty arms of the revolting soldiery must be overcome, and this without the King's help. For I would have him mount to the castle gate smiling and saluting,

his horse a-prancing and all the people shouting welcome from the battlements with my father there to
throw wide the portals in greeting, as becomes a
loyal subject.   That is the way it should be, and it is
for this that I have summoned you, that taking
advantage of the King's presence and the fear it
excites we may accomplish what I have declared —
and this ere to-morrow's dawn.   For the night is one
to favour our enterprise and the secrecy with which it
must be conducted, the Gods as if to favour us, having
sent a furious storm to hide our purpose in its tumultu-
ous oubtursts," she proclaimed, her voice lost for the
moment in the shrieking of the wind and the crash of
thunder that echoed and re-echoed from the neighbouring mountains.   "And the King," she continued,
when she could again make herself heard, "as if foreseeing our efforts, has drawn off his forces so that the
rebels no longer fearing immediate assault are less
watchful than they otherwise would be.   Everything
thus favours the attempt, but I, being a woman, can
do nothing and so come to you for advice and aid, you
who are born to bold exploits and familiar with the
craft and subterfuge of war's alarms and quick sur-
prises," she concluded, in tears, her eyes fixed on the
countenances of those who listened as if she must there
find favourable response to what she proposed.   But
when each, reluctant to speak, waited upon the other,
and the night was advancing without anything being
done, she turned impatiently to Ossa, exclaiming:

"Surely, you, whom the King loves and trusts and to whom danger is as an inheritance, surely you can devise some plan by which we may regain possession of the fortress in welcome of our lord."

But when he would have answered, Ossillia, who had returned to the fortress with her father some time before, and now sat moping in the corner, sprang up, stammering and blushing:

"I have a plan, please you, mistress, if you will listen to me."

"You, Ossillia?" Roxana frowned, impatient at the interruption.

"Yes, and one that cannot fail!" the other cried, coming forward.

"Tell me what it is," Roxana acquiesced, humouring her, thinking it the quicker way.

"It is to lower me from the wall," the other said, excitedly.

"For what purpose?" the Princess asked, surprised.

"That Itanes being advised of our forlorn state, may lead a body of soldiers to the rescue, as he did in the plains of Babylon," Ossillia explained, glancing with some alarm at her father.

"That the King will himself assuredly do if our efforts fail," Roxana smiled, indulgently, stroking the dimpled face of her brother's young and trusting wife.

"And I would then be with my love — and could tell them why the gate is shut — a thing that must seem strange to the King," Ossillia went on.

"Would you not fear to be lowered from so great a height?" Ossa questioned, eying Ossillia as if seeing in her proposal an object to be attained, far different from what she thought.

"What is there to fear — if the thong be stout and you hold tight?" she laughed.

"What she plans, my mistress, however absurd it may appear to you, fits in with a purpose I have had in mind," Ossa smiled, turning to the Princess.

"Go on — tell me what it is!" Roxana exclaimed, her face lighting up as if any project conceived by this brave man must of necessity succeed.

"It is to apprise our friends without in the way she suggests, and with their aid regain possession of the fortress ere the night passes."

"But the gate — the key to the rock?"

"That we will ourselves secure, and through its possession and the help of our friends, overcome those who hold the fortress and the guarded path."

"What you propose is absurd, a thing impossible, Ossa," Zapetes, who had in years past been entrusted with the guardianship of the gate and knew its strength when defended by resolute men, impatiently interposed.

"The King, our master, says nothing is impossible to resourceful and resolute men," Ossa mildly rebuked, "and now while we talk nothing can be more certain," he went on, confidently, "than that he is himself planning some way of taking the rock, however impossible it may seem to others."

"And so striving will succeed, as he does in every-thing," Roxana murmured, "but in this we must fore-stall him, good friends, that he may come in honour and as a welcome guest."

"That we may accomplish by opening the gate and clearing the narrow path, but we are too weak except by the aid of our friends without to overcome the garrison or anyway impede its defence of the fortress," Ossa explained.

"And you can effect both?" Roxana questioned, resting her hand in confidence on the other's arm.

"Yes, but should we fail nothing will have been lost of advantage to the King."

"Nothing save your life and that of your compan-ions! No, no, Ossa, I will not consent to such sacri-fice after so many acts of devoted service," Roxana cried, breaking down.

"They have been services lovingly rendered, oh Princess," Orestes interposed, blushing, speaking now for the first time.

"And therefore the more precious to me," Roxana responded impulsively, her eyes wet with tears.

"No danger is too great in the service of our beloved King, or those he treasures," Ossa affirmed, simply, as if it could not be doubted.

"You seem to think highly of the King," Zapetes interrupted, turning to Ossa, who had always been more or less of an enigma to the denizens of Arimazes.

"And well I may, Zapetes, for to him I owe my life — and honour, and my beloved wife," the other cried, aroused, recalling the Vale of Tempe and what followed.

"And well have you repaid the service," Roxana exclaimed, lifting Ossa's hand to her lips.

"But about lowering me from the wall — that seems to be forgotten?" Ossillia here interposed, with mild impatience.

"Were you serious in what you said concerning that?" Roxana questioned, turning to Ossa.

"Yes, in this that the gate gained, our friends must come to our aid on the instant, for we cannot alone hold possession assailed by the garrison from within, as we shall be."

"And you would use her to forewarn them?" Roxana questioned, her face aglow.

"Yes, there being no other way."

"And I would risk it hanging by a thread to be the sooner with my love," Ossillia cried, with flaming cheeks.

"And you have no fear?"

"What is there to fear when bundles are lowered that way every hour of the day. Let's play I'm a bundle or a bucket of mortar if that will make it seem the easier," she added, with whimsical humour.

"Cease your foolish babbling, child, you talk as

one bereft of her senses," Zapetes, her father, reprimanded with scared face, frightened lest some accident should befall her in the attempt.

"I care not how foolish it may be; or if you refuse and Itanes be long in coming," she sobbed, "I'll throw myself from the wall."

"Peace, child, you shall soon see him," Roxana soothed — "as I hope soon to see the King, Iskander, my lord," she murmured under her breath.

"Come, come, we lose time if anything is to be attempted! Out with your plan, Ossa, ere the night's gone!" Zapetes demanded impatiently, ill at ease.

Whereupon Ossa, without further interruption, explained how he hoped to gain possession of the gate and the path leading to the fortress.

"But why may not my father's soldiers, encamped at the foot of the pass, aid you rather than those of the King?" Roxana suggested, when Ossa's plan, by which he proposed to call on the King for help, had been explained.

"They may if you would have it so," Ossa assented.

"Yes, that it may not be said by the ill-natured that the garrison denied the King entrance to the castle or received him otherwise than with favour."

"And so it shall be," Ossa smiled, pleased at the high spirit of the Princess, usually so gentle and yielding.

Thus the recapture of the fortress was planned by the little group of determined spirits, and everything connected with the hazardous enterprise having been agreed upon no time was lost in carrying it into execution.

And first of all Ossillia, eagerly lending herself to the plot, was lowered to the valley below. And in this there was no difficulty, as the house of Zapetes rested against the wall where he had caused it to be placed years before when the security of the fortress-gate was entrusted to his care. When this had been accomplished, and sufficient time had elapsed for her to warn the soldiers of Oxyartes encamped at the foot of the path, Ossa and his companions stole from the hut and hid themselves in the shadow of the guard-house, a massive stone structure that enclosed the gate-way of the fortress. When they had thus concealed themselves and as prearranged, the hut which they had just left suddenly burst into flames, and simultaneously the slaves and attendants emerged from the burning building, screaming with fright and calling for help at the top of their voices. Hearing the outcry the soldiers in the guard-house, surprised and alarmed, rushed forth, thinking the hut had been struck by lightning. And the cries continuing and the flames increasing in violence, they one and all hurried without thought to the rescue of the imperilled occupants of the isolated building.

When in this way the guard-house had been left unprotected, Ossa and his companions emerging from their hiding-place were able to secure possession of the coveted structure without striking a blow. Barricading the entrance, Ossa threw open the door that shut off the path without, and bidding his companions defend what they had gained, he plunged down the rock-cut road, hoping to surprise the guard stationed midway of the ascent. And in this he was completely successful, for the soldiers not expecting to be assailed from above, and indeed thinking little of attack from any direction because of the storm, were huddled in a mass beneath the overhanging cliff. Reaching the platform hewn out of the solid rock on which the guard were stationed, Ossa rushed upon them sword in hand with furious outcry, and the attack being unexpected and coming from above, the bewildered group, thrown into confusion, made at first no defence whatever. However, quickly recovering themselves, those who were unharmed charged Ossa in a mass, driving him back to the narrow path by which he had descended. Here, where only one man could attack him at a time, he held his ground, and having the advantage of position quickly overcame the assailant in advance, hurling him headlong from the height.

Meanwhile loud and angry cries from above apprised him that an attempt was being made by the garrison to regain possession of the protecting guard-house. In this situation, uncertain of the outcome, he knew not whether to maintain his ground or turn back to the assistance of his companions. But as the latter course would be without avail in the accomplishment of the object on which they had set out unless the path was cleared, he determined to sacrifice his life if need be in attaining this necessary purpose. Springing forward, therefore, with a cry of fury he cut down the soldiers in his front, and awaiting the one who followed, thrust him through the body with his sword. Unable to withdraw his weapon on the instant, he sprang upon the guard that followed and grappling him about the body hurled him from the precipice, the despairing cry of the doomed man resounding high above the roar of the storm. Grasping the spear the soldier let fall, he charged afresh, his stalwart form looming in the uncertain light like some malignant spirit of the night. In this situation, and while those who defended the pass knew not why nor by whom they were assailed, Oxyartes' soldiers suddenly emerged from below and attacked the guard from the rear, at which, overwhelmed and panic-stricken, they threw down their weapons and begged for mercy.

The path being thus freed, Ossa calling to Oxyartes' men to follow quickly, mounted to the guard-house, where he found Orestes and Zapetes in deadly conflict with the soldiers of the garrison who had meanwhile burst open the door and so gained entrance to the building. Joining his companions in the murderous fray, and being presently reinforced by Oxyartes' followers, the rebels were finally put to rout, Ossa

and his party following to the open streets of the
fortress. Here, raising the fierce war-cry of Macedonia, they charged the surprised garrison with sword
and spear, upon which the bewildered rebels, believing
the army of the King had found entrance to the
fortress, threw down their arms and sought safety in
flight. In this way and as planned, Arimazes was
retaken, and Oxyartes, who had been held a prisoner
in the citadel, was instantly reinstated as its governour.

Thus it came about that when the sun arose on the
succeeding morning and Alexander's soldiers appeared
on the summit of the overhanging mountain,¯ as
already related, Roxana was able to wave the King
welcome and submission from the lofty wall of the
great rock. Answering her signal, the overjoyed King
spurred his horse at a gallop up the narrow path, and
entering the fortress hastened to the Princess, who
awaited him beside the moss-grown wall where she
had passed so many sorrowful hours in expectation
of his coming.

Thus the young King at last came a-wooing, and
presently, and as it should be, there were great doings
in and about the fortress; feasts and gorgeous spectacles following each other in quick succession interspersed with games and friendly bouts at arms.
Unexampled in the history of men were the honours
and largesses of gold showered upon his followers
by the happy King, no one being overlooked in the
generous favours. And when this had continued

many days there was wondering throughout the camp,
but he, from whom all these things came was as if
lost to the world, for no one could so much as catch
a glimpse of his person or knowledge of his whereabouts. But one day when expectation had grown
to uneasiness because of his prolonged absence, he
came forth on horseback clad in silk garments, with
nodding plumes, and by his side, on a Nisæan steed,
the Princess Roxana. Seeing them the soldiers stared
open-mouthed, looking each other in the face, for the
King had never been known to do such a thing before.
But when on the next day and the days that followed
he continued to ride forth, and with him always the
same entrancing being; and when it was seen that he
rode not as the King, but as a Bactrian Prince, paying
no heed to the camp, his eyes intent upon her beside
him, then the soldiers understood and cheered till
their lungs were hoarse. And still he did not look
up, but she, all beauty and gentleness, bowed to the
right and left, always smiling and often with open
laughter, supremely happy, it was apparent, in the
possession of her love.

Such was the King's romance as the soldiers and
the world knew it, and then the meaning of the remarkable things that had gone before, the feastings
and the honours, were clear as the sun at noonday.
But there needed no other incentive to the rejoicing
than the knowledge that the King was in love and
had at last found a Queen in this far-off fortress. And

because of it, there was no longer word or thought of war or conquest, nothing indeed but laughter and feasting and the King's wooing.

Thus the dream of the King came true at last: he to find a contentment that had been denied him, and she happiness unutterable in his single and devoted love. For so it was to be as the years passed, each day adding to his admiration and love, and she finding something new to treasure in the chivalrous character of the mighty King.

Following the days and nights of revelry and rejoicing, a great festival was given by Oxyartes on the solemnization of Roxana's marriage with Alexander. On that eventful night the great rock and the majestic mountain high above were aflame with light, and as the King and Queen slowly made their way among those who feasted, the soldiers lifting high their tankards cried with one voice:

"Long live Alexander the King, King of Kings!"

"Long live Roxana, Queen of all the World!"

Following the King and Queen amid wild huzzas there marched the heroes of the fortress, now princes of the realm, Ossa and his brave companions. And in immediate and loving attendance upon the Queen, and forming a part of the regal court, came the King's friends of other days, Theba and the Princess Eurydice, and with them their devoted and loving husbands. In a group near the royal couple, and in conspicuous honour, happy in the King's happiness, were his companions in arms, Hephestion and the others, including his trusted physicians, Jaron and Philip.

Mingling obscurely with the throng of exalted officers and Persian nobles, unnoticed by all, with no thought of rank or precedence, came Itanes and Ossillia, their arms about each other, laughing and whispering, oblivious of everything, seeing and hearing nothing. And that there might be no friend of the King missing on that eventful night, Lysimachus, now old and feeble, was borne forward in an open chair, bowing and saluting the throng as if the festival were in his honour.

Thus the romance of Alexander's life was fulfilled through his marriage with the gentle Roxana, the daughter of the Bactrian noble, displaying in the act the chivalrous character of the great conqueror — the avowal before the world that the all-sufficient dower of woman is the woman herself.

HISTORICAL NOTES

BEING AN ACCOUNT OF THE LIFE OF ALEXANDER
THE GREAT FROM THE TIME OF LEAVING
MACEDONIA FOR THE CONQUEST OF
PERSIA UP TO THE TIME
OF HIS DEATH

Having subdued the barbarous nations to the north, east, and
west of Macedonia, and again quieted Greece, Alexander set out
from Pella in April, 334 B. C. on the long-contemplated invasion
of Persia. His march to Sestos, on the western shore of the
Hellespont, a distance of three hundred and fifty miles, occupied
twenty days, his fleet of one hundred and sixty triremes following
along the shore. Reaching the Hellespont, he gave orders for
the transfer of the troops to Abydos, on the Asiatic shore, after
which he set sail for Ancient Troy. There he offered up sacrifices and libations to Achilles, his ancestor, and made propitia-
tory gifts to the manes of Priam, the murdered Trojan King —
dead a thousand years — lest somehow his august shade should
bring to naught the contemplated conquest of Persia. Strange
contrast of superstitious belief and common-sense resolve. But
in this Alexander was not more strange than in other things.
A poet and dreamer, he was yet a man of definite purpose; an
idealist, yet a man of practical accomplishments; amiable and
complaisant, yet of iron will; an enlightened scholar, yet a bigot
in his religious observances. For in this last respect the Christian
of our day believes not more devoutly in the ethics of his faith
nor observes its precepts more regardfully than did Alexander
accord the belief of pagan Greece. He was fond of quoting the
sayings of one of the philosophers, that all men were governed
by God, because in everything that which is chief is divine. It
was a philosophic saying of his that God was the common Father
of all, but more particularly the best of men. A resolute foe,
terrible in battle, he was generous and forgiving beyond belief.
A youth in years, yet with wisdom and accomplished purposes

355

never surpassed in the world's history — a King, born to rule, who often simulated passion, but rarely felt its force. In such mood he put to death Clitus, whose traitorous utterances threatened the discipline of the army and menaced the Macedonian power in Persia, by destroying respect for the kingly office — all-important to the authority and personal safety of an Oriental Monarch.

War was Alexander's natural element, the turmoil of battle his delight, peace but a preparation for war — the end, domination of all the world. Yet withal, he was in heart, a lover of men. The purpose of his conquest aside from the gratification of his ambition was to instill neighbourly relations in place of aversion and hatred. To make men live in peace with each other regardless of their nationality or previous habits of life. Thus he not only conquered Persia, always at enmity with Greece, but put down with an iron hand the murderous tribes that infested the mountains and waste regions of the kingdom, preying on the peaceable communities and making both life and property insecure. It resulted from his enterprise and moderation that at the time of his death security everywhere prevailed throughout the Empire, something never known before. These conditions he would have made permanent, but, dying at thirty-three, time was not permitted him in which to cement the power of the kingly office and make secure the beneficent fruits that followed his conquests.

---

334 B. C.

Having accomplished the object of his religious pilgrimage to Ancient Troy, Alexander lost no time in rejoining his army, which had meanwhile been transferred to the eastern shore of the Hellespont. Serious, if not successful, opposition to the crossing might have been offered by the Persians as their fleet greatly outnumbered that of the Macedonians, and was supported, moreover, by an army of one hundred thousand men. Their failure to do this seems to have been due to the slight importance they attached to the invasion. Having but recently forced Parmenio to raise the siege of Pitané and defeated Calas in the open field, compelling him to seek safety in Rhæteum, they appear to have thought there would be no greater difficulty in driving back the army under Alexander.

The Persian force of one hundred thousand men, collected to repel the invasion, established itself on the heights of Mt. Ida, some distance from the coast. But Alexander, conscious that a direct attack would be attended with great sacrifice of life and be of doubtful result, determined to force the enemy to give battle where the advantage of position would not be so unequal. He accordingly directed his course to the north beside the Hellespont, and thence eastward along the southern shore of the Propontis (now known as the Sea of Marmora).*

Observing the wide detour of the Macedonian army, and fearing an attack in their rear, the Persians hurriedly evacuated Mt. Ida and concentrated their forces on the eastern shore of the Granicus, a stream having its source in the mountains and flowing north into the Propontis. Reaching the Granicus, facing the position of the Persian forces, Alexander, contrary to the advice of Parmenio, ordered an immediate attack, he himself leading the charge at the head of seven squadrons of the Companions. The superb cavalry of the Persians, twenty thousand strong, confident in their strength, awaited him on the eastern shore, supported by their infantry. As the Macedonians forded the stream they were assailed with a shower of javelins and spears, but protecting themselves behind their bucklers as best they could, they made no response, pushing forward, cheered on by the King. Reaching the shore far in advance of his followers, Alexander was twice repulsed in his effort to ascend the steep bank, but the third attempt being successful and the Companion Cavalry forming about him, supported by the Phalanx, a secure foothold was at last effected. The Persians having meanwhile unwisely wasted their spears and javelins in vain effort to stay the progress of the Macedonians had now only their scimetars to oppose the stout thrusting-pikes of Alexander and those who followed him; and the thrusting-pikes proving the more effective weapon the Macedonians, after a desperate struggle, compelled the enemy to give way.

Forcing the attack, the centre of the Persian army was at last pierced and its force divided, and Parmenio presently coming up on the flank of the enemy from the north, the latter, discouraged and broken, gave up the struggle, leaving many of the most exalted of the Persian nobles dead or wounded on the field. In their flight the Persians abandoned the Greek mercenaries, a part of their force, twenty thousand strong, who, placed far in the rear, had taken no part in the battle. These Alexander surrounded and attacked with all his forces, and with such

---

* The army with which Alexander invaded Asia was as follows:

HETAIRAI. Companion Cavalry; armour clad.................	1,800
HYPASPISTS. Companions; royal foot-guards; armour clad......	3,000
PESETÆRI. The Phalanx; sarissa (long spear) bearers..........	9,000
PELTASTS. Light Infantry.................................	12,000
PSILOI. Slingers, darters and bowmen......................	6,000
THESSALIAN CAVALRY......................................	1,200
DIMACHIAS. Dragoons — light cavalry — who fought on foot or on horseback as required	2,200
To the above should be added the troops awaiting Alexander on the eastern shore of the Hellespont	5,000
Total...	40,200

success that as the day waned and those who still held out against him laid down their arms, only two thousand of the gallant array remained alive. These he sent to Macedonia to till the soil, in punishment for having taken up arms against their countrymen.

It is to be said in connection with the contest at the Granicus (as with every great battle in which Alexander encountered the Persian forces) that while he fought with inferior numbers, his victories were not due so much to the greater bravery and training of his soldiers, as to his incomparable tactics and genius in determining the vulnerable point in the enemy's formation. It was this and his skill at arms, and lion-like courage in forcing an opening in the enemy's lines at the Granicus, as afterward at Issus and Arbela, that finally gave him the victory. His troops were without doubt superior, man for man, to those of the enemy, but the latter possessed many tried leaders and soldiers, the equal in courage of any in the world. That they were defeated was due neither to cowardice nor lack of patriotism, but to the superior genius of Alexander and his presence, always in the forefront of the conflict, spurring his followers on to prodigies of strength and valour.

334 B. C.

When the funeral rites of those who fell at the Granicus had been solemnly celebrated, Alexander continued his march to Sardis, the capital of Lydia and for many centuries the centre of commerce and wealth in the far West. As he neared the stronghold with its impregnable citadel, he was met by the Persian governour, Mithrines, who tendered submission and delivered up the keys of the ancient city. This greatly surprised Alexander, for the stronghold was practically unassailable and would have required months in its reduction, during which time the Persians might have recouped their forces and re-formed their line of defence.

Taking possession of the city, he established a form of government satisfactory to the people, granting them such privileges as seemed likely to gain their favour and add to their contentment and prosperity. Afterward he continued his march to Ephesus of biblical memory, which city opened wide its gates on his approach, craving his friendship. This he granted, and in token of his good-will re-established the Grecian customs and forms of government existing prior to the domination of the Persian Kings. While here, Tralles and Magnesia and other Greek communities lying along the Ægean Sea came to him yielding submission and begging to be favoured as in the case of Ephesus. These requests he complied with, re-establishing the ancient forms and freeing the Grecian inhabitants of the ills that had oppressed them under Persian rule. Thus it became his settled policy from the first to grant acceptable forms of government, and deal in all gentleness with those who yielded to his authority.*

Leaving Ephesus, he directed his march to Miletus, where he found the gates closed and its walls guarded at every point. He responded by storming the outer works, which the enemy, finding it impossible to hold, abandoned and retired to the more important defences of the inner city. Setting his engines, the King lost no time in assailing the interior walls, and at last making a breach stormed the city, and after severe fighting accomplished its capture, putting all who had opposed him with arms to the sword.† After the taking of Miletus and under cover of its secure harbour defences, Alexander dismantled his fleet that he might add those who manned the ships to his depleted army, the vessels being of no present use to him.

From Miletus he continued his march along the coast to Halicarnassus, a wealthy city on the Ægean Sea, accepting on his way the submission of the different towns through which he passed. Halicarnassus, like Miletus, confident in its strength, refused to open its gates on his approach, treating with scorn all his conciliatory advances. He responded as before by storming the stronghold, but the resistance being stubborn, the conflict for many days alternated between savage attacks on his part and futile efforts on the part of the enemy by sorties and otherwise to beat him off. Finally, however, effective breaches were made in the wall, which, the Persians being unable to repair or successfully defend, they hastily abandoned, to seek refuge in a strong citadel situated on an island in the harbour. Unable to force the enemy to give up this stronghold without great delay and loss of life, Alexander, not deeming it worth the sacrifice, rested content with setting fire to the city proper and razing it to the ground.

334–333 B. C.

With the destruction of Halicarnassus the conquest of the west coast of Asia Minor was complete, all of which was accomplished in the summer and autumn months following the departure from Pella. Dividing his army as winter approached, Alexander sent half his force back to Sardis under Parmenio, with directions to meet him at Gordium in Phrygia in the follow-

* For details of Alexander's campaigns, see map.

† Readers of history of the age of Alexander the Great should bear in mind that human life at that time was regarded very differently from what it is in our day. Men sought to protect or avenge their kin, or those belonging to the same tribe, clan, or people. Further than that there was no interest or obligation, and if any were spared after a battle or the storming of a city, or the capture of a ship, it was because of their value as chattels, or for some political or sentimental reason.

ing spring. With the remainder of his troops he determined on a winter campaign in the south and east, personally leading the invading force. Continuing his march along the coast he took peaceable possession of Hyparna, Telmessus, Pinara, Xanthus, Patara, and some thirty other towns and cities, Marmara alone refusing submission. This last he stormed, but when the inhabitants found further resistance hopeless, they heroically set fire to their homes, and under cover of the conflagration made their way undiscovered through the Macedonian lines and escaped. Greatly admiring their resolute spirit, Alexander resumed his march to Phaselis, which city, with the intervening communities, presented him with gifts and offers of submission, according to the custom of the time. From Phaselis he made a winter campaign against the Pisidians, a savage tribe of robbers who possessed a mountain stronghold in the immediate vicinity, and were in the habit, from time to time, of descending from their fastness and plundering the peaceful denizens of the neighbouring plains. In this brief and effective foray, Alexander gave the first intimation to the world that his was a mission of peace as well as war; that it was his purpose to establish law and order throughout the land; to protect the peacefully inclined against the predatory bands that everywhere infested the Empire, and which the Persian rulers had been too weak or indifferent to hold in subjection.

With the completion of the campaign against the Pisidians, the King determined to spend a part of the winter at Phaselis, recruiting his strength and indulging his troops in games and religious festivals. While thus engaged word was brought him of the discovery of a treasonable correspondence between the Lyncestian Prince, Alexander, and Darius, the Persian King. As the traitor was then in command of the Thessalian Cavalry — a trust second only to that of the command of the Companions — the situation was dangerous, indeed. Accordingly the King hastened to Sardis secretly, under cover of a small escort, that he might personally investigate the matter. Finding to his great regret and sorrow that the story was true, he caused the offender to be put under restraint, but would not allow him to be executed, as the soldiers decreed. In this way the traitorous nobleman remained under surveillance until the time of the conspiracy of Philotas, some three years afterward, when finding it unwise to further temporize with treasonable practices he responded to the renewed demand of the army by putting the Lyncestian to death.

Returning to Phaselis, the King presently resumed his campaign, his objective point being Pergé, a mountain city of great strength and strategical importance farther to the east. Sending a part of his force by a roundabout mountain road, with the remainder he marched along the coast, encountering on his way the pass lying between Mt. Climax and the sea. This path, always partly submerged, could only be traversed when a north wind beat back the waves, and at such times was exceedingly dangerous because of the likelihood of the wayfarer being surprised by the returning waters. However, as the stronghold the King sought to surprise could only be reached in this way without the enemy becoming aware of his purpose, he boldly led his troops forward beside the perpendicular cliff, the water reaching to the men's waists. What historians term his usual good fortune, however, attended the movement, the column emerging without the loss of a man, and so was able to achieve the object of the dangerous venture. And not only Pergé, but the cities of Sidé, Syllium, and Aspendus, lying beyond the pass, astonished and terrified at his unexpected coming, yielded without a struggle — the latter, however, only after Alexander had occupied the approaches to the mountain fortress with a strong body of troops.

Directing his march now toward the interior, he approached the Taurus Mountains in the direction of Phrygia, surprising, on his way, by a quick night attack, the impregnable defiles of Termessus, thus opening up the road to Sagalassus, one of the great mountain strongholds of the warlike Pisidians. This city lay along the topmost terrace of the Taurus Mountains, and the inhabitants, confident in their strength, marshalled their forces before its walls to oppose the King's advance. Boldly attacking the heights, Alexander was assailed on both his flanks from cunningly contrived ambushes, his troops in consequence being thrown into great disorder. But a part of the force holding their ground, the Phalangites hurried up, headed by the King in person, and thus the day was saved. Brave to rashness, the mountaineers threw themselves against the impassable ranks of the invincible corps, but unavailingly, until at last, unable to beat down the long, protruding spears, and convinced of the futility of further effort, they sought safety in the fastnesses of the surrounding heights.

Continuing his march, Alexander next attacked the stronghold itself which the Pisidians, after some further attempts at defence, at last surrendered. From this place of vantage he made expeditions against the remaining strongholds of the courageous enemy, until, through capture or by negotiations, he at last brought the barbarous people under subjection to law and order.

Continuing his march into Phrygia, he reached Celænæ, a fortress built on an inaccessible rock at the headwaters of the Mæander. Here, loth to sacrifice the men that the storming of the stronghold would involve, he arranged terms of surrender for a future day, and these being perfected, continued his march to Gor-

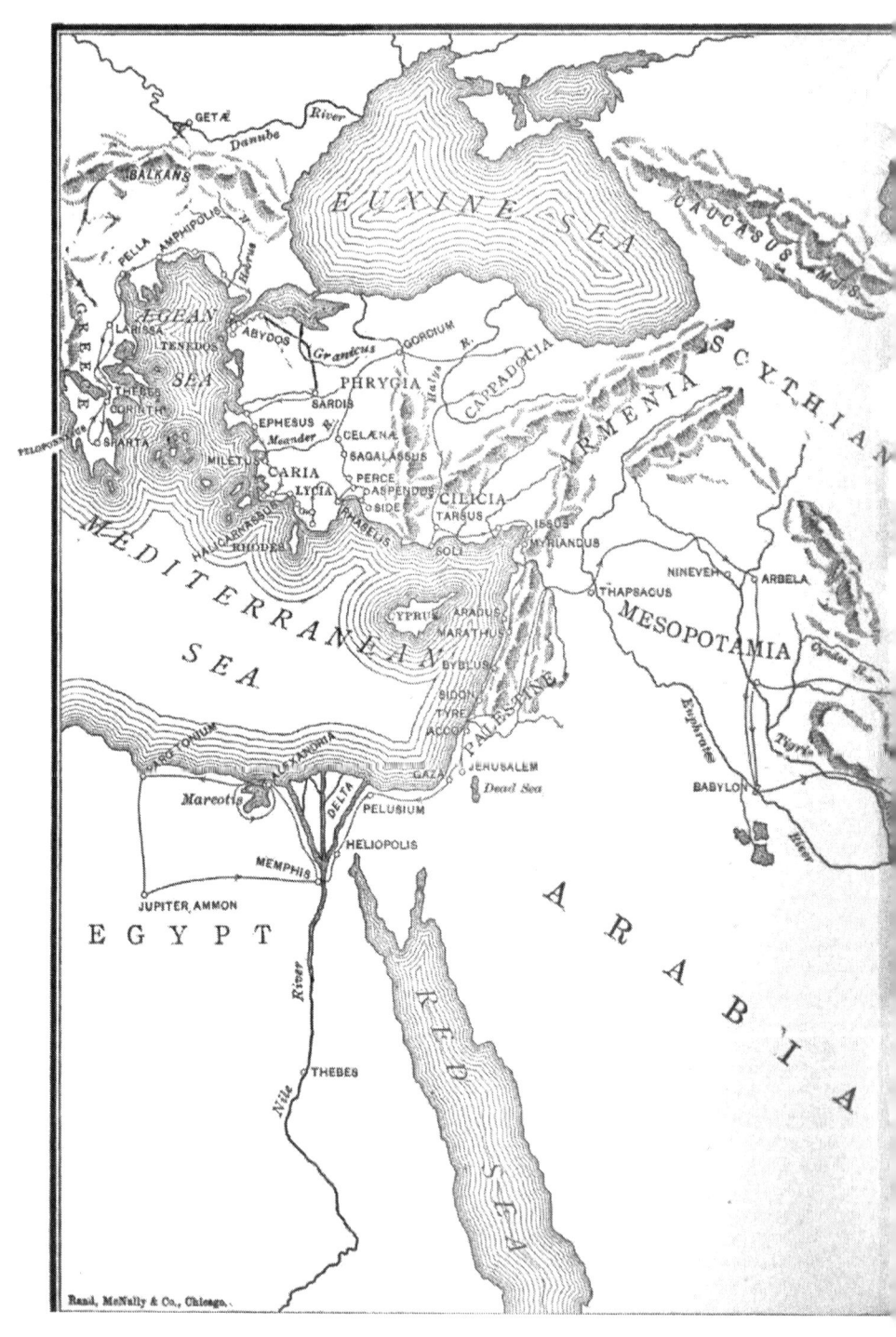

GETÆ

River Danube

BALKANS

PELLA AMPHIPOLIS
GREECE LARISSA
ÆGEAN
TENEDOS
SEA
THEBES CORINTH
SPARTA
PELOPON

ABYDOS

Granicus
PHRYGIA GORDIUM
SARDIS
EPHESUS CELÆNÆ
Maeander
MILETUS SAGALASSUS
CARIA PERCE
LYDIA ASPENDOS
HALICARNASSUS SIDE
RHODES PHASELIS

EUXINE SEA

CAUCASUS Mts.

Halys R.

CAPPADOCIA

ARMENIA

SCYTHIA

CILICIA
TARSUS ISSUS
MYRIANDUS
SOLI
CYPRUS ARADUS NINEVEH ARBELA
MARATHUS THAPSACUS
MESOPOTAMIA
BYBLUS
SIDON
TYRE Euphrates
ACCO PALESTINE Tigris R.
JERUSALEM BABYLON
GAZA
Dead Sea River

MEDITERRANEAN

SEA

PARÆTONIUM ALEXANDRIA
Mareotis DELTA
PELUSIUM
HELIOPOLIS
MEMPHIS

JUPITER AMMON

E G Y P T

River

THEBES

Nile

ARABIA

RED SEA

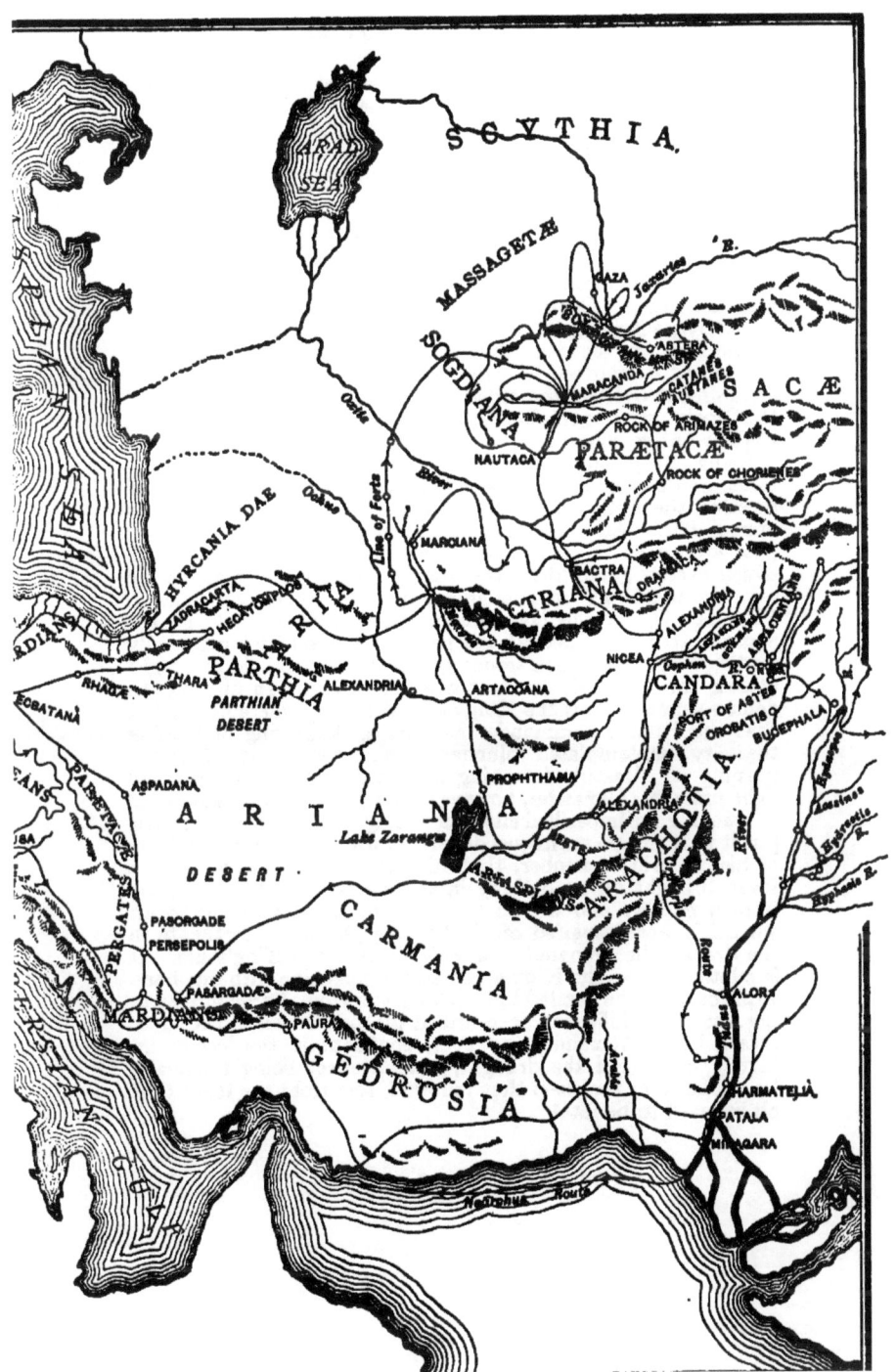

dium, where the forces that had wintered at Sardis — with returning soldiers and recruits from Macedonia joined him, thus uniting the whole army. While at Gordium, Alexander is said to have untangled — or cut — the Gordian knot, the solution of which, so the legend ran, foretold the domination of Asia.

---

333 B. C.

From Gordium Alexander marched with his whole force to Ancyra, where the Cappadocians, a high-spirited people, tendered their submission under reservations which he gladly accorded them. Continuing his course to the east, he crossed the Halys, subduing the countries beyond the great river as far as the Iris. In the cities thus acquired, as in all those that had previously submitted, he established liberal laws, turning the government over to the enlightened party, and, in the case of the Greek towns, re-established the ancient practices and customs of their native country.

Being now master of all Asia Minor west of the Taurus Mountains, he determined to cross the great range with the view of meeting the army which the Persian King was collecting to oppose him. An obstacle to be overcome, however, was the pass known as the Gates of Cilicia in the Taurus Mountains, which narrow gorge, three thousand six hundred feet above the sea, was practically unassailable if guarded by an alert enemy. But, happily for the Macedonians, the Persians made no adequate attempt to defend the pass, and Alexander personally leading a body of chosen troops against the stronghold in a night attack, the force left for its protection was driven off and the defile secured. Thus the King entered Cilicia, where he learned that the Persian commander at Tarsus, despairing of holding the city, contemplated plundering the town and afterward burning it. Hastily detaching a strong force of cavalry and light infantry, Alexander, however, by a forced march succeeded in reaching the imperilled city and taking the garrison by surprise put it to flight ere harm was done. It was in this city, students of history will remember, that Alexander was stricken with a fever, brought on by bathing in the icy river while overheated from a midday march. In the crisis of the disease, however, when life was despaired of, Philip, the physician, fortunate in the draught he prepared, was able to save the King's life. It is related that as the King accepted the medicine with one hand with the other he handed the leech a letter from Parmenio warning him that Philip had been bribed by the Persian Monarch to poison him. Alexander, however, confident in the leech's integrity, swallowed the draught, and its effect being fortunate, he awoke from the sleep that followed, free from the fever that all believed to be fatal.

After his recovery, Alexander made an expedition to Anchialus and Soli in the west, both of which cities yielded to his arms. From thence he continued his march against a savage tribe of outlaws and murderers who occupied the mountain fastnesses of rugged Cilicia, and by their presence threatened his communications by the Cilician Gates.

It was amid the dangers and hardships attending these minor campaigns that Alexander, quite as much as in his battles, displayed the heroic qualities of a great leader. For in these isolated expeditions, aside from the harassments of command, he was compelled to submit to all the hardships and dangers of a common soldier. To the lovers of the great King it will ever be a source of regret that they cannot follow him in these wanderings through wastes and trackless mountains in pursuit of the savage hordes which for centuries the supineness of the Persian government had permitted to despoil the more peaceful part of the community. But the scribes who followed the army to recount its doings had no taste for the hardships and dangers of such expeditions, and so rested in camp, telling us merely that the King went on such and such an expedition against this or that savage people. Thus we are left to conjecture his doings and those of his brave followers as they traversed hidden fastnesses, accessible only by rude paths, and threatened at every step by ambuscades and pitfalls prepared by the alert and cunning enemy they sought.

---

333 B. C.

Returning to Tarsus after his campaign in rugged Cilicia, Alexander continued his march to the east, occupying Megarsus and Mallus and establishing in both governments conformatory to the desires of the inhabitants. It was while at the last city that he learned of the presence of Darius with an army of six hundred thousand men encamped on the plains of Sochi, beyond the Amanic range of mountains that bordered the eastern shore of the Mediterranean. Calling a council of war, the officers concurred in his advice to the effect that no time should be lost in seeking the enemy and giving battle. The army acccordingly resumed its course along the coast, passing the Syrian Gates, a narrow defile between Mt. Amanus and the sea, two days' journey from where Darius was supposed to be encamped. While making preparations to continue his march through the mountain gorge that led to the plains of Sochi above, Alexander learned that Darius, (impatient at his delay in coming to meet him, and not understanding the Macedonians' long pause at Tarsus), had descended to the valley bordering the sea and now occupied the town of Issus, in the rear of the Macedonian army. At this town Alexander had left his sick and disabled soldiers, and these the Persians, in conformity with their usual practices, had cruelly misused and afterward put to death. This outrage, as may be readily supposed, steeled the Macedonian's arm and did not incline him to mercy in the battle that followed.

Greatly surprised at Darius' unexplainable action in leaving the plains of Sochi, where his vast force could be manœuvred to advantage, to seek the narrow valley bordering the Mediterranean, Alexander nevertheless instantly turned about and re-occupied the Syrian Gates. Marshalling his forces, the succeeding morning he marched straight for the enemy, coming upon the Persians about midday as they were drawn up in battle array beyond the Pinarus, a little mountain stream that crossed the narrow plain some miles south of Issus. In marshalling his forces to meet Alexander, Darius, avoiding the mistake at the Granicus, placed his heavy armed Greek stipendiaries, thirty thousand strong, in front, facing the river. On either side of these were thirty thousand shield-bearing guards, trained to fight hand to hand, and on his extreme left twenty thousand light troops were stationed to threaten Alexander's flank. The Persian iron-clad cavalry, thirty thousand strong, Darius placed on the extreme right, their flank resting on the sea. Behind the Greek mercenaries were the Immortals and kinsmen of the Persian King, picked troops, twenty thousand strong. In the midst of these last Darius took his station in a chariot drawn by four horses abreast. Behind the forces thus described were his mixed troops, four hundred and forty thousand in number. Opposed to this force the Macedonian army numbered, all told, thirty thousand men.

Approaching the waiting army of Darius, and acting as usual on the offensive, Alexander charged with a body of cavalry against Darius' extreme left, putting the enemy stationed there to instant flight. Refraining from pursuit, he ordered the Phalanx to charge Darius' centre, he himself leading the Companions and Hypaspists. When a foothold had been gained on the opposite bank, Alexander circled Darius' left and attacked the Greek mercenaries on their flank. These presently giving way, unable to resist the strength of the onslaught, he pursued his advantage, attacking with incredible fury the Immortals and kinsmen guarding the person of Darius. Here the contest raged for some time with varying fortune, but ever increasing advantage to the Macedonian King. Seeing this, and that his retreat was likely to be cut off, Darius, fearful for his personal safety, turned and fled, followed, as his flight became known, by his demoralized and panic-stricken army. In this way the victory of the Macedonians was made complete.

After the pursuit which followed, Alexander returned wounded to his camp, and on being conducted to the abandoned tent of the

Persian King, he found in a room apart, to his great surprise, Statira, Darius' Queen, and her young son and two daughters; also the mother of the Persian Monarch. Sending word to the Queen of the safety of her husband, Alexander, on the following morning, paid her a visit of ceremony, assuring her that he did not make war on women, and that she should be treated with the same dignity and consideration she had received as Queen of Persia. In this he was better than his word, as thereafter he would never allow himself to see her lest it might be construed to her disadvantage. In this determination he chivalrously persisted up to the time of her death, which occurred immediately before the battle of Arbela, some two years later. He, however, would not consent to deliver her or her children up to the Persian King, holding them to be necessary hostages for the safety of his people, it being the practice of the Persians, as at Issus, to mutilate and put to death any Grecians so unfortunate as to fall into their hands. Nor would Alexander negotiate for a division of the Empire, as Darius desired, but wrote to the Persian King that if he would come to him he should have whatever he asked, but that the Kingdom belonged to him, Alexander, by right of conquest, and that only as its King would he treat with Darius.

The chroniclers of the time, in describing the battle of Issus, say that when word was brought Alexander that the family of the Persian King was among the prisoners he was more lively affected with their misfortune than with his own success. In his subsequent treatment of them he diminished nothing of their equipage, or of the attentions and respect formerly paid them, and allowed them larger pensions for their maintenance than they had before received. But the noblest and most royal part of their usage was, as Plutarch recounts, that he treated these illustrious prisoners according to their virtue and character, not suffering them to hear, or receive, or so much as to apprehend anything that was unbecoming. So that they seemed lodged in some temple, or holy virgin chambers, where they enjoyed their privacy, sacred and uninterrupted, rather than in the camp of an enemy. Darius' wife was accounted the most beautiful princess then living, and the daughters were not unworthy of her, but Alexander, it is related, esteeming it more kingly to govern himself than to conquer his enemies, sought no intimacy with any one of them. When Darius, the Persian King, heard of the treatment accorded his Queen, he is said to have lifted up his hands, exclaiming: "Ye gods of my family, and of my kingdom, if it be possible, I beseech you to restore the declining affairs of Persia, that I may leave them in as flourishing a condition as I found them, and have it in my power to make a grateful return to Alexander for the kindness which in my adversity he has shown to those who are dearest to me. But if, indeed, the fatal time be come, which is to give a period to the Persian monarchy, if our ruin be a debt that must be paid to the divine jealousy and the vicissitude of things, then I beseech you grant that no other man but Alexander may sit upon the throne of Cyrus.''

333–332 B. C.

Following the battle of Issus, Alexander continued his march to the south, following the Mediterranean coast. In his progress, the petty kings who ruled over the different cities and islands sent embassies or came themselves to offer submission. This was thought remarkable, for some of these ancient strongholds had never yielded to either the Assyrian or Persian kings. But now, as if recognising a power greater than any known before, they yielded up their cities, and with them expressions of confidence and friendship. In some cases princes came to represent their rulers, for many of the kings were absent at the time under mandate from Darius. But the people, fearing Alexander's might and hearing of his generous treatment of those who yielded, one and all compelled their rulers to make peace with the conquering King. In this way the great island strongholds of Rhodes and Cyprus yielded, and so also the cities of Aradus and Byblus and Sidon. Thus the King advanced, and his progress was not unlike that of the Persian Monarchs. for the people, knowing no difference, prostrated themselves beside the road, and this to the great disgust of the Macedonians, who had not been accustomed to see such homage accorded their Kings.

Approaching the great city and fortress of Tyre, a deputation met Alexander offering submission, but refusing him permission to enter the city. This he construed to mean that they were desirous of maintaining the position of armed neutrality, siding, from time to time as might be to their advantage, either with him or with the Persian King. He therefore determined, on their again refusing to open their gates, to lay siege to the stronghold situated on an island half a mile from the mainland. The impregnable city — for so it was thought — was surrounded by a wall of cut stone one hundred and fifty feet in height and fifty feet across at the top. As Alexander had no ships it was impossible for him to reach the stronghold except by a mole, and this he at once set about constructing, the embankment being two hundred feet in width. The undertaking was one of incredible labour and difficulty, and as it neared completion, the Tyrians suddenly emerged from the harbour and set fire to the machines and engines, and other inflammable material on the made land. This misfortune was followed the same night, and as if in complement to it, by a great storm which washed away the huge filling, practically destroying all the work that had been done. Setting his force to reconstruct the great embankment, Alexander hastened to Sidon, and the cities to the north being now free from service with Darius, voluntarily tendered him their warships, three hundred in number, so that he was able to sail back to Tyre with a fleet outnumbering that of his stubborn enemy. This superiority was presently still further increased by an engagement which the Tyrians were so uncautious as to invite, and in which the greater number of their vessels engaged were captured or destroyed by the ships which Alexander led against them in person. Having now the advantage, he assailed the walls of the city night and day, until at last, a breach being effected, he led the assault, and beating back the enemy mounted the wall from which he descended into the city. Here the struggle continued with incredible ferocity, ending at last in the victory of the Macedonians and the slaughter or enslavement of the entire population. This after a siege of eight months.

Alexander's base being now made secure by the capture of this last remaining stronghold on the sea, he continued his march to Gaza, which fortress blocked the way to Egypt and stood guard over the vast territory to the southeast bordering the Red·Sea. The governour, Batis, a trusted eunuch of the Persian King, refusing Alexander submission, the latter at once laid siege to the place. This lasted four months, ending in the breaking down of the walls and the putting to death of the entire garrison, as not one would yield. In this slaughter, however, contrary to the account of some historians, Alexander took no part, as he had been severely wounded shortly before, and in consequence was compelled to view the final assault from a litter on which he lay, cared for by his physicians.

While conducting the siege of Tyre, Alexander made a successful winter campaign against the robber hordes infesting the Lebanon Mountains. These had long disturbed the peace of the country by their forays, and now harassed his soldiers and stole his supplies. It was during this winter campaign, amid the snows of the mountain heights, as students of history will remember, that Alexander's life was endangered in his effort to save that of Lysimachus, his ancient tutor, whom he had good-naturedly allowed to accompany him on the expedition.

Shortly after the capture of Gaza, Alexander continued his march to Jerusalem, which city, warned by the fate of its neighbours, sought not to defend itself. But taking time by the fore-lock, the high priest, attended by the inhabitants, clothed in white, went forth to meet the young conqueror; and accepting submission, he went into the city, and visiting the sacred temple in company with the high priest, there offered up sacrifices to the

God of Israel, according to the Israelitish rites. After this, returning to Gaza, he continued his march to Pelusium, in Egypt, and from thence to Memphis, the capital, no opposition being offered him. Accepting the submission of the people in good faith, he lingered in the city some days, offering up sacrifices to Apis, the Egyptian deity, and indulging his army with musical entertainments and sumptuous festivities attendant upon the Grecian games, which he caused to be celebrated with untold splendour. Afterward he visited the mouth of the Nile, where he laid out the famed city of Alexandria. Having now been successful in all his undertakings, he determined to make a religious pilgrimage to the shrine of Jupiter-Ammon, located on an oasis in the Libyan Desert. Accordingly he set out with a small force, marching two hundred miles to the west along the southern shore of the Mediterranean, and from thence a like distance across the trackless desert. Reaching the sacred spot, he offered up sacrifices and libations, visiting the temple of the Supreme God, and consulting the oracle regarding the past and future, asking among other things whether all those implicated in the murder of his father, Philip, had been punished. Having accomplished the purpose of his pilgrimage to the temple of Jupiter-Ammon, he returned to Memphis, marching straight across the desert a distance of three hundred and forty miles.

When it became known that he had visited the shrine of Jupiter-Ammon and had consulted the oracle of the great God, his enemies gave out that his visit was for the purpose of having himself declared the son of Jupiter — in other words, that he was born of a God, and not of Philip. When this story and his unexampled march across the desert (a similar attempt on the part of Cambyses, two hundred years before, having cost the Persian King the loss of his entire army of sixty thousand men) became noised abroad, the ignorant, misunderstanding the purport of the slander, came to believe that the Supreme God had really proclaimed Alexander of divine origin. The story greatly amused Alexander, but because of the political advantages that would accrue to the Macedonian cause from its belief among the superstitious people of the East, he would by no means contradict it. On the contrary, by ornamentation of his helmet and in other respects he encouraged the absurd belief, until at last the more enlightened thought the story to be true.

---

331 B. C.

While at Memphis, Alexander reorganized the government of Egypt, giving it over, as in the case of other provinces, to the hands of the natives, except in so far as was necessary to safeguard the interests of the Empire. He also here, as elsewhere, re-introduced the customs and ancient forms of government that

the natives loved, and that were far more to them than the
nationality of their King. While engaged in this way he learned
that Darius was collecting an army of a million men beyond the
river Tigris to give him battle and thus settle forever the question
of domination. Alexander accordingly hastened his departure
from Memphis, and directing his course to the northeast reached
the Euphrates without opposition, and crossing the river at
Thapsacus, directed his course to the Tigris, which stream he
forded some miles above the ruins of the ancient Nineveh. The
march from Memphis to the Tigris — eleven hundred and fifty
miles — occupied several months, embracing as it did many
cities and petty provinces, in all of which matters of administration claimed the attention of the King. After crossing the
Tigris, Alexander turned to the south, where Darius' army was
marshalled in the open plain some distance away. In the battle
of Arbela, which followed, Alexander's forces numbered forty
seven thousand men; those of Darius, one million men.

The Persian order of battle was in three lines, formed of oblong
masses or squares, the different classes of troops and nationalities
forming the several chains, presenting in their warlike fittings
and picturesque costumes a scene of unexampled splendour. In
the centre of the Persian force, the high chariot and person of
Darius were visible to both armies, surrounded as at Issus by
the Immortals and kinsmen, fifteen thousand in number.

Observing Alexander turn abruptly to the right as the battle
opened (in avoidance, it appeared, of obstacles the Persian engineers had devised to obstruct his progress) Darius, fearful that
the combat might thus be transferred to ground unfavourable
for manœuvering his vast army, ordered his centre to charge,
preceded by one hundred scythed chariots, designed to confuse
and break Alexander's line. With them (to the wonder of the
Macedonians) were fifteen war elephants, from the backs of which
soldiers showered arrows and javelins on the advancing enemy.
Not, however, with the resulting panic Darius had been led to
expect. For the Macedonians beat off the huge beasts, and opening wide their ranks, (as Clearchus had done at Cunaxa seventy
years before) allowed such of the chariots to pass through as they
were unable to intercept or turn back in flight on the Persian
front. Alarmed at Alexander's continued oblique movement
to the right, Darius ordered Bessus, who commanded the Persian
left, to move forward his first line of troops to intercept and stay
the Macedonian King. Doing as he was commanded, the Persian nobleman beat back an auxiliary column of cavalry Alexander had caused to threaten Darius' extreme left. But in the
forward movement Bessus' second, or reserve line, for some
reason failed to take the place of the line he had advanced to stay
Alexander's progress. Thus there was a weak spot in the Per-

sian left centre, which Alexander, perceiving, instantly charged, forming for the purpose a wedge of the Companion Cavalry, supported by a part of the Phalanx.

For a time the Persian troops bravely held their ground, animated by Darius' encouraging presence, but the armour-clad Companions, charging again and again with thrusting-pike and sword, supported by the long protruding spears of the Phalanx, at last broke through the weakened line. This accomplished, Alexander turned abruptly to the left and charged the serried ranks formed in a mass about the chariot of Darius, and beating down those in front directed his course straight for the person of the Persian Monarch. At this moment, when the battle hung in the balance, Alexander, having approached near to Darius, hurled his spear full at the Persian King, but missing his mark transfixed the charioteer of Darius instead. Whereupon the followers of Darius thinking it was he who was stricken raised the cry that the King had fallen. And the cry spreading, the timid instantly took flight, and this disorganizing the array of those more courageously inclined they in turn gave way, leaving the unhappy King alone and unprotected. With the Persian centre and left wing broken, and those about him in panic-stricken flight, Darius, having no other resource, wheeled about and reluctantly left the field. Seeing this, Bessus no longer sought to stay the failing battle, but turned and followed upon the heels of his master.

Meanwhile Mazæus in command of Darius' right wing, observing the gap in the Macedonian centre caused by Alexander's wide divergence to the right in the early part of the battle, ordered his cavalry to charge the weakened line. Beating down all opposition the Persian troops passed through the Macedonian line reaching at last the camp beyond, where they found the members of Darius' family. These they would have rescued, but frightened at the wild turmoil of the field and fearful of the result of the battle, the royal children would by no means accept the friendly offer. Gratified at the success of his manoeuvre and the desperate plight of Parmenio, who commanded the Macedonian left, Mazæus hurriedly collected his remaining cavalry and charged full upon Parmenio's weakened line, and with such fury that the Macedonian, fearful of the result, dispatched couriers to Alexander to come to his rescue lest the army be destroyed and the day lost. This summons reaching the King, he turned reluctantly from the pursuit of Darius, and presently encountering those who had penetrated his centre a fierce struggle ensued, ending in their extermination. Taking fresh heart, Parmenio, massing his cavalry, now charged upon the hitherto victorious Mazæus, which assault the latter, weakened by the defection of Darius' centre and left wing, found it impossible to withstand. And so, evading the conflict, the gallant officer led off his troops in the direction of Babylon, of which city he was governour.

When in the way described victory was at last assured, the King set out afresh in pursuit of Darius, reaching Arbela, seventy miles distant, the succeeding day, but too late to catch the flying Monarch, who had passed on his way to Ecbatana some hours before.

It is claimed by military critics that the victory that attended the battle of Arbela (one of the most notable of history) was the direct fruit of Alexander's incomparable genius. Its immediate result was to open up to his arms all central Persia, including Babylon and the southern capitals of the Empire, Susa and Persepolis.

331–330 B. C.

On his return from the pursuit of the Persian King, Alexander caused his army to face about, and recrossing the Tigris directed its march on Babylon. Mazæus, the governour of the city, knowing it to be impossible to defend the walls against his victorious enemy, emerged from the gates as the King approached, and, kneeling, delivered up the keys of the city, offering submission for himself and all over whom he exercised authority. Graciously accepting the tender, Alexander entered the great metropolis, where he remained a month, re-organizing the government of central Persia and otherwise looking after the affairs of the mighty Empire, over the major portion of which he now held undisputed sway.

Having rested his army and afforded it a taste of eastern indulgences — for the Macedonians were a virile race, peculiarly susceptible to such things — Alexander directed his march to Susa, the winter capital of Persia, lying to the east of the Tigris. Here, on his approach, as at Babylon, the Persian governour, Arbulites, met him with the keys to the city and assurances of loyalty and submission. While at Susa Alexander assumed all the prerogatives and outward trappings of the King of Kings, installing with great pomp Darius' mother and children in the regal palace, where they continued to reside with the honours attached to royal station.

Having settled the affairs of government at Susa, Alexander determined to continue his march to Persepolis, the birthplace of the Persian nation, and still under the domination of Darius' governour. Setting his army in motion, he himself, with a strong body of troops, made a detour into the mountains of Uxii for the purpose of bringing under subjection a barbarous tribe of outlaws who had long harassed the peaceful people of the plains and who, moreover, had been in the habit of exacting tribute from the Persian kings in their journeyings back and forth between Susa and Persepolis. Agreeably to such custom they dispatched an envoy to Alexander asking him to conform to the ancient custom in his contemplated passage through the mountain defile which they guarded, and from whence they exacted tribute of all who passed. Listening to their demand with patience, he told them in enigmatic phrase to meet him at the defile and collect their dues. It was this demand and the cruelty and arrogance of the robbers that induced the King to make the campaign against them, and it being conducted with his usual celerity resulted in surprising them in their mountain retreat and putting them to flight. After accomplishing this he continued his march with all speed to the disputed pass, which he found heavily guarded by the mountain hordes. Attacking with such troops as he had at hand, the contest was long protracted and at one time threatened to be disastrous to the King's force, but finally overcoming their defences, he put them to rout. Exacting hostages for the future good behaviour of the robbers, Alexander continued his march and thus approached the summit of the last mountain range that intervened between him and the fertile plains of Persis. To reach the height, however, he had to pass the Persian or Susan Gates, a lofty defile protected on either side by perpendicular cliffs and defended by Ariobarzanes with forty thousand men, all that remained of the Persian force in the south, after the disastrous battle of Arbela. Unassailable, the King nevertheless made an effort to force the gorge, but being repulsed withdrew to the plain, where he established a camp as if meditating further effort. However, when darkness had set in, he detached a strong body of cavalry and light infantry and following the base of the mountain ascended the height by an obscure bridle path guided by a shepherd familiar with the country. Reaching the summit of the mountain, he lay still until the succeeding night, when making a forced march along the crest of the height, he reached the pass at dawn, attacking the surprised enemy on the instant with incredible fury. At the sound of his trumpet that part of his army lying in the plain below, charged anew at the foot of the pass, and the surprised Persians, attacked in front and rear, unable to resist the double onslaught, at last gave way. With the remnant of his force numbering seven thousand men, the Persian commander, Ariobarzanes, hastened to Persepolis with the design of removing the vast treasures stored there in the vaults of the Persian King. Warned of his purpose by Tiridates, the colleague of Ariobarzanes, Alexander set out with all speed for Persepolis, which he was so fortunate as to reach in time to prevent the governour from despoiling the treasury, as contemplated. In the battle that ensued Ariobarzanes was killed, but in the sack of the city that followed few lives were sacrificed, as the inhabitants had fled in a mass on news reaching the capital of the defeat of their army at the mountain pass.

Thus Persis, the birthplace of the nation, fell into Alexander's hands and with it the palaces and vast treasures of the Persian King, including among the latter one hundred and fifty millions of dollars in coined money and ingots. Such was the treasure hoarded here by the frugal Monarch, a part of which expended in corrupting and arming Greece against the Macedonian King would have delayed or forever prevented the latter from crossing over into Asia.

Alexander throughout his conquest made a distinction between native Persians and their subjects, and at Persepolis and Susa refused to recognize the religious customs and prejudices of the Persian race. At Memphis he had rendered honour to Apis, the Egyptian deity; in Jerusalem, to Jehovah, the God of the Israelites; at Babylon, to Belus, the local deity, and so in all the different provinces and cities he paid homage to the accepted gods of the country, but at Susa and Persepolis would recognize no gods save those of Greece.

Of the reason for Alexander's destruction of Persepolis, the hearthstone of the Persian people, with its innumerable palaces and altars, there has been much idle and irrelevant comment; many untrue and scandalous stories that still pass as of value in current literature. In truth, the act was drastic in the extreme, but so were all things in that rude and wildly superstitious age when coloured by the fervour of religious hatred. For although one hundred and fifty years had passed since Xerxes' time, the zealots of Greece still treasured in vengeful remembrance their temples and sanctuaries burned by him as if it were but yesterday. In the destruction of the Persian capital Alexander executed the vengeance so long threatened by the Grecians for the sacking and burning of Athens by Xerxes, the Persian King. Of the many fables connected with the event that have existed to our time, one is to the effect that the destruction of Persepolis with its palaces and altars was precipitated by the courtesan, Lais, at a banquet given by Alexander to his generals. This story, falling in with others of a like nature concerning Alexander, manufactured by his enemies, and being everywhere repeated by them, at last found lodgment in the history of the conquest. This notwithstanding the fact that everything mankind knows regarding Alexander's character and his avoidance of women and freedom from their control utterly forbids belief in the story. The despoiling of the city had long been meditated, and was intended to emphasize the resentment of Greece and at the same time strike terror into the heart of the nation that had so long persecuted the Grecian people.

It was an act of reparation and warning, and the riches and gorgeous splendour of the palaces and the sacred traditions that surrounded Persepolis made it all the more acceptable to Greece and her outraged Gods. But that nothing might be wanting to precipitate the vengeful act, the soldiers of Alexander were stung to madness as they approached the ancient capital by being met by four thousand Greek captives, who, after being mutilated in every conceivable manner by their cruel oppressors, had been hidden away, unknown to their countrymen, in this sequestered valley. On beholding them Alexander was moved to tears, and dismounting mingled with the disconsolate throng, offering to send them back to Greece and there provide for them out of his private purse for the remainder of their lives. But, ashamed of their hideous deformities, they one and all refused the kindly offer. Sorrowing over their fate, he assigned to each a measure of land with attendant slaves in the fertile valley of Persis, bestowing upon them every necessary thing to enable them to pass the remainder of their days in peace and comfort.

Such were the causes that led to the destruction of Persepolis, about which some of the early historians gave currency to so many romantic and unsavoury fables.

330 B. C.

While resting his army at Persepolis, Alexander made a winter campaign against the Mardians, a savage tribe of outlaws that occupied the mountainous region between the valley of Persis and the Persian Gulf, and who among other iniquities had destroyed the great commercial highway between Persepolis and the sea. Perhaps no mountain campaign that the heroic King ever undertook against a barbarous foe was attended with greater hardships. For the savages had their homes in caves and huts in the remote mountains, and in the battles that ensued the women fought in the open field with the same hardihood and bravery as the men. However, at last bringing them under subjection and exacting fitting guarantees for the future, Alexander re-opened the great highway, after which he returned to Persepolis.

With the advent of spring he resumed his pursuit of Darius, who was collecting an army at Ecbatana, the summer capital of Persia, three hundred miles distant. On the march north, Alexander tarried to make a campaign against the Parætacæ, a tribe of robbers who had their homes on the eastern slope of the Oxii. Having brought the turbulent people under subjection, and exacted the usual guarantees, he continued his march to Ecbatana. Nearing the great capital he found that Darius, having failed in his effort to collect an army, had fled to the far East, with the purpose of continuing the struggle amid the mountains of Sogdiana and Bactria —modern Turkestan. Taking possession of the walled city and the ancient palace of Deioces, the first Median King, Alexander rested his army for several days, at the expiration of which time, leaving Parmenio as governour of the city, he set out with a well-appointed force in pursuit of the flying King.*

Of Alexander's pursuit of Darius there is nothing in the annals of kings or of royal adventure to be compared to its hardships and unique features, conducted as it was without cessation amid mountain snows and desert wastes. The prize was the possession of the Persian Empire without further strife; for on the capture of Darius alive depended the yielding of every part of his extended kingdom. But as the pursuit continued, Bessus, a kinsman of Darius, feeling assured the Persian King meditated submission, conspired with his companions and dethroned his sovereign, following this act by putting him in irons. On news of this being brought to Alexander by two Persian noblemen who had abandoned Bessus' train, he set out with a small body of troops with renewed energy, fearing Bessus, who aspired to the throne, should be led to put Darius to death. But all too late, for Alexander having come upon Bessus after an all-night ride across a waterless desert, the Persian Prince hurried to the cart in which Darius lay chained, and bringing him forth bade him mount a horse and continue the flight. For only thus, it was apparent, could he prevent his falling into the hands of the Macedonian King. But this Darius positively refused to do, whereupon Bessus and those with him, disappointed in their purpose, plunged their javelins in the King's body, and mounting their horses escaped. The body was found by a Grecian soldier as Darius lay dying, but raising himself the unfortunate Monarch bade the soldier thank Alexander for his chivalrous treatment of the Queen, Statira, adding a grateful prayer to Ahura-Mazda, the God of his country, that the throne was to pass to so generous a man. Alexander himself shortly approached, but was too late to hear the King's words, or offer him aid of any kind.

It is not difficult to picture the great conqueror's rage and regret at this unfortunate ending after his unexampled march of twelve hundred miles. For to have taken the Persian King alive would have quieted the whole Kingdom, as Darius, wearied

---

* The gold and silver in coined money and ingots found by Alexander in the vaults of the Persian King at Susa, Persepolis, and Ecbatana amounted to $207,000,000. The balance of this, after making princely donatives to his officers and soldiers, he deposited in the treasury at Ecbatana, making Harpalus treasurer — a most unfortunate appointment, as the officer afterward defaulted for a huge sum. In addition to the above he also acquired vast treasures at Damascus, after the battle of Issus, and also at Babylon on the capture of that city.

of the struggle, was disposed to yield without further effort. Taking charge of the remains of the fallen King, Alexander caused them to be embalmed and taken in state to Persepolis, where they were interred with the Persian Monarchs who had preceded him.

While attending to these matters, Artabazus, an exalted Persian noble, and his two sons came into camp and tendered submission; and this greatly to Alexander's delight, for the nobleman had previously been a part of the entourage of the Persian King and had remained loyal to him to the last. But finding himself unable to prevent Bessus' treasonable act in putting the King in chains, and fearful for his own life and that of his followers, he had detached himself with the small force under his command and sought safety in the neighbouring solitudes.

The escape of Bessus, who was satrap of Bactria and Sogdiana, and his determination to continue the struggle, not as viceroy but as King, compelled Alexander to reorganize his army for the long and hazardous campaign that the uprising of the eastern provinces would entail. Resting for some days after the death of Darius, in order that those who had fallen behind in the long and forced march from Ecbatana might rejoin his command, Alexander directed his course northward to the Caspian Sea, toward which the main army had been ordered to proceed. To reach the sea, however, it was necessary to traverse the intervening mountains, and while doing this the King quelled the savage hordes that inhabited the heights and were a scourge to the neighbouring people. This pursuant to his fixed determination to reclaim the country throughout from the barbarous tribes that infested the mountains and deserts, and which the Persian Monarchs — too weak or too intent on the indulgences of their court — had permitted to terrify the outlying districts of their vast kingdom.

Arriving at the Caspian Sea, the southern shore of which was a vast morass, interspersed with half-sunken rivers and dense forests, Alexander turned to the east, where he subdued the Mardians, a cruel tribe who had their haunts in the fastnesses of the mountain district. Having by this expedition made secure the great highway bordering the sea, and the remainder of his army having now rejoined him, he turned his face to the east where Bessus, meanwhile, had proclaimed himself King of Asia, under the title of Artaxerxes.

When, however, Alexander had advanced five hundred miles he was compelled to turn back because of the revolt of the Persian governour he had left in charge of Aria, one of the provinces traversed. Making a forced march he fell upon the surprised forces of the recreant satrap like a whirlwind, killing three thousand of his followers and putting the remainder to flight. Installing a loyal governour, he directed his march to the south, to forestall an uprising threatened in Zarangeia, by one of Bessus' followers. Successful in this, he made a march of a thousand miles to the southeast, to bring under subjection the nomadic and other tribes of that remote and little-known region which had been led to take the field against him. Having effected this, he directed his course to the valley of the Cophen (modern Cabul), where he went into winter quarters preparatory to crossing the Parapamisus Mountains in pursuit of Bessus, who occupied the Bactrian territory to the north.

330 B. C.

It was during the terrible marches and attendant warfare of the far East, amid trackless deserts and mountain snows that occurred the notable conspiracies of Alexander's reign. The first was that of Philotas, the trusted commander of the Companion Cavalry, who with other members of his family had occupied throughout the places of greatest honour in Alexander's gift. Unsuspicious of danger, Alexander was resting in camp, when a trusted attendant brought him word that a conspiracy existed to murder him on the following day. It appeared on investigation that the plot was made known to Philotas, but he doing nothing and the day passing, it had again been brought to his notice. But another day passing and he failing to warn Alexander or arrest the conspirators, and the need of action being pressing, it was at last brought directly to the attention of the King. Upon Philotas being questioned, he replied that he had not regarded the matter as serious, but upon being put to the torture confessed the names of those implicated in the plot, and among others his father, Parmenio. Thereupon he was condemned after trial by the army and put to death. Dimnos, a brave and resolute man, who it appeared had been selected as the agent to kill the King, escaped the disgraceful fate of Philotas by committing suicide at the moment of his arrest, confirming by the act the truth of the conspiracy, if further confirmation had been necessary. The great importance of the command held by Parmenio as governour of Ecbatana, the key to all central Persia, made it necessary for Alexander to exercise the greatest caution in the execution of the death-sentence pronounced against that officer by the army after his son's confession. He accordingly dispatched a secret messenger to Ecbatana, eight hundred and sixty miles distant, ordering his generals there to put the traitorous governour to death, which command they at once proceeded to carry out.

It is probable that Philotas had long meditated his treasonable act, for he had been outspoken in his criticisms of Alexander, openly ascribing the success of the latter to himself and his father, Parmenio. These malevolent carpings were well known to Alexander, but being tolerant of such things, and because of the long service of Parmenio, he had refused to seriously notice the treasonable utterances of the arrogant young noble.   However, the dangers that now surrounded the army and its remoteness from succour in the event of disaster made it impossible longer to condone open or covert treason among those surrounding the King, or who were entrusted with high command.   The inadvisability of this led the army at this time to condemn anew the Lyncestian prince, Alexander, who was accordingly executed.

The need there was for prompt and drastic action in such matters was illustrated later by what is known as the conspiracy of the pages, fostered by Callisthenes, the philosopher and scribe and the open enemy of Alexander.   In this case it appeared that a youth named Hermolaus, one of the pages, having been flogged for some offence and being incensed at the act, had prevailed upon his associates to join him in an attempt to murder the King when they next watched by his bedside.   And their purpose would have been effected, it is believed, had it not happened by chance that the King did not return to his tent during the night they were to guard his person.   Afterward, becoming frightened at the contemplated act, one of the pages confessed, whereupon those implicated, three in number, were subjected to trial, and upon being proven guilty were executed.   Of the final fate of the cynic, Callisthenes, who was imprisoned, historians are, however, in doubt.

The treason of Clitus that culminated in his death about this time had no such immediate and sinister purpose as the other conspiracies, but was, however, quite as much to be feared because of its effect on the prestige and authority of the King with the army and the Persian nation.   This brave but choleric man seems never to have been able to view the glory of Alexander as King of Kings with kindness or complacency.   But made it a practice in season and out of season to publicly remind him of his lowly Macedonian origin, vehemently boasting that his successes were due not to his own ability, but to the late King Philip, and Parmenio.   Alexander's disposition to conform to the ceremonial observances of the Orient in order to rule the Persian people acceptably also deeply incensed Clitus, as it did Callisthenes.   On the night the disaffected and traitorous officer met his death, he entered the presence of Alexander at a great banquet where many Grecians and high Persian dignitaries were assembled, and standing forth abused the King in the most bitter and scurrilous manner.   Professing to treat the matter lightly, Alexander laughed, and turning to one with whom he was conversing, said: "You must look upon us Macedonians as mere savages."   However, on Clitus continuing to shout out his abuse, to the shame of all present and the great disparage-

ment of the King's dignity, Alexander arose from his seat as if
to punish the offending officer. Allowing himself, however, to
be restrained, the friends of Clitus laid hold of the irate officer
and hurried him from the tent. But being full of venomous
hatred he hurriedly re-entered the room by another door, com-
mencing anew and with still greater vehemence to revile and
defame the King. Whereupon, the situation being intolerable,
Alexander grasped a spear and killed the traitor on the spot.
This exercise of kingly authority, however much the manner of
it may be criticised, was just, and above all imperative — according to Eastern usage — if Alexander's prestige as Persia's
ruler was to be preserved. And while the act seemed to be
dictated by passion, it was undoubtedly calculated and its
effect clearly foreseen. Clitus, in his malign efforts to outrage
the sensibilities of the mighty King, also twitted him with the
fact that had he, Clitus, not intervened to ward off a blow intended for Alexander at the Granicus (a common occurrence in
every battle) Alexander would not then be alive to take on the
Oriental forms and ostentatious trappings of Persian royalty.
In fact, it appears the unfortunate officer left nothing undone to
render his death a political necessity.

Such are the facts surrounding Clitus' execution, stripped of
all sentimentality. As King of Kings Alexander could not,
any more than his Persian predecessors, recognize a distinction
between the greatest prince and the lowest peasant, so far as
personal equality was concerned, inasmuch as both were required by the etiquette of the court to treat him with respectful
homage. He stood alone, and it was apparent that if his kingly
prestige was impaired all authority over Persia would vanish
and chaos reign. It is not strange that Alexander should have
afterward retired to his tent, and denying himself to all, mourn
for days in bitter anguish the loss of his friend of other and
happier years. And when the soldiers in their rage would have
cast the traitor's body to the dogs, denying it sepulchre, the
King, intervening, gave the dead such honourable burial as he
would have received in the days of his greatest strength and
glory.

329–328 B. C.

With the advent of spring Alexander determined to break up
his camp on the Cophen and resume his campaign against Bessus,
but in order to reach the object of his pursuit, it was necessary to
cross the Caucasus Mountains. This great range was traversed
by three roads, and thinking Bessus would expect him to take
the easiest, Alexander chose another, or what was known as the
easterly pass. Impatient to begin the campaign, the army set
out on its way to the north in the early spring. Because of the

genial warmth the crossing of the lofty mountain was seemingly easy of attainment, but on the second morning the rugged heights were swept by a furious hurricane, which lasted many days, clogging the rude mountain roads and filling the passes with snow and ice. Harassed and delayed, the army made little progress, so that ere the summit was reached the provisions were exhausted and the wearied soldiers compelled to subsist on the flesh of their half-starved animals and the roots of the stunted shrubs they found amid the rocks. In consequence of this and the bitter cold great numbers perished. Many crazed or in despair of life hurled themselves from the dizzy cliffs; others blinded by the snow wandered away and were lost in the cañons and crevasses of the mountains. Still greater numbers perished from weakness and hunger or were frozen where they lay asleep, wood with which to build fires being unobtainable. It was amid such hardships, the horror of which was added to by frequent and destructive avalanches of snow and ice, that the soldiers slowly surmounted the storm-swept height. To add to their dejection, on reaching the plain beyond they found it devastated by Bessus' troops and void of shelter or food. Encouraging the drooping spirits of his followers, the King, who marched among his men sharing the hardships of a common soldier, led them on at last to a more hospitable land where they were rested and refreshed. Fretting at the delay, so destructive to his plans, Alexander waited until the army had regained its strength, when he again set out in pursuit of the regicide Bessus. But that wily Prince, apprehensive of the result, did not wait his approach, but fled northward to a more secure region beyond the Oxus (Amu Daria or Jihon). In the pursuit, and as if the presence of the traitorous Persian brought disaster, many of Alexander's soldiers lost their lives in crossing a waterless desert that lay to the south of the great river beyond which Bessus had sought safety. For in the march across this desolate waste great numbers perished from thirst and the intolerable heat. But the more hardy, pushing on and at last reaching water, hurried back to those who had fallen, Alexander himself aiding; nor would he take off his armour until the last survivor had been rescued.

Having no boats with which to cross the Oxus in pursuit of Bessus, Alexander made use of his tent-skins — as at the Danube — filling them with straw and using them as floats. When the Bactrian cavalry with Bessus saw that he could not defend their country they abandoned him, whereupon his other followers, becoming disheartened and fearful of the King's vengeance, delivered the regicide up to Alexander who condemned him to death. In the indignities Bessus suffered preceding his death, which occurred at Ecbatana, Alexander followed closely the customs of the Persian kings in dealing with the Greeks so unfortunate as to fall into their hands, and more particularly the Thessalian general, Menon, of Xenophon's time.

After the capture of Bessus, Alexander continued his march to Maracanda (modern Samarcand) which he garrisoned, proceeding from thence to the Jaxartes (Sir Daria) having its outlet in the Aral Sea. In this march, the country being hostile, one of his foraging parties lost its way and was cut to pieces by the predatory bands that infested the mountain districts. Halting his forces, he demanded redress, and on its being refused marched against the enemy. Whereupon the hill tribes, mustering their whole strength, met him with a force of thirty thousand men. In the battle that ensued, in which the enemy was put to rout with a loss of twenty-two thousand men, Alexander was severely wounded, but refusing to delay the march of his army caused himself to be carried forward on a litter. As he approached the Jaxartes, the boundary line between Persia and Scythia, he was met by embassies from the latter offering submission. This appeared, however, to be only a ruse, for on reaching the Jaxartes he found the nomads of the desert drawn up on the opposite shore awaiting favourable opportunity to cross over and devastate the country to the south. Feeling it would be unwise to leave these restless and warlike enemies in his rear, Alexander crossed the river on rafts made of inflated skins, as at the Oxus, and attacked the Scythians with cavalry and heavy infantry, driving them back after a severe battle to their native wilds. Humbled, the Scythians sued for peace, which he gladly accorded them. The Massagetæ, (a kindred people who had defeated and put Cyrus the Great to death two hundred years before) unmindful of the fate of their neighbours to the east, shortly attacked a Macedonian force under Andromachus and put it to ignominious rout. Afterward Alexander, in command of a force of cavalry and infantry, marched against them, and in the battle which followed utterly destroyed their army, and following up the victory with relentless energy, drove the barbarous horde back to the desert from whence it came.

In order to protect the frontier provinces against these and other enemies, Alexander established fortifications along the border of his kingdom, and in this way, after many vicissitudes, sometimes resulting favourably to him, but often the reverse, finally perfected an adequate system of defence. Anxious to establish a stable government in the further provinces before continuing his march to the south, he called upon the inhabitants to meet at Maracanda, the capital, and agree among themselves upon a form that would be acceptable to them. But it being maliciously reported by the disaffected that the only purpose of the meeting was to enable Alexander to entrap the nobles and put them to death, the whole country revolted. Furious with

rage and despairing of all gentle measures, the King marched into
the rebellious country, and traversing its broad extent swept
it from end to end with fire and sword, not one being spared who
in any way opposed his will.   Thus at last amid flaming cities
and sanguinary battles the turbulent and half-savage provinces
of the East were stilled.

It has been impossible with any certainty to follow the movements of Alexander's army in its marches and counter-marches
amid the deserts and mountains of Bactria and Sogdiana.   All
we surely know is that in the end peace was secured and stable
governments established.   In instituting these Alexander showed
the same genius for affairs that he displayed in the conduct of
his campaigns, introducing governments acceptable to the people
and sweeping away the purely Persian forms instituted by
former rulers.   His measures, moreover, were such as to protect
the peaceably inclined against the half-barbarous hordes which
had hitherto terrorized the country.   Nowhere, however, do
historians give him proper credit for his efforts in this direction,
seeing in the isolated and hardy campaigns he was compelled to
carry on only the activity of a hunter of men.   Similarly, they
have not regarded with the attention they should the diverse
nationalities of which Persia was made up, and the wisdom displayed in organizing local governments to conform to the particular desires and habits of the people, retaining only such
authority in his own hands as was necessary for the common
good.

328-327 B. C.

Having at last quieted Bactria and Sogdiana, Alexander
returned to Nautaca, where he was joined by the various scattered
detachments of his army.   Continuing his march in the early
spring to the northeast, through a mountainous country still
heavily clogged with snow and ice, he at last approached the
lofty fortress known as the Rock of Arimazes.   To the offer
of pardon and free exit he made the unfriendly garrison if it
would yield, the denizens of the lofty height shouted down that
the rock was unassailable and that they would only surrender to
winged soldiers.   In this dilemma Alexander issued a proclamation to his army, offering prizes to those who should scale the
apparently inaccessible mountain that looked down from a
lofty precipice on the fortress from the rear.   In this the efforts
of the hardy climbers were successful, though of no avail, so far
as the capture of the rock was concerned had the garrison stood
out.   However, upon reaching the summit the adventurous
soldiers looking down from the impassable cliff raised and lowered
the wide sleeves of their tunics in mockery as if they were indeed
winged men.   Although the rock was unassailable from the

height, the fortress yielded the same morning without further adventure.

Following possession of the rock was consummated the most romantic event of Alexander's warlike life; namely, his espousal of Roxana, the beautiful daughter of Oxyartes, a Bactrian nobleman and governour of the fortress of Arimazes. She was at this time, so historians recount, the most beautiful woman in all Persia, and interesting traditions concerning her and Iskander or Iskender (by which name Alexander was known in middle Asia) still linger in the more remote districts of the far East. It was a love-marriage, pure and simple, and every way like the great conqueror, the only dower of the bride, being the bride herself. In his unselfish choice of Roxana, and in his admiration and love for the beautiful woman, Alexander's ambition found fitting culmination. Up to that time his thoughts had been wholly occupied with the acquisition of empire and the establishment of orderly governments in the provinces and cities conquered. But with the taking to himself of a Queen, whose choice had been dictated by affection, there entered into his life another and gentler element, the love of woman, the most priceless heritage of man, be he king or peasant.

The accounts of historians differ widely as to the particulars of Alexander's marriage to Roxana and the events leading up to it. Intent upon giving an account of his marches, sieges, and battles, his marriage was thought a trivial thing. They looked upon it as a private matter of no historical importance, and ignoring its romantic features (so much more interesting to us than much they have to say) give but a meagre account of the great event. Plutarch, who wrote four hundred years after Alexander's death (while the traditions of the great King were still matters of current report) gives us of all historians the clearest insight into his remarkable character. Although often in error — as in regard to the meeting of Alexander and Roxana — his statements are always intelligent and unprejudiced. He has this to say of the marriage: "It was indeed a love affair, yet it seemed at the same time to be conducive to the object in hand. For it gratified the conquered people to see him choose a wife from among themselves, and it made them feel the most lively affection for him, to find that in the only passion which he, the most temperate of men, was overcome by, yet he forebore till he could obtain her in a lawful and honourable way."

327–326 B. C.

After his marrage, Alexander lingered for a time in the northeastern provinces, undertaking in person the siege of Chorienes, the last of the Persian strongholds to stand out against him. This fortress, like that of Arimazes, was situated on an unassailable rock, but following a siege of several weeks, the governour, through Oxyartes' friendly efforts, was induced to accept the generous offer Alexander made him.   Here the King rested two months, attending to the affairs of his vast Empire, happy, we may believe, in the society of Roxana, his beautiful Queen. Afterward resuming his career of conquest, he marched to the south with an army of one hundred thousand men, intent upon the subjugation of India.   But of this conquest and the over-coming of the savage mountain tribes that intervened we have even fewer details than of Alexander's campaigns in the far northeast.   And because of this obscurity, historians have little to relate save the bare outlines of the marches, sieges and battles.

In seeking an entrance to India, Alexander followed the Cophen, in the valley of which he had wintered ere setting out in pursuit of Bessus.   Afterward he followed the Choaspes and its tributar-ies, and traversing their rugged defiles finally surmounted the chain of mountains that now separates British India from Afghan-istan.   His march lay through the countries of the Aspasians, Cursæans, and Assacenians, a savage and warlike people who met him with resolute courage at every step.   But, undeterred by their fierce opposition and the almost insuperable natural ob-stacles of the country, he at last made his way to the level plains of India.   Of the particulars of this long and hazardous march we know little, save that the barbarians who inhabited the mountains and secluded valleys, after being overcome in the open field, fled to their fortified retreats, where they continued the struggle with courageous though unavailing persistence. Throughout, the campaign, we are told, was one continual skirm-ish or hand-to-hand battle amid deserts and mountain retreats, followed by sieges which ended always with toppling walls and devastated strongholds.

As he approached the Indus the famed Rock of Aornus — said to have resisted Hercules — barred his further progress. This stronghold was twenty-three miles in circumference and lifted its height five thousand feet above the plain, the path by which the summit could be reached being effectively blocked and guarded.   However, after weeks of resolute investment and many disastrous reverses the King effected the capture of the stronghold, celebrating the victory afterward on the summit of the rock with fitting sacrifices to the Gods.   Reaching the Indus, Taxiles, the King who ruled over the country, approached him with offers of submission.   He at the same time begged Alexander as a favour to assist him in a conflict he was waging with Porus, a warlike monarch who dominated the country to the south and east.   Listening to his request, Alexander would do nothing until the temper of Porus could be ascertained.   But when that King curtly refused submission and marshalled his army to prevent Alexander's further progress, the latter crossed the Indus and continued his march to the Hydaspes, behind which Porus' troops were concentrated. In his progress he encountered the army of Spitakes, which was entrenched in a narrow defile through which the King must pass. Skillfully manœuvering his forces, Alexander, however, finally took him by surprise, and after a severe encounter compelled him to seek safety with the army of Porus. Reaching the Hydaspes, Alexander deemed it unwise to attempt to cross in the face of Porus' army, as the river was rapid and greatly swollen by recent rains. He, however, made vast pretence of doing so, clamorously marching a part of his army back and forth day after day as if seeking a fit place to cross. When this had been continued for a long time and Porus had been lulled into security, Alexander secretly moved a part of his force seventeen miles up the river. Here, boats having been prepared, he crossed with fourteen thousand men in the night, his movements concealed by a storm and the presence of a wooded island that lay near the opposite shore. Apprised of the movement too late, Porus drew out his army, facing his enemy and having a front of four miles. In the foreground he placed two hundred elephants, designed to crush Alexander's infantry and stampede his cavalry. The huge beasts were placed one hundred feet apart, and each bore a complement of men armed with bows and javelins. In addition to this terrifying array, he had three hundred four-horse chariots, each carrying two mailed drivers and four heavily armed men. Behind these came his infantry, thirty thousand strong, armed with spears and javelins and bearing long bows carrying arrows three feet in length. Having thus admirably arranged his forces, Porus waited, acting on the defensive. This, it is believed by military critics, cost him the battle, as it left Alexander with his smaller force free to choose the place and manner of attack, an advantage which he availed himself of with his usual genius for offensive movements. Sending his cavalry by a roundabout way to circle the enemy's flank, Alexander charged with his heavy infantry, wherever there was an opening. Overturning the chariots and plying the elephants with darts, he drove them maddened with pain and rage back on Porus' army, where they trampled friend and foe alike.

The Indian King fought throughout from the back of a towering elephant, and although clad in armour suffered many severe wounds. Yet he would not leave the field, but continued to the last to cheer his soldiers by his presence and courageous behaviour. While he could plainly see as the battle progressed that his army was doomed to defeat, yet for eight hours he kept it in order, and not until his last armed retainer had fled did the brave King himself seek to escape. In the pursuit Alexander would not suffer Porus to be slain, but sent first one messenger and then another to the heroic King, bidding him yield and promising that no harm nor indignity should be offered him. This Porus was at last led to do, and dismounting from his elephant approached Alexander with lofty mien and as a brave man should, even though suffering defeat. Welcoming him, no way irritated or angered by his obstinate resistance, Alexander asked him what he expected, whereupon Porus answered, yet without bravado, that he desired to be treated as a King. This answer of the potentate greatly pleased Alexander, and afterward on acquaintance he was led to continue him as ruler over the country he had until then governed, adding to his territory as much more.

In the pursuit of the Indian King, Alexander's war-horse, Bucephalus, then thirty years old, fell dead from heat and over-exertion. This historic beast, ancient writers tell us, always knelt for Alexander to mount or dismount, and at last, sinking on his knees as he died, permitted his master to leave his back unharmed. The horse when naked, it is said, would amiably permit his groom to ride him, but when fitted with his harness would allow no one but Alexander to come near him to mount. In commemoration of the noble steed which he had conquered as a youth, and as a token of love, Alexander caused a city, ten miles from the scene of battle, to be created and named Bucephalus in his honour.

326–325 B. C.

Alexander did not attempt to incorporate India as a part of the Persian Empire, but sought to make allies of its numerous rulers, so adjusting the power they respectively exercised that one would counterbalance the other. In pursuance of this he accorded Taxiles and Porus equal authority over the territory they respectively governed, having first brought about a reconciliation between them. When, however, he found it impossible to make an ally of a petty Indian king or ruler, he put one that was friendly in his place, or added his territory to that of one he could trust. In this way, conformably to the interests of the Empire, he settled the affairs of the vast territory bordering on the Indus and its tributary streams.

The battle with Porus was followed throughout the year's stay in India with great activity, so that the eye is scarcely able to follow the marches and counter-marches of Alexander's forces. There were, however, no more great battles, but a multitude of lesser encounters in the open field followed by sieges, in which the walls of cities were undermined or scaled and the places taken by storm. Thus it was at Sangala, before the walls of which stronghold there were three rows of breastworks, behind which the defenders fought with herioc courage. These Alexander finally overcame, seventeen thousand of the enemy being slain and seventy thousand taken prisoners.

The capital of the Mallians, a warlike people, also offered many obstacles, and in its taking Alexander came nigh to losing his life through his impetuous courage. For upon there being some delay at the time appointed for scaling the wall, and only two scaling ladders being forthcoming, he impatiently mounted to the top of the rampart with three companions. Seeing the King's danger, and in great fear for his safety, the Macedonians followed in a mass, unfortunately breaking down the ladders in their attempt. Meanwhile Alexander and his companions had leaped from the height to the street below, where they stood, sword in hand, with their backs to the wall, facing the enraged enemy. In the struggle that followed two of Alexander's companions were killed, he himself being prostrated by an arrow which penetrated his lungs. The remaining soldier, Peucestas, a shield-bearing guard, not in the least intimidated, however, fought on with courageous heart, protecting the body of the fallen King, from which position of peril he was rescued by the half-crazed Macedonians who hurried to his assistance.

While the invading army appears to have been engaged throughout the campaign in continual conflicts there were none — save in the case of the cities mentioned — that approached in severity those it had previously undergone. When the dense population that crowded the valley of the Indus was in some measure overcome and quieted, the army being then on the bank of the Hyphasis, Alexander made known for the first time his intention to continue the conquest to the Ganges in the far East. The Macedonians, however, weary and heavy of heart — having now been seven years from their homes — refused to proceed farther. In their refusal to follow him, after vain pleadings and after having secluded himself for three days, he reluctantly acquiesced. It was undoubtedly, however, the greatest disappointment of his life. Thus it fell out in August 326 B. C., that the veteran army, now numbering one hundred and twenty thousand men, set its face in the direction of home.

Many petty tribes, however, remained to be overcome, and a wide stretch of country to be traversed ere the sea was reached. Over this vast territory Alexander made Oxyartes, Roxana's father, viceroy. Reaching Patala, near the coast, the King divided his army, giving Craterus a part with which the latter took a course to the north, while Alexander marched straight for Persepolis in the northwest, and having in his way to traverse the Gedrosia Desert, eight hundred and fifty miles in width. A fragment of the army he sent under Nearchus by water through the Persian Gulf, an expedition that was thought to be fraught with especial perils, but, happily, found to be the reverse.

Historians have sought in vain to find words to describe the horrors of Alexander's march across the Gedrosia Desert to Paura, and thence with lesser suffering to Persis. "In this land of Gedrosia," says Dodge in his admirable history of Alexander's military expeditions, "there was an abundance of myrrh and other spices, but naught else but suffering and death. As the army marched onward, the desert grew sandier and more sterile — brooks dried up in the sand — the heat became intolerable — vegetation ceased. Not a path of any kind existed, and the marches had to be made at night. The men were scantily provided with rations, and these were finally exhausted. . . . . . Water was often sixty and eighty miles apart. The sand was like the waves of the sea for tracklessness. Discipline broke up. The men killed the cattle used as beasts of burden, and even mules and horses, and ate their flesh, saying that they had died of thirst and heat. The very animals which drew the wagons on which lay the wounded men were killed for food and the wounded left behind. Worse than the thirst was the terror of reaching water, followed by the agonizing death of those who too freely drank of it. . . . It is said that but a quarter of those who started reached Paura; and these in rags and without weapons. The beasts of burden almost all perished mostly from lack of water, but many dropped from weakness and were engulfed in the sand. The marches had to be made from water to water, and . . . the progress was no more than ten or twelve miles a day. When they could reach water by a night march, they did well enough; but when the march had to be by day the suffering was indescribable. . . . The sick and weak had to be abandoned, and the stragglers were rarely able to regain the column."

It is recounted by historians that Semiramis, the Assyrian Queen, in attempting to cross the Gedrosia Desert, lost her entire army. Alexander, though more fortunate, was often overcome by despair, but giving no expression to his fears shared in the sufferings of his soldiers, affording them such succour as he was able throughout the frightful struggle.

325–324 B. C.

Alexander passed the winter of 325–324 B. C. in Persis resting his army and attending to the governmental machinery of his vast Empire. Afterward he continued his march to Susa, where thirty thousand young and vigourous native Persian troops joined him, organized and armed after the Macedonian fashion. These, under his direction, had been collected and drilled at the various satrapies with the view of making every portion of the Empire bear its just part of the burden of the army. Another purpose he had in view was to relieve him, as King of Persia, of subserviency to the Macedonian contingent which had no sympathy in many things with the native population over which he was now called upon to rule. This commingling of the different nations was a part of his far-seeing determination to amalgamate the kingdom of Persia with that of Macedonia. And in further-ance of this he now formally recognized for the first time the customs of the Orient in respect to marriage and its attendant plurality of wives. To this political necessity those immediately concerned made no great objection, but when the army beheld the thirty thousand Persian levy, the Macedonian officers and soldiers (ever jealous and exacting) cried out that his purpose in thus recognizing the native population was to rid himself of his old and tried followers. And when he declared that it was his purpose to send home the infirm and aged veterans, and there make provision for their comfort, the troops mutinied, demanding that he send them all home, bidding him with bitter scorn to call upon Jupiter-Ammon for aid in his future conquests. Incensed beyond measure, Alexander took them at their word, and after having punished those who had incited the revolt retired into his palace, where he refused the malcontents further recognition or direction. After this had continued for some time, during which period he communicated only with his Per-sian subjects, the Macedonians, heartbroken and repentant, came to the palace gate, and prostrating themselves begged for pardon. For two days and nights he refused to receive them, but on the third day came forth, shedding tears in the reconcil-iation that followed. The reunion was succeeded by rejoicing and sumptuous festivals and the offering of sacrifices and liba-tions to the Gods. Thus he accomplished his object, which was to prepare the way to the building up of a great and homo-geneous Empire — a thing that would assuredly have followed had his life been spared the allotted period of man. For in all his administrative acts he displayed the same genius for affairs that he evinced on the field of battle, it being noticeable that he brought to questions of government no preconceived passions or prejudices, but sought only that which would bring the greatest prosperity and contentment to the people.

Alexander, who was generosity itself, made wise use of the vast treasure of the Persian Kings. While at Susa, among other notable things he paid the debts of his officers and soldiers, amounting to twenty-five millions of dollars. This in recog-nition of their patriotism and the manifold hardships they had suffered in his conquests. In addition to this he granted largesses of gold to those who had distinguished themselves, these donatives, with what had gone before, being sufficient to enrich all who had fought under his standard. In further provision for those who had served the state, he continued the pay of all who had met death in his service to their children.

Alexander's habits were temperate in all things, though his enemies sought to make it appear that his indulgences in wine were greater than they should have been. It appears on the contrary that he was much more abstemious than the men of his age. Plutarch, the most discerning and fair of all the ancient chroniclers who have written of the Great Conqueror, says: "He was much less addicted to wine than was generally believed; that which gave people to think so of him was, that when he had nothing else to do, he loved to sit long and talk, rather than drink, and over every cup hold a long conversation. For when his affairs called upon him, he would not be detained, as other generals often were, either by wine, or sleep, nuptial solemnities, spectacles, or any other diversion whatsoever; *a convincing argument of which is, that in the short time he lived, he accomplished so many and so great actions.* When he was free from employment, after he was up, and had sacrificed to the Gods, he used to sit down to breakfast, and then spend the rest of the day in hunting, or writing memoirs, giving decisions on some military questions, or reading. In marches that required no great haste, he would practise shooting as he went along, or to mount a chariot and alight from it in full speed. Sometimes, for sport's sake, he would hunt foxes and go fowling. He never cared to dine till it was pretty late and was wonderfully circumspect at meals, that every one who sat with him should be served alike and with proper attention; and his love of talking, as was said before, made him delight to sit long at his wine. He was so very temperate in his eating, that when any rare fish or fruit were sent him, he would distribute them among his friends, and often reserve nothing for himself. His table, however, was always magnificent, the expense of it still increasing with his good fortune, till it amounted to ten thousand drachmas ($2,000) to which sum he limited it, and beyond this he would suffer none to lay out in any entertainment where he himself was the guest."*

Alexander possessed many of the common frailties of mankind; some of them inherited, others the outgrowth of his youth and the environment of a Monarch of transcendent aims and am-

---

* It is a noticeable fact that the farther we recede from the rancorous and venomous period of Grecian misrepresentations and spite the more enlightened and unprejudiced the view we get of the Great King. The Romans never had any sympathy with the petty efforts of the Greeks to slander or belittle Alexander. They thought him incomparably great. Plutarch, a Grecian, wrote when the passions of his countrymen had cooled, and if he sometimes repeats the perversions of the early Greeks it is qualifiedly. Later writers like Plutarch, reading between the lines, judge Alexander honestly. And among them is Colonel Theodore Ayrault Dodge (United States Army), of whose great military history I have been glad to avail myself, an indebtedness I most gratefully acknowledge. Colonel Dodge's education as a soldier makes Alexander's military genius comprehensible to him and otherwise enlists his enlightened sympathy, as his exhaustive and admirable characterisation of the Great Conqueror evinces.

bitions. His temper, always high, was in later life imperious. The devotion and affection of his followers, with the exception of a few envious and disaffected leaders, however, evince his loveable qualities and exalted sense of justice. No autocrat ever looked upon those about him with so little distrust. His punishment of Philotas and Clitus and other traitors who sought to create divisions in the conquering army when remote from succour and surrounded by enemies, the Grecians severely commented upon. It was, however, like everything he did, wise and effective, and mankind was benefited by the peace and unity that followed his measures.

There was no Monarch of ancient times whose character was more moderate than Alexander's, and none of later days of whom more that is great or good can be said. Altogether too much was written in his disparagement. The explanation is simple, Philip, King of Macedon, had many enemies in Greece; Alexander still more; many of them outspoken slanderers and back-biters. Their misrepresentations were carefully preserved and spread abroad. Every scintilla of ill that could be suggested by his acts was set down in malice by some detractor, and by hosts believed. What Alexander's admirers said was doubtless sometimes overdrawn. Arrian and Ptolemy have, however, described the Great Captain's methods and deeds — and those things susceptible of exaggeration are no part of them. Thus Alexander's losses may sometimes have been diminished, or the numbers of the enemy slain exaggerated, but as to what he himself did all men agree. Its simple telling serves to make him in intelligence, force, character, achievements, and splendour of manhood incomparably the first of men.

The life work of Philip had been transcendent; that of Alexander greatly surpassed it. His attributes as a soldier and administrator cannot be exaggerated. Leaving Macedonia without resources and in debt, in four years he had possessed himself of practically all the treasures of the earth. Thence with marvelous courage, endurance, and skill he completed the conquest of the then known world, and this ere he was thirty-two years of age. There is no other instance in the world's history, it has been pointed out, of so small a nation over-running the earth, and impressing itself for all time on the countries conquered.

Alexander was possessed of great personal beauty, being of fair complexion and kingly bearing and gracious manners. He read much, and loved to surround himself with men of comprehension and affairs. Aristobolus confirms Plutarch's statement that he did not drink much in quantity, but was fain to talk over his wine and sit long at table, chatting with friends. He was able to endure heat, cold, hunger, and thirst beyond the strongest of his followers, and his strength and moral and physical courage were exceptional. Quintus Curtius tells how he saved his father's life in a mutiny among the Triballi, when a lad, by his undaunted courage and gallantry. He was oblivious of dangers which terrified other men, his bravery excelling that of all, even of those who had no other good qualities. Wounds did not cause him to complain or change colour, and when the Mallian arrow which had penetrated his lung was cut out it was without expression of pain or change of countenance.

When young he refused to enter the Olympic games, because he had not kings or their sons to compete with. An athlete, he disapproved of professional athletes, saying that they should place their strength at the service of their country. In his campaigns he marched much on foot with his troops rather than make use of a horse or chariot. Disposed to sleep but little, he increased his wakefulness by habit. His intellect was transcendent in clearness, and his heart animated by noble impulses. He was ambitious, but from exalted motives; one desire to conquer the world being coupled with the thought of furthering the influence and civilisation of Greece. He loved the roar of battle, and its turmoil raised his intellect to its highest grade of activity. His instincts were keen, his perception remarkable, his judgment all but infallible. As an organiser of an army he was without a rival; as a leader, unapproachable in exciting the ambition and courage of his followers. He stilled the apprehensions of men by his own fearlessness. Polybius says his soul was fashioned on a superhuman pattern.

He was noted for his high honour and faithfulness in keeping his agreements. His generosity, which was kingly, was coupled with inimitable grace in giving. He lavished money on his friends, but cared little for it himself. He had the rare gift of making men hang on his words, and do great deeds afterward. To Hephæstion, with whom he had been brought up, he clung with never-ending devotion, and to him confided his every secret. His affection for his mother, Olympias, nothwithstanding her cruel excesses, never waned.

While of exalted dignity as a King, Alexander was intimate with his soldiers and shared their toils and dangers. He never asked of them an effort he himself did not make; never ordered a hardship of which he himself did not bear a part. His eagerness was such that he could not see another perform deeds of valour without taking a part. At the end of his heroic pursuit of Darius, the Persian King, after a march of four hundred miles in eleven days, and at the close of which but sixty of his men were able to rally beside him, he himself led the charge on the Persian ranks, cheering his followers to victory. Such actions, of which his life was full, endeared him as a leader beyond the power of words to portray.

324–323 B. C.

From Susa Alexander marched to Ecbatana, where Hephæstion sickened and died. Inconsolable in his grief, the Great King caused the most sumptuous funeral ceremonies that could be devised to be celebrated in honour of the dead. Late in the fall he set out for Babylon, stopping by the way to make a winter campaign against the Cossæi. This tribe of barbarians and robbers had their habitation in the mountains from whence for centuries they had defied the Median and Persian Kings, preying upon the inhabitants of the plain as need or humour dictated. Successful in his undertaking, he continued his course to Babylon, his march attended throughout by the visits of envoys and rulers, who sought his presence from every quarter of the world.

In selecting Babylon for the capital, Alexander looked, it is apparent, to the easy communication it afforded by water with his Empire in the far southeast. And in this connection it is highly improbable that he had given up his purpose to extend his conquests at some future day to the Ganges, as contemplated while in India. But all his energies were now directed to the subjugation of the little-known country lying between the Persian Gulf and the Red Sea, a thing necessary to assure him free intercourse with India, and uninterrupted use of the great waterways that border the Arabian peninsula on either side. It is apparent that he esteemed the acquisition of Arabia necessary to round out his kingdom and free it from the depredations of the fierce predatory tribes that occupied the warlike and inhospitable country. In these preparations he found it necessary, following his arrival at Babylon, to visit the lower Euphrates, to personally explore the river and waterways that permeated the marshes and lowlands bordering the great stream.

It was while making these explorations, with a view to their future utility, that it is probable he sowed the seeds of the malignant fever from which he shortly died. Years of warfare unparalleled in results, filled to the full with hardships and anxieties, followed by the horrors of the Gedrosian Desert and the death of Hephæstion, had so weakened his body, scarred by wounds and exposure, that he was unable to withstand the strain of the severe sickness. And so he sickened and died, leaving the work of consolidating his Empire unfinished. Yet was he supreme in all he did. Monarch at twenty of a kingdom shaken by the throes of a murderous conspiracy and threatened on every side by alert and warlike enemies. At thirty-two master of the world. A herculean labour, in which it is apparent the mind and body of the labourer had little rest. The soul of the army, bearing the brunt of every battle, the builder and guardian of the State, in achievements unprecedented, no man before or since has done so much with implements so inadequate.

By preference a soldier — in accomplishments a just and wise governour, he died undisputed ruler of a far-reaching Empire, in which no murmur of discontent was heard, and in which life and property were everywhere secure.

Such was Alexander, dead at thirty-two.

Yet to the last he had no thought that he was to die thus early. Conquests still occupied his mind, and it is plain that he believed there was abundant time to build upon the secure foundation he had laid. Thus he made no provision for the succession of his Queen, Roxana, or another, to power; nor thought of it, except indefinitely. So that at last when he felt the hand of death upon him he had only strength to give Perdiccas his signet ring in token of some desire he was too weak to voice. For no one can believe the incredible story that he gave utterance at that time, or at any other period of his life, to the expectation or desire that his kingdom should fall "to the strongest." Such belief is too absurd to think of in the successor of a long line of kings who for four hundred years had striven to perpetuate and aggrandize their dynasty. The expression, it is more probable, was given currency by his generals in excuse for what followed his death. For Alexander, it is apparent, had no thought that the succession would be different in his case from that of his predecessors. Yet so it was, for those he left behind would yield to no arm less strong than his. And thus, after a little chaos reigned, in which ambitious military chiefs struggled with each other, each for himself — save Eumenes — the turmoil ending as we know in the dismemberment of the Empire, the scattered fragments falling to the more fortunate.

The ambition of Alexander's generals after his death is not, however, to be too severely criticised. They had served their master with unquestioning courage and loyalty, and when he died they could not forego their individual interests to further the Dorian Monarchy or the scheme of the Greco-Persian Empire Alexander contemplated, and would have undoubtedly achieved except for his early death. Yet it is clear in the light of subsequent events that the individual interests of the generals, with one or two exceptions, would have been better served had they remained loyal to the kingly house. There was indeed a pretence of doing this, and accordingly Aridæus, Philip's half-witted son, was made King under Perdiccas' tutelage; and afterward when Roxana gave birth to a posthumous child he was made joint king with Aridæus. But it was only a pretense, and intended merely to give those to whom the guardianship of the different provinces of the vast Empire was allotted time in which to so shape their affairs as to make the domination permanent. But fearful that their tenure would prove only temporary or inconsequential if any Dorian heir survived, they became a unit in their determination to exterminate the line, root and branch. And as hungry wolves follow their prey, so these ambitious chiefs, who owed their fortunes to the generous conqueror, forgetful of his favour, pursued with deadly fear every one who had in their veins a trace of Dorian blood. And in this great stress of fortune, and the submerging of the kingly house, the hapless Roxana and her son, most pitifully, and Olympias the queen-mother, most justly, perished with the others.

The chroniclers of the period, generally, concur in their account of Alexander's sickness and death, which last occurred in June, 323 B. C., in his thirty-second year, and when he had reigned twelve years and eight months.

On the morning following the beginning of the fever, so they tell us, he was unable to rise, and after having been carried out on a couch to celebrate the sacrifice, was obliged to lie in bed the remainder of the day. Nevertheless, he summoned his officers and prescribed the details of the impending expedition (the conquest of Arabia), ordering that the land force begin its march on the fourth day following, while the fleet, with himself aboard, should sail on the fifth day. In the evening he was carried on a couch across the Euphrates into a sheltered garden, where he bathed and rested for the night. In the morning, the fever continuing, he bathed and was carried out to perform the sacrifices, after which he remained on his couch throughout the day. In the evening he bathed and again sacrificed, but endured a bad night with heightened fever. The next two days passed in the same manner, the fever increasing. Nevertheless, he summoned Nearchus (his admiral) to his bedside, and discussed many points regarding his maritime projects, ordering that the fleet should be ready by the third day. On the ensuing morning the fever being violent, he reposed all day in the garden, calling the generals to discuss the filling of vacancies among the officers, and directing that the armament should be in readiness to move when required. The next day his malady was still more violent. On the succeeding day he could with difficulty support himself, being lifted out of bed to perform the sacrifice. He, however, continued to give orders in regard to the expedition. The day following, though alarmingly ill, he made an effort to perform the sacrifice, being carried from the garden-house to the palace. In this weakened state he ordered that the officers should remain in permanent attendance in and about the hall. Thus he remained for two nights and a day, without amendment or repose, incapable of utterance. News of his malady reaching the army, it filled the soldiers with inexpressible grief and alarm. Many of them, eager to see him, forced their way into the palace, and were admitted unarmed, passing beside his bed and expressing their great affection and sympathy. The King recognized them, and in return made demonstrations of love, but was unable to speak. He succumbed to his sickness on the afternoon of the same day.

Thus died untimely one whose achievements have never been surpassed. Only Napoleon and Cæsar are comparable with him. Napoleon died broken-hearted and in exile, bereft of all his possessions. Cæsar was assassinated at the acme of his power. Alexander died a natural death, surrounded by his friends and in peaceful possession of his own kingdom and the vast Empire he had conquered.

THE ROMANCE
OF GILBERT HOLMES

By MARSHALL MONROE KIRKMAN

"Each chapter contains something of interest . . . The love-story gently and gracefully pervades the whole book."—*Vanity Fair (England).*

"Of the beauty and delicacy of the author's touch there can be no question."—*Chicago Tribune.*

"An historical novel. Ranks with the best of its kind . . . The plot is of the strongest, the most stirring adventures being interwoven with a love-story which is idyllic and full of charm."—*The Manchester Courier (England).*

"The real strength of the book lies in the life-like portrayal of Abraham Lincoln and Stephen A. Douglas as well as Jefferson Davis. The daring venture of introducing these men in a romance has been crowned with success."—*The Philadelphia Press.*

"The bygone days of Illinois in the early days of its settlement pass before our eyes in vivid array. Abraham Lincoln, Jefferson Davis, and the pathetic figure, Black Hawk, the great Sac Chief, live once more and throw over us the spell of their commanding personalities."—*The Literary World (England).*

"A vivid and stirring picture of adventure, incident and romance that holds the interest of the reader from the start. A pretty love-story runs through the book, told with so much delicacy and tenderness that it is a distinct charm."—*Baltimore American.*

"A striking picture of a romantic period of American History . . . Possesses the primordial attraction of a really idyllic love-story developed with a delicate charm which stamps the writer as a literary artist."—*The Empire (England).*

"Winning golden opinions on all sides."—*The Chicago Times-Herald.*

"Wherever opened, something beautiful is found."—*The Christian Nation (New York).*

"A choice romance, peopled with characters as real as those of Dickens. It has not a dull page in it; no one who has begun it will lay it aside unfinished."—*The Book World (New York).*

Cloth 12mo., gilt top, deckle edges, illustrated. Price $1.50.

PUBLISHERS
CROPLEY PHILLIPS COMPANY
CHICAGO

Primitive Carriers

BY MARSHALL MONROE KIRKMAN

This unique and rare work of art embraces fifteen hundred beautiful engravings, portraying the Primitive Peoples of the world and their methods of carriage in every age and quarter of the globe. It also contains an historical account of the peoples of remote antiquity, among others the Aryans, Chaldeans, Phœnicians, Carthaginians, Grecians and others. It appeals alike to all classes, ages and conditions: king and peasant, bishop and layman, philosopher and peasant, rich and poor, all find it equally interesting and attractive. Cultivated men and women in every walk of life, and in every part of the world, express their high appreciation of its rare beauty and interest.

"A more interesting series of illustrations it would be difficult to imagine, or one that could give more clear and positive instruction in the history of humanity."—*New York Sun*.

"A work of great merit and beauty."—*Boston Globe*.

"A superb volume, original in conception and unique in literature and art."—*Chicago Tribune*.

"For originality of design and thorough treatment of its subject, it is unique among books. Disraeli would have enshrined it among his 'Curiosities of Literature' as a stroke of genius."—*Right Rev. Wm. E. McLaren, D. D., D. C. L., Bishop of Chicago*.

"It treats well and artistically a comparatively new field of literature."—*His Eminence, James, Cardinal Gibbons, D. D.*

"It was a most happy thought that conceived such a work, and in its execution it becomes a most instructive and suggestive contribution to our best literature."—*Right Rev. Henry C. Potter, D. D., L. L. D., D. C. L., Bishop of New York*.

"A very beautiful book. It is not only classical and historical, but also a work of great interest and usefulness."—*Most Rev. Patrick A. Feehan, Archbishop of Chicago*.

The august rulers of the world find this work quite as fascinating as do their more simple brethren. Among the more exalted of these who have commended its worth, beauty and artistic merit may be mentioned Her Late Most Gracious Majesty, Queen Victoria, the Czar of Russia, King Humbert, the King of Belgium, the King of Greece.

The prices, delivered, are:

Portfolio Size, Edition de Luxe, Seal Grain Leather, Padded Sides, Gold Center and Back Stamp, Gilt Edges $11.50

Portfolio Size, Seal Grain Leather, Flat, Gold Center and Back Stamp, Gilt Edges 10.50

Portfolio Size, Best Cloth (Combination), Gold Center and Back Stamp, Gilt Edges 8.50

PUBLISHERS

CROPLEY PHILLIPS COMPANY

CHICAGO

The Science of Railways

By MARSHALL MONROE KIRKMAN

REVISED AND ENLARGED

In Sixteen Volumes:

Organization of Railways, and Financing
Building and Repairing Railways
The Locomotive and Motive Power Department
Locomotive Appliances
Engineers' and Firemen's Handbook
Shops and Shop Practice
Air Brake — Construction and Working
Cars — Construction, Handling and Supervision
Electricity Applied to Railways
Operating Trains
Passenger Traffic and Accounts
Freight Traffic and Accounts
Collection of Revenue
Safeguarding Railway Expenditures
General Accounts
Railway Rates and Government Ownership

In writing these books the author has had fifty-three years' practical experience as a railway employe and officer, and has been aided throughout his work by the advice and co-operation of railway men of genius and extended experience in every department of the service.

"A work having the unique distinction of being both comprehensive and thorough. It presents in an equally meritorious manner the theoretical and practical aspects of transportation. It will never cease to be of great value." — *Marvin Hughitt, President Chicago & Northwestern Railway.*

"There is nothing in railway literature to be compared with these books in extent or value. I cannot think of anything better that I can do for our employes than to bring such a fund of information within their easy reach." Referring to the revised and enlarged edition, he says: "I congratulate you heartily on the great improvement you have made in your unique railway library."— *Sir Wm. C. Van Horne, Chairman Board of Directors, Canadian Pacific Railway.*

"The full and exhaustive examination of the multitude of conditions that surround and apply to the subject. 'The Science of Railways,' as set forth in the work, required such knowledge, experience and patient application as very few men are capable of giving. Mr. Kirkman's railway life has especially fitted him for the task, and the work is a splendid monument to his ability."— *James J. Hill, President Great Northern Railway.*

"Even the casual reader can not fail to remark the fertility and capacity of a mind whose observations have given him a mastery over such a mass of detail." — *Railway Journal.*

"The author has a great reputation. His books are especially valuable to the profession."— *Journal of the German Railway Administration Society.*

"Mr. Kirkman is an authority in the highest sense on the matters treated in his works."— *Banker's Magazine.*

"Useful to all who desire to gain some insight into the arcana of railway management."— *Herapath's Railway Journal, London.*

"Mr. Kirkman is a recognized authority in America, and his views are accepted in England."— *Commissioner of Railroads of New South Wales.*

This great work of *Reference* and *Instruction* portrays the methods and principles connected with the Organization, Location, Capitalization, Construction, Maintenance, Equipment, Motive Power, Operation and Administration of Railroads. It is profusely illustrated with plates and engravings of railway appliances prepared expressly for the work.

PUBLISHERS

CROPLEY PHILLIPS COMPANY

CHICAGO

THE ALEXANDRIAN NOVELS

By MARSHALL MONROE KIRKMAN

PUBLISHED 1909

THE ROMANCE OF

"ALEXANDER THE PRINCE"
"ALEXANDER THE KING"
AND
"ALEXANDER AND ROXANA"

These stories of love and adventure follow the career of Alexander the Great, but each lies apart, and such interest as attaches to one is in no way dependent upon the others. The romances were suggested by studies of the times of Philip of Macedon and Alexander, and it was because of the interest they excited, and not a desire to write an historical romance, that they had their origin. Each novel is followed, however, by a chapter giving an historical account of the life and deeds of the heroic prince during the period covered by the love story. These chapters cover the whole career of the Great King, a career that has hitherto been little more than a myth to the majority of mankind, no great character in history indeed being so altogether vague, illusive and indeterminate.

The romantic nature of Alexander's life and conquests makes his history in itself as interesting as the most absorbing novel.

PUBLISHERS
CROPLEY PHILLIPS COMPANY
CHICAGO